Praise for

ALISON DELAINE

"A fearless debut! Alison DeLaine
pens a stand-out romance."
—*New York Times* bestselling author Julia London

"Unusual and engaging…
DeLaine keeps the pages turning."
—*Publishers Weekly* on *A Gentleman 'Til Midnight*

A Wedding by Dawn

ALISON DeLAINE

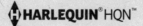

Recycling programs
for this product may
not exist in your area.

ISBN-13: 978-0-373-77868-3

A WEDDING BY DAWN

Copyright © 2014 by Black Canyon Creations, LLC

Printed in U.S.A.

To my parents, for their support.

CHAPTER ONE

FOR FIFTY THOUSAND pounds, Nicholas Warre didn't give a damn what his bride looked like.

He curled his hand around the jamb of the tavern's side door, with Malta's night breeze at his back and a host of raucous Mediterranean drunks shoving their way past him, and glanced at William Jaxbury. "You're absolutely certain?"

Jaxbury's gaze leveled on their prize, Lady India Sinclair. His gold earrings glittered in the muted candlelight that spilled through the doorway, and his dark red Barbary turban made him look like a corsair devil. "Recognize that tricorne anywhere," he said, and ducked quickly out of view on the other side of the doorway. Amusement danced in his eyes, damn him. Always laughing when there wasn't one bloody thing to laugh at.

Inside the tavern, Nick's betrothed perched on a stool, deep in conversation with a companion who could only be Miss Millicent Germain. Lady India's full attention was fixed on something—someone?—across the room. That tricorne blocked her face, and a black waistcoat obscured her figure, but he had a clear view of a shapely leg clad in breeches and a white stocking. Her black buckled shoe tap-tap-tapped the stool's leg.

"Second thoughts?" Jaxbury asked, eyes gleaming.

"No." A man didn't have second thoughts about a bank draft that would finally put an end to his misery. "I shall go in through the main door, while you stay here and wait for my signal." And then—

Good God.

She'd turned her head, and he found himself staring across the tavern at her profile. Even as he watched, she glanced at something over her shoulder and gave him a quick but full view of her face. His hand constricted around the doorjamb. "Jaxbury, you bloody bastard. You could have warned me she's got a mouth that'll have every man in London reaching for his breeches."

The words scarcely left his tongue before Jaxbury had his fist clenched in Nick's shirt. "Besmirch Lady India again, and you'll answer to me." There was no laughter in those eyes now.

"Did I besmirch her? I could have sworn I merely commented on her beauty." And beauty was the dead last thing he needed in a wife. He thought of Clarissa— so lovely yet so deceptive—and checked a sudden urge to lay his fist into something. Jaxbury's jaw, for example.

Even from this distance and dressed like a man, Lady India screamed sensuality. The men in that tavern were either sodomites or blind.

"Let me make one thing clear, Warre." Jaxbury's blue eyes glittered like cold sapphires. "Lady India's a virgin, and whatever else happens, you'll go easy on her even if I have to stand by the marital bed and watch."

Nick curled his lip. "Enjoy that, would you?"

Jaxbury's fist tightened in Nick's shirt. "Careful, or you may find I've changed my mind about this folly."

"This 'folly' does not require your approval." Enough

was enough. Nick pushed Jaxbury away and started forward.

Lady India's days of wanton adventure were about to come to an abrupt end.

"FOOL'S ERRAND IS an insulting way to speak of something as profound as my deflowering, Millie." India took a swig of ale and studied a square-jawed, dark-haired sailor through the crowd. Finally setting foot on Malta was a blessed relief for so many reasons.

"Nothing profound originates in a waterfront tavern," Millie said.

India felt her foot resume its tapping. The tavern roared with conversations in every language, teemed with whores, barmaids and men who were too drunk to see past her waistcoat and breeches.

But she would make sure one of them saw the truth. Tonight.

Millie gripped her tankard as though she were the one about to invite the carnal knowledge of a Mediterranean stranger. "If you're smart," she continued to warn above the din, "you'll keep your flower intact."

"*Smart* is merely another word for *prudent, dull* and *biddable*." And *accomplished, well-versed* and *literate,* but this sailor was one person who wouldn't care that India was none of those things. He laughed at something his hollow-cheeked companion said, revealing an intriguing gold tooth. India leaned across the table toward Millie. "Do you think he's Egyptian? I think I might like to be deflowered by an Egyptian."

"*I* think I'm going to be sick."

India snorted and pulled her tricorne hat lower across her eyes to better conceal her surveillance. If anyone was going to be sick, it would likely be her. Her lady's maid Frannie had warned her that women of quality sometimes vomited after their virtues were taken.

Already the ale soured a little in her stomach, but she couldn't help smiling. There was little of quality left of her, so she'd likely come through the event without disgracing herself.

Ha. *Disgracing herself* was the beginning and end of the entire endeavor.

The Egyptian sailor lifted his glass with a large hand that was no stranger to rope and canvas. Gold gleamed from the fingers that would unlock the last door to her freedom.

For freedom, she could endure a bit of vomiting.

She drew in an unsteady breath heavy with salt air and tobacco smoke, sailors and alcohol, and slipped a crust of bread to a brown-spotted mongrel who sat begging beneath the table. A loud trio of men jostled her from behind, sloshing a bit of ale onto her hand.

She licked it away and shifted on her stool but couldn't quite make herself stand. "You'll send the longboat back to shore for me?" she asked Millie.

"By the devil, India—" Millie huffed. From beneath her giant misshapen peasant's hat, she frowned at India through a carefully applied layer of grime that almost completely hid her gender. "You cannot do this."

She could, and she would. Now, before she lost her nerve completely. "I shall meet you back at the ship."

"I'll not return to the ship without you!"

"You can't stay here by yourself!"

"India...." In Millie's eyes India saw all the arguments Millie had already made against this plan: pain, pox, pregnancy.

The sailor didn't look like a brute, and Millie swore all men were poxed, anyway. As for the third...

"I've got my vinegar sponge in my pocket."

"For God's sake, India—"

"Must you be so bloody contrary about everything? Always?" India's palms began to sweat. She forced herself to her feet. Even now, Father's lackeys could be afloat in the Med looking for her. He would have dispatched them the moment he'd learned she and Millie had borrowed Katherine's ship. They would very likely find her, but she would not allow them to drag her back to England to marry whatever disgusting, fleshy fish-belly Father had paid to wed her.

If her father's men succeeded, she could well find herself with Millie's three *P*'s in spades regardless.

"If you catch his eye dressed like this," Millie warned, "it won't be deflowering that's on his mind— at least, not the kind you're thinking of."

"I have a plan." *Pardon me, sir,* she would say, *there's a gentleman outside asking to see you.* Once outside, she would whisk off her hat, let her blond hair tumble free and tell him what she wanted.

On hearing this, Millie grabbed her arm. "We're leaving. I absolutely will not allow you to commit such a folly. An utter stranger, who could have any manner of disgusting ideas—"

"Don't be such a pill." India wrenched her arm free. "Auntie Phil beds whomever she pleases. It can't be so terrible and disgusting." It probably could, but she'd already told herself to stop remembering the more shocking details Frannie had described.

"Your aunt's deflowering took place in a marriage bed," Millie hissed.

"Which can hardly happen to me as I have no intention of marrying."

"I'll never know how you've survived being such a dullard."

The accusation stung more than Millie had intended. "Perhaps I shall marry the Egyptian." India laughed. She might be a dullard, but she would soon be a dullard whom her father could marry off to absolutely nobody.

An especially rowdy bunch at a table in the far corner exploded in guffaws. The dark sailor punctuated his conversation with the kind of dramatic gestures that always accompanied an exotic tongue.

India reached for her tankard to take one last swig and hoped a deflowering didn't take much time.

Millie grabbed her arm. "I'm serious, India. Ruining yourself won't solve anything."

"But it will most certainly solve one thing." She set the tankard on the table and fixed her gaze on the sailor. "I have nothing to lose and everything to gain." Every nerve came alive in an alarming swarm of anticipation.

"Nothing to lose! You'll throw yourself away—"

"Oh, fie." Virginity was the last virtue she had left *to* throw away. Everything else—her friends, her reputation, her popularity—was already gone. "I'm a woman of the high seas now, Millie. What does it matter if I give my virtue to a handsome sailor?"

But suddenly Millie wasn't looking at her anymore. She was looking past India's shoulder, and her eyes had grown as big as silver crowns.

"It matters, Lady India," came a cold voice from behind her, "because you are betrothed to me."

CHAPTER TWO

BETROTHED.

India whipped around and looked up into heartless green eyes set like flints above an arrogant nose and grim mouth. They were eyes so cold they could have belonged to an executioner, in the kind of face that could command the attention of an entire ballroom.

And he wasn't alone. Next to him stood—

"William!" Freedom collapsed like a sail in a dead breeze.

William grinned and crossed his arms. "Such a disappointing welcome, Indy. Not happy to see us?" India thought she might end up vomiting with her virtue still intact. William shifted his laughing blue eyes to Millie. "Why, Millicent, you've gone pale. At least, I think you have. Difficult to tell beneath all that—what *is* that on your face?" He reached a finger toward her cheek, but Millie swatted it away.

India glanced away from them at the Egyptian sailor. At Millie, whose eyes had grown sharp with alarm—and that bloody pessimism that was the bane of India's existence. There was no question what Millie was thinking: They would never escape William, the man who had taught their own mentor to survive on the high seas.

But India wasn't above trying. "We're overjoyed to

see you, aren't we, Millie?" she said brightly. "We absolutely are. What a stroke of good fortune— Millie, was I not just saying how much I wished we had friends in town? And now here you are. Join us, and let's toast your return to the Mediterranean." It took all her willpower not to look at William's companion.

William laughed. "Very well. We'll play that game if you wish."

Game? Millie and India had sailed with William on the *Possession*. He knew how important their freedom was to them. Yet he thought this was a *game?*

"For God's sake, Jaxbury," the betrothal-announcer muttered irritably.

From the corner of her eye she could see he was dressed impeccably, conservatively, as though he'd just emerged from Westminster. Except no respectable man would be desperate enough to enter into an agreement to marry her, which meant he was what—a slave to the gaming tables? The holder of an empty title? A merchant with a mountain of debt?

Even now she could hear her father's voice. *You will choose one of these men, India, or I will choose for you.*

The tavern seemed to close in on her. It would take seconds to dart across the room to the Egyptian, seconds more to reveal that she was a woman, a moment or two to convey what she needed. They would need to leave the tavern and go—where? Where would they go?

"Forgive me." William laughed. His gold earrings glittered terrifyingly in the light from candles sputtering in an iron chandelier. "I see my new shipmate is growing impatient. Introductions and all that—terrible manners on my part. Lady India, may I present Nicholas Warre, Lord Taggart."

Millie's eyes snapped up from the table.

Nicholas *Warre!* In an instant India surveyed everything from the top of his greedy head to the toes of his debtor's shoes. Father had betrothed her to a man so desperate to save his own estate he'd tried to steal someone else's?

"Pillock!" she spat.

That grim mouth did not so much as twitch. "Be that as it may, Lady India—" he calmly reached inside his waistcoat, let her catch a glimpse of a small sheaf of papers and tucked them safely away "—it is incumbent upon me to inform you that we are contracted to wed, pursuant to an agreement I've made with your father." Now the corner of that mouth curved slightly, and those heartless green eyes wandered briefly over the front of her coat. "Which means the only recipient of your virtue will be me."

India looked him straight in the eye. "Dead men take no one's virtue, *Mister* Warre." He did not deserve the respect of his title. All her senses homed in on the Egyptian, but she didn't dare glance his way. Didn't dare look at Millie, who would surely be able to escape amid the commotion India was about to cause.

Before anyone could stop her, she dashed away from the table, barreling blindly through the crowd toward the Egyptian.

"India!"

The tavern noise swallowed William's shout. She whipped off her hat and felt her braid tumble down her back. Her pulse thundered and she lunged for the sailor, gripping his arm. "Sir, you must help me. I beg you. I need you. I need you to—" *devil take it, words! words!* "—compromise me. Carnally." The mix of interest and confusion in his eyes told her he didn't speak English. Desperately she switched to Italian. "Come with me. I need you. My body—" now there were even fewer words "—my *body* needs you." Her frantic fingers fumbled with the buttons on her waistcoat, her vest. But now it was clear he understood. That gold tooth flashed with his grin. His arm snaked around her, and his hand took possession of her left breast. There was a light in his eye—no, she didn't like that light, but it was better than—

"India!" William's voice bellowed above the crowd.

"We must go!" She tried to pull him off his stool, but he wouldn't budge. He laughed and said something to the men around them—where had all these men come from? Moorish. He was speaking Moorish. "Now!" She couldn't speak much, but Rafik the boatswain had bellowed that word constantly aboard Katherine's ship.

Apparently thinking he was obeying her order, he pulled her closer and buried his face against the side of her neck.

"No, not here!" She only knew the Italian. *Moorish, Moorish—what was Moorish for—*

But then it was too late, because Nicholas Warre was on them. He grabbed the sailor by the arm. The sailor pushed her aside and launched himself at Mr. Warre. A dozen men reached to take the sailor's place, pulling and yanking on her, groping her breasts and her buttocks. Her own scream pushed bile into her throat.

The sailor's hollow-cheeked companion threw himself at William, as the sailor landed a solid fist across Nicholas Warre's murderous face.

William and the other man fell together against a chair. Above the chaos she heard Millie scream. Desperately India fought the men who grabbed her, but there was no escape. Her pistol—she couldn't let them find her pistol! She used her elbow to jab, defend, keep groping hands from closing around her prize. Its weight dug into the waistband of her breeches. She tried to wedge herself against the table, but the hands and bodies and shouting and stench were everywhere.

The hollow-cheeked sailor struck William on the side of the head. He stumbled into a fallen stool, and she heard herself scream again. They couldn't hurt William! Oh, God—this had to stop! Her pistol—it would be useless against this mob even if she could manage to draw it out.

Nicholas Warre sent the gold-toothed sailor flying. A hand sneaked between her legs and she tried to shove it away but couldn't.

William lurched off the fallen stool and threw a right, left, right. Blood spurted from the hollow-cheeked sailor's nose. The commotion inside the tavern was deafening. Another man took a swing at Nicholas Warre, but he ducked and someone else took the hit. A new fight erupted, and the chaos grew. Hands closed sickeningly around her waist, an inch from the pistol's grip.

And then, suddenly, Nicholas Warre had her by the arm and wrenched her free.

"This way!" he shouted in her ear.

"Millie—"

"Jaxbury's got her. Run, damn you!" His hand clenched hers painfully as he dragged her out of the tavern. She stumbled on the cobblestones, trying to keep up with him as they raced down the street. Moments later, he yanked her into a pitch-dark alley and shoved her against the wall.

"Don't you *ever*," he seethed at her, nose to nose and out of breath, "do anything that stupid again."

"Leave Malta this instant and I guarantee you I shan't." She tried to push him away, but he was solid stone.

"Your recklessness could have gotten both me and Jaxbury killed—never *mind* the fate that would have befallen *you*." He drew in a sharp, ragged breath. "Is that how you planned to bestow your virtue? In a tavern with thirty sailors taking turns between your legs?"

She told herself she was trembling out of anger, not fear. "You'd best return to the safety of your London drawing room, Mr. Warre," she taunted. "It's clear you haven't the constitution for Mediterranean life." Except it was clear he had the constitution for any life he might choose. Faint light from the street caught the white flap of his torn shirt and a gleam of blood near his mouth. His wig was gone, and his dark hair stuck out everywhere.

"Then what a blessing that you and I will be returning to London posthaste," he drawled.

No. They would not. But arguing that point would get her nowhere. "You are wasting your time here," she told him flatly, and reminded herself that if not for him the danger never would have arisen in the first place. "I will not marry you. I'll kill you first."

"Will you." His eyes were nothing more than shadowed hollows.

His hands burned through her sleeves. He smelled faintly of cologne—something spicy and aristocratic and much too expensive for someone in his financial condition. Faint light from the street brought his face into chiseled relief, and a renegade nerve flared to life in her belly.

Betrothed. He fancied he had captured her as his prize. Perhaps he wasn't so wrong after all.

The weight of her pistol sat heavy in the band of her breeches. "Yes. And after what you did to Katherine Kinloch—" India began.

"If bringing a bill of pains and penalties against her was a capital crime, I have little doubt my sister-in-law would have murdered me herself."

"I shall happily take on the responsibility."

"Bold words from one who actually has committed a capital crime against the lady in question. You *do* realize you could hang for stealing her ship?"

Her pistol would put a quick end to this if only she could grab it and fire before he had time to react. There would be seconds, no more. There might be opportunity for nothing more than to gut-shoot him.

A queasy spell dizzied her head.

"We merely borrowed the *Possession,* Mr. Warre. Every moment you waste here with me is a moment you could be searching a way to satisfy your debts. You have greed and selfishness enough for ten men. I have every confidence that you will soon find an alternative method of relief."

"Praise, indeed. Fortunately for me, my search ended the moment I found you in that tavern."

"Your search, Mr. Warre, will end when your body lies cold at my feet." She inched her hand toward her pistol. "I demand that you let me go. *Now.*"

"Nothing in the world would please me more."

"Then—"

"But I have a vested interest in keeping you."

"I'll not give my consent to a marriage with you."
She raked him with disdain and gave a laugh that
sounded more like choking. "Not ever."

"I don't need your consent."

"Yes, you do. A marriage requires—"

"The only thing our marriage will require, Lady
India, is an officiant and a consummation. The first
will be easy enough to find, and it's clear you are desperately in need of the second. Once all that is complete,
I assure you our marriage will not be put asunder—not
by me, and certainly not by your father." His port-laced
breath feathered her lips. "Forgive me, but I cannot
think who else might be interested in challenging it."

"*I* will challenge it." Closer, closer…she nearly had
the pistol now. "If you drag me back to England—which
you will never succeed in doing—I shall file suit the
moment we return."

"And may I wish you much success, waddling before
the court with my babe rounding your belly."

Another strangled laugh escaped her. "You are just
like all the rest that my father attempted to fob me off
on these past months—going at me with their eyes before Father's money landed in their greedy, fat hands."
Except he did not have fat hands, and he was as handsome as the devil. Perhaps Father imagined he was
doing her a favor.

"Spoken as if any of those hands would have been
pleased with their catch once they realized what they
had captured," he said.

"Are you disappointed, Mr. Warre? Surely my father
did not fail to mention that I am a sailor."

"He did. And that you are spoiled, hoydenish and a—"
Disgrace.

"—disgrace. All of which can be easily corrected."

Oh, yes. Father had thought the same, and only look how he had succeeded.

If she was going to be a disgrace, she would be one from the deck of her own ship. There would be no returning to England, no being locked away in isolation, no endless tirades about her shortcomings—and *no* unwanted marriage.

Her fingers brushed the pistol grip. If Nicholas Warre succeeded in taking her, she may as well use the pistol on herself. The consequences of what she was about to do made her palms sweat. "Whatever my Father has offered you, I will pay you more to leave me be."

A shadowed brow rose. "If you have more, then I am a lucky man indeed, for once we are wed I shall have both."

"We are not going to be wed," she said flatly, and closed her hand around the pistol's grip. Her stomach rolled. Shooting him would make her a fugitive and guarantee she would never see England again.

So be it. She never wanted to see England again, anyway.

"Enough of this." He stepped back, keeping hold of her arm. "We shall return to—" His eyes fixed on her hand.

Now!

"We shall return nowhere." She tried to whip the pistol from her breeches but his hand was already there.

"Give me that!"

"No!" She fought with him to cock the hammer.

"Let go, before you—"

"No!" The pistol discharged into the alley with a deafening roar, and he wrenched it from her grasp.

She tried to run, but he caught her easily and shoved her against the wall once again. Now his hands were on her everywhere—inside her waistcoat, searching, groping, skimming over her hips, her buttocks, even between her—

"Stop!"

"And allow you to murder me in cold blood?" he growled, drawing his hand across a place he had no business touching, then shoving it inside her pockets. "God's blood, I got the sorry end of this bargain."

"You did indeed. And if you insist on keeping it, you will spend the rest of your life sleeping with one eye open."

"I shall do nothing of the kind." His fingers bit painfully into her arm, and he yanked her away from the wall. "Now. We shall proceed to my room at the inn, where we will wait for William and your associate. You will say nothing—not a single word—unless you wish to be bound and gagged. Do I make myself clear?"

CHAPTER THREE

THE ONLY THING truly clear to Nick was that it would be a short leap from marrying Lady India to being committed to an asylum.

"I suppose you've brought my things from the ship," she said. Sixty seconds. Possibly less. That was all it took for her to ignore his warning.

Not for the first time since embarking on this hellish voyage, Nick wondered if there might not have been an easier way to get his hands on fifty thousand pounds.

They rounded a corner, and the inn came blessedly into view. He didn't give a bloody damn about her things. His jaw hurt, his eye throbbed and the byblow from her pistol had singed one of his fingers—all of which meant little compared to the real problem.

"Well, I can't imagine how you expect me to prepare for my wedding without my things, Mr. Warre," she scolded. "Or to travel, which raises another question. How, precisely, do you plan to convey me back to England? By ship, I hope. The roads on the Continent are devilish rutted. Auntie Phil and I took weeks upon weeks to travel to Venice, but of course that was years ago. Oh, I would *love* to see Venice again. And Vienna. All cities beginning with *V,* in fact. Perhaps we can—"

"That's *enough.*"

"Am I bothering you, Mr. Warre?" she inquired with

false concern. "*Do* accept my apologies. Truly. One does so hate a yammerer. Such a nuisance. Of all the qualities one might find in a person, I daresay chattering has *got* to be the *least*—"

"*Silence.*" He pushed her inside the inn, ignored the frowning concierge, hauled her upstairs by the arm and managed to drag her into his room.

"Well, since you hadn't the foresight to collect my things—" Good God, he *would* have to gag her "—we shall simply have to return to the *Possession.*"

He went to the pockmarked bureau. "By all means, let us proceed there directly." The looking glass in this third-rate inn was so shoddy it was good for little more than guessing where the blood was as he inspected the damage from the bar brawl.

"Sarcasm is an ugly thing, Mr. Warre. Everyone says so. You really ought to be more sincere, if not for me then for the sake of your soul, because—"

"Lady India," he said sharply, and turned on his heel to face her. She observed him craftily with eyes better suited to a courtesan. "For the sake of *your* soul—" he pointed at the fraying sitting suite behind her *"—sit."*

There was a beat. A little twitch at the corner of her too-full lips. And then she turned away and sprawled herself in a shabby velvet armchair like a man, except there wasn't one bloody thing masculine about her—a fact his hands were having difficulty forgetting.

"I wish he'd broken your nose," she said, staring him directly in the eye.

"A charming sentiment." He turned back to the glass. He'd lost his peruke in the tavern, and his hair—too long for the damned thing anyhow after nearly five weeks aboard that godawful ship—lay in a mess of

near-black waves. He'd have a black eye by morning.
That, a bloody lip and sore ribs were the perfect cap to
an endless bout of seasickness.

No. No, the perfect cap was sitting in an armchair
behind him, observing him disdainfully.

He checked his pocket watch. Where the hell was
Jaxbury?

"You did not succeed in ruining Katherine's life to
pay your debts," she told him haughtily, swinging a
small foot back and forth, "so you've decided to ruin
mine. You will not succeed."

Ruining Katherine's— Of course. Lady India was
loyal to her former captain, and apparently the fact that
Katherine was now Nick's sister-in-law carried little
weight. But Lady India would not want to hear that ruining Katherine Kinloch's life had never been his objec-
tive, and that sometimes one pursued options in one's
desperation that one would never consider otherwise.

Such as agreeing to pursue a young hellion and force
her into marriage.

"Your life is already ruined," he told her.

"It isn't."

Yes, it is. No, it isn't. There was no doubt Lady India
would be able to keep up *that* conversation for the better part of an hour.

In the glass he watched her rise from the chair and
approach him. She had the kind of shapely mouth that
could earn a fortune doing unspeakable things at Cov-
ent Garden.

He refused to think of what Lady India might do with
that mouth. Leave a man singing two octaves higher,
most likely.

"My *life* isn't ruined, of course," she said conversationally, "but my body—well, that is another matter entirely. I regret to inform you, Mr. Warre, that I am not a virgin." She put a hand to her belly. "At this moment, I could well be carrying a child. An Egyptian child, if you must know, although strictly speaking I suppose Ottoman is the better—no. No, in truth he was from Tunisia, I think, so if one wants to be strictly factual—"

"And I do, Lady India. I do wish to be strictly factual. Which is why I must remind you that less than an hour ago you spoke of giving your virtue to a sailor."

Her mouth curved in a bemused smile. "I really don't consider anything properly done until it's been accomplished a *minimum* of three times, so—being *strictly* factual now, mind you—tonight would have marked the final demise of my virtue. I was referring to the coup de grâce. The triple cut, one might say."

My daughter is a wild harridan, Cantwell had said. The man had a talent for understatement.

"Well, then." He dropped the cloth in the basin and turned toward her. "You won't mind if I have a taste of what I may look forward to once we've celebrated our nuptials."

The quick apprehension in her eyes told him everything he needed to know about whether she might be carrying a Tunisian sailor's illegitimate child.

Those eyes were blue—real blue, not gray-blue like Clarissa's. Nor was her hair the pale, flaxen shade of Clarissa's. It was pure honey, alive with ten shades of gold.

Desire ripped through him. Devil take him, he was an idiot.

But those eyes had taken on a decidedly less bold

light, so he let his lip curve. "Not so adventurous as you claim, I see."

She laughed, and it transformed her face in a way that wasn't helpful at all. "My, Mr. Warre, you *do* think highly of yourself. You've already seen my taste in men. You're hardly exotic, and much too old. I could never bring myself to bed someone so ancient."

Fifty thousand pounds. Cantwell suffered from a severely overinflated view of his daughter's worth. Or, depending where one stood, a severely underinflated one. "Indeed. God knows how I manage to stay upright with thirty-four years behind me."

"Thirty-four!"

"Fortunately, our relations will be more of the lying-down variety."

"Thirty-*four?*"

"Shocking, isn't it?"

"Ought you to remain standing? You mustn't tax yourself on my account." She gestured toward the sitting suite. "Please, do be seated."

"I find that I am particularly fit for my age," he said drily. If only someone were transcribing this priceless conversation. "As for exotic, if you like, I shall wear a turban when I 'bed' you." He regretted the words the moment they left his tongue.

"What a generous offer, Mr. Warre. But I worry about engaging in anything so vigorous as bedding with a man of your age. My Auntie Phil once spoke of a Lord Garth who dropped stone dead in the middle of—"

"Lord Garth was two and eighty." Something like a laugh escaped him, and he went to his portmanteau because it was too easy to imagine her splayed across that bed, and his dropping dead would not be part of the entertainment. Good God. Lady India's *Auntie Phil,* the young and widowed Lady Pennington, should have a care what she discussed with impressionable minds.

"Regardless, one can't be too careful when one gets up in one's years," she said. "I would *hate* for anything to befall you."

His hands itched to open the door and toss her out. Let her go back to her stolen ship and her lusty sailors. Let Jaxbury deal with her, while Nick finally, blessedly got some sleep after the hellish weeks of sea travel.

But he was in too deep to turn back. Holliswell had granted him time to pursue Lady India and collect the money from her father, yes. But if Nick did not succeed by their agreed-upon date, Holliswell would take ownership of Taggart. It was either marry Lady India or lose Taggart.

And he'd be damned before he'd lose Taggart.

"I assure you I shall take the utmost care," he told her. "At least we may content ourselves that the marriage will be short, as I have one foot in the grave already."

"There will be no—"

"Marriage. Yes, I understand your position thoroughly. Unfortunately, you've got no say in the matter."

"You cannot force me to say the vows," she informed him.

With the right priest and enough money, she could recite bawdy tavern songs for all he cared. "I have a signed contract and assurances from your father that I may do whatever is necessary to carry it out." He pulled Cantwell's contract from inside his waistcoat and unfolded it. "You may read the contract if you like, but you will understand if I hold it for you while you do. I would hate for anything to happen to it."

She wrinkled that shapely little nose that would have been perfect were it not dusted with a handful of freckles. "That contract means nothing to me."

"Perhaps that will change when you read it."

"I don't need to read it, because I shan't be agreeing to its terms."

"Then it's a good thing its terms don't require your agreement," he said, and tucked the contract away. Once again he checked his watch. *For God's sake, Jaxbury—* Perhaps the man had gone to the church instead of coming back here.

He looked at Lady India.

She narrowed her eyes at him. "I will make you regret the hour you decided I was the answer to your problems, Mr. Warre."

"Believe me when I say you already have." Did he dare drag her through the streets again in the hope Jaxbury would be waiting at the church? He glanced irritably at the door. There wasn't much choice. "I've waited long enough. Let us be off."

"Off." A spark of fear lit her eyes. "Where?"

"To see this business finished." He walked toward her, and she backed away.

"We scarcely know each other, Mr. Warre. Certainly it would benefit us both if we had the opportunity to become better acquainted. For instance, how deeply in debt you are to a certain Mr. Holliswell."

"I have all the information I require. And you may ask me anything you like on the way to the church."

"You're free to change your mind, you know." He watched her struggle valiantly for composure. "Nobody would think less of you if you allowed me to escape. You could salvage your pride by saying how grateful you are that I *did* escape, as you realized your ill fortune the moment you set eyes upon me."

For a moment she looked so young and frightened he almost felt sorry for her.

But she wasn't an object to be pitied. She was a hoyden and a pirate and much too comfortable with a pistol.

"I realized my ill fortune long before that. But I have no intention of allowing you to escape." He smiled tightly. "You, Lady India, are as good as a bank draft to me. And you can imagine how well I would safeguard one of those."

If it weren't for Nicholas Warre *safeguarding* her by the arm as he dragged her once again down the street, India wasn't sure she'd be able to stand. Her knees trembled violently as she frantically tried to think of a way to stop him.

"This is not at all how I envisioned my wedding day," she told him as they closed in on the shadowed hulk of a church at the end of the street. "Surely we have time to find some flowers. Or a gown—you can't possibly imagine I could marry without a new gown. It's a disgrace to both of us, and only imagine what the guests will think."

He didn't even bother to tell her to be quiet. She didn't dare glance at his face and risk meeting those eyes, not after the way he'd—

She exhaled. After the way he'd looked at her. At the inn.

She'd come very close to pushing things too far. But

now every step over the uneven cobblestones brought him closer to victory, while bringing her closer to—

"Devil!" She stopped short.

"Keep walking."

"A moment—"

"Understand me well, Lady India," he practically growled into her ear. "I'll not fall for your tricks. You may either walk the rest of the way, or I shall carry you."

"It seems only appropriate that you *do* carry me," she managed, "being as this is our wedding day. One does expect one's wedding to be romantic, and one does so bemoan the lack of chivalry displayed by the modern male in general. Although the older generations do seem to have a better grasp of the concept, so I suppose I may expect more from you than I might otherwise. Indeed, if I weren't afraid you might come to harm I would *insist* that you carry me."

He ignored her and kept walking, while she tried to slow their progress by taking the tiniest steps she could. If only he and William had arrived tomorrow, at this moment she would have been becoming intimately acquainted with that Egyptian sailor, and her tale of lost virtue would be fact and not fiction and Nicholas Warre would not want her as his wife.

They passed a narrow alley, a street that led to the harbor, another that led into shadows. Where had William taken Millie? There had to be an escape. It could not end this way—him forcing her into marriage, dragging her back to England, locking her away—

Oh, God. Her legs buckled, and cobblestones bit into her knees.

"Stand. Up."

"I will. I certainly will. Only give me a moment—"

He didn't. Instead, he hauled her to her feet and hooked her around the shoulders— "Wait!" But it was too late, and she struggled uselessly in arms that disproved her assertions of his frailty.

"Your antics will get you nothing but imprisonment under lock and key," he told her sharply. "Where you will remain until you—"

Stop behaving like a spoiled child.

"—stop behaving like a spoiled child."

Panic made a grab for her lungs. He was exactly like Father. Exactly. And why shouldn't he be? Hadn't Father been the one to choose him? *Breathe. Breathe.* But when she did, there were only lungfuls of *him*— that expensive cologne emanating off warm, male skin that badly needed a shave.

"Oh, Mr. Warre," she managed, resting her cheek against his shoulder, "what a romantic you are." She pressed a palm against that same stony chest she'd been unable to budge in the alleyway. Beneath her hand, his muscles flinched.

Pain?

"I do hope you're not so battered from your tavern brawl that it hurts you to carry me." She shifted a little, curled one arm around his back, slid the other higher on his chest and squeezed. She felt his fingers splay across the side of her thigh. "Not at all, Lady India."

Her breath caught, and she snatched her hand away from his chest.

Now the church loomed just ahead, and she could make out William and—thank heavens—Millie, standing by the door.

If she were going to escape, she would have to think—*think!* Could they really be married if she refused to say the words? She could appeal to William's conscience. Behave calmly inside the church, waiting for any kind of opportunity.

There was still hope.

That hope died when she saw William's battered face. His turban was gone, and even in the shadow of night she could see his left eye was dark red. He had one hand locked around Millie's arm. "God's blood, you're a thrice-over fool," he said to India. "We could have been killed."

"Open the door," Nicholas Warre bit out at William, and transported India across the threshold. Inside the cavernous sanctuary, he deposited her on a pew near the front.

"India…?" Millie's anguished tone said she feared the worst—that Nicholas Warre had pressed his advantage since leaving the tavern.

"I'm all right, Millie. My dearest betrothed has been most solicitous, haven't you, darling?" Nicholas Warre wasn't paying any attention. He was scowling toward the front of the church looking for a priest. India sat up and looked dreamily around the shadowed church. "It's lovely. Everything I always hoped my wedding would be. Isn't it perfect, Millie?"

She waited for Millie to tell William to go to the devil, to unhand her, but Millie only stood woodenly in his grasp, gripping and regripping her own wrist. And now India was too aware of William's hold on Millie's arm, the possibility that he might be angry enough to thoughtlessly hurt Millie even knowing what she'd suffered in London. He would show no mercy—they may have been shipmates once, but Katherine was William's closest friend in the world, and he would not easily forgive India and Millie for taking her ship.

She looked pointedly at his hand on Millie's arm. "I *am* the bride, William—at least allow Millie to attend me."

William didn't budge.

Millie's eyes darted about the church for a possible means of escape, already dulled with the conclusion that there would be none.

India dragged in a breath. "So far this day has been everything a wedding day should be. In fact, even had I dreamed it I could never have hoped for something this unsurpassed in beauty and…" Nicholas Warre stalked off toward the church's recesses. "And splendor."

She tried to stop herself from shaking, but her whole body trembled. Millie's silent conclusion was correct: there was no chance for escape now. Nicholas Warre would offer the priest money, and they would be wed in a sham ceremony. And then they would return to that inn—

"William," she hissed the moment Mr. Warre was out of earshot, standing up, abandoning all pretense. "You cannot possibly be a party to this. After what he did to Katherine? Do I mean nothing to you at all?" The dark tomblike church swallowed her plea. It was deathly quiet, with the eerie flicker of candles sputtering in small banks next to a dozen shrines.

William forced Millie onto the pew. "At least he tried to take from Katherine in broad daylight—unlike the two of you, who sneaked away under cover of night."

"She wasn't using the ship."

"That didn't make it yours to steal," he bit out.

"At least give us a fair hearing!"

"The kind of hearing you'd receive if I hauled you back to England and accused you of piracy? You'd be hanged." William may have laughed in the tavern—William *always* laughed—but he wasn't laughing now, which was worse than anything he could have done. "You have a fine way of showing your thanks to Katherine. Would have expected more loyalty from you, under the circumstances." He looked at Millie. "Especially you."

Millie stared up at him, still working her fingers mechanically around her wrist. "I won't return to England," she said. "I can't. You know I can't."

"Millie and I apologize about the tavern," India said, more desperately now. From somewhere in the dark recesses of the church came the sound of Nicholas Warre knocking on doors and calling out. "Don't we, Millie. We never meant to put you in danger. And we know taking the ship was wrong—" depending on one's point of view "—but you've secured it once more—" unless she and Millie could somehow find their way back on board "—and this goes too far. You can't possibly approve of this marriage, William. You can't possibly. And it can't be what my father intended." But it could be, and it probably was.

What she wouldn't give to know what that contract said. If only she weren't such a muttonhead. If only those books in the *Possession*'s great cabin had done her any good. But she was, and they hadn't. Some people were easy to fool—Nicholas Warre would not be. She would have pretended to read the contract, understanding nothing, and he would have understood very clearly how stupid she was.

"Past time someone took you in hand," William said.

"Daresay Warre is better than having the crows peck the rotting flesh from your bones at the mouth of the Thames."

"You would never allow that."

"Not here on my own behalf, and the law is the law."

For a split second the image of a stinking, crowded room at Marshalsea paralyzed her lungs. "I won't say the vows," she warned, trembling harder now.

"You'll say them, or you'll suffer the consequences."

"Dear God—" Millie made a sudden dive to exit the pew, but William caught her by the shoulder.

"Sit."

"I'd rather you kill me now than return me to England," Millie seethed at him.

"And I shall kill Nicholas Warre if you do not stop this wedding," India warned. From the back of the church there was another knock, another call. "You know I shall." She would not be taken to England and locked away again—not in prison, and not by Nicholas Warre.

"You're a pair of fools," William barked. "Millicent—" He struggled against her. *"Enough."*

Millie kicked him. "Let *go* of me."

India scooted out of the pew. William snatched her arm but imperiled his grip on Millie. "Warre!" he shouted.

Almost immediately Nicholas Warre was there, pulling her away from William, who now held a wild, struggling Millie by both arms. "Where's the bloody priest?" William barked.

"There's nobody here."

"Got to be. Devil take it—" He turned Millie's arms

behind her back and held her head down, immobiliz-
ing her.

"Let me go!" Millie shrieked.

"William, you're hurting her," India cried.

"I'm not bloody hurting her."

"Anyone would have heard us long before now,"
Nicholas Warre said, holding India tightly against his
body. "There are other churches—"

"Can't drag this one through the streets like this. I've
got to get her to the ship."

"I've got my bag at the inn, and I'll be damned before
I'll leave this island unwed," Nicholas Warre snapped.

"Listen here," William said. "I'm— Millicent,
cease!" He adjusted his grip on her. "I'm taking this
one to the ship. You want to be wed? Then stay and
take care of the bloody business yourself."

CHAPTER FOUR

OH, YES. NICK would take care of this bloody business, and he would do it just as soon as dawn broke and a priest could be found.

"What a shame our wedding did not turn out as you hoped," Lady India was saying as he steered her back to the inn. "But you mustn't be too disappointed. Sometimes one's best-laid plans are put asunder for reasons much higher than mortal understanding can grasp. It seems clear—we did just leave a house of worship, after all—that Someone is attempting to keep you on the straight and narrow path, Mr. Warre."

"Indeed. The straight and narrow path to an early morning wedding."

"A *morning* wedding." He could hear the gears turning inside that lamentably pretty head. "Excellent idea. I always did think a morning wedding would be so charming."

To think, he'd imagined saying the vows, sending Lady India to the ship with William and devoting a few motion-free hours in that lumpy bed.

"You'll secure me a room of my own tonight, naturally. It isn't proper for a bride and groom to pass the night together before the wedding."

He ignored her.

"I'm sure my father will want to know that everything was done as it should. Nothing unseemly—Father has always been dedicated to making sure one does what ought to be done." She missed a step, and he tightened his grip to keep her from falling. "I would hate for you to produce me as your wife, only to find your reward withheld because you overlooked a bit of common propriety."

The word *propriety* falling from her lips might have been laughable if anything had been laughable, which at this moment it was not.

"I shall be very well behaved, of course. In my own chamber. You needn't worry about a thing."

Yet for some unfathomable reason, Nick bypassed the desk clerk and hauled India once more up the stairs to his room.

At the first ray of dawn, he would rouse a pair of sailors and pay them to spend a few minutes in the church as witnesses. But until then, he was going to rest. Not sleep—he wasn't a fool, no matter how exhausted he was—but rest. It would have to do.

He pointed at a chair. "Sit."

"I am not a dog, Mr. Warre."

An hour—perhaps less—and he was already dreading the rest of his life married to her. "Sit *down,* Lady India," he repeated.

She flashed him a smile that—devil take it—shot raw lust straight through him. She put her hands on her hips and stared at him. "What are you going to do to me if I don't, Mr. Warre? Shout at me? Beat me? Or heaven forbid—no. You wouldn't." She widened her eyes at him in mock horror and put her hand on her heart. "You wouldn't *call off* our *wedding,* would you, Mr. Warre?"

He went to the bureau, intent on ignoring her, but she was having none of it.

"It would be so disappointing if you changed your mind about our nuptials. My thoughts are already filled with plans for our life together in London—soirées, card parties, dining with *all* of my friends. And of course there will be the theater, the opera, musical performances of every variety and I shall expect you to accompany me for a long and romantic walk in the park at *least* four times each week." She clapped her hands together. "Oh, Mr. Warre, I daresay I am half in love with you already."

He saw those lips smirking at him in the glass. If he survived the night locked away with her in this hellhole, it would be a miracle.

He pulled at his neckcloth, loosening it, and turned. "Are you."

"Once we are wed, I shall never leave your side. Not even for a moment."

"How intimate that will be."

And how mistaken. He would endure the voyage to England, collect his money and once the mortgage on Taggart had been lifted, he would lock her away where she could not injure his person or his reputation.

"Let me make one thing very clear," he said, turning now. "You have been apprehended. And unless you'd care to be tied up, you will sit. In. That. Chair." He pointed at it. "And I shall sit in the other. We shall pass what remains of the night, and in the morning you will become my wife. Depend on it."

THERE WAS A time and a place for defiance, and that time and place ended when he threatened to tie her up.

And so she sat.

Minutes ticked into an hour. More than an hour, though it was impossible to tell for sure, except for the candles slowly, slowly shrinking.

India fixed her eyes on Nicholas Warre, barely daring to breathe. It couldn't be possible. After all his threats, his manhandling, his confident declarations—

She sat perfectly still and watched. Yes, he was falling asleep.

From somewhere in the distance, a drunken sailor song lilted through the open window across the room. She didn't dare glance at the window.

His eyes drifted shut, only to open again and fix on her. "Go to sleep," he said. In that hard face with its purpling bruises, those eyes were like chips of green winter ice.

Very fatigued winter ice.

"I'm trying," she murmured, and shifted in the lumpy armchair. She let her own lids droop closed and flutter open, exactly as his had, so he might assume she, too, was drifting off.

If there was one thing that could be learned from a childhood spent locked away until the impossible was accomplished, it was how to wait.

After a moment she shut her eyes completely. The street below was silent. The only sound was the distant swoosh of waves coming ashore in the harbor. His scent came to her on a puff of breeze.

Falling asleep! Could he really be that foolish?

No. Which meant either he was pretending, or he was as tired as he seemed.

Her hands tightened in her lap. A glance out the window earlier had revealed a drainpipe not two feet from their room. It hadn't seemed possible that the opportunity would present itself.

Until now.

She opened her eyes just a little and found his still closed. Dark lashes lay against sun-kissed skin, and his lips had relaxed into a less grim shape. A moment passed, then another, but those eyes did not reopen. Small creases at their corners testified that he was no mere youth, but with a face like that... No, *ancient* was hardly accurate.

Fascinating.

He was incredibly handsome. There was no denying it.

But she'd spent too much time locked away in rooms, too many years at the mercy of a man who showed no mercy. She would not exchange Father's unyielding lack of compassion for a husband's—not now, not when she was finally mistress of her own life.

Her toes curled restlessly inside her shoes while his chest rose and fell, rose and fell, a little more deeply with each breath. *Wait. Just wait.*

Minutes passed.

More minutes

Slowly, carefully, India sat forward. A fresh puff of night air was just cool enough to make her shiver.

Silently she rose to her feet, tensing, fighting off a sudden nervous tremor as she fixed her eyes on Nicholas Warre.

His hands lay slack on his lap. No movement. Nothing.

She crept toward the window. It was torture knowing her pistol was tucked into his breeches, but there was no help for it. She paused at the window and stared at the back of his head, willing him to stay asleep. Between them, the bed sat untouched. Whatever might have happened on that shoddy bed behind him wasn't going to happen tonight. Or ever.

Slowly, quietly, she stuck one leg outside.

Listened.

Swung the other leg around.

Listened.

The only thing she heard was her own heart thundering in her ears. *Hurry!*

She sprang into action, reaching for the drainpipe, gripping it with both hands as she swung out of the window and landed with both feet against the building. Through the window she could see his arm and the top of his head.

She willed him to stay asleep and began her descent. The distance to the ground was nothing compared to a ship's crow's nest. Every scrape of her feet against the building sounded like the drag of twenty saws, but already she was near the next floor. The guests in the room directly below theirs had left the window open. She prayed the sound of her feet would not wake them.

One more floor and she would be on the ground.

And then, from above, a shout.

"India!"

Nicholas Warre's angry bark shot into the night from inside the room.

No!

She glanced up but he hadn't come to the window—not yet. There were only seconds to spare.

"Lady India!"

There was only one escape. She dived toward the

open window to her left and clambered through it just as
Nicholas Warre's voice came more clearly from above.

"Lady India!"

She tumbled through the window and onto the floor,
bruising her elbow. A woman screamed. A man shouted.
A large form leaped from the bed just as India scrambled to her feet and darted half-blindly toward the door.

"Arretez!" the man shouted.

"Excuse me!" No—French! *"Pardonnez!"* India
stumbled over an open trunk. The woman in the bed
screamed loud enough to wake the entire city.

A pistol shot exploded in the darkness. India
screamed and dropped to the floor just as the ball
whizzed past her head and slammed into the door.
"Don't shoot! *Don't shoot!*"

"Henri!" the woman shrieked. *"Tirez! Tirez!"*

"No! *Don't* shoot!" Thank heaven she could speak
French—thank heaven she hadn't needed to read to
learn it. There were shouts from other parts of the hotel.
Doors slamming.

A match flared. *"Ne bougez pas!"* the man ordered.

"I won't—I won't move!" She kept her head buried and her faced pressed to the floorboards. Footsteps
pounded upstairs, outside the room, and she needed to
leave *now* or the chance would be lost. "It's a mistake,"
she told him in French. "You must let me go. Please—
quickly! I must *go!*"

Candlelight sputtered to life. *"Un voleur, eh?"* He
snorted. *"Vous allez le regretter."*

"I'm not a thief. And I *am* sorry—very sorry. But I
must go!" She started to sit up.

"Henri, idiot! Tirez!"

"Tais-toi!" There was a mad rustling as though he

were struggling into his clothes. Footsteps thundered outside the room. A crescendo of voices poured through the paper-thin walls. Someone pounded on the door.

"What is going on in there?" came an angry voice in Italian.

"Please—you must let me leave by the window. There is a man trying to abduct me, and I was only trying to escape—"

"*Silence!* The authorities will make quick work of you."

The authorities! "No, you must listen. I am not a thief—ouch!" He yanked her to her feet, not listening at all. "I am staying upstairs with a man who is trying to abduct me!"

He dragged her to the door.

"I am not a thief!" If he summoned the authorities, she could end up in gaol.

He wrenched the door open. Nicholas Warre burst into the room followed closely by a man who could only be the innkeeper. There was a commotion of angry voices—the innkeeper furious over the damaged door, the Frenchman outraged by India's invasion, the woman screaming and huddling beneath the covers, the onlookers exclaiming from the hallway.

"I must ask you to release my wife," Nicholas Warre told the man in French.

"Your wife!" the man exclaimed.

Faced with a choice between being mistaken for a thief or being mistaken for Nicholas Warre's wife, she broke away from the Frenchman and launched herself at Mr. Warre.

"Oh, Nicholas!" India cried, clinging to him. "Tell this man I'm not a thief."

He offered the Frenchman a grim smile. "You have my deepest apologies. I am discovering that my bride has unconventional ways of showing her displeasure with me. The lady was not nearly so eager for our nuptials as her father, I'm afraid."

"Nicholas, how can you *say* such a thing? I was perfectly eager until you brought that...that *awful woman* into our room and tried to make me— Oh!" His grip tightened painfully. "Would not any bride climb out the window under such circumstances?"

"You can imagine that whatever justice you might hope to exact, she exacts from me tenfold daily," he told the Frenchman grimly, and gestured toward the pistol. "In fact, perhaps I ought to beg a favor and ask you to put me out of my misery."

The Frenchman made a noise.

"Shame on you, Nicholas. Sir, perhaps you would be so good as to explain to my husband that a wedding night is meant to be a private evening involving only *two* people."

Laughter erupted in the crowd, and India silently thanked Auntie Phil for being a bit too free in describing her friends' amorous liaisons.

Nicholas Warre reached into his pocket and held out a sovereign. "For your trouble—again, with my deepest apologies and my sincerest request that you not summon the authorities."

India held her breath.

The Frenchman narrowed his eyes at the coin, and finally lowered his pistol, stalked forward and snatched it. "*Bien.* Take her away." He gestured as if India was a pile of refuse in Nicholas Warre's arms and turned his anger on the crowd. "All of you, *allez! Allez!*"

Nicholas Warre dragged her mercilessly into the crowded hallway.

"If you would rather be shot than marry me," she told him under her breath, "I would be happy to arrange it."

"If you can find a way to escape your cell aboard the ship," he growled into her ear, "I invite you to try."

CHAPTER FIVE

INDIA LAY ON a hammock watching candlelight dance on the wooden walls and letting her mind go numb, while Millie stood with her forehead and hands pressed against the door. Their prison was a cabin on the same deck as William's, bolted across the outside with a heavy wooden slider India had barely glimpsed as William shoved her into the cabin with Millie.

"I can't let them put me on trial for piracy," Millie said against the wood. And then, "William!" Millie's voice cracked as she cried out and pounded on the door. "William!"

India had learned years ago that pounding, clawing and shouting would not make a locked door open.

"Millie, *please.*" A cold wisp of panic snaked through her, and India snuffed it out quickly.

Millie stopped shouting. "Are you all right?" she asked quietly.

"My stomach hurts." It always hurt when she was locked away, probably because being locked away usually meant going without a meal.

"I'm sure William will send us dinner," Millie reassured her. She knew what India had endured as a child—she just didn't know the full truth of *why* India had been punished so severely.

And India wasn't going to tell her. She wasn't going to tell anyone, ever, if she could help it.

At least William would not be entering the cabin every few hours to make irate demands that India do the impossible.

"I knew Father would send someone after me," India said now, "but I never thought…" About what that would mean for Millie. Truthfully, she'd never really considered that whomever Father sent might actually succeed in capturing her. "Please forgive me."

"It isn't your fault," Millie said, turning to lean her back against the door.

The old Millie, the pre-London Millie, would have snipped that it *was* India's fault. The two of them always bickered aboard the *Possession*. And they still bickered plenty. But ever since London…

It was as if Millie had built a great stone wall around herself that even India could not break through.

Perhaps that's what people did after they'd been beaten nearly to death.

"The money," Millie said now. "It was everything I had." Her tone said she already believed their stash of money hidden aboard the *Possession* was lost forever.

"We haven't left Malta yet," India said, pressing fingers carefully into her belly, trying to relieve the cramping. "We're still a stone's throw from the *Possession*."

Their entire plan rested on Millie's money: it would let them make a start in shipping, which would enable them to make enough profits for Millie to attend the surgical school at Malta while India carried on their trade routes. Eventually, India would buy her own ship and return the *Possession* to Katherine.

"She may as well be anchored in Bristol for all the good that does us now."

"She's *not* in Bristol," India said irritably. "She's a hundred yards away. We can swim a hundred yards. We could not swim to Bristol."

"We won't have the opportunity for swimming."

"Not unless we look for one."

"William's crew will be crawling the ship like ants."

"There won't be that many of them. If we can escape while it's dark—"

"That will only make it more dangerous."

"Fine," India snapped. "We won't escape. We'll be locked away in this cabin forever, and William will likely *not* bring us any dinner—" her stomach spasmed a little "—and we shall waste away until we starve to death and he throws our bones to the fish."

India reminded herself that Millie was afraid, had *always* been afraid even though she would rarely admit it, and that it was only natural for the fear to grow worse after what she'd suffered at her brother's hands. But still...

She imagined having Gavin Germain at the business end of her pistol. It would be less than he deserved.

"Or until Lord Taggart marries you," Millie said, "and I am hanged or thrown in prison."

She hadn't come all this way only to be captured and dragged back to England, where she would exchange one gaoler for another: her father for a husband who would have complete control over her, would do with her as he pleased, would own her. Who would discover how useless she was and be ashamed of her, but by then it would be too late.

No. She could not let that happen. At sea, she felt

useful. Knowledge came easily. The ropes, the pistol…
Father would never, ever have allowed her to touch a
pistol.

"You know what happens to women in prison," Millie said now.

"Stop it, Millie."

"The same thing that will happen if we manage to
escape but can't retrieve the money."

India knew Millie well enough to know exactly what
she was thinking. "We're not going to end up as pros-
titutes."

"*You* won't—you'll be married to Lord Taggart."

"The devil I will," India said sharply, reaching for
anger as a lifeline, and finally she sat up, steadying herself in the hammock with toes that barely touched the
floor. "We haven't failed yet. We're on a ship, aren't
we?" It wasn't logical, but being on a ship seemed better than not being on a ship.

Millie let out a strangled laugh. "As if we could take
a ship from William."

Under no circumstances could they possibly take the
ship from William. But, "We could take a longboat. We
could float in a barrel if we must. Or perhaps we'll
attacked and captured."

"Being taken captive by Barbary pirates is your solution?"

"We only have to escape. We'll find our way back
to the *Possession* before William has a chance to re-
provision it for sailing. We'll sneak aboard—at night if
necessary—and we *will* get the money." Already half
a dozen new thoughts tumbled through India's mind.
"Someone will bring us a meal, and that someone will

have to open the door. And that someone—" hopefully not William "—will likely be male."

"How is *that* supposed to be comforting?"

How much would Nicholas Warre want her if she bedded one of William's crew? "If our chance for freedom equals my opportunity to ruin myself—"

"What fascinating mathematics!"

"—then the odds that we can—"

"It's your father's money Lord Taggart wants, not you. You'd wait until some poor sod delivers our gruel, bed him in the hammock and discover that Lord Taggart still plans to wed you and we are as far from that money as ever." Millie exhaled. "You'll likely not have the chance to ruin yourself anyhow. Lord Taggart will do the deed himself at the first opportunity—only wait."

India grew warm, remembering how he'd touched her in the alleyway. She rubbed her arms, pacing a little. "What else can I do to deter him?"

"Likely nothing. God, I hate men," Millie said bitterly. "I hate them, India." Those normally soft brown eyes grew hard and cold. "Arrogant sods, expecting everyone to submit to their whims."

"Indeed."

"A pox on them all."

"I shall show him, Millie. I shall show Lord Taggart exactly what kind of wife he would have if he goes through with this, and believe me, he will quickly find some other way to pay off his debt."

NICK PACED THE quarterdeck, already feeling a little queasy from the roll and sway of the ship, and stared at the near-dark city where that blessedly motionless bed would never see use now—at least, not by him. The injustice of it made him want to cry. Or kill someone.

If that someone weren't the key to his financial solvency, he might have done just that.

Climbing out the window—God's blood, he'd been careless, letting himself fall asleep with her there. He was lucky she hadn't slit his throat.

There were footsteps behind him, and Jaxbury's voice cut through the night. "India said you threatened to shoot her. Threaten her with your pistol again, and you'll find your own way back to England."

Nick didn't bother to turn. "Now that we're aboard, there won't be a need to threaten her."

"Believe that, and you *are* a damned fool." Jaxbury laughed and crossed his arms, joining Nick at the railing.

"We'll be underway in the morning, soon as I find the rest of my crew."

"Can't make England come quickly enough to suit me," Nick muttered, and contemplated taking a longboat to shore for half a night's rest.

"Then you'd better hope the roads through France are passable."

Nick's gaze shot to Jaxbury. "What are you talking about?"

"Change of plans," Jaxbury said.

Now Nick straightened. "Devil there are. You'll return us to England as you promised."

"Happy to, if you'd like to wait a few years."

"Now listen here, Jaxbury." Nick advanced on him. "The agreement was you would help me find her and return us to England along with that ship you were hunting. Immediately."

Now Jaxbury's expression hardened. "Helped you find her, and I don't care to do anything more. Damned unpleasant business, Warre. Ought to leave you here to find your own way, but I've got to get those two away from the *Possession*. After that—" He shrugged. "Got a mind to stay here awhile and do a bit of trading."

"That was not the agreement!"

"Ought to be plenty of priests in Marseille to do your job for you."

France was absolutely, positively out of the question. "You know bloody well a trip through France will present a thousand opportunities for her to run off and get into God knows what kind of trouble." And would require passage through Paris.

"Not my problem, Warre."

He'd spent fourteen years avoiding Paris and the man who lived there—a man he never cared to meet. Whose existence he tried to forget, but couldn't.

"What about Miss Germain?"

"Miss Germain is *my* problem. Not yours. We require passage directly to England," he bit out, knowing there wasn't a damned thing he could do if Jaxbury refused. "As agreed."

"Then I suggest you return to shore and find another ship."

Jaxbury knew bloody well that wasn't an option. On Jaxbury's ship Lady India was safely locked away; if he arranged for passage aboard a different ship, he would have to try to control her without being noticed. He couldn't hold a pistol on her from the folds of his greatcoat for an entire voyage—especially not when he would likely be bedridden the entire time.

It would be no different in France, riding in jolting

coaches from one inn to the next while those devious blue eyes plotted death and destruction at every stop, where she would have plenty of opportunity to beg, cajole, win support…even divest herself of her virtue.

Hell.

IT WAS WILLIAM who brought their breakfast the next morning. And William again, an hour later, who came with other news.

"Warre is sick. Had to set sail without my surgeon, thanks to you two, and I need *you*—" he pointed at Millie "—to tend to him."

"Is he going to die?" India asked hopefully from the hammock.

"Not going to die." William looked at her pointedly. "Not by your hand, either."

That remained to be seen. "I'm sure I don't know what you mean." She pushed the hammock idly with her toe. "The thought of killing someone never crossed my mind. I'm quite content. I can't think when I've enjoyed a voyage more, if you must know—"

"Devil that," Millie said irritably, facing William with her hands clenched. "If Lord Taggart's ailment isn't life-threatening, then he can tend to himself."

"*I* could tend to him," India offered.

William barked a laugh. "*You* will stay as far away from Warre as the ship allows. And *you*—" he pointed at Millie again "—will tend to Warre, or you'll not leave this cabin. You'll find what you need in the infirmary."

There was a small commotion in the passageway, and two sailors wrestled India's and Millie's trunks into the cabin and dropped them on the floor with a thud.

"Don't get any ideas," William warned when they

left. "Been all through those trunks. Nothing more dangerous in there than—well, might have said a petticoat, but neither of you own one. Best put on something warm," he said to India. "I'm sending you up the yards."

"You are?" The promise of freedom got the better of her, and India jumped off the hammock.

"In a merciful mood. And we're a man short. My boatswain is under strict orders that you're not to have a moment's rest."

India narrowed her eyes at him. "I can't believe Nicholas Warre approves your releasing us from this cabin." She studied his expression for any hint that there had been a falling-out, that William might have become an ally.

"Not Warre's ship," he said flatly. "You'll not throw yourselves overboard without somebody seeing it, and if you try, you'll not see the outside of this cabin until we reach France."

"France," Millie said sharply.

"We're not sailing for England?" India asked. New hope flooded through her so fast she felt light-headed.

"Marseille," William said. "And once you go ashore, you'll be Warre's problem and not mine."

"You're going to *leave* me with him? In *France?*"

"Aye. Now hurry up—Warre's green with mal de mer, a stiff breeze is coming up and we're about to go full sail."

CHAPTER SIX

MAL DE MER. They expected her to spend her life tied
to a man who suffered from mal de mer? For the next
two days, India watched Nicholas Warre emerge from
the cabin for short reprieves on the upper deck, where
he would stand with his hands curled around the railing
and his elbows locked, staring at the horizon, braced
against the ship's motion—the glorious, magnificent
roll and sway that made the wood and ropes creak and
splashed sea spray into the air to mist her face.

From the lower deck India watched him emerge
again, making his way up the stairs wearing no wig,
no hat, no turban. His dark hair ruffled in the breeze
and glistened in the sunshine. Without a waistcoat, his
shirt stood out white like the sails against the sparkling
sea. He was remarkably steady despite his affliction.
She watched him brace himself at the railing, followed
the line of his arm to his shoulder. She already knew
he was as strong as any sailor on board.

She pulled a line with Tommy, one of the youngest
of William's crew, who smirked. "There's 'is lordship
again, going to empty 'is stomach over the side."

If there was one thing Nicholas Warre had *not*
done—heaven be praised—it was empty his stomach
over the side. "I hadn't noticed him," India lied.

"Got no business on a ship, that one."

It took a double effort not to stare. The temptation was a matter of morbid fascination, nothing more. What woman would not stare at a man who was threatening to force her into marriage? She glanced at Tommy, who was much, much too young for her purposes, and looked past him to the other sailors.

Not one of William's crew was as exciting as the Egyptian sailor. They were like most other sailors— dirty, coarse, loud. She kept her hair pinned up and her tricorne pulled low and her waistcoat firmly buttoned. For now. But beneath her shirt, her unbound breasts strained against clothes that were not made to accommodate them, awaiting the right moment.

In another day or two, she would choose one of these sailors and orchestrate a tête-à-tête, as Auntie Phil might say. There was a Lorenzo who wasn't quite as awful as the rest. And he was Italian, which wasn't quite as exotic as Egyptian, but it counted for something.

Nicholas Warre remained at the railing for his usual fifteen minutes or so and disappeared below. He would be in William's great cabin again—had been there every day and evening since they'd set sail, despite his illness.

And sure enough, when she went below a while later to find Millie, there he was. She paused in the passageway, out of sight in the shadows, and watched him study a large scroll of paper he'd unfurled on the table and weighted with books at each corner.

A map?

Her eyes followed the line of his arm to the large hand splayed out, the solid finger guiding his study.

Betrothed. The word sliced hotly through her mind.

Husband. The too-real possibility shot by on its heels.

She studied the broad shoulders encased in the simple dark waistcoat he favored. The hard line of his chin, the shadow of beard on his jaw, the angle of his nose that was slightly too irregular to be called aristocratic. A quiet, pressing tug made her want to look at him, and keep looking.

As if Auntie Phil were sitting on her shoulder, a laughing voice invaded her thoughts. *I daresay this one knows how to conduct himself in a tête-à-tête.*

He exhaled sharply. India tensed. He rubbed the back of his neck and closed his eyes, then reached for a book that had more papers stuck between its covers than pages. He scratched a few notes with a pencil and returned his attention to the map.

He looked miserable.

He frowned at the map, pinpointing something with his finger, making a few more notes with a pencil on a leaf of paper. If only it were as easy as it looked. What would he think if he knew she could not even pen an invitation for tea?

He might decide she was unsuitable for a wife and return her to Malta. More likely, he would think her a disgrace, curse his increasing bad fortune and marry her, anyway.

He glanced up. Spotted her in the passageway.

Her breath hitched. And then she forced herself into the cabin, because the alternative was running away.

"We're in the Mediterranean Sea," she informed him breezily. "South of Sardinia. We'll be passing along—" It wasn't a map. It was a giant drawing of some kind of mechanical device—a mill, it looked like.

"*What* do you *want*." He said it as a statement, not a question, and rubbed his hand across his forehead. He looked at her as though he wanted to murder her—or possibly vomit on her, considering the greenish pallor of his skin.

"Ideally, I would like to be returned to Malta," she said even though it was obvious he was short on patience and feeling very poorly. "If Malta isn't possible, then I suppose Italy would do."

"If you haven't got anything intelligent to say, then I suggest you return to your duties."

"Oh, I have many intelligent things to say, Mr. Warre. A *great* many intelligent things. And not to worry—a lifetime together will allow you to hear every last one." She hopped onto the table and perched there, crinkling the corner of his drawing.

"Get down."

Instead, she rested her toes on the edge of his chair and studied the drawing. "Surely, if you plan to make your fortune constructing a mill, you don't need my father's money."

He ignored her and took a measurement, jotting the figure on a chart.

She leaned closer. "Three and an eighth."

His eyes shifted to her, and he stared, expressionless.

"It was three and an eighth," she said. "You wrote three."

"It was an estimate." Oh, yes—there was definitely a spark of irritation just now.

"An estimate. Oh, I see. Do forgive me. One doesn't *estimate* aboard a ship, or one could end up in Alexandria instead of Athens." She dove her brows and cocked her head to the side. "You haven't been merely estimating the size of your debt, have you? Because I would hate to live beneath my standards even after you've pocketed my father's money."

"Get down," he repeated. "Now."

"Such a tremendous effort you're making to win my hand. Very commendable."

He waited for her to obey his command.

"I must say it is flattering beyond all description," she went on, "being pined after with such heartfelt devotion and such puppy-dog eyes. It's only too obvious that you love me to distraction."

"Lady India." He leaned forward. "As much as I burn endlessly for you body and soul, as I suffer in lovesick torment, as I can scarcely keep my wayward mind from composing spontaneous sonnets in your honor—" he pushed to his feet and braced his hands on the table, looming over her "—I must request that you *remove yourself from this table* else I shall do the removing for you."

"Will you."

His face was inches from hers. "One."

One?

His gaze touched on her lips, raked across her breasts, returned to her eyes. "Two."

"Are you *counting,* Mr. Warre?" Her pulse leaped a little. Those eyes were nothing like a puppy dog's. They were predatory and on fire with thoughts that would make Frannie sound like someone reading from a ladies' companion.

"Control yourself, Mr. Warre." She slid off the table and onto unsteady legs, but refused to break his gaze. "Wearing one's heart on one's sleeve is dreadful unseemly."

"Were I not overcome by love and adoration," he

said, still much too close to her face, "I would certainly be capable of greater discretion." The ship banked and lolled with a wave, and he gripped the table, clenching his jaw.

"Overcome by seasickness, rather," she scoffed. Trapped in the space between his body and the table, the subtle scent of his cologne teased every breath. "If you're feeling that ill, I can't imagine why you aren't in bed instead of sitting in here."

"For the same reason you study every empty barrel and piece of potential flotsam aboard this ship." He returned to his chair and seated himself.

"Why, Mr. Warre, if this mill can help me escape an unwanted suitor, you must explain it to me at once."

He picked up his ruler, silently took another measurement. Wrote it down.

One and three-eighths.

She went to the door. Turned. "Do not insult me by suggesting that we have even a single motive in common," she said with her hand on the jamb to steady herself. "I merely want my freedom, while *you* are motivated purely by—"

The desire to escape? Escape what?

"—greed."

She left him, frowning to herself, and returned to the quarterdeck.

A FEW HOURS later, Nick stood on deck, staring at the horizon as Miss Germain suggested, telling himself it helped when it didn't, wondering how in God's name he was going to survive a life wed to Lady India, hating that he had no choice.

This was what it had come to: an arranged marriage—

no, forced. Definitely forced. She was right about that much. A *forced* marriage to a young woman who had strayed so far from the usual expectations that she was hardly recognizable as a lady.

A wave of nausea gripped him and he let his head fall. He needed to accept that his life was not going to turn out the way he'd hoped, and that he would be doing well if he managed to save Taggart.

His shipping operation was defunct—destroyed by storms and pirates in the space of two months. All that remained was his debt, and the deadline he'd agreed to with Holliswell was fast closing in on him. Holliswell had "graciously" given Nick enough time to pursue Lady India and collect the dowry—Nick much preferred to think of it that way—from her father. But if Nick didn't manage it in…God, a few more weeks, Holliswell would take Taggart. That was the agreement: more time to pay off the debt, with Taggart itself as collateral.

There would be little left after that, and he would need to make the most of it. He would not risk another investment on the seas. He needed to have the plans for the new mill works ready by the time they reached London, which meant he needed to prepare drawings for each mill site and lay out projections for how quickly the new corporation—if the other men agreed to form it—might turn a profit.

It wouldn't be much of a profit. Barely enough to make all the repairs Taggart Hall desperately needed and pay the cost of maintaining Lady India in the standard that the wife of a peer should maintain. He'd already been forced to sell his house in London, which meant he had nowhere to keep Lady India while they were in town, except with James or Honoria.

What kind of man had to lodge his wife with his siblings?

Wife.

The thought made his lungs constrict, a bit like the thought of being locked in prison for the rest of his life. This forced marriage ran both ways. Most of the time he managed not to think about all the things that would be lost to him forever once he married Lady India. But sometimes…

God, he was a fool for wanting something most people didn't even have.

Something like the marriage his brother James had— companionable, passionate, loving.

You love me to distraction.

He couldn't imagine ever loving Lady India to distraction. But he could damn well imagine *making* love to her, which only made him more furious—mainly at Jaxbury, for releasing her from that cabin when she should have stayed safely locked away. She should not have been allowed to roam the ship. To sit on the table, giving him a view of shapely thighs encased in those breeches. Leaning forward so that her unbound breasts—God, her breasts—moved freely beneath her shirt and peaked against the fabric, scarcely hidden at all beneath her ridiculous waistcoat.

Even now, her raised voice drifted from somewhere near the bow of the ship.

He looked up, saw her climbing the yards. Bloody hell. Cantwell would have a fit of apoplexy if he could see her running amok like a common sailor. And Nick…

He would force her to marry him, collect the money her father had promised, take her to Taggart…and then what? Stand by while she swung from the chandeliers like an ape? While she ran about the estate dressed in a waistcoat and breeches?

A large wave rocked the ship, and he gripped the railing as his stomach rolled. *Deep breaths, deep breaths...* a few moments, and the nausea subsided. He reached into his pocket for a piece of the candied ginger Miss Germain had given him.

Footsteps sounded behind him. "Contemplating a good French wine?"

"Sod off, Jaxbury." Nick didn't bother to turn. But he did glance at Lady India, who was working a line up in the yards. High above in the rigging, he caught a glimpse of long legs and tight buttocks clad in a pair of old breeches. One fall, and his chance at fifty thousand would be gone.

Jaxbury grinned. "At least you're enjoying the view."

IF THE MOON hadn't been half-full, she would not have been able to see a thing in Nicholas Warre's cabin. Any fuller, and it would have been too bright.

His sleeping form was a dark heap on the bed as she tiptoed by. Across the cabin his trunk sat open with his coat and waistcoat draped over the edge. She crept toward it, pausing to make sure his breathing was slow and steady. One of the floorboards creaked with the ship's rocking. He showed no sign of waking.

There was nothing inside his coat. Nor his waistcoat, blast him. He must have hidden the contract inside his trunk. The moonlight was too dim to let her see anything but a black pit, so she plunged her hand inside and blindly groped around, feeling for paper. Her fingers touched linen. Silk. Wool. Velvet, covering something—coins! She was no pickpocket, but she would remember this. One might say he owed her, after all.

A book, then another book. She slipped them from the trunk and fanned the pages, but no papers fell out. She groped some more. Leather—a shoe. Another shoe. Cold metal—

"Whatever you're searching for, Lady India," came a gravelly voice from the bed, "you won't find it."

Damn, damn, damn! She inhaled sharply, and her head whipped around, even as her fingers touched cold metal. He hadn't moved, and it was too dark to see that his eyes were open, but clearly they were. She felt the length of the metal—a pistol! She closed her fingers around it and smiled.

"Perhaps not, but you will find it for me." She stood quickly, taking the pistol with her and pointing it at the bed.

"I don't think I will."

"I suppose you'll tell me no ball has been loaded, but I am convinced I could find your powder and load one before you could lurch over here to stop me."

He groaned and rolled to his back. "You threaten nothing but blessed relief."

She crouched down, still facing him, and groped for the powder and shot. "That's twice in our brief acquaintance that you've expressed a desire to see your life end. Hardly a noble sentiment."

He inched toward the edge of the bed. "I've long since dispensed…with being noble."

First one of his legs swung out of the bed, then the other. She still hadn't found the shot and powder. "Stay where you are," she warned.

"Hardly an effective threat under the circumstances."

"I shall hit you if I have to."

"Will you."

"Yes."

"With the pistol, I suppose."

That hadn't occurred to her, but, "Yes."

He was standing now. Blast it all, where was the shot and—powder horn! Her hand closed around it and she whipped it from the trunk, plunging her hand back in for the shot. This time she found it immediately.

"Aha!" she said, scooting farther away from him to the dressing table, while he steadied himself against the edge of the bed. "I have them now. If you would prefer to save us time and trouble, you may simply tell me where the contract is and I will retrieve it."

"Ah. The contract."

Loading a pistol was one thing she could do in her sleep. He took a step forward. She loaded a ball. "Yes. The contract."

"You do realize, of course, that destroying it would change nothing."

She tipped the powder horn and jammed the ramrod hard. He was halfway across the cabin. "That remains to be seen." She hoped. At the very least, if he had no copy of the contract, he could not prove he had her father's consent for the marriage. She leveled the loaded pistol at him. "Find the contract and give it to me."

He reached the dressing table. "Very well. But you'll have to move so I can open the drawer."

She stepped back. In the faint moonlight she watched him reach inside, careful not to get close enough for him to grab the pistol from her hand. He held a document up—but not out.

"Here," he said. "You may have it."

"Hand it to me."

"Come and take it."

"Ha." He thought she was stupid. "I'll not fall for your trap."

"Nor I for your threats. Which leaves us…where? You'll shoot me, I suppose, then tear up the contract and mop up my blood with the pieces."

"If I shot you, there would be no need to tear up the contract."

He gripped the dressing table and pressed his other hand to his stomach. "Devil take these waves."

Was he going to be sick right here? Now? "Give me the contract and return to your bed."

"I don't think I can—"

Oh, God. He was. "Quickly!"

He doubled over. "Christ—"

"No!"

He lurched forward, but all that projected toward her was his arm, snatching the pistol from her hand. He grabbed her with his other hand and held fast, standing upright now, and plunked the pistol on the dressing table.

"Pillock!"

"I believe that has already been established."

"Release me."

"I'm not a complete fool."

He did not smell sick. He smelled of the candied ginger Millie had been giving him to settle his stomach. His grip was warm and tight around her arms. "I do hope you don't intend to continue burgling into people's rooms after our marriage," he growled. "It would be a pity to have to keep you locked away for the rest of your life."

It was no less than she would have faced if she'd stayed with Father. "You would need a fortified tower to keep me imprisoned," she warned. "Or a dungeon." She would not be locked away again—not by him, or Father, or William or anyone else.

He eased his grip, smoothing his palms down her arms an inch or two. "Perhaps I shall build a tower just for you." In the dim light she saw his lips curve, and the hair prickled on the back of her neck.

"With the fifty thousand pounds you get from Father? I should think most of that will go to Mr. Holliswell."

"Indeed it will." His thumbs moved lightly, caressing the place where her arms pressed against her breasts, and—

Oh. The sensation of his touch against the sides of her breasts shot through her like fire, and for a moment she couldn't breathe.

"I—" Suddenly it was a struggle to form words. "I shouldn't think, in the long run, it would be worth it. You've endured weeks at sea when you obviously can't stand even five minutes on the waves. Now you're set to endure weeks more. You're willing to commit an illegal act—and forcing someone into wedlock does *not* create a legal marriage, Mr. Warre—and even more than that, once your debt is paid you will still have me to contend with." His thumbs ventured lower, whispering around her fullest curves. She swallowed. Hard. "You will have me for the rest of your life, which promises to be a considerable amount of time despite your advanced age. You will regret it bitterly, I assure you."

"No doubt I will."

"A sensible man would change his mind about wishing to marry me." The ship lolled, creaked. Outside, the nighttime sea splashed against the hull. Her breasts grew heavy with an odd kind of ache.

"Let us have one thing perfectly clear between us, Lady India. I do not *wish* to marry you. I *need* to marry you." His caress circled up, around. A nerve pulsed in a place much lower, much more secret. "No amount of your hoydenish tricks will change that fact."

"Oh, yes—I'm fully aware that I'm to be a casualty of your embarrassed circumstances," she breathed. His touch lulled her, made her want more, tempted her toward him in ways she couldn't quite resist.

"If you choose to see it that way," he said.

"That is the only way *to* see it." She needed to pull away from him. Now. But the sensations he was creating held her transfixed, rooted to the floor, too willing to debate him. "At least do me the honor of explaining what, exactly, I am to be sacrificed to save."

"I have a vision of you trussed like a pig and stretched across an ancient pagan altar." And *oh*—his thumbs brushed the tips of her breasts, shooting pure sensation straight to a point between her legs. He leaned close, lowered his voice. "We are talking of *marriage,* Lady India—a simple contract. In exchange for my protection, you agree not to bring me shame."

His words cut through her pleasure-fogged mind even as her breasts screamed with need. She broke from his grasp. "*That* is your idea of marriage?" Her voice felt thick, clogged with the pleasure he'd stoked.

"I rather think it's most people's idea."

It wasn't hers. Not that she had *any* idea of marriage— quite the opposite. Dread coursed in, lapping icily at the desire burning across her skin. "I need protection *from* you," she managed. "And as for my bringing you shame…perhaps you should have considered that before you agreed to marry a young lady as well acquainted with the ways of the world as I am. I'll not return easily to a life of drawing rooms and embroidering cushions."

She'd told Father as much in London, but he hadn't cared. A daughter married was a daughter tamed…or so he thought. And so Nicholas Warre thought, as well.

"It's all too clear you need protection from *yourself*," Mr. Warre said calmly. "Little wonder your father was reduced to such desperate measures. But know this…" His voice turned flinty. "You will not shame Taggart, Lady India. I'll not allow it."

You'll not bring shame on this family, India.... The echo of her childhood pooled coldly in her belly. She would not endure that again—she couldn't. "From the sound of things, it's too late for that," she scoffed. Anger flashed dangerously in his eyes. "If you insist on forcing our marriage, I daresay I shall only be adding to Taggart's shame. What will happen if you cannot pay your debt to Mr. Holliswell?" she taunted.

"Oh, it will be paid," he said flatly. "It's merely a question of whether he'll be paid with the dowry I receive from our marriage or with Taggart itself—and Holliswell will *never* seat his greasy, self-satisfied arse at the head of Taggart's table." He pointed at her. "No matter if I've got to drag your pretty behind in front of a priest and have an altar boy move your jaw up and down while reciting the vows in falsetto. This wedding *will* take place."

"And you accuse *me* of shameful behavior."

He made a dismissive gesture. "For God's sake— you've got nothing to lose and everything to gain."

"Gain?"

"For the price of a few meaningless vows, you'll have Taggart's name and you'll live as any other young woman would be content to live, and in ten years at least *some* of Society will have forgotten your transgressions. It's more of a chance at redemption than most ever receive."

"I don't need redemption." She made herself laugh. "But you will, sir, if you do not quickly repent the grave mistake you're making."

"Oh, I don't know that I would call it a mistake," he said. His shadowed eyes dropped to her breasts, lingering. Her breath hitched, and her sensitive peaks came alive with fresh, unwanted desire. "Especially if I am to find such pleasure at my fingertips," he added huskily.

A heady yearning curled inside her. She never should have allowed him to touch her. But it was too late to take it back now, and it was too clear that he may not have wished to marry her—but he did want something else.

She forced her feet to move and went to the door. "Good night, Mr. Warre." The ship banked with a large wave, and she turned, smiling back at him. "Do sleep well."

CHAPTER SEVEN

INDIA LET HERSELF into the passageway and crept back
to her cabin, trying to ignore that her body hummed
with the lingering effects of Nicholas Warre's touch.

Gain. He thought she would *gain* from marrying
him, when he'd made his expectations perfectly clear.

Oh, God. She stopped, suddenly, in the middle of
the passageway. Leaned against the wall outside her
cabin, taking a moment to compose herself, aware of
her breasts in a way she had never been before—but
even more aware of the things he'd said, and the fact that
she could never, ever allow this marriage to take place.

She knew all about the things a man would do to
avoid being shamed.

Your hoydenish tricks...that was how he saw her. He
did not see her accomplishments, her skills. He was
already ashamed to take her to wife—just as Father
had been ashamed when she'd returned to London and
locked her up in her apartments.

Only imagine how Nicholas Warre would treat her
if he discovered her biggest failing. Except she didn't
need to imagine, because she had an entire childhood
of memories to draw on.

*You may redeem yourself, India—and have your din-
ner, as well—the moment you decide to apply your efforts and read me these stanzas from Pope.* It hadn't

mattered to Father that applying her efforts had never done any good.

It wouldn't matter to Nicholas Warre, either. When he learned she couldn't read, he would try to force her just as Father had, and withhold every pleasure from her, and it wouldn't work because no matter how hard she tried it *never* worked. And he would prevent her shaming Taggart by keeping her hidden away, and Taggart would become her prison, just as surely as her childhood rooms had been.

Her stomach twisted. She needed to do something now—*tonight*. But the only person who could possibly save her now was William.

Yes. Yes—she could talk to William. Tell him everything—make him see how imperative it was that she be in charge of her own destiny. She would promise anything in exchange for his forgiveness. Then perhaps he would let her and Millie join his crew, and then they would have protection instead of needing to make their way alone. And it would be just like before when they'd sailed with Katherine—

"India!" Millie's voice hissed through the darkened passageway.

India turned. "Millie?"

Millie hurried from the darkness and grabbed India's arm. "Come—come quickly!"

"What's happened?"

Millie didn't answer. India practically ran after her down the corridor to William's cabin, through the door, and—

Oh, God. "What have you done?"

"I don't know—I don't *know!*"

India fell to William's side, where he lay motionless on the floor.

"It isn't as bad as it looks—"

"How can it not be as bad as it looks?" Oh, God. Oh, *God.* India shook him.

"No! Don't try to rouse him!"

"We have to!" She listened for breath—yes! He was breathing.

"No, we don't." Millie grabbed her arm and tried to pull India to her feet. "India, *this* could be our opportunity. I didn't mean to do it—I didn't—but we won't escape any other way...you know we won't. And even if we do, what then? But if we take this ship back to Malta now, we can retake the *Possession*—"

"We can't return to Malta. When William's crew finds him like this, we'll be killed." She felt behind William's head, encountered a bump wet with warm blood. Pain fisted in her stomach. "Mutiny? How could you? He'll kill us himself when he awakes!"

"Not if we lock him in here."

"We can't do that! Not to *William!*"

"Have you forgotten he came here on Katherine's orders?"

"You know bloody well the crew will never accept our leadership."

"Did you not hear their complaints as we boarded? These men are not loyal to William. They were hired two months ago. They thought they would be a week at Malta, but instead they're back at sea after only a day. Believe me, the promise of returning to Malta will have them in the palm of our hands. But in case it doesn't..."

She held out a pistol, shot and powder.

The metal glinted in the moonlight through the windows of William's cabin. India looked at the pistol. At Millie.

"I can't do this. Millie, you should have *told* me first."

"It wasn't something I planned!"

"We'll be pirates. *Real* pirates."

Millie's hands were trembling. She quickly set the pistol and shot on a chair. "He's come to no real harm."

"Aye," India said sarcastically, "That is *precisely* the definition of piracy. As long as nobody comes to harm—"

"We shan't be stealing William's ship." Millie sounded terrifyingly determined. "We shall merely divert it back to Malta and then return it."

"If we return to Malta with William and Nicholas Warre aboard, there will be no way to keep them secured until we make our escape. We'll be apprehended before we can weigh anchor out of Valletta."

"Then we shall leave them off somewhere before Malta."

India's breathing turned shallow. Leaving them off was different from keeping them safely aboard.

"What are we going to do when William awakes?" India asked.

"There are things I can give him to keep him calm—"

"Millie, we can't *do* that."

"Do you have a better solution?"

Yes. They could wake William and beg for his mercy. But even William had limits, and they had already exceeded those limits by taking the *Possession* from Katherine.

Now there was no turning back.

Millie hurried to dress William's wound while India held his head with shaky hands. "Is there any chance he would wake up and think he fell and hit his head?" India asked.

Millie answered with a look.

"You *confronted* him?"

"I went to ask him a *question*."

"And knocked him *unconscious?*"

"I didn't care for his answer! Hold his head higher."

William's slackened features were terrifying. "What if he dies? How can you be certain he won't die?"

"Stop asking questions and help me put a pillow beneath his head!"

"What good will a pillow do us now?" None. A pillow would do them *no* good. But India stuffed one beneath him anyhow and grabbed up the pistol and shot.

Nick awoke to the sharp pounding of a hammer.

What the devil—

He pushed himself upright in the darkness, realizing at the same time that the hammer was pounding against his door. He bolted out of bed and tried to wrest the door open, but something on the other side held it fast.

Bang! Bang! Bang!

"What the devil is this about?" No answer. "Jaxbury! Jaxbury, you sodding bastard, *open the bloody door!*"

The hammering stopped, and it wasn't Jaxbury that answered.

"How does it feel to be locked away, Mr. Warre?" Lady India's voice singsonged through the door.

The implications raced through his mind. "Where is Jaxbury?"

"William is none of your concern. From now on you shall answer to me as your captain."

"Tell me what's happened to Jaxbury." Lady India, and presumably Miss Germain, could not have taken over the ship unless—

"You need not fear for your safety, Mr. Warre, as long as you cause us no trouble. You shall be let off at Sicily—it should be easy enough for you to find passage back to England from there."

Nick's blood ran cold. "Is Jaxbury dead?"

"I do not care to answer any questions. You will remain in your cabin. Of course, that shouldn't present any additional hardship for you with your ill health. But I intend to keep the door locked just in case."

"So you will put me off at Sicily, and then what? You and Miss Germain will sail the Mediterranean in a stolen ship? Once the line of piracy is crossed, it can't be undone."

"If I tell you I fully intend to cross that line, will it make you less inclined to marry me? Only imagine what shame it will bring upon Taggart to have a pirate as its mistress." Nick did not bother to answer. "Ah, well," she said after a moment. "I thought not. But only consider, Mr. Warre, how much *you* could profit by piracy. More than fifty thousand, I daresay."

"You and Miss Germain are as good as dead, Lady India. And anyone else out there—" he thought of the crew and called louder, in case any might be listening "—do you imagine you'll not be counted as pirates, too?"

"Enjoy your voyage, Mr. Warre," she called, and he heard her footsteps fading down the passageway.

He stared at the door.

A wave of nausea rolled through his stomach, and he breathed deeply through his mouth until it passed. When it did, he lurched to the dresser for another piece of candied ginger and stumbled toward the pot in the corner of the cabin.

God, he hated ships. Despised them and everything they stood for.

With just enough moonlight to see, he slid the pot aside with his foot, gripped the wall for balance, and retrieved the pistol he'd hidden there. Loaded a ball, and replaced the pistol behind the pot with his reserve of shot and powder. Under these circumstances, having an extra pistol hidden away could become very useful.

He returned to the bed, sinking into the mattress and staring at the ceiling while his stomach threatened another rebellion.

In the space of—what, half an hour? Longer?—he'd gone from stroking her breasts, God *damn* it, to being imprisoned in his cabin with Jaxbury possibly dead. They couldn't actually have killed him. Could they?

Whatever they'd done, Lady India would have had the opportunity for none of it if he had alerted Jaxbury and returned her to her cabin like he should have instead of standing there captivated by the womanly swells beneath her shirt. Putting his hands on her was a misjudgment of incalculable proportions. Yet he'd scarcely touched her at all—so much less than he'd wanted to do, and so much more than he should have.

And she'd reacted. Bloody devil, he'd seen exactly the moment it had happened, had seen the way her lips had parted a little, had noticed how she stumbled over her words as he'd caressed her full, heavy curves.

A strangled laugh pushed into his throat. Perhaps *that* was the way to tame her. Good God.

The ship pitched now with a large wave, and he braced himself to keep from rolling.

He'd thought her foolish and stupid. Had wanted—*needed*—to believe it was true. But that was just as much of a mistake as touching her. There'd been something else in those eyes tonight—something he'd been in too much of a hurry to notice in Malta, or perhaps just unwilling to acknowledge: a dark shadow.

Evil?

No. It was the dark shadow of desperation one saw in the eyes of street urchins. Except that Lady India was no urchin. She was the spoiled daughter of an earl.

And she was a pirate. And according to his agreement with her father, his fiancée.

If he were smart, he would let her put him off at Sicily and be grateful to see the last of her.

But he wasn't smart. He was nearly fifty thousand pounds in debt. And she may have been desperate, but she was forgetting one thing.

So was he.

CHAPTER EIGHT

THEY MANAGED FOR a day, and then another, and another, until India began to wonder if they might succeed at this after all. They'd known William was all right when he'd begun pounding on the door and shouting before the first night was through.

The carpenter had filed enough of a space beneath each door to slide plates of food and low-lipped trays filled with water, like one might give a cat.

"I'm worried that there's been no sound from William's cabin since this morning," India said to Millie, as the setting sun spilled into the captain's great cabin at the end of the third day.

"Did you expect him to pound at the door without ever giving up?"

"I don't know *what* to expect." India rubbed her arms and paced by the windows.

"We'll make Sicily by tomorrow midday," Millie said testily. Already the wind had softened, and they both knew they would be lucky to reach Sicily by nightfall tomorrow. "We'll put them out, and they'll be ashore in an hour or two. Nothing will happen to them."

"I only wish I could say the same of us," India snapped.

But by noon the next day, the wind had died completely overnight, and it showed no sign of returning.

India licked her finger and anxiously held it up, but the only sensation was the warm Mediterranean sunshine. "Nothing."

"It will pick up," Mille said, working her fingers absently around her wrist.

"Is that optimism I hear?"

"Pragmatism," Millie snipped. "The wind has to blow sometime."

But above them the sails hung limp while the ship floated calmly on a sea disturbed by the barest ripples. Below, the crew lolled about on deck with nothing to do but watch her and Millie stand helplessly on the upper deck and wait for a breeze to catch the sails.

India held William's spyglass to her eye and studied the distant green ribbon that was Sicily.

"The crew is getting restless," Millie said under her breath.

"I *know* that." India cast a wary glance toward the bow, where fifty men controlled only by their desire to return to the Valletta taverns had stopped lolling and now milled about impatiently. She caught the boatswain's eye and lifted her chin the way Katherine had always done, and was satisfied when the boatswain turned away.

India studied Sicily once more. "How far do you suppose it is really?"

"Too far. Putting them in the longboat here would be murder."

"You're right—the wind will pick up. It's got to." India said it mostly to reassure herself. "Perhaps I should order another keg opened."

"A third keg? They'll all be drunk."

"But occupied."

"Oh, yes. That's the perfect—dear God." Millie's hand flew to her chest, and she gripped her wrist tightly. "India, look there."

At the bow, the twenty-seven crew members had all gathered together in a huddle. Without the crash of waves and the snap of canvas, the voices carried easily to the upper deck in an increasing crescendo of discontent.

India touched her pistol. "If they mutiny..." There would be little she and Millie could do to stop them.

Millie watched the group through eyes that had grown fearful. "They could do no more in charge of this ship than we can—nobody can control the wind."

India thought of the brawl in the tavern at Valletta and felt a chill despite the warm sunshine. It would take mere seconds for hell to break loose aboard this ship, and the crew could throw them overboard or simply kill them and be done with it. Or worse.

From somewhere below deck came the sound of a small explosion. India snapped her attention to Millie. "A pistol shot."

"Who could be shooting?" Millie asked frantically.

And another.

Moments later—too soon to reload—another.

India counted heads rapidly. "All the men are on deck." Which meant it had to be William...*and* Nicholas Warre. "Bloody hell—it's them."

Bang!

Fear surged through Millie's voice. "We can't let them escape. We can't!" Her frantic eyes fixed on the deck below. "What's happening now?"

The group broke up, and the entire horde of men was heading toward the upper deck.

Bang!

India judged the distance, but she would never get past them to the stairs to see who was shooting. And at what. But it was a good guess the target was the door. A loud pounding—louder than any fist could make—confirmed it.

India's heart raced. Millie was absolutely right: they could not allow William to escape. India drew her pistol at the same time Millie drew the one she'd taken from William, and together they rushed to the stairs and aimed down at the men gathered on the quarterdeck below.

"What is the meaning of this?" India called down.

"Just want to talk about this wind," the boatswain called, taking the first step with a dozen men behind him.

"Do not come any closer!" Millie aimed her pistol at the boatswain's chest.

There was another pistol shot from below. More violent pounding. If they did not go below quickly, William and Nicholas Warre would soon come above.

"There's nothing to discuss, as you well know," India told the men. "We shall be underway as soon as we have a breeze." Angry faces outnumbered them six to one. "Return to your posts at once, and as soon as we are underway there will be more rum for everyone!"

Bang! Another shot from below.

"Clear off," India commanded. "Can't you hear those shots? If I don't go below immediately, you'll all be strung from the yards for piracy when Captain Jaxbury escapes." Oh, God. Oh, *God.* And she and Millie would be strung with them.

"T'aint us that locked up the captain," someone called out.

They didn't clear off. Instead they crowded up the stairs. Too late she realized she should have resorted to her pistol while they were still gathered below. "Do not cross me," she shouted. "One of you will die—who will it be?" She only hoped it wouldn't be her—her and Millie both, moments after she fired a shot. But if she waited...

Below, more pounding. And hacking.

The sound of ripping, splintering wood.

A burly sailor stepped forward, and she shifted her pistol toward him. "Are you volunteering to die for the others?"

The sailor stopped.

A warm bead of perspiration trickled from her temple to her jaw. Stalemate. The glassy sea shone behind the men as far as the eye could see. The ship made no sound.

Except for voices from below. Male voices.

And hard, solid footsteps.

"India..." Terror edged Millie's voice.

"I know."

"We've got to go over the side."

"And then what?"

Suddenly the sailors' attention shifted behind them, to the stairs—the quarterdeck. A shot fired, and all hell broke loose. Millie fired back. A man screamed, and the crew rushed them. For two heartbeats India had a dead bead on a man's chest—Lorenzo's chest. A voice in her head screamed, *Murderer!* In her hesitation, the moment was lost. Angry hands grabbed her, tore her pistol away, shoved her roughly toward the stairs. Above the voices she heard Millie scream.

And then— *"Enough!"* William's deafening command rose above everything.

At first they ignored him in their frenzy. But he pushed onto the upper deck, bellowing at them to cease. Right behind him was Nicholas Warre—with a pistol.

Men were explaining, pushing her and Millie toward the front of the crowd, calling out "We got 'em, captain" and "Kill the pirates!"

A moment later they faced Nicholas Warre and a William she scarcely recognized as the lighthearted sailor she'd known for years. Fury had turned his eyes cold, his face expressionless. He barely spared them a glance before descending to the quarterdeck. He stalked to a massive coil of rope, took up the end and began winding.

Nicholas Warre stalked after him. "What the bloody hell do you think you're doing?"

Now the crew shoved and crowded down the stairs, dragging India and Millie with them. India lost sight of William, but not before she'd seen the noose taking shape in his hand.

An uproar went up among the crew—shouts of "Hang 'em!" and "Let 'er swing!"

The world constricted to a small red spot in her vision. Perspiration ran down her face. Hands—men's hands—she barely noticed them.

Millie's screams came to her through a muted fog.

"Have you gone mad?" Nicholas Warre demanded. "You can't kill them."

William ignored him and kept winding. His usually laughing mouth was grim, and she knew him well enough to recognize that he did not want to kill them.

Breathe. *Breathe!* She fought for control, to stand tall instead of dissolving into hysteria. But William could rightfully kill them, and he would, because it was the only way to prove his authority in front of the crew.

Nicholas Warre yanked India from the sailor's grasp. "You will not murder my wife, Jaxbury."

"I'm not—" The protest leaped to her tongue despite her fear.

He silenced her with a violent yank. "Quiet!" he hissed in her ear. "For once in your blasted life." And then, "My wife is *my* responsibility," he said fiercely. "*I* shall mete out the consequences for what she's done." He looked down at her with the most awful expression and added loudly, "And I assure you they will be severe."

The fog of terror cleared just enough to realize what he was doing: he was trying to give William a way to change his mind.

He dragged her toward William amid cries of "Hang 'em!"

He jerked her even closer. "When I threaten him, beg him for your life," he ground out under his breath. "And prepare yourself."

For what?

Nicholas Warre raised his pistol and leveled it at William. "You will not touch my wife. I shall take her below and punish her as she deserves."

Beg. "William, *please*—"

"Silence!" Nicholas Warre's arm lashed out, and he backhanded her across the face. The force of the blow knocked her to the deck amid wild cheers from the crew.

Prepare herself to be *struck*. Hot, burning pain shot through her cheek, and she didn't have to pretend to cry.

William stopped winding the rope. He looked at her, and he laughed as though there was nothing more amusing in the entire world. "She can suffer for moments," he said to the crew at large, holding up the noose, "or she can endure a lifetime of punishment. Very well, Warre. Not going to interfere in the business between a man and his wife. Take her below and do your worst. But keep her out of my sight until Marseille, or I'll not be responsible for what happens."

Nicholas Warre yanked her off the deck. But now William turned his attention to Millie.

"No!" India screamed. "Millie!"

Silent tears streamed down Millie's face. As William approached, her wide brown eyes rolled in terror like an animal sensing slaughter.

"Quiet," came Nicholas Warre's command in her ear.

"William, *please!* You know what she's been through! You saw it with your own eyes!" Nicholas Warre shook her hard, dragging her toward the stairs. She fought him rabidly. *"Millie!"* Let Nicholas Warre strike her again—it didn't matter. "Will you finish what her brother started?" she screamed, crying so hard she choked. "Will you?"

But now Nicholas Warre had her in the stairwell, shoving her down the hatch, and she grabbed for the stairs to keep from falling while desperately trying to stay on deck. "I can't leave her," she sobbed. "I have to stay!"

Nicholas Warre held firm. "You will not stay and watch this. *Get your arse below.*"

"Millie!"

MILLIE STARED AT William, unable to speak. Unable to feel. It was as if she watched him from somewhere else, coming toward her. Behind him, the noose lay like a dead snake on the pile of rope.

There was a hot sensation on her face. Hot and wet. Tears.

She saw herself crying as though observing herself from the upper deck.

Sounds rushed through her ears—so many sounds. Voices, voices, voices. Screams—India's screams as Nicholas Warre dragged her away.

She needed to say something, *anything* to change William's mind, to at least show she was not afraid, but her throat would not work.

Forgive me.

The words raced through her mind, seeking an escape, but her mouth would not open.

"William, no!" India was screaming. Barely coherent, barely intelligible. "Millie!"

Millie looked at William and saw her brother Gavin. He came at her like before, and there was no way to stop him. She could only prepare herself for the blows. This time, she did not have to wonder if she would die. She thought absurdly of the school at Malta, that she would never see it now, and felt fresh tears slide down her cheeks.

William stopped in front of her, and she made herself meet his eyes. Dear William, who had stood by her bedside with Katherine and Philomena while she lay nearly dead from Gavin's fists. They had shown her nothing but kindness. But she could not live on their charity—she could not.

So she had stolen from them instead.

William's lips curled, and he crossed his arms across his chest. The crew began to chant.

Hang her!
Hang her!
Hang her!

But William silenced them and laughed the demand away. "Only look how small and frail she is," he called. "If I allowed myself to be taken by this woman, *I* am the one who should hang for my weakness."

A roar of protest went up from the crew. Her mouth was so dry she could not even moisten her lips.

"Silence!" William bellowed. "I will give you your satisfaction yet." He looked at Millie. In those blue eyes she saw a mixture of rage and regret. "Bring the lash."

CHAPTER NINE

BRING THE LASH.

The order sent chills down Nick's spine and sent India into hysterics. He felt sick to his stomach—sicker than any waves could have possibly made him. Jaxbury was taking this too far. Yes, they'd committed an act of piracy, but they hadn't injured anyone.

Well, except William.

He dragged India kicking and screaming toward his cabin, veering past it when he saw the mangled door that he'd shot and hacked to pieces in his escape. He went to hers instead.

"Release me! I must go above!" She was a dervish in his arms, kicking and wrenching violently this way and that. "Let go of me, you bastard!"

"Be still!" he barked. "Would you go above and meet the lash yourself?"

"Yes—*yes!*" The warning became an idea in those panicked blue eyes. "I shall take Millie's place!"

"Don't be a fool!" The idea of India under Jaxbury's lash made him feel a protectiveness he'd sworn never to feel again after Clarissa's betrayal. He cursed and kicked the door shut.

"He can't lash her. He *can't!*" India broke free and lunged for the door, but he grabbed her away. She flung out a fist and caught him in the shoulder.

"Enough!" He grabbed her arms.

"She almost died, and he *knows* she did—he *saw* what she looked like when her brother was done with her. Get out of my way!"

"You are *not* going up there."

She kept struggling. "Cretin! You will have to strike me again to stop me!"

"Do not tempt me!" But God knew he'd barely been able to force himself to do it the first time, and if her life had not depended on it—

A bloodcurdling scream filtered through the boards above.

"Millie!"

Somehow he managed to keep hold of India.

"He's going to kill her!" she screamed. Rage burned bright red on her cheeks beneath a stream of tears. She was close to breaking completely—it was there in her eyes. Vulnerability. Helplessness. Terror.

"He won't kill her. Jaxbury himself has spared her life—surely you see that. He cannot do more, not and maintain control of the ship. You know that as well as I do."

There was another horrifying scream.

"I can't stand it!" India let go of him and covered her ears. "I can't!"

Nick wanted to plug his ears, too. There was a roar— a cheer from the men, and he wanted to be sick. And suddenly India wasn't fighting anymore, she was cowering like a child with her hands over her ears trying to block out the awful sounds.

The need to protect her churned up from a place very deep—a place he'd never been quite able to control. A woman in distress wrenched him like nothing else.

He braced her head in his hands the way one might do when scolding a child, making sure his palms covered hers over her ears.

It wasn't enough. He needed something more—some kind of noise to block out the awful sounds.

"It's past time you surrender," he shouted. Perhaps it would be enough. "All this bloody nonsense, stealing ships and sailing around the world—you're bloody lucky anyone is willing to marry you at all. You're damned near spinsterhood as it stands—"

Another scream.

"—and everyone knows a girl's marriageability decreases exponentially with every month that passes, never mind all this nonsense about giving away one's virtue—but of course you're too naive to know what *that* entails."

She just blinked at him, so he kept shouting, louder—hopefully—than the sickening clamor from above.

"I ought to let you go—straight back to your father, who can find some other fool willing to marry you! Would you prefer that? Some fat, old lecher with a taste for deviance—" Good God, what was he saying? "—who will want to do things to you most whores wouldn't do? Someone who truly *is* ancient, and *then* you'll find out about the degradation of a man's body, and don't I wish I could see your face when you get a first look at *that*—"

India's blue eyes fixed on him in horrified desperation as she clung to his shouted nonsense.

"—but of course I shan't, because we shall be wed the moment we set foot in France—"

The men shouted even louder on deck. Tears welled up in her eyes. Ah, God—he needed some other way to distract her, so he did the only thing he could think of that was sure to infuriate her beyond reason.

He kissed her.

A full-on plunder of a kiss that was guaranteed to enrage. He dug his fingers into her hair, keeping his hands over her ears, and invaded her so completely she would have nothing left to wonder about kisses when it was through.

No working up to anything, no taking anything slowly.

Just him consuming her—ah, Christ, she tasted better than he'd imagined—and forcing her to engage with him and regretting it when she did, because her lips were as soft and sensuous as they looked…and too late he realized he couldn't do this and forget about it later, and he had no idea what the bloody hell to do next if this didn't get her fighting again.

Which it wasn't, because she wasn't struggling or kicking or trying to bite him. She was leaning into him. Letting him devour her.

Another tortured scream shrieked through the deck above.

And he couldn't do this anymore, because he was ravishing her innocent tongue, and her untutored response was killing him, and his body had no conscience. It didn't give a damn about torture and lashings. It was responding to her, and nothing could be more wrong.

He tore his mouth away, breathing harder than he should have been. In her stunned blue eyes he saw confusion, outrage, despair and—God *damn* it—desire.

He aimed straight for the outrage. "The moment we set foot in France," he said harshly, "you shall be mine. And *then* you will discover the true meaning of—"

"I don't care." Instead of running for the door she grabbed his shirt and tried to shake him. "She doesn't deserve this—you must do something! You must! All she ever wanted was to be a physician, to attend that devil-blasted school—"

"What? What school?"

"The surgical school. At Malta. All she's ever wanted was to be a physician, but then Katherine returned to England because of *your stupid bill of attainder*—" *now* she was fighting him "—and Millie went home, and her brother nearly killed her because she'd sailed with Katherine, and you've got to *do something* to—"

Another scream. What if Jaxbury was so angry he *did* kill her?

"—*stop him!* I'll do *anything*—I'll marry you the moment we reach France. I won't protest, I won't fight you, if you will *go above and stop the lashing!*"

It was a desperate promise she would never keep. But Jaxbury was taking this too far, and the sounds coming from above were more than he could take—never mind that if anything happened to Miss Germain, life with India would be a special level of hell all its own.

But those desperate blue eyes were staring at him as if he were her only hope in the world—God, but he was a fool—and it didn't matter anymore that she wasn't as vulnerable as she looked. "Stay here," he finally told her. "Do *not move.*"

He opened the door, but just as he stepped into the passageway there was a commotion in the stairwell. They were coming down. Jaxbury had Miss Germain by the arm. Men crowded at the top, and Jaxbury barked at them to return to their posts or they'd get the same.

Miss Germain's shirt was still on, but she clutched

her waistcoat to her bosom. Her knuckles were white in
the black fabric, and her face was strained and ghostly.
Jaxbury barely spared Nick a glance as he brushed by
and ordered Miss Germain into the cabin where India
waited. The back of Miss Germain's shirt was cut to
ribbons and seeped with blood.

Jaxbury ordered a cabin boy to bring ointments and
bandages from the infirmary and to tell the ship's carpenter to come and repair the lock.

Nick didn't need to ask if that was necessary. The
expected shrieking and pounding from inside the cabin
never came, and the silence was worse than India's
worst fit.

"Breeze is starting to come up," Jaxbury told him.
He looked about ten years older than when they set sail,
and there was no trace of his usual humor. "Putting you
and India out at Marseille, Warre—one of the men will
row you to shore."

"What of Miss Germain?"

Jaxbury's lips thinned. "She's none of your concern."

The hell she wasn't. The past half hour had made it
clear she *was* his concern—at least, if he ever hoped to
keep India in check. As dangerous as the two of them
were together, trying to manage India if she were separated from Miss Germain would be next to impossible.

But there might be a way to work this to his advantage, and if the situation was as he suspected, he was
not above profiting from it.

MILLIE STUMBLED INTO the cabin, and India's voice failed.
It was too awful. There was no way Millie could lie in
the hammock, so India snatched a pillow and blanket
and started to spread them on the floor.

"Just let me sit in the chair," Millie whispered.

India positioned it for her and helped Millie lower herself to the edge of its seat. This was not the time to cry—it would only make Millie feel worse—but sobs she couldn't control shook her chest. "Forgive me." She backed away, fisting her hand against her mouth trying to gain her composure, but the sight of Millie torn to shreds and the memory of her awful screams was too much. "I couldn't stop him…. There was nothing I could do." And then, "I will kill him." Rage exploded through her, and she rushed for the locked door. "I will kill William with my own hands!" The rough boards bit her skin as she pounded with her fists. "Do you hear me, William? I'll kill you!"

"India, *stop.*"

Millie's hoarse voice cut her to the quick. India's hands stilled against the wood, and she stood there, breathing hard with her hands pressed helplessly against the boards. She didn't want to stop. But there was nothing more to be done.

She let her forehead fall against the door, felt the grain press into her skin. "What can I do?"

"There is nothing left to do."

There had to be. There *had* to. Finally India turned away from the door.

"Oh, Millie—your back." India couldn't stand it. She looked away. "I wanted to die, listening to you."

"He told me to scream," Millie said quietly. "Before he started. He told me to scream as if my limbs were being torn from my body, and he would stop at five."

"To satisfy the men," India realized.

Millie nodded. Tears of anger leaked from her eyes, and her quiet voice broke. "I didn't want to scream.

I never did when Gavin hit me—not once." Her face burned with anger and shame. "I would rather have had twenty and kept quiet. But I knew—" Now she began to cry. "I knew I could well die…from twenty."

And William had known, too.

As dreadful as this was, it could have been so very much worse. And William would have had the right. They *were* pirates. On any other ship, their bodies would be swinging from the yards.

India sank onto the bed, leaned forward and buried her face in her hands.

It was too much—she couldn't take this anymore. She couldn't have the kind of life everyone else had, and she couldn't be left alone to have the only kind of life she wanted, and Nicholas Warre had no right to destroy what she'd worked so hard trying to accomplish—not that it would ever have worked, or that she and Millie would not have failed completely even with a new crew.

But she had nothing else. Nothing.

Millie sniffled. "Did he punish you terribly?"

"No." She took a deep, steadying breath. "No, he did not." And she could scarcely think of what he *had* done.

What it felt like to have his arms around her. To lean on him. To have him pull her close and—oh, God—*kiss* her. Deep inside there'd been a feeling that she wasn't alone, and that somehow he could make the horror go away and everything would be all right.

She'd felt…protected.

"I suppose he decided the situation was punishment enough," she said, picking at a fingernail while a new feeling curled inside her, sneaking into secret places she'd always made certain nobody could find.

"Your eye will be black by morning," Millie said.

Already it was swelling shut, and India's face throbbed and burned where he'd hit her. "He could hardly marry me and collect Father's money if I was killed by a mutinous mob," she said. He had only been defending his hope of the money he would receive by marrying her—he wasn't defending her for her own sake.

Except that he hadn't needed to cover her ears and try to keep her from hearing the horror of Millie's punishment.

But he had.

And now there was no going back and un-feeling what it was like to have someone defend her, no matter the reasons.

Millie let out a long breath and closed her eyes. "Perhaps you ought to negotiate with him."

"*Negotiate?* He'll accept nothing less from me than marriage, Millie." *The moment we set foot in France, you shall be mine.* That was what he'd said.

And she'd told him she didn't care.

It wasn't true.

She'd told him she would do *anything.* Even marry him.

He couldn't possibly have believed her.

"If you agree to stop fighting him—" Millie sighed "—he might agree to give you some of that money and allow you to live independently."

"Oh, yes—and renege on that agreement the moment he's got the money in hand." She could still taste him. The skin beneath her lower lip still burned a little from the scrape of his unshaven jaw, and her lips felt a little bruised. "We'll escape as soon as we arrive in Marseille," she told Millie. "We'll find a way to quickly return to Malta before William can ready the *Possession* to sail. We could yet steal it from under his nose—or at the very least, sneak aboard long enough to retrieve your money."

"We won't," Millie said raggedly. "Because once we reach Marseille, Lord Taggart will take you away, and we'll likely never see each other again."

MILLIE LAY ON her stomach in the cabin William had moved her to, with her back on fire. She tried to muster some kind of resolve, but all that was left inside her was an empty chasm.

The ship rocked and lolled in a newfound breeze, steadily making its way toward France.

In a day or two she would find herself alone in Marseille—left behind when Lord Taggart took India away. She would be forced to sell her body to disease-ridden sailors, earning no more than a few pence each time. The prospect curled around her lungs, making it difficult to breathe against the musty pillow.

A tear slid down the side of her nose and dropped into the ticking. An unholy thought crept like a finger of black fog into her thoughts:

Poison.

It would be quick. Easy.

And a terrible, horrible sin. But did that really matter now?

The scrape of the bar being lifted snapped her attention to the door. Quickly she swiped at the tear, cursing when the motion pulled at her wounds, cursing again when the door opened and Lord Taggart came in.

"Leave me," she said. "I do not want you here."

"I have a proposal," he said flatly, and shut the door behind him.

"Nothing you have to say could possibly interest me." Never mind everything that had transpired since Malta… If it weren't for Lord Taggart and his bloody bill of attainder, Katherine never would have left the Mediterranean to sail for England. They would all still be aboard the *Possession,* and soon Millie would have had everything in place to attend the School of Surgery.

"That remains to be seen." He spoke in that even, unperturbed tone that was his hallmark—as if nothing could disturb him, not even the sight of her wounds. "When we arrive in Marseille, I plan to hire a carriage and return to England traveling north through France. I have every expectation that Lady India will attempt to escape me." He paused, watching her. "I am prepared to take you with us, if you will assist me during the journey."

"To hell with you."

"In exchange, I will offer you a hundred pounds and a letter of introduction identifying you as a personal acquaintance under any name you like. I would claim to be your patron."

Now Millicent stared at him.

Go to the devil. Those were the words she should say. Instead, she thought she might vomit.

"You refuse? Very well." He started to turn.

"Wait." Her voice betrayed far too much.

He turned back. Crossed his arms. Stood staring at her with those cold eyes—India was right about that—while her mind spun in mad circles.

"What do you mean by *assistance?*"

"I have every expectation that my journey through

France will be marked by one escapade after the next wherein Lady India attempts to run off. I would expect you to foil those attempts and encourage her in a more lucrative direction."

Lucrative for him, at least.

She was supposed to say, *How dare you imagine I would betray India? I've never heard anything so offensive.* "India hardly listens to me as it is," she said instead.

"I'm aware this is a calculated risk. You may well decide to help her escape."

But he did not believe she would, because he knew how very desperate she was, and he was not above taking advantage of it.

But *she* should be. For India's sake, *she* should be.

She felt a little sicker. "Once you collect your money, you could go back on your word."

"True. But it will be in my interest to have you a continent away from my wife."

Unless Millie found a way to bring India with her. "And what if India manages to escape anyhow?"

"I feel confident India will not go anywhere without you. And forgive me, but you are in no condition to be traipsing about the French countryside." His gaze flicked to her back, hardened briefly, and his nostrils flared ever so slightly. If she didn't know better, she would think he disapproved of William's punishment.

I shall take her below and punish her as she deserves. But he had not punished India at all. Was he waiting until France?

"I will pay your room and board during the journey, of course," he added.

He thought the school meant more than India's friendship.

It didn't. It didn't. But... Dear God. It wasn't as if India would somehow escape this marriage. He would have his way in the end anyhow, and when he did, she would be left alone and penniless.

"If I help you..." Her lips suddenly felt paper dry, and she moistened them. "Will you promise never to lock her away?"

"Lock her away?" His brows dived.

"In her rooms. She cannot be locked away—she hates it more than anything."

"I shan't allow her to run wild and make a fool of me," he said flatly.

"I must have your promise."

She heard her own voice, bargaining with him, but it didn't sound real.

But with what he offered...she could disguise herself in men's clothes, attend the school and achieve a level of independence that would be impossible as a woman.

She thought of India and what *her* life might be like married to Nicholas Warre. Of the alternatives, of India flinging her virtue away to a sailor in a tavern, of hiring aboard a ship, where she would be discovered as female the first time one of the sailors got a yen for buggery with a cabin boy.

Or India could marry Nicholas Warre, endure his fists from time to time, look the other way while he diddled with the help. There were worse fates. At least she'd have money, a home.

Still... "Married or not, you should know I'll not stand by while you press your advantage in the adjacent room."

His cautious expression dived instantly into anger. "I'm not going to *press my advantage* against Lady India."

"Aren't you? How else do you propose to consummate this marriage you're so eager to complete?"

"Your opinion of me is lower than I imagined," he bit out.

He was a man, and he was a noble. Of course her opinion was low. She stared at him and waited for a promise he would be unlikely to keep.

"I assure you," he said coldly, "my interest in Lady India is strictly financial."

Oh, yes. She'd seen that strictly financial interest burning in his eyes when he looked at India.

She thought of India's fate. Of her own. Of what it would be like even if they managed to escape.

"May I count on your assistance or not?" he said.

Go to the devil. The words sat on her tongue.

"You may." She was the worst friend in the entire world.

CHAPTER TEN

MARSEILLE WAS CROWDED and damned hot to be wearing a greatcoat, but discomfort was a small price to pay with success this close. Which, of course, was an offensively liberal use of the term *success*.

Nick kept one hand locked around India's arm and the other wrapped around the pistol inside his pocket. It was probably an unnecessary precaution. And his conscience kept reminding him of that awful afternoon, and how small and vulnerable Lady India had been in her terror.

But he'd be a fool to forget what had happened aboard the ship a week ago. Lady India and Miss Germain were pirates, plain and simple, and now that he was alone with these two, he would be ill-advised to consider anything but how easily they had managed to take over that ship—and how much more easily they could overpower him if he wasn't careful.

He had fifty thousand reasons to be on his guard.

They made their way along the streets—Lady India eerily silent in the middle, Miss Germain a grim pallbearer on her other side. "Cross the street," he ordered. Lady India's lack of protest made him bloody nervous.

That thick rope of a braid hung down her back, glistening like gold in the sunshine. Her pert little nose was pointed stubbornly forward, and her mouth—God, he didn't dare think about her mouth. A fading bruise still darkened her cheek and eye—a bruise, he reminded himself yet again to assuage the guilt, that represented the only real consequences she'd endured for a crime that under any other circumstances would have ended with her death.

He steered them toward the first church he saw and told himself to stop thinking about what happened that day. Most of all, to stop thinking about the way Lady India had looked to him for help, and the terror in her eyes that had struck him where he was most vulnerable. He'd been prepared to interfere with Jaxbury's discipline—a foolhardy undertaking if there ever was one.

But he'd have done it. For her.

Just as he'd been prepared to sacrifice his honor for Clarissa, who—it turned out—cared nothing for him at all and had not even wanted his help. This vulnerability toward women in anguish was a personal flaw he would do well to remedy before he let his guard down and Lady India managed to escape. Because her silence could only mean one thing:

She had a plan.

"Do not scream," he said under his breath as he escorted her into the church. Inside, it was dark and a good deal cooler. It took a moment for his eyes to adjust.

Lady India didn't utter a word. But she was not going to say these vows without a fight—he'd lay his life on that. No doubt she intended to appeal to the priest for help. Which meant they were about to witness a prime example of the power of money.

A dozen people littered the pews. But up in front,

fussing with something inside a gilded box, was the man Nick was looking for.

The three of them walked down the aisle, and he caught the priest's attention. "Might we have a word with you in private?" he asked in French.

The priest inclined his head and gestured toward a door in the shadows. *"Bien sûr, mon fils."*

They followed the priest into a small chamber off the left transept. The door shut behind them with a solid click, and the priest turned to him. "What may I do for you?"

"This woman and I have met with unusual circumstances," Nick began, "and we need—"

"This man is trying to force me into marriage." There it was, in perfect French straight from those tantalizing lips. "I beg of you," Lady India continued firmly, "please give my friend and me refuge in your church. *Please.* You must help us."

The priest frowned at Nick. "Is this true?"

Nick gave India what he hoped was a shocked and wounded look. She was not going to evade him this easily. "My love, what can you mean?" He slipped the contract from his vest and handed it to the priest. "My apologies," he told the man. "She and I are contracted to wed, and I can only imagine that last-minute jitters—"

"He is holding a pistol to my side."

"A pistol!" The priest's eyes shot to Nick's other hand, buried as it was inside his greatcoat.

Nick withdrew his hand and let the pistol lie in his pocket. "Such a wild imagination."

The priest was frowning at the contract. "I know little English," he confessed, "but it does appear to say—"

"That contract is forged," Lady India informed him.

"This man wrote it himself in the hope of marrying me and exacting money from my father."

"My apologies again," Nick said to the priest. "Nothing could be further from the truth." He turned to Lady India and murmured, "My dear, what are you about? After last night, I would have thought— But forgive me. What happened between us is a private matter."

She glared at him with murderous blue eyes. "Nothing happened between us, as you well know."

He called their kiss to mind and let the full effect of it smolder in his gaze as he looked at her. "Didn't it?"

The spark of that memory caught fire in her eyes, and her cheeks flushed a particularly attractive shade of pink.

Nick smiled apologetically at the priest, even as he fought a fresh onslaught of desire. "As no doubt you can see, the circumstances demand a certain amount of discretion."

The priest eyed Lady India's tricorne, waistcoat and breeches for perhaps the sixth or seventh time, and Nick cursed his decision to visit a dressmaker after the wedding and not before.

Nick reached into his pocket once more and drew out a small sack of coins that represented a portion of the sum India's father had fronted him for travel expenses. The priest eyed the sack exactly the way Nick had hoped he would.

"I shan't say the vows," Lady India said testily. "You cannot make me. Please," she begged the priest, "you are a man of God—you cannot be a party to this."

Over top of Lady India's head, Nick met Miss Germain's eyes and gave her what he hoped was an unmistakable look: *do something to help.* She looked away, and he decided to refresh her memory about their agreement at the first opportunity. He returned his attention to the priest.

"Indeed, you appear to be involved in a most unusual situation." The priest held his hand out for the sack of coins.

"Your blood money cannot force me to speak," Lady India warned.

The priest's hand closed around the coins and he turned away. For the amount Nick had just given him, there should be no need for Lady India to say a word.

The priest went to a cabinet and turned a key, opening a small compartment. "Given the highly unusual nature of this marriage," he began slowly, "I will of course need to consult the bishop about the propriety of the matter before anything can be done." He looked sideways at Nick. "You would have no objection to that, would you, monsieur?"

Yes, he bloody well had an objection. Nick clenched his teeth. "I don't see the necessity—"

"Please do consult your colleagues," India interrupted wholeheartedly. "Surely you have a spare room, a small shelter where my friend and I might take refuge while you do."

"—but rather that time is of the essence," Nick went on. "Which, of course, I assumed you understood."

The priest turned an unmistakably disapproving look on Lady India. "I am afraid, mademoiselle, that we do not have such a room available." And then, to Nick, "*Oui*, monsieur. I understood you perfectly. If you will tell me where you are staying, I shall inform you when I have discussed this with the bishop."

"There is no need. We shall be on our way." Nick started forward, held out his hand for the coins.

"May I wish you a safe journey," the priest said, ignoring him and placing the sack inside the cabinet. "And may the Lord bless you for your most generous donation to our humble church." He shut the door and turned the key.

Bloody hell. "I'm afraid there's been a misunderstanding," Nick said coldly, knowing full well the priest misunderstood nothing.

The priest clasped his hands together. "My apologies. You would like me to speak with the bishop after all?" He smiled. "I thought not. I shall see you both out the side door."

"How many times must you fail at this before you realize what you're doing is wicked and wrong?" Back on the street, India wasn't sure whether to celebrate or panic.

There'd been no wedding, and Nicholas Warre had just lost a precious sum of money. But she had only one plan left, and it was the most terrifying of all.

"I shouldn't count myself victorious just yet if I were you," he told her. "That was not the only church in France."

"The question is," she said archly, "how many sacks of coins can you afford to lose?" It was a good bet the answer was not many.

They marched along the street, dodging people and dogs and carts going this way and that. His hand gripped her arm, and his face—the face she'd spent too much time thinking about while imprisoned in her cabin—was pure stone. Inside his greatcoat, his pistol pointed directly at her.

Which only made it more frustrating that those awful moments a week ago—his true horror, his earnest efforts to help—made it impossible to see him exactly the way she had before.

"Where are we going now?" India asked.

"To get you some proper clothes," he said.

She barely managed to hide her alarm. "I prefer the clothes I have."

"Of course you do." He steered them across the street, and India spotted a dressmaker's sign.

The moment she put on a gown, her ability to run from him would drop to practically zero.

The busy street teemed with activity—the perfect cover for an escape. One singular effort could be enough for her and Millie to lose themselves among the crowd. But Millie was in no condition for dodging through streets or climbing over walls or whatever else they might have to do in flight from Nicholas Warre.

Which is why your plan is not to run from him.

No. She planned to gain control an entirely opposite way. She'd thought it all through during those long hours in her cabin, but planning was different from doing, and now that the reality was upon her—

"Wait!" India stopped and put a hand to her stomach. Perhaps if she bought herself a few minutes to think…

"What now?"

"I'm feeling ill…"

"The hell you are."

"It's been happening every morning." She looked at

Millie. *We must do something!* "Do you think I could be...?"

"What are you talking about?" Nicholas Warre demanded.

She looked up at him, rubbing her hand lightly across her belly. "Mr. Warre, I must inform you that if you marry me now, I shall almost certainly bring forth a great shame upon you and your household."

His eyes narrowed, and he yanked her forward. "You are not enceinte."

"We can't know for certain."

"I daresay we can."

"There was an Italian deckhand on board William's ship. Lorenzo."

"Whom, naturally, you invited into your locked cabin at every opportunity for hours of glorious lovemaking."

"Please, Mr. Warre, if you are going to describe Lorenzo's skill at lovemaking, at least *attempt* to do it justice." He had her arm in his grip, but now she curled her hand around his and leaned into him, gazing dreamily into the distance, which in this case consisted of a donkey urinating in the street.

There was an alleyway, an open shop door, a giant, lumbering wagon piled with hay... But it was no use.

He turned his head just as she turned hers, and suddenly she was inches from his face. His green eyes dropped to her mouth. Her own gaze followed suit, dropping to his lips, which she remembered very, very well.

"What a relief to know I needn't take precautions for your inexperience on our first night together," he murmured.

A shiver dropped down her spine and crashed in

her belly, way down low. "Oh, dear, Mr. Warre." She laughed. "Now I am doubly sure you shall never live up to Lorenzo."

"And *I* am sure that, being the benevolent man that I am, I can be persuaded to overlook your indiscretion."

He opened the door to the dress shop and steered her inside.

"I SHALL HAVE him wrapped around my finger in no time," India told Millie in the back room of the dressmaker's shop, trying to sound more confident—and less anxious—than she felt. The dressmaker issued a string of instructions and gestured India toward a tall looking glass while Millie perched on a nearby chair that had fabrics piled across the back.

For Millie's sake—for both their sakes—her plan had to work.

"I can see you have him half-wrapped already," Millie said a bit glumly, wincing a little as she shifted on the seat.

"Doubt me if you wish. Only think what Auntie Phil would do if *she* wanted to escape from a man."

"Philomena? Want to *escape* from a man?"

"Voilà!" the dressmaker exclaimed, pushing a light blue gown into her assistant's hands, then a green, then a serviceable gray stripe.

"She would gain the upper hand through seduction," India said.

"Good God. You can't possibly be thinking—" Millie cut off abruptly.

Yes. It was exactly what India was thinking. And

what she'd been planning—but only as a last resort. A desperate measure.

They were at the point of desperation now.

"I shall seduce him, Millie, and have him eating from the palm of my hand, and then we shall be able to make our move."

She watched in the looking glass as the dressmaker's assistant helped her out of her beloved men's clothes and into a simple shift. She thought of Nicholas Warre, who waited at the front of the shop, and suddenly he may as well have been standing next to her, watching in the glass as she stood in nothing but her shift while the dressmaker measured her arms, legs, waist, hips.

"I already know it will work," she added. He hadn't been able to resist touching her that night in his cabin, and she'd been fully covered. A gown would not be nearly as modest as the men's shirt she'd been wearing that night.

"So your plan is," Millie began slowly as the dressmaker's assistant laced India into a set of stays, "that you will seduce him and he will suddenly bow to your every command?"

"He will be struck powerless," India corrected, and tried to believe it. "Isn't that what Auntie Phil says? That a man is rendered powerless by the sight of a woman's breasts?" She surveyed her breasts now and smiled. They practically spilled from inside the whalebone.

"I don't think she meant the way a pistol shot renders him powerless," Millie scoffed.

"A chance of rendering him powerless—or distracted enough for us to escape, in any case—is better than no chance." Although that night in his cabin, standing there while his hands wandered over her, she'd been rendered practically powerless herself.

The memory of it came alive, smoldering across her skin with fresh yearning, and now she thought of how possessively he'd kissed her, and how good it had felt to be held that tightly, and—

"Let us *hope* it will work as quickly as a pistol shot," she said. "Every moment of delay only takes us further from an easy means of escape." And escape was what she wanted—not the feeling of being in Nicholas Warre's arms. She may have succumbed a little before, but now she knew what to expect, and there would be no more weakness.

"I shall do it while we're still close to Marseille, so it will be easy to find our way onto a ship." She watched in the glass as the dressmaker pinned her smartly into a gown that, if she'd been at Father's house, would not have even done for her lady's maid. The gown took shape, molding to her form. Her breasts sat high above a blue ribboned stomacher pinned over her stays, and panniers caused the paler blue jupe to flare at her hips, accentuating her waist.

"I don't suppose you'll actually bestow your virtue on him," Millie said doubtfully.

Bestow her—

India exhaled. Felt a trembling of nerves deep inside, much different from what she'd felt in that Maltese tavern. "Perhaps I will," she said. "Depending on the exact…situation." Millie watched her in the glass with unhappy eyes, and India bolstered her resolve. "And I'll not listen to your objections this time. If bestowing my virtue upon Nicholas Warre will secure us a means of escape—" a whisper of heat feathered her skin "—then I shall simply see it as killing two birds with one stone."

Yes, that was exactly how she would see it. She would have given her virtue to that Egyptian sailor in Malta… There would be little difference in giving it to Nicholas Warre.

Millie smoothed her palms across her breeches. "Well, in that case…" She fiddled with the button on her jacket sleeve.

India waited. "In that case, what?"

Millie looked at her in the glass and raised her chin a little. "I was only going to say that if you're going to do *that,* you ought to do it sooner rather than later."

"So you do *not* object?"

"Of course I object. Only…" Millie fussed with her sleeve once more, and India knew exactly what she was thinking. Millie couldn't see any alternative, either.

"Only nothing. You mustn't feel guilty. You know how I've been anxious to be rid of this vexatious virtue." Butterflies converged behind her belly button as the dressmaker pinned a tuck near India's hip.

"Your husband will appreciate this gown very much," the dressmaker told India in French.

"I do not want him to merely appreciate it," India replied as confidently as she could, ignoring the dressmaker's misunderstanding. She smoothed her hands down her sides and hips, studying her reflection intently. "I want it to drive him to distraction." Literally.

One thin, dark brow rose. "In that case…" The dressmaker pinned a quick adjustment to India's stays and stomacher so that now, were it not for the short lace trim, a shadow of nipple would be visible.

India smiled at her reflection. Oh, yes. Once Nicholas Warre saw her, the seduction would be as good as complete. And *then* they would see who was in control and who wasn't.

THEY WAITED IN the back while the dressmaker and three assistants quickly stitched up the alterations to this and the two other gowns. A short while later the dressmaker helped her dress, and her assistant pinned India's hair into a simple chignon instead of her usual braid. In private, India helped Millie put on one of two ill-fitting gowns she'd accepted as-is rather than expose her wounded back during a fitting. India gave herself a last glance in the looking glass and turned away, confident that the pale blue gown would do everything it needed to.

The dressmaker opened the door to the front, and India swept out of the room with Millie in her wake. Nicholas Warre stood in front of the door looking out the window, and now he turned.

His eyes grazed her from head to toe, and his expression darkened. "No."

Her knees felt a little weak, but she forced herself to approach him. "Why, Mr. Warre," she said sweetly, "I thought you wanted me to dress like a woman." She pushed her shoulders back a little, and his gaze dropped.

Her skin tingled in response.

"Cover yourself." Now he was staring straight into her eyes, and he looked furious.

"I don't think I will." Whatever effect the sight of a woman's breasts was supposed to have on a man, so far it wasn't working. And it certainly would not work if she covered herself.

"Is the second gown the same as this?" he barked at the dressmaker.

"*Oui,* monsieur."

"Fix it. And bring the lady a fichu for this one."

"But I don't want—"

"Bring a fichu."

One of the seamstresses was already bringing a length of gauze. Nicholas Warre snatched it from her hand and shoved it toward India. "Put this on."

"No." India took a breath that pushed her breasts nearly to the point of full exposure.

"If you do not put this on," he ground out, clutching the fabric in his fist, "I shall put it on for you."

She raised a brow at him even as her pulse throbbed wildly in the base of her throat. "By all means, Mr. Warre. Your assistance would be most welcome."

A heartbeat later he had the gauze hooked around her neck and was crossing it in front of her bosom. The backs of his hands grazed her skin, and he took the ends of the fichu in his fingers, and her lungs stopped cooperating. His expression had turned positively black. Whatever Auntie Phil had meant about a woman's breasts, it wasn't working on Nicholas Warre. He wasn't supposed to be looking at her like this. He was supposed to be...

Slathering. That was the word Auntie Phil sometimes used.

"It will never stay after the fact," she managed. "You'll have to tuck it in very securely."

He raised his eyes and observed her for a moment with his hands hovering at the edge of her stays. "Will I."

Already her breasts felt heavy with desire, and it

was so, so difficult to breathe. But this was no time to give up. "Unless, of course, you *want* it to come loose."

There was a flicker—a lightning-quick bolt of intensity before amusement touched his eyes. "Oh, Lady India," he said, and slipped the fichu inside her stays. She gasped as his fingers slid against her peaked nipples, trapped by the pressure of tight whalebone, softened by the fichu's gauze. "I most definitely would *not*—" he pushed his fingers deeper "—want that to happen."

She couldn't think, couldn't speak, couldn't feel anything but a screaming need for him to keep touching her this way, except that they were standing in a dressmaker's shop and Millie was ten feet away staring pointedly out the window, and devil take it, she wasn't *supposed* to want his touch—

And just that quickly, he pulled his hands away.

She tried to speak, but her mouth had gone dry. She moistened her lips. His gaze dropped. His face seemed strained, and his green eyes seemed on fire. And then the dressmaker emerged with the second gown, which now had an extra strip of lace stitched across the top of the stomacher, and he turned away.

"Excellent, madame," he said. "Oh—and if I might have two lengths of your widest ribbon…"

CHAPTER ELEVEN

His sanity for fifty thousand pounds. That was to be the bargain.

The French countryside passed in a blur. Olive groves and vineyards hugged the terrain. High above, a medieval fortress town perched on a hilltop. The hired coach jolted so badly Nick could hardly read the words jumping across the page of the open book on his lap. The draft interest schedule on the seat next to him kept sliding to the floor, and directly across from him—nestled snugly beneath that blasted fichu—India's breasts sang a siren song straight to his cock.

He should have insisted—*demanded*—that she return to her breeches and waistcoat. But no, in his infinite wisdom he'd decided she should dress like a woman. And somehow, between the robbery at the church and the fiasco of her new wardrobe, they had gone from *I shall kill you in your sleep* to *Please do touch me*.

Holy mother of God.

He shifted the book on his lap. Focused on the words. And still, all he could think of was the firm peak of her nipples crushed against his fingers. Not that these thoughts were anything new… He'd been thinking about those soft, full globes ever since that night she'd sneaked into his cabin.

You'll have to tuck it in very securely.

She hadn't expected he would really do it.

He hadn't expected he would really do it.

And now all he wanted was to tear the stays away entirely and fill his hands with her flesh. But she had no skill for subtlety, and her game was only too obvious. She thought she was going to distract him with her feminine charms. Perhaps she imagined she and Miss Germain would be able to run off while he sat dazed in the throes of passion.

"People will see me like this and know I've been abducted," India warned now, raising her bound wrists. Three-inch ribbon, it turned out, made surprisingly strong bonds.

He was a fool to feel even the smallest amount of guilt over tying her up. His cheek still stung where she'd scratched him—a shift back toward *I shall kill you in your sleep.* The look she gave him now could have felled an entire regiment.

"With a cloak around you, they'll see nothing," he said. Next to her, Miss Germain sat staring out the window with her body contorted into an unfathomable shape to avoid having her wounded back slammed against the seat with every rut.

Lady India glared at him. "I need to use the pot."

"No, you don't."

She didn't respond to that, so he returned his attention to his book.

Fifteen minutes passed without another word. Thirty. An hour, as the sun sank lower in the afternoon sky thanks to their late start out of Marseille. But he could not have risked an overnight stay in a port city, not with these two women. They would travel as far as they could into the countryside and find an inn for the night far away from the blasted sea.

They were traveling through a picturesque valley when Lady India suddenly stood up.

"I think I should like to face the other direction," she said.

"Sit down."

"But the valley behind us is so lovely in the sunshine." She wobbled a little, standing with bound ankles.

"Sit *down*." The carriage jolted, sending her sprawling onto the seat next to him. His book slipped to the floor while Lady India struggled to right herself. She finally sat up, flailing a little with her bound wrists. One end of the fichu had come entirely untucked, and he now faced a crest of pink nipple peeking from behind light blue lace trim.

"Mr. Warre," she said, settling in next to him in a way that involved squirming on the seat such that her entire right side moved against him, "if we are to be married, I think it only right that we take every opportunity to become better acquainted, especially since our courtship will be so brief." This looked suspiciously like an attempt at seduction, and if it was, the journey to Paris had just taken a turn for the worse. "So many couples scarcely have a chance to become intimately acquainted before the wedding—in private, I mean, without prying eyes—but thanks to our unique situation, we may do as we wish." She gazed up at him, so close he could see the smattering of freckles on her nose.

Oh, yes. They'd come full circle once again.

"I never for a moment doubted that we could," he told her, fully aware they were *not* alone—the ever-helpful

Miss Germain continued to stare out the window across from them—and even more fully and painfully aware of Lady India's right breast pressed against his arm.

"Tell me your dreams, Mr. Warre. I want to know everything about you—absolutely *everything.* I want there to be no secrets between us. There should be nothing about each other that hasn't been laid entirely bare. No depth that has not been plumbed." He thought Miss Germain made a choking sound.

India moistened her lips in a way that was clearly unconscious, and Nick didn't know whether to laugh or cry. God, what he wouldn't give to feel those lips close around his—

"Indeed," he managed. It would take days to reach Paris. Days of enduring her attempts at seduction that were all the more intoxicating because she didn't know what in God's name she was doing.

He met India's gaze and immediately regretted it, because behind her faux adoration lay a yearning she wasn't quite able to hide.

If he wanted to...

He could win this game she was playing. He had a good deal more experience with *plumbing depths* than she had, and if he did this right—if he could stand it— he could snare her in her own trap.

THE SUN HADN'T yet set when Nick finally couldn't stand it anymore. It was only five o'clock—they could be at least three hours closer to England if they kept going. But devil take it, he needed to get out of this carriage. Now.

He pulled the bell and ordered the coachman to stop at the next inn, which turned out to be twenty minutes farther in a picturesque village that might have been a charming place to spend a few days with a willing companion. Instead, he found himself surveying the inn's stone walls for drainpipes and contemplating the wrought-iron balconies outside each room.

They pulled behind the inn to the carriage yard and finally, thankfully, came to a stop. India's cloak sat next to him on the seat and he shook it out just as a footman outside opened the carriage door.

"Stand up," Nick ordered, blocking any view of her with his body so nobody would see that her hands were tied.

When she stood, the fichu sagged open and gave him a clear and unhelpful view of the cleft between her breasts. He bundled the cloak around her and wondered how he was going to endure the rest of this journey.

"I shan't be able to walk with my ankles tied," she purred. "You will need to carry me."

Excellent. And it was too late now to untie her without calling attention to the fact that she'd been tied in the first place. Already a footman was handing Miss Germain out of the carriage and into a small chaos of barking dogs, footmen taking their trunks from the roof and two children offering to carry coats and bags.

"A single cry," Nick reminded her, pulling her to the door.

"I shan't be able to climb out."

"Bonsoir, sir, may I carry your coat?" A small boy tugged on Nick's waistcoat, while another struggled with a smaller bag the footmen had left on the ground, and a shaggy mongrel nosed Nick's leg.

"Mr. Warre, I'm losing my balance," India said.

Rarf! Ruff! Ruff!

Lady India was hanging back inside the carriage. "Come here," he ordered. She resisted.

Enough was enough. He shoved his hand into his waistcoat and tossed each boy a coin then grabbed Lady India around the shoulders, hooked his arm under her knees and lifted her out of the carriage.

"Oh, *thank* you, Mr. Warre," she murmured. "I was so afraid I might fall from the carriage, but only to see how chivalrous you are." Now he was close enough to smell the exotic scent that he already suspected was some kind of foreign soap she used, and even her cloak, stays and gown weren't enough to keep him from feeling every curve against his body as he walked.

A footman held the door and he edged in sideways, addressing the innkeeper more sharply than he might have. "My wife is feeling poorly. Have you a room she may use while I settle business with you?"

Within moments they were upstairs and the innkeeper was turning the key in the door to a small room with a giant bed.

INDIA'S HEART POUNDED furiously when the chamber door shut behind them. This was the moment she'd waited for—the moment she needed.

And she was already failing.

It was the moment to say something saucy, something seductive, but being in his arms was bringing back all those dangerous feelings she'd experienced before and all she could think of was how much she wanted him to keep holding her.

It only proved what a ninny she actually was. He carried her so she wouldn't escape, not because he wanted to hold her.

He set her down in front of the fireplace—slowly, so that every part of her body touched every part of his body before her feet met the floor. And still he held her against him, and still the sensation of it touched a place that she desperately tried to slam shut.

"Surely you can remove the ribbons now," she managed.

"Given that you've likely spent the entire carriage ride plotting a new plan for escape, I think I shall leave them in place."

Naughty. Say something naughty! "But surely we can entertain ourselves more without them."

"The ribbons are no obstacle to entertainment, Lady India," he murmured.

They weren't? He kept his hands on her upper arms, slowly moving up and down in a way that sent a shiver along her spine. His eyes searched her face.

She looked into them and got a little lost. They were beautiful eyes—so green, framed by dark lashes and dark brows, and at this moment, alive with desire.

For *her*.

A hot rush sizzled through places she'd scarcely been aware of before now. She raised her bound wrists and tried to put her hands against his chest, but she couldn't turn them, so she raised them farther and dared to caress his jaw. "But they make it so difficult to touch you," she said. Butterflies careened wildly through her belly.

Something dangerous flashed in his eyes, and a smile bent the corner of his lips. "Yet they create no difficulty for my touching *you*." He traced a finger down the side of her neck and along her collarbone. "Hmm," he murmured. "I daresay I was mistaken about the need for this." He took hold of the fichu and slowly, deliberately pulled it away.

Her breath caught. "I tried to tell you." She watched his eyes feast on the swell of her bosom, and a heady sort of thrill caught her chest.

This was going to be even easier than she thought. He was enjoying this. He *wanted* her. She didn't need Auntie Phil's experience with men to see that.

She became acutely aware of the bed against the far wall, of his hands now moving up and down her sides, brushing the outside of her breasts. Of the rise and fall of his chest, of the thundering rush of her pulse in her ears.

She traced his lips. They were firm. Warm.

He kissed a fingertip and took it in his teeth.

She fought back a gasp, and a lick of fire reached up from her belly to her throat.

He trailed his lips along each finger, while his hands feathered across the tops of her breasts. His touch was maddening—he did not dip his fingers inside her stays like before, but her nipples practically ached with wanting him to.

"I shall need help removing my gown for the night," she breathed, even though Millie was the obvious assistant.

"Will you." Those fingers moved farther from her breasts, not closer, and began a soft caress along her neck and shoulders. He dipped his head and touched his lips featherlight to the spot where her jaw met her ear.

She shivered.

"Cold?" he whispered in her ear.

"No."

He skimmed his hands down her back and trailed

his lips along her jaw, her neck. His hands spanned her waist and moved up, up, until she felt them cover her breasts, but the bloody stays kept them caged from any real sensation.

Between her legs, sensitive flesh throbbed. Her passage—the very place Frannie had said a husband would penetrate—felt warm and open. Even the brush of her thighs together had become an aching torment.

She turned her face to kiss him, but he moved at the same moment and brushed his lips against her other cheek. An involuntary sound of frustration escaped her lips.

He pulled back a little. The look he gave her could have set the sea on fire. "My apologies," he breathed. "Did I hurt you?"

"No, I—" *I what?* She couldn't tell him she wanted… Wanted *what?*

I want you to touch my breasts again, like you did before. And kiss me like you did on the ship.

He stepped back. "I'd better go settle things with the innkeeper," he said.

"Must you?" *Hold me. Please just hold me.*

A smile touched the corner of his mouth. "We can't have him tossing us into the night."

"No. Of course not." She smiled, but her body was tight with so many yearnings that the curve felt unsteady on her lips. "I shall be waiting."

What was she thinking? *She* wasn't supposed to want *him.*

The door shut behind him, and she lowered herself carefully into a chair by the fireplace. Her bound hands trembled in her lap.

He was supposed to want *her*—and he did. Knowing

that filled her with a need she could scarcely describe. He wanted to touch her, wanted to kiss her. *Her.*

Did I hurt you? His soft question whispered through her mind and lodged somewhere behind her heart. Did he really care if he hurt her?

Good God—of course he didn't care. Her hands and feet were *tied,* for heaven's sake. He'd held a pistol on her in Marseille!

You'll not shame Taggart, Lady India. I'll not allow it. Those were the words she needed to remember, every moment of every day if that's what it took. She must remain in control because his desire would lead to her freedom.

When he returned, she would take full advantage of that desire to regain the upper hand. And then she would finally give away her virginity—and receive Nicholas Warre's slavish attention in return.

NICK SHUT THE door behind him, and in the tiny corridor, leaned against the wall and closed his eyes.

Holy God. Holy *God.*

Tight need filled his breeches. Pure lust like he hadn't felt since school days.

His plan was working. Oh, yes, it bloody well was, but at a very high cost.

Because hers was working, as well.

He wanted to kick the door open and tumble Lady India on the bed beneath him. Yank those damned ribbons off her so she could put her arms around him and do everything he imagined she might do.

But he wouldn't. Not even if it killed him, which it bloody well might.

He had the advantage, and he would use it to the fullest. He would tease her until she became a whimpering putty of need in his hands.

He thought of those huge blue eyes, full of desire and questions and budding comprehension, looking at him—at *him,* Nicholas Warre, sworn enemy and scourge of the earth—for satisfaction.

But he would *not* satisfy her.

Absolutely not.

He inhaled. Exhaled. Pushed away from the wall and went downstairs to find the innkeeper.

He would think of Taggart, of the money and he would leave her burning and begging for more.

INDIA HADN'T BEEN waiting five minutes when a knock on the door startled her from her thoughts.

"Oui?"

A maid came in with an armload of wood. "For tonight's fire, madame."

Not him. Her breath left in a shaky exhale. *"Merci."*

They would need a warm fire. Because they would be nude. Wouldn't they? She felt her cheeks flame, as if the maid might read her thoughts.

"Oh!" The maid cried out, losing her balance as she bent forward to fill the wood bin. The wood tumbled from her arms into a pile at India's feet. India started forward to help, forgetting her bonds, and immediately fell to the floor.

"Madame! Are you all right? *Oh, là*—your hands. Your feet!" The maid scrambled forward to help, and clutched India's bound ankles. *"Qu'est-ce que c'est?"* she cried, horrified.

"C'est rien. I merely—" Nicholas Warre could return

any moment. "It is nothing," she repeated, trying to tuck her ankles beneath her skirts. "I am fine."

"Nothing! *Mais, non!*" Already the maid was yanking at the knot in the ribbon that bound India's feet. "There is nothing to fear, madame. I will help you."

"No, please— This isn't—"

The maid dismissed her protests with a hiss just as the knot came loose. "Your hands—quickly!"

"But I can't—" Another moment, and her hands were free.

If Nicholas Warre walked in and found her untied, he would be in no mood for seduction. It could ruin her entire plan. But the maid wasn't listening.

"*Venez!* Quickly! The servant's stairs will take you out. I know a place you can stay—do not fear!"

It could never work. Could it?

Did she really have a choice now? What about Millie?

"Madame!" The maid grabbed her arm and pulled.

"*Mon amie,* I can't leave her behind."

"I will tell her where you have gone. Now quickly. Quickly!"

They hurried into the hallway. India glanced over her shoulder, but Nicholas Warre did not appear. The corridor was empty. They flew down the servants' stairs and she half expected him to be magically waiting at the bottom, but there was only an empty hallway leading out a side door. "Here," the maid said, untying her cap and apron. "Put these on." She covered India's hair with the cap, tied the ends beneath India's chin and tied the apron around her waist. "Go to the abbey. You saw it on your journey here, yes?"

The abbey—yes. Yes, she'd seen an abbey.

"You will be safe there. Come— *Vite!*" The maid pulled her out a side door and into the carriage yard, where they skirted the edge of the building in plain view.

Oh, God. Oh, *God.* They could be seen at any moment.

They hurried to the road.

"That way," the maid said, pointing in the direction they'd come this afternoon. "It should take you— Oh!" The maid stopped short and waved to a man driving a hay wagon. *"Là!"* She pulled India forward, speaking to the man so quickly India could only snatch bits and pieces. Young woman—terrible cruelty—sister—bed—abbey—

"C'est mon cousin, Jervase," she explained quickly, while drops of rain soaked her cap. *"Vite!"*

Jervase—there was no time to assess him beyond his dark eyes and quick smile before the maid was pulling her, pushing her toward the wagon, practically shoving her up on the seat. *"Vite!"* the maid hissed. "He will take you where you can hide."

Jervase gripped her hand and pulled India up and into the shelter of his arm beneath a bulky brown overcoat. The wagon lurched forward, the maid ran back to the carriage yard and just that quickly India was free.

CHAPTER TWELVE

"Do NOT BE afraid, mademoiselle. Martine is forever rescuing things, and we shall rescue you, as well— from a tyrant of a husband, perhaps?" Tucked beneath Jervase's greatcoat, India jolted against both the man and the wooden seat while a steady rain pattered and the donkeys plodded through the mud.

"No." And then, when his brow rose in interest, "*Oui*. Yes, my *husband*. He is a terrible tyrant."

He only laughed, easily guessing which was the truth and which the lie. "I shall take you safely to the abbey… mademoiselle."

"*Non*—not the abbey." She realized now it was the first place Nicholas Warre would look.

"*Non?*"

"He will surely look there. My brother's man of business." Jervase didn't believe she was married anyhow, so she reached for a story more likely to win sympathy. "He will not be easy to hide from. He will search everywhere."

He raised a dark, interested brow. "Your brother's man of business."

"My sister and I have been living in Marseille with our aunt. But my brother doesn't approve—he sent his man of business to find us and force us home. We only just left Marseille this afternoon. My sister is still with him at the inn. I tried to tell your cousin I could not leave without her, but then it was too late. If he finds me, he will be furious. There is no telling what he will do."

Jervase made a noise, but it was impossible to tell whether he believed her story. If Nicholas Warre could not find her after a day or two, or three, or five…a week…how long would he pursue her before giving up?

If he did give up, he would certainly abandon Millie here in this village. Which meant if it really was possible to hide, all she needed to do was wait.

Except that in a valley this small, it would be impossible to hide. And for fifty thousand pounds, he was not likely to give up the hunt.

"Do not be afraid, mademoiselle," Jervase murmured, scooting a little closer—as if that were possible. "I shall take you to my sister's. She will not like it, but…" He shrugged. "She will have a place for you, and possibly some work—" he grinned "—if you do not mind milking cows."

Already India's mind whirled with the possibility: hiding on a farm in disguise as a milkmaid while she waited for Nicholas Warre to admit she had indeed escaped…or while she figured out a way to get Millie away from the inn.

"Of course, there is plenty of room at my house," Jervase went on. His dark eyes skimmed over her nose, her lips. "But I fear you would take offense if I offered you shelter there."

And suddenly India realized exactly what kind of opportunity she now had.

She should leap at the opportunity. It would turn Nicholas Warre off her permanently, wouldn't it? What greater shame could there be than to be cuckolded by the woman one intended to marry? The problem was…

She didn't *want* to throw her virtue away to this stranger. She wanted—

Everything inside her stilled.

No. She *couldn't* want that.

Giving her virtue to Nicholas Warre would be a sacrifice for strategic purposes only. Not because she *wanted* to.

Except that half an hour earlier, she'd awaited his return while her body ached and tingled, and she *had* wanted to. Give her virtue. To him. Nicholas Warre.

She swallowed. "I will be fine at your sister's."

He reached out and touched a raindrop that slid down her nose. "Too bad."

Twenty minutes later they slopped into a muddy farmyard, where a squat, ruddy-faced woman came out to meet them.

"Oh, c'est pas vrai!" the woman exclaimed, looking angrily at India. "Another of your *putains?"*

"Non, non!" Jervase practically shouted with an angry gesture, already on the ground and pulling India from the wagon seat while he explained. "I told Martine I would find her a safe place to stay."

"Ici? What kind of place do you think this is?" The woman looked India up and down, narrowing her eyes at India's wet décolletage.

"Don't be stupid, Collette," Jervase snapped. "Give the girl a meal and a bed in the barn."

India stepped back, only to run into Jervase. "Perhaps it would be better if—"

"Non, non!" Jervase said, hushing her. "You will stay here." He pushed her toward his sister. "Since when

have you denied anyone your hospitality? Anyone can see the poor girl needs help. A meal," he repeated. "And a place in the barn."

The woman pursed her lips. "One night," she snapped. *"Une seule. Et après—c'est fini!"*

Jervase grabbed his sister by the shoulders and planted smacking kisses on both her round cheeks. *"Merci,* Collette."

"Va t'en!" She shooed him away. "Go on with you!"

Jervase gave India a triumphant smile.

"And you," she said, turning on India. "If you steal so much as a single blade of straw, I'll have you charged as a thief."

"Perhaps you will change your mind, now that you have seen where you are to spend the night?" Jervase grinned at India.

Yes, I have changed my mind. Why not? It was no less than she'd planned all along, and it would solve any number of problems. But instead, "This will do perfectly. Thank you."

Ninny!

Jervase's sister looked as though she were on the verge of changing *her* mind.

"Mademoiselle, you are killing me." Jervase's dark eyes roamed over her. "But I shall check on you later to make sure you are indeed comfortable."

His sister threw her hands into the air. *"Mais, non! Non!"* she cried, shooing him away. "None of your playing here. *Va-t-en! Va-t-en!"*

Jervase winked at India and left.

NICK MIGHT HAVE described Lady India as mad, but in fact *he* was the madman. Riding through the valley, asking everyone he could find if they'd seen a young woman traveling alone…he was likely creating the biggest stir this part of France had seen in years. He stopped at one farmhouse after the next—not that there were very many—looking for her.

Knowing Lady India, she could be tucked away in a wood somewhere curled up inside a hollow log.

It was almost dark, and it had been an extremely long day. And to top it off, it began to rain. One more try, and he would quit for the night—but not for good. If Lady India thought she would escape this valley and return to Marseille, she was extremely mistaken.

He turned his horse down a muddy lane off the road, where a small stone house sat nestled against the side of a hill at the edge of an olive grove, barely detectable in the fading light. Nearby, an empty hay wagon sat in front of an asymmetrical stone barn.

After two knocks, a tall, dark-haired man answered the door.

"Bonsoir," Nick said. "Forgive my intrusion, but I am looking for my sister who has run off. I fear for her safety, alone on a rainy night. Perhaps you've seen her?" He held his hand up to his shoulder. "She is about this tall. Blond hair."

The man gestured him inside. *"Venez, venez."*

Impatiently Nick ducked in from the rain. Droplets from his greatcoat fell to the rough-hewn floor.

"A young woman alone?" the man repeated, rubbing his jaw. *"Non. Non, je n'ai rien vu."*

Nick didn't miss the man's eyes giving him a quick once-over. "Are you absolutely certain?"

"I would have noticed a woman such as you describe. Please—sit." He gestured Nick toward an immense pocked table near a giant hearth that yawned at the side of the main room. "Your sister, you say?" he asked, stabbing at the fire with an iron poker.

"Yes. You can imagine my concern."

"*Mais oui.* A grave situation indeed. I am lucky that I do not have any sisters. They are nothing but trouble— one is forever getting into fights keeping the men away."

Nick imagined how his sister Honoria would laugh at the idea of him fighting off a man. *La, Nicholas, one flick of my finger and he will be off like a pesky gnat.*

Lady India, on the other hand... Even now she could be tucked into a cottage bestowing her virtue on a French vintner.

Bloody hell.

"You are distressed," the man observed, glancing at Nick's hands. Nick forced them to uncurl. "Sit—I will pour us some wine."

"No. Thank you. I must—" What? Return to the inn? Continue the search, never mind the dark and the rain and the slim likelihood of finding her before morning?

"Sit," the man said again. Already he was pouring a pungent, dark red wine into two heavy glasses. He pushed one toward Nick.

A moment's more hesitation, and Nick finally sat. At this point, a few minutes drying out by the fire wasn't going to change anything. The wine was rich on his tongue, and he rested his forearms on the table and sighed. "*Merci,*" he told the man. "I think this was exactly what I needed."

Perhaps he would be fortunate if he never found Lady India. Perhaps fate had intervened just in time.

"*De rien, de rien.*" The man recorked the bottle and sat across from Nick. "My apologies—I have not introduced myself." He extended his hand. "My name is Jervase Favreau."

INDIA SAT IN the dark hayloft with rain hitting the roof and the night still young, huddled inside a smelly old blanket that did little to keep out the draft. A cup of tea would have been just the thing, but imagining it would only make her want it more. The barley soup and dark crusty bread Jervase's sister had reluctantly given her may as well have been ambrosia—but that was at least two hours ago. Now all she could do was wait for morning.

An occasional skitter in the hay told her she wasn't alone. She pulled the blanket more tightly around her and bit her lip.

I shall check on you later to make sure you are indeed comfortable.

A mad urge to laugh bubbled up to her lips. Comfortable? There was straw stabbing her in places she'd never even—

A noise came from outside, and she stilled. Held her breath. Listened, fearing Jervase's return.

After a long moment, she exhaled.

By now Nicholas Warre had discovered her missing. She imagined him returning to the room, expecting to find her there waiting to finish what they'd begun. He would be furious. He might even blame Millie and tie her up while he rode the countryside looking for India. Except...

He wouldn't hurt Millie. And the fact that he wouldn't—and she knew it with near certainty—only made her think of *why* he wouldn't. And that, at least where Millie was concerned, he wasn't quite as ruthless as she expected. He'd brought Millie with them when he hadn't needed to. He'd even bought her dresses. India could have hugged him for that, except that the only reason he was doing any of this was to force India into a prison of wedlock.

Rain pattered on the roof. If not for that maid, she would be in his room right now giving him her virtue. And what would it have mattered if she'd wanted to? If she desired him?

Desiring him would only make the entire business more pleasant. Nobody wanted to give their virtue to someone hideous.

It didn't mean she had to soften her opinion of him.

It was all beside the point now, anyway. She'd escaped, and first thing in the morning she would figure out how to attract Millie's attention, and before long they would be making their way quickly back to Marseille.

A FEW MORE minutes, and he would go. It turned out a glass of wine was just what he'd needed. Two glasses, rather. Or…well, damn. He'd lost count.

"Encore?" Jervase asked, holding a bottle—the third bottle?—over Nick's glass.

Nick nodded. Yes, exactly what he needed, and no bloody harridan driving him mad. "She's insane," he declared.

"All women are insane, are they not? As are we, for loving them."

"Love!" Nick swallowed more wine.

"Oui." Jervase grinned. "We love their breasts, their hips." He drained his glass. "Their welcoming thighs."

"God, yes." No. An image of India with welcoming thighs had him draining half his glass. "What I wouldn't give to part those thighs."

"The thighs of your sister?"

His sister? Nick grunted, shook his head. Drank more wine. "I lied," he confessed, while images of what those thighs might look like danced in his head.

"Eh?" His host wiped his mouth with the back of his hand.

"The girl is not my sister."

Jervase laughed and leaned across the table. "I lied as well," he said, and took another swallow of the wicked juice he called wine. "She is in *my* sister's hayloft at this very moment."

"Your sister's!" Nick tried to stand up but banged his knee against the table. God's teeth, they were drunk. "Hayloft?" The thought of India sleeping in a pile of hay struck him as unbearably funny, and he began to laugh. Jervase laughed, too, and soon Nick was gasping for breath. "Good God, it's less than she deserves."

"Beautiful girl," Jervase slurred a little. "I plan to pay her a visit tonight."

"You must take me there at once." But then Jervase's meaning sank in. "A visit?"

The man grinned. "She was not as encouraging as I might have hoped, but I feel confident I can convince her."

"Do you." The implication swam around in his brain, trying to settle somewhere. No doubt Lady India would welcome the encouragement. Had she not been trying to cast off her virtue from the moment he met her?

"But if you are already her lover…" Jervase trailed off, awaiting confirmation.

Nick grunted, imagining making the truth out of it—tonight, in Jervase's sister's hayloft.

"A quarrel, perhaps?" Jervase prompted.

"She's damned quarrelsome." Bloody damned quarrelsome. Perhaps he'd be better off letting her go. What was Taggart, anyhow, but a drafty old house with smoking chimneys and a leaking roof?

"That type is always fiery in bed." Jervase drank more wine and grinned. "She will be very lonely and cold in that hayloft."

"Indeed." Nick imagined it with satisfaction, as the wine flowed heady and sweet across his tongue. He should forget Taggart, forget Lady India, forget her father's money. Sod the whole bloody mess and stay here.

He took another swallow of wine. Perhaps he could learn to be a vintner.

Jervase leaned across the table with a gleam in his eye. "*Viens*—let us go find your young lover, *oui?*"

Nick banged his glass on the table. *"Oui."*

SOMEONE WAS IN the barn.

India tensed inside the smelly old blanket and listened while straw poked through her gown and a thread of cool, damp air whispered through the cracks in the barn wall. It had to be midnight at the earliest. Moonlight glowed through the spaces between the boards, but it would be too dark to see more than a shadow. Still she sat frozen, not daring to peek down from the hayloft in case whoever it was glanced up at the same time, and in case that someone might be Nicholas Warre.

Which was nothing but paranoia, because he would never find her here. He would have to knock on every door in the valley.

Which, given his determination, he might well do.

There was a scuffle, a low voice, some laughter—light! She sucked in a breath, only to suppress a sneeze. There were more muffled voices, one male and one definitely female. It could not be Nicholas Warre. She relaxed a little and dared a quick peek over the edge—

Oh, God!

She snapped back and sucked in a lungful of dust. It was the farmer and…a woman who was most definitely *not* the wife.

Oh, God.

There was more laughter, more whispering, more… *sounds*. She shouldn't look. She should absolutely, positively, definitely *not* look.

She looked.

The farmer and the woman were tangled in a mad kiss. Were they really going to… Here? In the barn? Dark curls tumbled over the woman's shoulders, bathed in the glow of a candle sputtering inside a lantern. The farmer grabbed the woman around the waist, and she laughed as he yanked at her blouse and—

She needed to look away. *Tried* to look away. But the more she tried, the more she couldn't tear her eyes from the scene while the farmer sank with the woman into a pile of hay.

Watching was shameful. Mortifying. But the scene below held her transfixed. There was a tangle of petticoats and trousers. A woman's moan, and a pair of white buttocks bobbing between a pair of bent knees.

The groan and scrape of the barn door.

More light. Another lantern—

People!

The woman screamed. The farmer scrambled off her just as the wife and two men walked into the barn.

It was Jervase, and…

Nicholas Warre!

India scrambled backward into the hay. Below, a

huge commotion erupted between the farmer's wife, the farmer and the woman. Great shrieks filled the barn, punctuated by the farmer's shouts. Oh, God. Oh, God. If she was quiet enough, they might forget she was here.

But they must have already told Nicholas Warre where she was, or else why would they have brought him to the barn?

Quietly, desperately she tried to cover herself with hay. Every handful seemed to rustle more loudly than the last. Quickly! Quickly!

There was a creak. And another. The ladder!

Oh, God! She dove headfirst into the pile—dust, vermin, lice, come what may—but it was too late.

"You never cease to fascinate me, Lady India."

CHAPTER THIRTEEN

INDIA SAT UP with hay clinging to every part of her. Nicholas Warre stood on the ladder, peering into the loft.

She eyed the ladder and wondered if she could manage to give it a shove.

His mouth was a grim line as he climbed the rest of the way into the loft. Below, the commotion faded as the combatants moved outside the barn—guests apparently forgotten. She watched Nicholas Warre come toward her and knew that after this there would be no escaping him again, unless—

"Oh, Mr. Warre—Nicholas—I am so overwhelmed with happiness at the sight of you I feel compelled to call you Nicholas—what a relief that you've found me!" She threw her arms around him. "No sooner did you leave me behind than the maid came in with a load of firewood, which she spilled on the hearth and of course I tried to help her but couldn't, and so she saw the ribbons, and before I knew what was happening she had untied me. I was so afraid you would be angry that I didn't dare stay, and she practically dragged me down the servants' staircase and out the door, but I *did* want to stay, Mr. Warre. I wanted to stay very much."

"As I very much wanted you to stay." His arms came around her, too, strong and holding her fast against him, flush against his chest on her knees in the straw.

And everything she'd felt at the inn came crashing back.

For a heartbeat the relief she claimed to feel became much too real. She swallowed, acutely aware of every single place their bodies touched.

Seduction. *Seduction.* That was the goal. Escape had failed, and now she was right back where she'd been when they first arrived at the inn.

And just as it had at the inn, her body came alive beneath hands that roamed over her back, warm breath that feathered her skin as he nuzzled the hair at her temple. "If circumstances had not prevented it," she breathed, "I would certainly have been in the room when you returned. To continue our becoming better acquainted." Her senses filled with his scent—the hint of his cologne, the warm muskiness that was purely him. And…wine. He smelled very strongly of wine. "But the maid's cousin just happened to be passing at that very moment in his hay wagon—"

"Jervase?"

He knew about Jervase? "Yes, that was his name. And once upon the seat there was no convincing him to let me down again."

"Don't suppose there would be."

Only now did she realize his speech was a bit slow. She pulled back and tried to look at him in the dark. "Mr. Warre, are you intoxicated?"

There was just enough light to see a flash of white teeth. "Your friend Jervase makes an exceedingly potent wine. Also has a damned loose tongue."

She swallowed. "Does he?"

"Don't suppose it was I you expected here tonight, was it."

"I didn't dare expect it, after what happened." His

lips roaming over her face and neck felt like heaven. "But I hoped." Right now, she almost believed it.

Nicholas didn't. He laughed. "I rather think you were hoping for a vintner's touch tonight."

"Don't be ridiculous," she said quickly. "How could you imagine such a thing, when you've already seen how I long for you?" She dared to brush her lips across his jaw, found his skin warm and rough, and oh—it was true. She *did* long for him. "As I know you long for me," she added huskily.

Yes—she could begin again where she'd left off at the inn.

His soft, deep laughter rumbled against her. "Oh, Lady India, whatever it is you imagine I might wish to do to you, you haven't even a fraction of the picture."

"Then paint it for me, Nicholas," she breathed.

"It would shock you."

It wouldn't, thanks to Frannie, but, "All the better."

"Very well," he murmured against her ear. "I want to taste you." Instantly she recalled their kiss aboard the ship. "I want to kiss your breasts until your nipples are hard little peaks between my lips." She inhaled sharply. "How are you enjoying the shock so far?"

His words touched her like hands—like *lips*—and her nipples puckered and ached inside her stays exactly the way they had when he'd touched her at the dressmaker's. She could hardly breathe. "Forgive me, Nicholas—was that the shocking part?"

There was more drunken laughter. "And then I want to lay you back and part your thighs—" she thought of the farmer's lover "—and taste your quim." His words seemed to explode between her legs. He planted kisses against the side of her neck, and her body caught fire.

"I want to explore every delicious little crevice," he said, and she felt his tongue against her skin. "I want to flick my tongue across your tiny—" flick "—little bud of pleasure—" flick "—and drive you mad with it until you cry out my name, and then savor the inside of your body while you climax."

Climax? Frannie hadn't said anything about a climax. Or…buds of pleasure. Or tongues, or tasting, or—

He pushed her back into the straw and practically collapsed on top of her, drawing her skirts up, reaching beneath them. His hand brushed the inside of her thigh, sending a torrent of sensation straight to the juncture above.

It was working…the seduction.

"Is that all?" she managed.

"God, no." He nuzzled her neck and—*oh*—his fingers found her intimate flesh, and there was a pleasure so sharp she cried out with it. He caressed her with tiny circles that had her gasping, straining her legs apart as if they had a mind of their own, clinging to his shoulders as if she might drown otherwise. "I've yet to describe the best part." He stilled. Pulled back a little. "But perhaps you don't want to hear."

Between her legs she was slick, wet, pulsing, throbbing with his touch. She could barely breathe, could scarcely let herself think about *where* he was touching. "By all means," she panted. "Describe it."

A low groan escaped his lips against her neck. She strained against his hand, wanting—needing—*something.*

"Very well." His fingers left her then to trail maddeningly along the insides of her thighs once more, while the place he'd been touching—her bud of pleasure?—

screamed with need. "I want you to ride me, Lady India. Astride. Straddling my hips, with your bare breasts falling in my face, and my cock spearing up inside you."

An image of what he described raged to life in her mind. Now his fingers returned, but to a new place, and suddenly she felt him breaching her, pushing his finger inside her, a little at first, then a little more, penetrating her farther. Deeper.

He raised himself onto one elbow, hovering over her. Let his lips linger against hers, barely touching. "Like this," he whispered, and slid his finger completely home. It seemed to fill her, and she strained against the sensation, wanting...*more.*

"Like that," she echoed, nearly out of her mind with some incomprehensible need.

"Only not like this," he said against her lips, and drew his finger out. Slowly. Then pushed it back inside again, deeply. "More like this." Out again, then in. "And this." Out. "And this." In.

"Nicholas." His name escaped her on a wild gasp. Her mind was slipping, spiraling, emptying of everything but the pleasure he was stoking between her legs. She strained her hips, pushing to meet his touch while she clung to him and inside her something was building...

Keening...

"Perhaps I ought to do it right now," he said.

Tightening... "Yes."

"Right here."

Constricting... "Yes— *Oh!*"

Exploding.

Pure pleasure careened through her body in gripping waves. She cried out, and he covered her mouth with his kiss, driving his fingers deep inside her while she pulsed and throbbed around them and her whole body shuddered and tightened and sang.

And she couldn't think at all, except that now she would give him her virtue, and she wanted to more than ever because there was something inside her that still needed—

"But I shan't." He made a noise that sounded like frustration. "Because I've decided I don't want you after all."

He didn't— "But I want *you*." Oh, God—what was she saying? She squirmed and tried pulling him closer, helpless to think of anything except, *Please, please touch me again.*

"Do you." His lips brushed hers as he spoke, but his hand had left her. The flesh between her thighs ached, yearned.... But he was pulling her skirts back *down*. "Thing is, Lady India...I've decided you're a damned sight more trouble than you're worth." He pushed himself to his knees between her legs. "No doubt you'll find this welcome news."

"Welcome—"

"Fifty thousand isn't nearly enough compensation for the likes of you, even if I could do every bloody thing I wanted to you and then some." He stood up, and this time his laughter was a little sharper. "A *hundred* fifty wouldn't be enough."

"What are you saying?" She scrambled upright in the straw.

"You may be on your way, free from my interference." He bowed to her. "It's been a pleasure."

Free from his—

Right after he'd—

He climbed onto the ladder, and she scrambled forward. "You're *leaving?*"

"Farewell, Lady India," he called, already halfway down. "And safe travels."

FAREWELL?

Safe travels?

India watched him leave the barn, too dizzy with sensations to do more than stare as his shadowed form disappeared out the doors below. Her body hummed. Inside, low and deep, fulfillment and need mingled hotly together. Sensitive flesh sizzled and pulsed, as if the only part of her that lived was the part between her legs.

The part that he'd touched.

Stroked.

Penetrated—just like Frannie had described.

What did that mean? Had she just—

Good God. Had she just given him her virtue? Surely not. Frannie had very clearly described that a man was supposed to have his cock—

Spearing up inside you.

The words—Nicholas's words—sliced through her, deep and trenchant and piercing, bringing fresh waves of yearning. She shifted restlessly in the straw, listening. Anticipating.

He would return at any moment. He couldn't possibly have been serious about setting her free. It was some kind of trick.

Wasn't it?

Long minutes passed, and then even longer minutes. She hugged her knees in the dark, with his scent on her skin and his scandalous words whispering through her mind and his touch racing through her blood. She was supposed to be glad he'd left. She *was* glad. With any luck, he wouldn't return. But…

She flopped back into the straw. *Whatever it is you imagine I might wish to do to you, you haven't even a fraction of the picture.*

Hearing him say he wanted her was an intoxication all its own. She wanted to feel that again. Feel *him* again—feel him holding her. Touching her. *Wanting* her. In the secrecy of the darkened hayloft, she let herself whisper his name and savor the feel of it on her lips.

Nicholas.

Imagining she might be able to distract him with seduction was one thing—feeling him touch her with such a wicked and lustful passion was something entirely different. She saw his face in her mind, let herself get a little drunk on his handsomeness and the memory of his hard body pressed against her.

Her blood hummed with the heady feeling of being desired. She found herself hoping that he *would* return.

That he would do all the things he spoke of, and she would give him her virtue and it would be the most passionate, breathless thing she ever experienced, and then it would be too late to escape him and she would return to England with him, to Taggart, which would turn out to be a beautiful, old house with quiet rooms overlooking the trees, maybe with a gazebo tucked beneath their branches where sunlight would stream through on clear days, just like the one where she used to take refuge during the summer weeks at Auntie Phil's. And Nicholas would be too busy to care if she spent her afternoons curled up on its seat watching birds chase each other through the treetops, and there would be no expectations to fulfill and no tasks to bungle and no books to read.

And she could live the way she wanted to without having to run away. Without scrapping about the world, worrying what would become of her, knowing the only alternative was a life of confinement and shame.

More long minutes passed, and then certainly an hour had gone by and there was no sign of him—or anyone. Her body cooled. She curled up in the straw, tired but unable to doze off. Another hour surely passed, and then another. Overhead, shadowy wooden trusses speared toward the roof. An occasional rustle drifted up from the animals below, but nothing more.

The heady sensations gave way to scratchy straw and damp drafts sneaking through the barn's walls. And *I want to taste you* gave way to *Fifty thousand isn't nearly enough compensation for the likes of you.*

It was exactly what she'd wanted him to conclude. All that really awaited her at Taggart were expectations she would never be able to meet. Nicholas may have defended her a little during a moment of unspeakable horror, but the daily reality of marriage would be nothing like that. He would have what he needed—Father's money. He wouldn't need *her* for anything. He'd made it clear he didn't approve of her at all, and once they were married it wouldn't be long before all of her flaws would be exposed.

First thing in the morning, she needed to get Millie away from that inn. Millie was probably fearing the worst now that they'd been separated. If she was very careful, she might be able to speak with the maid who had freed her. The maid could take a message to Millie.

There was no possible chance Nicholas had been serious. He needed that money. He needed *her*.

Devil take it, that was not supposed to make her
feel *good*.

He was the last thing in the world that *she* needed,
and there could be no more silly longings for anything
different.

CHAPTER FOURTEEN

"LORD TAGGART."

Nick groaned into the mattress. Someone was shaking him. He wrested himself away and buried his face in the pillow.

"Lord Taggart, wake up."

"Go away."

"Where is India? Did you not find her?"

Lady India.

She lurked at the edges of his thoughts, reminding him of something, but his mind felt like cotton and his head hurt like the devil and all he wanted in the entire world was to sleep.

A hand shook him by the shoulder. "Lord Taggart, *where* is *India?*"

"Bloody devil, *leave me alone.*"

"I would happily leave you alone if you will only tell me where I can find India. She isn't here. Were you unable to find her last night?"

India. Last night.

Images came to him in fits and starts—the vintner's house, wine, more wine, a hayloft—

He groaned into the pillow. Good God. Good *God.*

Oh, yes. He'd bloody well found her.

Nicholas. Yes— Oh!

Soft gasps, even softer thighs, hot, welcoming folds. Her tight channel, clenching his fingers as she climaxed…

Bloody hell.

He'd meant to talk. Only *talk* about being inside her. But she'd felt so bloody good beneath him, writhing a little and breathing against his face, and talking suddenly hadn't been enough. He had to touch her.

And then…

"I believe I told her she could go."

"You *left* her?"

The sharp question pierced his head like a pistol shot, and he winced. The facts of the situation assaulted him. She'd been so hot with desire she'd actually begged him to take her. Had he really thought leaving her would— What, have her desperately following him to Paris in the hope that he'd finish the job?

"Bloody *hell*." He pushed to his feet, noticed he was still fully clothed. Hadn't even slept beneath the covers.

He was an idiot. And he'd been so foxed he'd walked away from fifty thousand pounds. Bloody, *sodding* hell. Men had *killed* for less.

"She's probably halfway to bloody Marseille by now," he muttered, stalking to the pitcher and bowl, splashing his face, bracing his hands on the dressing table and trying to think past the pain in his head.

"You can't possibly imagine giving up this easily," Miss Germain said sternly.

"Of course I'm not giving up. I never had any *intention* of giving up." He'd just gone temporarily mad, thanks to Jervase the vintner.

"You'll have a sorry time finding her now."

"But we *shall* find her. And when we do, you will

convince her that the best option is for us all to continue our journey to Paris."

"And you imagine she will simply agree and climb into the carriage?"

"What I imagine, Miss Germain, is that you know exactly what to say to convince her to do precisely that." Aided by Nick continuing to behave as if he really had decided India wasn't worth fifty thousand pounds.

Except he wanted her so badly he wasn't sure he could manage that.

But somewhere out there, Lady India was likely dancing a giddy jig. He ought to race back to that farm this instant, snatch her up and throw her over his saddle before she had time to devise a plan of her own.

"Convince her to return to the carriage with *you?*" Miss Germain said. "You ask the impossible."

Nick finally dried his face and tossed the towel aside. "I don't think so." And when he did find her, perhaps what he'd started in that barn could continue to work to his advantage. He looked at Miss Germain in the reflection. "I fully intend to coax the wayward Lady India back into the carriage, and if you ever wish to see our bargain come to fruition, you will help me."

IT WAS STILL dark when India left the barn—and just in time, as already a faint light glowed inside the farmhouse. A light rain fell as she made her way toward the road, and the sky changed from charcoal to pearl-gray.

There was no sign of Nicholas Warre. She'd been half expecting to find him waiting there to carry her off.

She stood there a moment, carefully studying the surrounding vineyards for any sign that he was hiding nearby. There was none.

Was it *possible* that he'd been serious?

No. Nothing was too much trouble for fifty thousand pounds. But even if he had no intention of actually letting her go, he *had* left her, and right now she was alone. She needed to get to the village quickly. She kept to the edge of the vineyard where she could dive into the grapevines if she spotted him. Not that it would provide much cover, but there wasn't much else. Up ahead, the vineyard gave way to an olive orchard, where there were even fewer hiding places.

Suddenly, she heard the clop of a wagon on the muddy road behind her—

Oh! A farmer!

She hurried to the edge of the road and flagged him down. Moments later, she sat next to him huddled in the blanket she'd taken from the barn, clop-clop-clopping toward the village.

India kept her eyes fixed on the road ahead while raindrops seeped through the blanket. She would have the farmer let her off the moment she spotted buildings. It wouldn't do to simply arrive in plain view. She would sneak the rest of the way into the village on foot, and then—

Oh, no. Up ahead, a carriage rattled and splashed toward them on the muddy road. A very familiar carriage.

Devil *take* it.

She yanked the blanket over her face, but now the carriage was upon them, and it lurched to a sudden stop. The door flew open.

"India!"

Millie. India turned abruptly and let the blanket fall. Millie leaned precariously out the door, and behind her

India could see Nicholas Warre's legs stretched out inside the carriage.

She grabbed the farmer's arm. "Stop! *Arrêtez, s'il vous plaît!*"

"Mais, non!" he complained, gesturing toward the sky.

"Une minute—une minute, je vous en prie!"

The farmer stopped the wagon with an irritated jerk on the reins. *"Une minute,"* he growled, holding up a finger. One minute.

"I thought we might never find you," Millie cried.

All her hopes for sneaking back to Marseille crumpled.

From inside the carriage came a bored command. "Miss Germain, you're letting rain into the carriage. Please close the door and let us be on our way."

Be on their way?

Instead, Millie leaned out farther. "India—"

"Miss Germain, *close* the *door.*"

"—come quickly! Lord Taggart will take us to Paris."

The devil he would. This was a trick indeed.

"Wait just a minute," came Nicholas Warre's terse voice from the carriage. "I agreed to take *you,* Miss Germain. Lady India has expressed a desire to continue her journey without my assistance."

Without his assistance? Hope took wing. "Hurry, Millie," India called now, even as Millie climbed from the carriage into the muddy road and hurried to the wagon. India gripped the side and leaned down. "Get in the wagon. If he's serious, then we need nothing more to do with him. Quickly—before he changes his mind." Which he would, if he hadn't already.

"Mademoiselle," the farmer warned, gesturing to the sky.

"I think I can convince him to take us both to Paris," Millie said in a rush, "only you must promise to act as if you aren't even here."

"If we are to go to Paris, we don't need Mr. Warre to take us there," India said. "This farmer will take us as far as the village, and there will be many others headed north."

"And what will they want in exchange? India, we have no money! We're far safer with Lord Taggart—"

"*You* might be safer."

Through the carriage door, those legs that had tangled with hers in the straw shifted impatiently. "I've had enough delay as it is, Miss Germain. Return to the carriage immediately or continue your journey with Lady India."

"Can't you hear what he's saying? He's had his fill of you."

"He is lying."

"He wants nothing to do with either of us, which is more than we'll be able to say about the likes of most men willing to offer us a place in their wagons. We'll be in Paris in a matter of days, and you need never concern yourself with him again."

"I need not concern myself with him now."

Millie hurried back to the carriage.

The rain began to fall harder, and the farmer picked up the reins, but India stopped him again. "Wait, please— *Attendez!*"

"Non! Allez!" The farmer launched into a lengthy complaint. He gestured sharply for India to get down

from the wagon. *"Allez!"* Now he actually pushed her to her feet, forcing her to the wagon's edge.

"No, please—" But there was no changing his mind, and it was either climb out or fall out, so she clambered to the ground. He made a dismissive gesture without looking back, hunched into the rain and flicked the reins.

"Wait!" she cried after him. *"Attendez!"*

He wasn't waiting. Raindrops plummeted from the sky, striking her head and shoulders. Water ran in rivulets across the road. In the carriage door, Millie was arguing with Nicholas Warre.

"Absolutely not," he said angrily. "It will be a deadly long journey to Paris even without Lady India's constant protesting. Good *God.*"

"She won't be bothersome. *Please,* Lord Taggart. I beg you!"

"Millie, we don't need him." But the road was a disaster, and her wet skirts clung heavily around her legs and dragged in the mud, and Paris was very far away. "Let him go." Her tone was hardly convincing.

Millie turned from the door and gripped India's arms. "Please," she said. "Please let us ride with him. It's wet, and awful, and the idea of begging rides from strange men—I can't bear it. You know I can't." The fear of what could happen was alive and real in Millie's eyes, making it impossible to insist that Millie go through with such an uncertain journey.

Rain dripped from India's lashes and fingertips. Cold droplets slid down her neck and into her bodice. Cautiously she moved behind Millie and peered inside the carriage.

Nicholas Warre flicked his gaze over her. If he was

thinking at all of what they'd done last night, it didn't show. Yet despite the rain and mud, every place he'd touched her—every single place—caught fire.

She lifted her chin. A drop of water fell into her eye. "You needn't worry about me being a bother, Mr. Warre," she said, wiping it away. "I'd like nothing better than to reach Paris posthaste. You shall hardly know I'm here." She told herself this was strictly for Millie's sake.

He exhaled with great irritation. "I thought I made myself clear last night."

"You're going to Paris anyhow. I don't see what difference it should make if we part ways here or there." She studied his expression for any sign that he was bluffing.

He regarded her with impassive green eyes. "A very dear one," he said, "each night for your room and board." It was impossible not to remember looking into those eyes last night, while he'd—

"My aunt Philomena will repay you when we reach Paris. She spends a good deal of time there, and is sure to be in residence."

"She can hardly repay me for the trouble of your company, can she."

"If you've truly changed your mind about marrying me, there should be no trouble at all." Except that already a sign of trouble pulsed hotly, deeply, in the places he'd touched her last night.

The corner of his mouth quirked up—Good God. Could he tell what she was thinking?

"Very well," he said. "I will take you and Miss Germain as far as Paris. But the smallest fuss from you—" he leaned forward and pointed his finger at her "—and you're out."

HE IGNORED HER. Completely, utterly ignored her.

"He is simply waiting for Paris," she told Millie when they were two days from the city, as she and Millie returned from an evening walk through the small village where they would spend the night. "And then we will see a marked reversal to his matrimonial ambitions."

"He doesn't seem to have any ambitions toward you at all," Millie said.

He didn't seem to have any desire for her, either. And that was maddening because *she* still desired *him,* and each day sitting across from him, taking his hand in and out of the carriage, fighting the urge to stare at him while the carriage rattled endlessly through the French countryside...

Each day her desire only grew stronger.

In the evenings, she and Millie walked to stretch their legs after endless hours on the road. Nicholas did nothing to prevent their escape—they could simply have kept walking. Fled into the meadows. Begged a ride back toward Marseille.

He didn't seem to care whether she stayed or left.

And it was the most aggravating thing in the world.

Now, after their evening walk, India and Millie climbed the narrow, dark stairwell to their room, passing by Nicholas's closed door. "You'll have Philomena to protect you in Paris," Millie said.

"He'll never hand me over to her," India said. "Mark my words."

Inside their room, Millie went straight to her trunk and dug out her nightgown while India stood at the small window and tapped her fingers on the sill. Outside, the light had begun to fade after the setting sun.

Nicholas hadn't given up. She wasn't fooled at all.

And as long as he pretended he'd changed his mind, there was nothing she could do to *actually* change his mind. Seduction would do her no good now—if the object of seducing him was to distract him so that she and Millie might escape, there was no *reason* to seduce him.

Other than that you want to.

She could talk to him, perhaps. Goad him a little— a very little, in case he followed through on his threat to leave her and Millie behind—and see if he might reveal himself.

Reveal that he still desires you, or reveal his intentions toward marriage?

She turned abruptly from the window. "I'm going to go ask Mr. Warre what time we should expect to leave in the morning," she told Millie.

"We always leave at five o'clock."

"That might change now that we're closer to Paris." It sounded ridiculous even to her, so she hurried from the room before Millie could point that out.

Outside his door, she nearly changed her mind. But she wasn't going to seduce him—she wasn't. Only talk to him.

"We're nearly to Paris," she said when he answered his door, and slipped by him into his room before he could stop her. "I wondered if we'll be keeping the same traveling schedule."

He observed her a moment with the door open and his hand on the latch, wearing only his shirt and breeches. His shirttails hung out, and the buttons at the top were…open.

"Yes," he said. "We will."

The unbuttoned V exposed a smattering of dark hair

on his chest. She looked at his throat, remembered the scent of his skin when he'd held her in the hayloft.

"I thought perhaps you'd want an earlier start. So we could arrive sooner." She made herself look away and saw that a small writing table was littered with the same papers and books he'd been studying ever since they'd sailed aboard William's ship.

"We'll arrive soon enough as it is."

Soon enough for what? she thought of saying. *To stop at the first church we see?* She didn't dare goad him that much, not when they were still two days from Paris and all this indifference might be genuine.

"Is that all?" he asked, so evenly that it was impossible to tell whether her visit was having any effect on him at all, except that he still had not closed the door.

"Millie and I just returned from our evening walk," she informed him.

"Yes, I heard you on the stairs." He finally shut the door. Crossing the room, he sat down at the writing desk and leafed through the papers.

"There's a small church just down the road. We saw the priest walking through the cemetery at the side."

"Did you." He dipped his pen and wrote a few words.

"And a public coach passed us, headed the other direction. No doubt toward Marseille."

"No doubt."

"It stopped at the inn down the street."

"Too bad for the passengers. Those rooms cost five derniers more." He reached for one of his books and began searching its pages, not bothering to look up.

She followed the strong line of his jaw to his ear. It was perfectly formed, not too large or small. He'd once kissed her just below her own ear, and now she imagined kissing him below his, in that shallow spot between the cords of his neck.

"I do hope you're not worried about the extra expense of having me and Millie along," she said, shifting a little.

"I trust your aunt will reimburse the cost of your travel." He still did not look up.

"She'll be thrilled to see us, I'm sure." Her gaze dropped to the place where his shirttails pooled on his legs and his muscled thighs strained against his breeches. "And ever grateful to you for delivering us into her care."

She could perch on the bed and see if he reacted. But what if he joined her?

She walked closer to the desk. "What are you working on?"

His fingers tightened around the edge of the book. "The same thing I've been working on during this entire journey."

"I so admire your determination. If there's one thing I've learned about you, it's that once you have an idea of something, you don't let it go."

He shut the book and stood up suddenly. "It's been a pleasure, Lady India, but I need to go to sleep. We leave early in the morning."

He was close enough that she could reach out and touch him if she wanted to. "It isn't dark yet."

"So it isn't."

His green eyes regarded her evenly. His lips were at ease—not thinned, not pursed. No muscle worked in his jaw, and his arms hung at his sides, hands open.

There was nothing—not one single thing—to betray even the slightest hint of desire.

Would that change if she touched him? Or if he really had stopped desiring her, and she touched him, might he want her again?

"Sleep well, Mr. Warre. I think I shall go ask the innkeeper about the stage to Marseille."

He walked past her, opened the door and held it for her. "Enjoy your evening, Lady India."

She went into the small corridor, and he shut the door behind her, and she squashed a mighty urge to give it a good kick. Enjoy her evening? That was all he had to say?

She inhaled. Exhaled. Reminded herself that the point was not whether he desired her. It was whether he still intended to marry her. Which he did. And once they reached Paris, once she had Auntie Phil on her side, he would be forced admit it.

CHAPTER FIFTEEN

"INDIA! DEAREST!" AUNTIE Phil's voice rang out as she swept through the entry in a cloud of light perfume, while a pair of footmen carried India's and Millie's trunks inside. "You wicked, wicked girl," she said, kissing India's cheeks. "And Millicent—I hardly know what to say. What the two of you did is too despicable for words."

India felt Nicholas Warre's eyes on her. Any moment, he would announce that he was actually taking her with him to the nearest church, where they would be married immediately. And then Auntie Phil would inform him that she would not stand for India to be forced into marriage.

This was perfect. Who was the fool now?

"And Lord Taggart." Auntie Phil turned her attention to him now. "What a fascinating surprise this is." She held out her hand.

"Lady Pennington." He bowed and raised it to his lips. "No doubt you are aware of my understanding with your brother."

"Lord Taggart, I cannot think of a soul who is not aware." She looked back and forth between him and India. "Are congratulations in order?"

"I'm afraid there's been a change of plans," Nicholas said.

"Has there?" Auntie Phil's slender brows rose, and she looked at India.

"Mr. Warre has come to his senses," she said breezily. Indifference? Even now? *For shame, Mr. Warre,* she silently scolded. "He has decided not to commit a grave moral wrong. But he has been kind enough to convey us here, for which I am very grateful." She smiled at him. "I'm sure now you will be able to continue your journey to London with a good deal more haste and comfort. You are continuing to London, are you not?"

"Indeed."

"Today?"

"No." His lips curved the tiniest bit. "Not today."

"Why ever not?" She cocked her head with false innocence. "Does Paris hold some interest for you, Mr. Warre?" Oh, yes, Paris held some interest for him. Only let him confess it now, here, with Auntie Phil to crush all his plans to dust.

She thought she saw a tiny flicker of something in his eyes, and triumph leaped in her blood. The man had abducted her. Undone all of her and Millie's efforts. He'd *ruined* her *life*.

And now he wanted to toy with her by pretending he didn't need her anymore.

But before she could press the point, Auntie Phil tucked her hand into India's arm. "I daresay respite from these horrid French roads holds some interest for him. Am I correct, Lord Taggart? But of course I am. Do not let us keep you from taking your ease."

He inclined his head. "Thank you, madam."

"In case we don't see you again...you have my eternal gratitude for conveying my niece safely to me. You have only to let me know what I may do for you while you are in Paris."

TAKING REFUGE WITH Auntie Phil should have brought relief, but it didn't, because somewhere out there Lord Indifferent was *not* leaving Paris immediately, and it wasn't because he needed a respite from the carriage.

"I don't know whether to turn you over my knee or embrace you for dear life," Auntie Phil declared a few hours later after all had been told—well, most, anyhow. She sat in front of her dressing table in a froth of silk, ribbons and lace, while India perched by the window in a spear of sunlight.

"So you see how it wasn't all Millie's fault," India said.

"Of *course* it wasn't all Millicent's fault. You are equally complicit in the entire affair. Reckless is what you are. And lucky to be alive."

India's chin jerked up a notch. "We had no trouble sailing that ship."

"Of course you didn't. But you are not Katherine, and I suspect you had more than a little trouble commanding a crew."

"Well I won't be commanding a crew now, will I?" She exhaled sharply. Besides, Auntie Phil knew a great deal about many things—especially men. "Why did you tell Nicholas Warre to call on us? He lied when he told you he's changed his plans. He's been pretending indifference toward me practically since Marseille, but he hasn't changed his mind."

Auntie Phil cocked her head and regarded India in the looking glass. "How do you know he's been pretending?"

"I know because I can see it in his eyes."

"Can you? How interesting. I confess I must have been too distracted by his physique. You must admit he is a very fine figure of a man."

"He is a man who is trying to force me into marriage. Surely you don't approve of that. *I* find it makes him quite ugly." On the inside, anyhow.

"I never approve of a forced marriage, and I told my brother as much, but as usual he wouldn't listen." Auntie Phil leaned closer to the glass and touched a beauty mark by her lip. "Are you saying you don't find Lord Taggart handsome?"

"Handsome is as handsome does, Auntie Phil," India said righteously, and was immediately confronted by the memory of Nicholas hovering over her in the hayloft with his hand between her— "But now that I'm here with you, I needn't think about him anymore at all. I needn't ever think about *any* man if I don't want to."

Auntie Phil smiled. "Surely you don't imagine you can simply never marry, dearest. Of course you will have to marry *someone.* The trick will be to find a man your father will approve of and that you will be satisfied with."

India stood up, alarmed. "Please tell me you're joking. Nobody could possibly fit that description—" she would *not* think of Nicholas "—and there's the matter of my freedom—"

"Dearest, often freedom comes *after* the wedding. But there's no need to worry—we are together in Paris again, and there is great fun to be had." She pushed at one side of her sable-colored coiffure and smiled reassuringly in the glass. "Now. I want to hear *everything* about your relationship with Lord Taggart. If he is as determined as you say, how is it possible that he has managed to convey you this far and you are as yet unmarried? Has he never touched you? Not once in all these weeks?"

"Of course he's touched me. I practically *forced* him to touch me—" and she'd suffered endlessly since, wanting him to touch her again "—but only as part of my strategy, mind you, and I feel certain it would have worked had I been allowed to follow it through." Almost certain.

"Your strategy? How intriguing. What was it?"

"Seduction." She tried to make it sound offhand but failed miserably. "To distract him so that Millie and I might make our escape somewhere along the road to Paris."

Auntie Phil looked at her in the glass. "Ingenious."

"You're laughing!"

"Good heavens, no… But how can it be possible you weren't allowed to follow through with a seduction, of all things?"

India told her about the first inn where they stayed, and how Nicholas excused himself to go downstairs and make arrangements with the innkeeper.

"Mmm," Auntie Phil said. "Perhaps he had a crisis of conscience at the thought of consummating the marriage before the ceremony."

"Nicholas Warre? A crisis of conscience? Auntie Phil, if you had been there—" No. "What I mean is, he was definitely not having a crisis of conscience. He had me tied up, for heaven's sake."

"Tied up!" Auntie Phil turned abruptly from the glass.

Finally—progress. "Do you see?" India stood up.

"He was so prepared to force me into wedlock that he *tied* my *hands* and *feet*." She crossed her wrists in front of her for emphasis. "And now he acts as if marriage is the furthest thing from his mind?"

"So I am to understand that you attempted to seduce Lord Taggart even though your hands and feet were bound?"

"*Because* they were bound," India corrected. "He would have had to untie me."

"Mmm."

"You don't think it would have worked?"

"Oh, certainly. Certainly." Auntie Phil went to her monstrous jewelry box and opened the lid. "But since he left the room, I presume you eventually came untied some other way?"

India told her about the maid, the firewood and the unexpected escape.

"Gracious!" Her aunt paused with a sparkling emerald bracelet dangling from her fingers. "But clearly he found you."

"He was nothing if not motivated."

"Ah, yes. The money." She clasped the bracelet around her wrist. "Let me guess. The second attempt at seduction occurred upon his finding you. And, as you've already indicated, he walked away again. My dear, there are only two reasons I can think of why a man in his prime would walk away from a woman in the middle of amorous pursuits. Either he knows he is doing the wrong thing and is making a desperate attempt to control himself, or…" She held out her hand and examined the bracelet. "Hmm."

"Or what?"

Whatever she'd been thinking, Auntie Phil waved it

away. "Nothing that could possibly have been the case, dearest. He must have been trying to control himself."

"*What* could not possibly have been the case?"

Auntie Phil unclasped the emeralds, returned them to the box and selected a ruby cuff. "Only that he could have been trying to turn the tables on you. But if you say he's actually changed his mind…"

Turn the tables on her? "I don't understand."

Auntie Phil slipped the cuff around her wrist. "No, of course you wouldn't, which is why it would work so beautifully if that *were* what he had in mind, but it would take a man of great calculation and self-control to introduce a young woman to, shall we say, *passionate embraces* and then walk away, leaving her helplessly yearning for more."

Nicholas Warre was nothing if not a man of great calculation and self-control. And when he had left that hayloft, he had definitely left her…yearning. For more.

"But of course," Auntie Phil went on lightly, "it would only work on a young woman who found the man attractive, which you have already said you do not, thus leaving us with the conclusion that he must be a man of deep moral fortitude."

"Indeed," India said tightly. "Unfathomable morals."

I want to taste you, he'd said. *I want to lay you back and—* He *had* been trying to seduce her—all the while letting her believe *she* was seducing *him*. "So everything he said was a lie?"

Auntie Phil raised a brow. "I don't know. What did he say?"

"Nothing." India's cheeks felt on fire.

"Men say all sorts of things in the heat of passion, dearest. Some true, some not, but all—and I *do* mean *all*—testifying to the simple truth that a man is incapable of touching a woman without falling prey to ravenous desire." Auntie Phil came forward and squeezed India's hands, while her blue eyes sparkled with wickedly amusing thoughts. "How scintillating to imagine that if he *were* trying to work a seduction against you, he would almost certainly have fallen into his own trap."

"He would?"

"Of course!" She tipped her head back, laughing. "Regardless of his motives, there's little doubt he lies awake at night positively *burning* for you, dearest. Isn't that an amusing thought?"

NICK STOOD IN his friend Charles Vernier's library, gripping a glass of cognac and forcing himself not to pace. He couldn't quite bring himself to sit—too on edge for that—but there was no need to give his unhappy state entirely away, especially not with the Duke of Winston's near-black eyes watching him lazily from an armchair.

He would have preferred to speak with Vernier alone, but so be it.

"I need a favor," he told Vernier.

"You have only to name it, *mon ami*."

"I need the name of a priest who would be willing to perform a marriage ceremony, under…less than usual circumstances."

Vernier raised a blond brow. *"Intéressant."*

"That would suggest Lady India is in Paris," Winston spoke up.

"Yes. At Lady Pennington's." Which was saving him the cost of room and board while he worked out the logistics of their wedding, and which—hopefully—would not turn out to be a serious miscalculation.

Winston leaned his head back and laughed. "And so it comes full circle! The bewitching Lady Pennington and the fair Lady India, together in Paris again. Last time they were here, they set off for Italy and ended up on a boat to Egypt and from there wound up playing pirates on the high seas."

"Lady India's days of playing pirate are over, I assure you." And it was past time for her days as Lady Taggart to begin.

"So you wish to…*ensure* that this marriage takes place," Vernier said. "Regardless of her desires."

Lady India's desires… Good God. He'd been seeing them in her virginal blue eyes ever since that disastrous night in the hayloft. His feigned indifference had worked beautifully, but his strategy also had unintended consequences, as illustrated two nights ago when she'd come to his room with that pitiful excuse of a question and spent the entire time watching him with innocent lust pinkening her cheeks.

Nick cleared his throat. "Understand, the girl is mutinous even at her very best. She is naive. Headstrong. A danger to herself."

Vernier nodded thoughtfully.

"When I found her, she was in a Maltese tavern preparing to bestow her virtue on a sailor."

One of Vernier's brows shot up. *"Dieu."*

Winston laughed and sipped his drink. "A danger indeed. I would have happily obliged her myself without the need for half so much travel."

A sharp response leaped to Nick's tongue on a hot lick of annoyance, but he bit it back.

"No need to look at me like that," Winston said, nonplussed. "I prefer my women to have a certain level of expertise."

Nick drained his glass and faced what he hadn't wanted to admit: somewhere on that endless road from Marseille, he'd begun to think of Lady India as his. Had begun to *want* her, and not because of any damned money.

He told himself it was the irresistible lure of her own obvious yearning. And he wondered, now, at what point her desire would intensify such that he would not be taking advantage of her if he actually seduced her. If he could pretend indifference a little longer, long enough to see where her own desires would take her...

Perhaps a *forced* marriage would be unnecessary, and he could manage with a merely *arranged* one. Besides which, it would be harder for her to object at the altar if he'd already claimed her virtue.

The sooner she's taken into hand, the better," he said. "I want this business finished."

Vernier nodded. "*Bien sûr,* I am beginning to understand why."

"I will need a priest who will be deaf to her protests."

Vernier laughed. "And attentive to your money."

"Precisely."

"You have come to the right city, my friend. I can think of several possibilities. There is Père Bouchard, who shows up at Madame Gravelle's more nights than not—" he ticked off one finger as if running through an easy list "—Père Valentine, who keeps a mistress in a small town house near the Pont-au-Change, and *mon Dieu,* Père Dechelle—"

Père Dechelle.

"—who has a daughter working in the laundry boats

on the Seine. No, you will have no trouble finding one who will do as you ask. For the right price, *bien sûr*."

Père Dechelle. Yves Dechelle. The name had his pulse thundering in his ears.

"Bien sûr," Nick echoed.

So the man not only lived, he ranked among Paris's most corrupt men of the cloth. It should not have been a surprise.

Vernier frowned. "Is something wrong? You look pale. Please, sit—"

"No. *Non. Merci.*"

A daughter working on the laundry boats. That meant…

A sister. Nick had another sister.

"You went pale as a ghost just now, as well you should," Winston said. "Virgin or no, Lady India's ruined herself beyond all recognition. Nobody would blame you for turning your back on your arrangement with Cantwell."

A bark of insane laughter pushed into Nick's throat and sat there. He raised his glass to his lips, but it was empty. Winston thought Nick was second-guessing his decision to marry India? What would he think if he knew the truth?

What would India think?

Somewhere outside the walls of Vernier's house, Dechelle's existence taunted him with exactly what kind of man Nick was. His elder brother James thought Nick an obstinate fool for not repaying Holliswell out of the Croston estate. But Nick had no more right to the family money than a street urchin. Whatever kind of man he was, he was not the kind to take what didn't belong to him.

Except when it came to India, who, if nothing else, at least made no pretense about *her* life.

Nick looked at Vernier. "This Père Valentine," he said. "Where do you suppose I might find him now?"

Two hours later, Nick returned to his lodgings to find an invitation waiting—an "intimate gathering" tonight at Lady Pennington's. Interesting. It would seem he had at least some level of Lady Pennington's blessing anyhow. Tonight he would attempt to find out for certain.

He tossed the invitation on the pockmarked dressing table and went to the window, staring through dirty glass at a cobbled back alley where two stray dogs nosed through a pile of refuse. A church bell rang nearby, and his fingers tightened around the chipped molding.

Yves Dechelle. *Père* Dechelle—a supposed man of God who had nonetheless found his way into a married woman's bed. Nick's *mother's* bed.

If only Mother had never told him the truth. But a deathbed was a damnable thing for more reasons than the obvious.

And Dechelle had a daughter working as a laundress on the Seine.

He had another sister. A *laundress*—and it didn't take much to imagine what other services she likely provided in order to make her way in this city. He thought of Honoria, his younger sister in London, who even now would be dressing for some spectacular soirée. He could see her so clearly, with dark hair and green eyes so like his own, always sparkling with some kind of shockingly mischievous remark. So bold, so sure of herself. Yet even so, sometimes he simply felt a need to protect her. From what, he had no idea.

This other sister would not be readying for any soirée. She would have hands that were red and raw from
the water, perhaps a pox from whatever nighttime activities she had to engage in to survive on a laundress's
pay. She would be gnarled from labor, aged beyond her
years, possibly ill—

God. He pushed away from the window, but there
was nowhere to go in the tiny room. He was *not* going
to conjure up an imaginary, suffering sister. But guilt—
horror—clawed at him, anyway. The life she had was
the life he deserved. He wasn't really a Warre. He had
no moral right to the honors bestowed on him through
his connection with Croston, because he was not the
Earl of Croston's son.

Would his other sister look anything like Honoria?

Unlikely. The woman probably had a husband and
a brood of children. And it wasn't difficult to imagine what would happen if she found out she had a half
brother who was a baron, never mind that he could
barely afford even these ramshackle lodgings.

The sum Cantwell had given him to finance the
search for India was being depleted alarmingly quickly.
There also remained the journey north, passage to
England, expenses during whatever time it took for
Cantwell to make good on their arrangement. And there
was Nick's own agreement with Miss Germain, which
would wipe out half his remaining purse as it stood.

Nick went to his trunk, took out the finest suit of
clothes he carried. Shrugged into his waistcoat and
buttoned it himself when every other man who would
attend Lady Pennington's soirée tonight was being buttoned by a valet.

He thought of Holliswell, waiting even now in London with his greedy eyes turned toward Taggart. If Nick took too long in returning, would Holliswell try to begin proceedings against Taggart even before the appointed date? It was possible.

He could afford a few days in Paris. Perhaps even a week, if things with India looked promising enough that an ugly scene in front of a priest might be avoided.

He latched on to that idea and shoved the others away.

His indifference had worked wonders on the road.... Tonight he would find out what effect it would have on Lady India in Paris.

CHAPTER SIXTEEN

IF NICHOLAS WARRE had fallen prey to ravenous desire, he showed no sign of it that night at the soirée.

India wore one of Auntie Phil's spectacular gowns— hastily remade that very afternoon—and watched Nicholas Warre across the room, very clearly not burning for her.

"If nothing else, Lord Taggart does have very fine attributes," Auntie Phil said, sipping a glass of wine and studying him with open appreciation.

He was using those attributes at this moment on a French coquette who kept touching his lapel and stretching up to whisper in his ear. He laughed at something, and India felt it in her knees.

"*Why* did you invite him?" she hissed.

"Gracious! How could I not, under the circumstances? He knows a great many people who are in Paris at the moment. It would have been terribly awkward not to invite him."

"It would be the least he deserves, after what he's done." India watched Nicholas touch the flirt's arm. He wore his best suit—she knew because she'd been through his trunk—but it was modest in comparison to the finery on display tonight. He was like a rooster in a house of peacocks. And yet, somehow, he managed to put every man here to shame.

Now the Parisienne was laughing and brushing something from his sleeve.

India tore her attention away and surveyed the crowd. "There are any number of men here tonight with fine attributes," she said, and spotted a particularly excellent example making his way directly toward them—tall, dark, wearing a burgundy coat made nearly black with embroidered designs. "That one, for instance."

Auntie Phil saw whom she meant, and smiled. "Ah, yes." And then he was within earshot, and Auntie Phil was holding out her hand in welcome. "I'm surprised you found my little fête to your taste this evening, Winston," she told him.

"Everything you do is to my taste, Lady Pennington." His eyes flashed, and a smile played at the corners of his mouth. "Although I do plan to enjoy the delights at Madame Gravelle's later this evening. Perhaps you'll join me?"

Auntie Phil laughed. "You grow more preposterous by the hour. I don't know that you've been introduced to my niece, Lady India Sinclair."

He raised a brow. "Cantwell's daughter."

"Indeed. India, His Grace the Duke of Winston."

He took India's hand and kissed it chastely. "A great pleasure, Lady India."

"Likewise, Your Grace." She'd heard of the wild duke, but it was the first time she'd ever set eyes on him. He looked like the devil incarnate. Behind him, she saw Nicholas had left the Parisienne behind and was closing in on them.

She gave the duke her best smile and said, "*I* might be persuaded to join you at Madame Gravelle's."

The duke's brows shot up, and Auntie Phil laughed. "That venue may be a bit ambitious for you, dearest."

"What a shame," India said as Nicholas joined them, and made a mental note to discover later exactly where and what was Madame Gravelle's. She looked directly at Nicholas as she added, "I've so been anticipating the delights of Paris."

"Ah, Taggart," the duke said. "I've just been acquainting myself with your lovely fiancée."

Nicholas's brows dived in a brief, not-certain-what-you-mean V, then smoothed. "Ah—you haven't heard. There is to be no wedding after all."

India tensed. He was telling his fabrication to the duke?

"Forgive me," the duke said smoothly. "I didn't realize."

"No apology necessary, Your Grace," India said. "Lord Taggart is only too eager to inform everyone of our change of plans. In fact, he'll be returning to London shortly. Perhaps, if you plan to leave Paris as well, the two of you could travel together."

"I'm afraid I shall be traveling the opposite direction," the duke said. "I journey to Greece next month."

"Oh, I *adore* Greece."

The duke smiled, a flash of white teeth against swarthy skin. "As I am sure Greece adores you." He offered Auntie Phil his arm. "Do show me the way to the refreshments, would you?" he murmured.

And then India was alone with Nicholas. Her belly fluttered a little, but she refused to succumb to nerves—or attraction. "You surprise me, Mr. Warre. I would not have expected you to go to such lengths to convince me of your indifference."

"I'm not sure I would call it indifference," he said, and sipped a glass of deep red wine while he watched a pair of ladies walk by. One cast him a long look from behind her fan. "I have simply abandoned any plan to marry you."

"How do I know this is not all a trick? That you haven't been pretending to have changed your mind, simply to lull me into a false confidence and then launch your attack?"

"Lady India, if I had wished to *launch an attack,* I would not have left you in that barn."

"If you had tried to take me from the barn, I would have screamed."

His eyes shifted to hers. "Do not think for a single moment that I could not have taken you from there had I wished it."

A shiver feathered her skin. "So if I went right now and brought a priest, you would not say the vows?"

"No."

"I do not believe you."

"Then by all means, let us go find a priest."

And if this was a trick, wouldn't that be the perfect way for him to accomplish his goal. "That won't be necessary."

"And if it will help convince you, I plan to return your pistol and shot tomorrow." He did? "Perhaps they will help you fend off hopeful suitors in Paris."

A couple walked by, and Nicholas's hand lighted for half a second on the small of her back, as if to guide her out of their way.

"I have no intention of fending anyone off in Paris," she told him, while little sparks danced up and down her spine even though his hand was already gone.

"No?"

"No." He wanted to continue this farce? She could toy with him just as easily. "Paris is the City of Love, not the City of Fending Off."

One of his brows quirked upward.

"A city full of young Frenchmen will suit my needs perfectly."

"Much like a tavern full of sailors, I suppose."

Her temper flared, but she managed to keep it in check and offer what she hoped was a secretive smile. "Oh, far more perfectly than that, Mr. Warre."

Let him believe she planned to finish in Paris what she'd begun in Malta. *Then* they would see just how long he would profess disinterest.

"Is that your plan for Paris, then?" he asked. "To tease the poor Frenchmen mercilessly until they are out of their minds with wanting to claim your innocence?"

There's little doubt he lies awake at night positively burning for you, dearest. Auntie Phil's earlier speculation shot through her mind and left her…smoldering. Just a little.

"You may have noticed that I am a woman of action, Mr. Warre. Not teasing." She spotted a handsome young man in a flamboyant blue and silver jacket, and— Oh. She recognized him. It was the Marquis de Bravard, a friend of Auntie Phil's who had expressed a particular interest in India when they were here three years ago.

How fortuitous.

"Mmm." Nicholas sipped his wine. "Indeed, I suppose you've proven that to be true." His tone was heavy with unspoken examples: the dressmaker's. The inn. The hayloft, where she'd practically begged him to— "Tell me," he went on, "what precisely is your plan of action?" The question was dry, delivered as he looked at the crowd.

"Mr. Warre, a lady does not discuss the details of her affairs." Her voice came out breathier than it should have.

He chuckled. "That is because a *lady* does not *have* affairs."

More people walked by, and now they'd been pushed so much together that her arm pressed firmly against his chest. Her mouth went a little dry. She looked down, realized her glass was empty.

"Please," he said, "take mine." He made the switch before she had a chance to respond. Her gaze dropped to the new glass in her hand, to the tiny drop of red wine where his lips had touched the rim.

Those green eyes followed the motion as she raised it to her lips. She sipped, and the heady liquid sang through her as if he'd touched his mouth to hers.

"I do hope I haven't offended you," she said, just as the marquis spotted her.

"Not at all."

The marquis bowed to her from afar, and she raised Nicholas's glass to him, and he started toward them. "I'm sure my plans are nothing to you—not anymore."

"Indeed not." Nicholas lowered his voice and leaned close—so close she began to tingle in her most intimate places—even as his eyes followed a pair of ladies walking by. "In fact, if you should find that you need any assistance with how to conduct your affairs, you have only to ask. I shall be happy to help you."

"Lady India," the marquis declared, joining them at last. "*Quel plaisir.* Paris has not been the same without you." His gaze swept the length of her body.

"A pleasure indeed," she said, and allowed the handsome marquis to kiss her hand. The marquis raised a curious brow at Nicholas, and India made the introduction.

"Lord Taggart," she said. "A family friend." She thought she saw the corner of Nicholas's lips twitch.

"How very fortunate for you to be a friend to such a magnificent young woman," the marquis said to Nicholas. And then, "You must honor me with a dance, Lady India. With Lord Taggart's permission, of course."

India laughed lightly. "I do not need Lord Taggart's permission."

"Nor would I dream of withholding it," Nicholas assured them, already shifting his attention to the crowd beyond them as if he was impatient to move on to more interesting company.

"Then by all means," India said, taking the marquis's arm, "let us dance." She held out the wine Nicholas Warre had given her. His fingers brushed hers when he took it, and a hot, quick yearning shot through her.

Already he was turning away.

"After you left Paris," the marquis told her dramatically as he led her to dance, "I despaired of your ever returning."

"Such flattery. But I am here now," she said loudly enough for Nicholas to hear, "so you needn't despair a moment longer."

"You do realize," Lady Pennington said a short time later, positioning herself gracefully at Nick's side, "that you have just left my niece in the care of the most profligate young marquis in Paris."

The countess, who was at least five or six years

Nick's junior, looked like the kind of woman for whom profligacy was a desired character in a man.

"You disapprove?" he asked.

"You do not?" she countered.

He more than disapproved. He wanted to cross the ballroom, grab Lady India out of the marquis's embrace, take her to his hotel and finish what they'd started in that barn.

But he could be patient.

"How interesting." Lady Pennington pinned him with eyes every bit as blue as India's, and he could see why she had men falling at her feet—and how easily India would be able to follow in her example. There was no way he would allow that to happen. But he was best served to let India think she could do as she pleased. "You are a clever man, Lord Taggart."

"Am I?"

"I suspected you had not given up."

"Forgive me, Lady Pennington. You have me at a loss."

"There's no need to pretend with me. There is nothing more attractive to a woman than a man who doesn't want her. I daresay you'll have her in love with you before the week is out."

His pulse sped up. He didn't want India in *love* with him—only married to him.

"I'm afraid you misjudge my intentions," he said evenly. But now he was thinking of the way India had felt pressed against him moments ago, the unguarded desire she was too open to hide. The glisten of his wine on her lips.

Married to him, with all the benefits that implied. That was what he wanted.

Lady Pennington laughed. "You cannot fool me, Lord Taggart. But if by some chance I do misjudge you, then I must warn you... You will not ruin my niece, and you will not break her heart."

Break the heart of the young woman who had just professed a desire to seek the attentions of every young Frenchman in Paris? Across the room, he watched her smile up at the young marquis.

Just once, he wanted to see that blazing smile directed at him, and not because she was trying to work another scheme against him.

"Then allow me to put your mind at ease," he told the countess, "as I have no intention of the first, and I would need to possess Lady India's heart in order to accomplish the second."

"I wonder that you did not accomplish the first already. You doubtless had ample opportunity."

"Perhaps you've failed to notice your niece's less than enthusiastic opinion of me. She would not have made a willing accomplice."

"Hardly a deterrent, for some."

He looked at her sharply. "But a very great one, for me."

"Mmm."

"Am I to assume you do not approve of my arrangement with your brother?"

She laughed. "It's never safe to assume anything, Lord Taggart. But know this. India's happiness is my sole concern."

"I would expect nothing less."

She studied him from behind her fan, then smiled and cast her eyes toward the dancers, where Lady India whirled in the arms of that damnable marquis. "But that's neither here nor there," Lady Pennington declared happily, "as she is not your responsibility any longer. But I've little doubt we shall see you at any number of soirées. Oh, what a wonderful unexpected surprise to be together with India in Paris once again. I daresay we shall have a very high time indeed."

CHAPTER SEVENTEEN

"IF I WANTED to marry someone," India said to Millie the next afternoon as they strolled along the shops on the Pont Notre-Dame, "that is, if I wanted to *force* myself *upon* someone in marriage, I would bide my time and assert myself when that person least expected it. Wouldn't you?"

"I can't honestly say."

"Well, wouldn't you want the element of surprise on your side? And what better way to do that than to convince the person that you did not want to marry them when in fact you did?"

Millie stopped and looked at her. "India..."

India stopped, too. Saw Millie's tired eyes and drawn mouth, and felt terrible. "Oh, Millie." She sighed. "I've been thinking of nothing but myself and my own fears, when you are just as affected by all this as I am. Please forgive me. I haven't forgotten that we need a solution."

There was a moment, and then, "What if Nicholas Warre *is* the solution?"

The question caught India behind the ribs. "You can't be serious."

Millie gave her a you-can't-fool-me look. "I think you have a fancy for him and you won't admit it."

"Very well. I admit it."

"I *knew* it."

"But it doesn't change anything."

"How can it not change anything? It's a good deal more than most women ever—"

"Millie, look there." Speak of the devil. "Do you see him? What a *convenient* coincidence." Nicholas Warre, here on the Pont, at exactly the same time she and Millie had decided to visit. She wondered if perhaps Auntie Phil was to blame, having stayed behind at the last minute to deal with a row between her butler and housekeeper.

Millie looked. "Perhaps it *is* a coincidence."

"You give him too much credit." India took Millie's arm. "We shall keep walking and pretend we don't see him. Let's go back this way," which would take them by several shops the girls had seen earlier on their walk, all of which were attended by flirtatious young artists.

If Nicholas Warre was here to keep an eye on her, she would give him an eyeful indeed.

They meandered back down the Pont, where rows of shops stretched out, each framed by a great stone archway and filled with a dazzling variety of artwork and other wares. She paused to study a collection of Greek replicas.

Three shops behind, Nicholas Warre paused to inspect a painting.

They moved to a shop with several large bronzes on display.

He shifted to study a collection of portraits.

"He's following us, Millie."

"Where else do you expect him to go?"

"Quickly, in here—"

"No, not *here*." Millie yanked her away from the shop full of nude portraits they'd bypassed earlier.

"Then over here." India hurried back to the shop filled with marble statuettes—only some of them nude—where a young sculptor had shown a particular interest in her. She lingered in the archway, making sure Nicholas saw her, then headed toward a table of small sculptures.

It wasn't long before Nicholas found his way to the shop's entrance.

She admired a miniature marble of Venus and glanced over her shoulder. Oh, yes. He was well within listening distance. She extolled the sculptor's talent, bestowed her most winning smiles, leaned forward to admire his sculptures in a way that would assure him an excellent view of her breasts.

"You are far more beautiful than any of these, mademoiselle," the sculptor said.

"You mustn't say such things," she protested lightly in French, and checked over her shoulder again.

Nicholas was gone.

Gone?

And so was Millie.

"*Pourquoi pas,* when it is the truth?" The sculptor's eyes sparkled with appreciation. "A figure such as yours should be immortalized in marble."

"You...you go too far, monsieur." They could not be gone. Nicholas would not *leave* her here. *Alone.*

Would he?

"Do I?" The sculptor smiled a little wickedly.

"Such flattery could hardly be sincere." She checked again. Definitely gone.

Surely any moment he would return.

"*Dieu,* you wound my honor, mademoiselle, by questioning my sincerity on such an important matter. But if you do not believe me, perhaps you will allow me to prove it to you."

"And how do you propose to do that, monsieur?"

He leaned closer across the table and lowered his voice. "I know somewhere close by where we can become...*plus intimes.*"

More *intimate.*

She exhaled. Smiled a little less brightly. Glanced over her shoulder yet again, and— Oh, thank heaven. Nicholas stood near the entrance once more, bent over, studying a trio of statues.

"That sounds...interesting," she said a bit loudly.

"Bien sûr," the sculptor agreed, and reached across the table to touch a lock of her hair. *"Très intéressant."* He reached behind him for a large canvas cloth and began to unfold it. "We shall go, eh?" The sculptor nodded across the shop to his friend, then draped the large cloth over the table of sculptures. "Fortune has smiled on me today," the sculptor murmured.

Her pulse was beating faster now, but she made herself smile. "On me, as well." Had Nicholas even been paying attention? "Although I can't possibly—"

"Pardonnez-moi," came a too-familiar voice behind her. India had to hold in her sigh of relief. "Your statues exhibit such excellent craftsmanship. I was just coming to observe them more closely when to my great disappointment you covered them over." He looked at India as though only just noticing her. "Oh, but do excuse me. In some circumstances, business must wait. I don't expect to remain long in Paris, but I may well have time to search you out again before I leave."

"Non, non," the sculptor said, already whisking away the canvas. "A few minutes, *ma cherie,*" he mur-

mured. And then, to Nicholas, "By all means, do take your time."

"Liar," India said under her breath.

"Not at all," Nicholas Warre said casually, leaning forward to study a replica of a discus-thrower.

"What have you done with Millie?"

"Miss Germain complained of a headache," Nicholas said. "I put her in a chair back to Philomena's."

Odd…Millie hadn't complained of a headache a few minutes ago.

"You are acquainted with mademoiselle?" the sculptor asked.

India answered quickly. "No."

Nicholas gave her a chiding look. "Indeed, our families are acquainted. I fear Lady India looks on me quite as an insufferable older brother. It would appear that I have ruined her fun." He gave the sculptor a quick, knowing grin that she felt in her knees. "Aha," he said then, reaching past the Venus and selecting a small marble of a bare-breasted woman reclining on—Good God—a bed of intricately carved straw. "This one."

"An excellent choice," the sculptor said.

India watched Nicholas's thumb pass lazily across pale marble breasts. "It reminds me of something…I can't quite place it."

Nicholas gave the artist a sum of money she knew he could not afford, and he turned away to wrap the statue in paper.

"You'll be pleased to know that I've delivered your pistol to Lady Pennington's as promised," Nicholas told her.

"Thank you, Mr. Warre. And apparently you inquired about my afternoon plans, as well."

"I don't recall any such inquiry— Au revoir, monsieur, *et merci*—" He accepted his statue from the sculptor. "Although the butler did assure me he would keep the pistol in a safe place for you." Now they were outside the shop without any further discussion of a possible tête-à-tête with the sculptor. "And I can see now that you are unlikely to be successful in parting with your virtue," he added, surveying the row of shops across from them.

"Of course you can, since you are the reason."

"Only half the reason, I daresay."

"No, you are the whole reason." She met his gaze directly. "But I shall indulge you by asking what you believe to be the other half."

"Your technique."

"Ah. We have returned to the subject of you assisting me with my affairs."

"We have? I meant only to point out a flaw in your strategy."

"Yes. And then I am supposed to inquire what exactly is wrong with my strategy, at which point you will offer to show me. Although for what purpose I can scarcely imagine, since you profess to have no interest in me. Unless, of course, that is a lie. Is it a lie, Mr. Warre?"

He laughed. "Hardly. But I'm thinking of a saying.… How does it go? Something about 'He who hesitates…' Oh—I've got it." He bent close to her ear. "'*She* who hesitates will not part with her virtue.' I have to wonder why, if a common sailor would have been sufficient mere weeks ago, a talented sculptor would not do for you now."

"He would have done nicely but for your interference."

"So you *would* have gone with him."

Absolutely not. "Of course." She turned on him. Looked him directly in the eye. "Do you find that objectionable?"

His expression did not flicker as he returned her gaze. "Not at all. In fact, let us return to his shop at once. Perhaps this time, with a bit of coaching, you might— Bloody hell."

He reached out and yanked her to him, pulling her suddenly into the nearest shop just as a trio of large ruffians barreled through the crowd, followed by a shrieking woman in a dirty apron and mobcap.

There was hardly time to consider that her hands were pressed against his chest and his arm had banded around her waist before the ruckus had passed, and Nicholas eased his grip.

"Are you all right?" he asked.

"I think a bit of my gown tore," she said, looking down. Sure enough, a small slice of fabric gaped open. "Nothing that can't be mended."

He was too close, looking at her too seriously, still touching her as if he actually cared whether or not she was run down in the street. As if she hadn't fended for herself dozens of times in Athens and Constantinople and Alexandria—well, William had been there, and Auntie Phil and Katherine and Millie, too—but even so. She'd spent time in markets much more colorful than the Pont Notre-Dame.

But being in Nicholas's arms was something entirely different. The need to press closer to him buzzed crazily in her head, but she couldn't. This was madness. And it needed to stop, somehow, before she lost her mind completely and did something irrevocably stupid like *agree* to marry him, because it would make things so much easier, and because there was a certain comfort in the idea of being mistress of her own home, and because it would mean that this incredibly handsome man would be hers.

She knew better than that, though. Easier? She would merely exchange the fight against his schemes for a lonely life married to a man who cared nothing for her. Her own home? Hardly. Taggart was *his* home, and he would carry the keys that could too easily shut her away as an inconvenience. And Nicholas Warre, hers? Quite the opposite. Once they wed, she would be nothing but a bit of unwanted chattel—the price he'd been forced to pay for the money he so desperately needed.

She pulled away from him, looking about for any possible distraction, and found it immediately.

"Mr. Warre," she said brightly, trying to sound mischievous even though she wanted him to enfold her once again in his arms, "I've just had an excellent idea." All around them hung portraits—the very nude portraits Millie had spurned with disgust. She headed toward a man at the back of the shop who was sketching a drawing on a large sheet of paper.

"Bonjour, monsieur," she said to him. "I would like to have my portrait painted."

He looked up, cast a critical eye over her, and smiled. "And I would very much like to paint it," he told her agreeably, then shifted his smile to Nicholas, who now stood behind her.

"When could I have an appointment?" India continued.

"For you, mademoiselle, shall we say…Thursday?"

The day after tomorrow. Perfect.

"You see, Mr. Warre?" she said, turning to him with a smile. "I do believe I am perfecting my technique already."

CHAPTER EIGHTEEN

How India thought having her portrait painted by a professional artist would lead to an affair, Nick wasn't quite sure.

And by the next day, he didn't care. Because he was too busy being a bloody fool.

The church was so quiet, Nick could hear his own heartbeat quietly swish-swish-swishing in his ears. It was cool inside. Tomblike. The sightless eyes of cold statues watched him silently as he avoided the center aisle and walked down the side instead. It smelled of candlewax and faded incense and must. At small shrines all around the perimeter of the sanctuary, dozens of candles flickered with the prayers of those who had lit them. With his eyes fixed on the area around the altar, he slipped into a pew near the front.

He knelt and pretended to pray, all the while watching, waiting for the preparations for mass to begin. All he wanted was a glimpse. One look at Father Yves Dechelle—that was all.

Nick's knees ached already and he shifted a little, only to have the kneeler let out a great creak that echoed sharply through the sanctuary. A confrontation would be entirely inappropriate, not to mention unnecessary. The man was probably wizened and frail and in no condition to be confronted about an indiscretion that had taken place more than three decades earlier.

Not that Nick wanted to confront him. It was just a fantasy he'd been finding himself indulging in ever since he'd left Vernier's house.

Père Dechelle?

Yes. I am he.

I am Nicholas Warre. My mother was Marie, Lady Croston. I don't suppose you remember her.

The fantasy broke down at this point. He might say, *No, I am afraid I do not. How may I help you, my son?* In which case Nick would want to murder him.

Or he might say, *Marie? No, I cannot say that I do,* with a gleam in his eye that said he was remembering quite clearly. In which case Nick would want to murder him.

Or he might say, *Ah, Marie. Yes, yes I do. And you— mon Dieu, it can't be!* In which case Nick would want to murder him.

Any way he looked at it, he wanted to kill Père Dechelle. But one could not kill a frail, elderly man of the cloth.

A door opened, and Nick's eyes snapped toward the sound. One priest emerged from a side room, and then another. Neither were frail or wizened. They went about their business, keeping their backs turned. And then one of them turned and looked out at the pews, his eyes colliding with Nick's.

Nick felt the blood drain from his face. It was like looking into a glass and being transported thirty years into the future.

He should let things well enough alone. For God's sake, if anyone ever found out…

But *he* knew. It was the reason he hadn't used the earldom's resources to pay off his debts during the weeks when he believed that James had died and he had acceded to the title. He had no real right to any title but his own, because the Earl of Croston had not been his father.

Nick and Mother were the only souls in the world who knew—except for the man he was looking at right now.

And suddenly Nick's feet were moving even though he willed them not to. He was exiting the pew even though he knew better, making his way toward the altar even though it would accomplish nothing.

"Père Dechelle." His heart thundered as he said the words.

"Oui." The priest narrowed too-familiar eyes at Nick—brown, not green, but with the same angle of brow, the same slight furrow between. Dechelle's hair was dark, the same shade as Nick's, but salted with gray. "May I help you?"

"I would like a word. In private."

The man gestured behind him. "I'm afraid I must prepare for the mass—"

"It will only take a moment." Nick's hands shook a little, but he didn't dare fist them. Dechelle had the shrewd eyes of a man who knew his way around the darker side of life. Nick would be hanged before he'd show weakness.

"Very well. Come with me."

Nick followed him through a door on the side of the church, into a shadowy corridor, and into a small room lavishly furnished with an ornate desk and bookcases on all sides. "There, now. We are in private," Dechelle said, facing Nick in front of the desk.

"My name is Nicholas Warre." It felt as though he were listening to someone else speak the words. "I am the youngest son of Margaret, Lady Croston."

For a long moment Dechelle observed him impassively. Suddenly Nick wondered if Mother had lied about having told the priest she was with child. It would have been a foolish thing to do, would it not? But having an affair with a priest was a foolish thing to do in the first place.

"I see," Dechelle said.

Anger flared. Somehow Nick managed to tamp it down. "Do you?"

"What is it you want? Money? I assure you, I feel no such sense of obligation."

"That much is obvious, with a daughter working as a laundress on the river." He spoke before thinking better of it.

Dechelle only shook his head and held his hands out to his sides. "You have me at a loss, Monsieur Warre."

"Lord Taggart," Nick corrected sharply, though why he should care that this man knew his title, he didn't know.

Dechelle nodded thoughtfully, smiled a little. "A nobleman. Of course. As I was saying, I have heard this rumor you speak of, but the young lady in question— Emilie, I believe her name is—there is nothing to prove that I am her father. And as I am a man of the cloth, sworn to celibacy—" he shrugged "—it is all very doubtful."

Oh, indeed. Very bloody doubtful.

THEY WERE IN Paris, and India had not run away, and as they strolled along a street of shops a short distance from Philomena's house, Millie wondered exactly when and how she was to receive her compensation from Lord Taggart.

If she would receive it.

The marriage could happen at any moment. Today, even. She'd wanted to talk to Lord Taggart yesterday about the money and letter he'd promised, but when he'd put her in the hired carriage at the Pont Notre-Dame—a gesture meant only to ensure that he would be left alone with India—he'd been in a hurry to return to the shop where they'd left India, and there hadn't been time.

And God help her if he made his move without paying her. Millie would be left alone in Paris, and she was not family to Philomena—Philomena's lack of attention testified to *that,* and once India was gone, Millie may well be out on the street.

There was only one way to earn a living on the street.

"India, wait." Millie reached for India's arm, suddenly short of breath.

"Are you all right? Do you have another headache?"

"No, I…it's nothing. I was only thinking of Lord Taggart. What if he decides not to accompany you to your portrait sitting?"

"Do not worry about *that.* He won't miss it."

"Perhaps you would be better served with a more subtle approach." One that would take a bit more time. This game India was playing with Lord Taggart…it could too easily result in Lord Taggart growing angry, and then all opportunity to speak with him about the payment could be lost.

"A less effective approach, you mean," India countered, and began a list of reasons why her current strategy was the best plan.

Millie took a deep breath and told herself to be optimistic. She was fulfilling her end of the bargain to the best of her ability. Lord Taggart would fulfill his. The problem was, optimism had never been a strong suit, and it was too easy to imagine him *not* fulfilling it.

Betrayer. Guilt clawed at her. She loved India, hated scheming behind her back, even if marriage to Lord Taggart did seem like the best life India could hope for.

And Millie needed what Lord Taggart had promised. Everyone she knew had someone. None of them knew what it was like to be fully alone, without a soul in the world who could truly be relied upon, who was bound by blood to honor and protect her.

Her brothers may have been bound by blood, but they had no honor, and the last time she'd gone to them for protection, Gavin had beaten her nearly to death.

"...might have pretended indifference," India was saying, "but he will be there tomorrow—mark my words—likely contriving a way to prevent my having my *full* portrait painted, if you understand my meaning, just as he intervened at the last moment yesterday as I was making plans with a very agreeable sculptor."

"You *wanted* him to intervene yesterday."

"That's beside the point, because he refused to *admit* that he was intervening. But he will admit it tomorrow, as I've arranged a very special surprise— Wait." India put her hand on Millie's arm, staring intently down the street. "It's him, going into that church. Look!"

Millie followed her gaze past a gentle curve of buildings with shops below and apartments above, to a stone church that broke up the line of buildings.

"For heaven's sake, India, how could you possibly tell from this far away?" A carriage trundled by, interrupting their view. "And what do you mean by a very special surprise?"

"It *was* him," India insisted, "and there's only one reason he might have gone in there."

In fact there were any number of reasons, but once India had latched on to something there was no use dissuading her from it. And not only that... "If you really think he's gone into that church, perhaps you ought to go confront him."

"And end up married for my trouble," India scoffed, her eyes glued to the pair of carved wooden doors.

"I'll go with you." If Lord Taggart was in that church planning a wedding, how grateful might he be if Millie brought the bride to the altar and enabled him to finish the business immediately?

Millie's palms grew damp, and she smoothed a hand down her skirt, staring at that church as intently now as India did.

"Your presence didn't stop him before," India said.

"Then don't go, and accept the fact that he's probably gone into that church for reasons of a more spiritual nature, and hope that whatever happens tomorrow will bring out the truth."

India looked at her then, blue eyes narrowed and calculating, and Millie saw that last argument had done the trick.

INDIA PUSHED CAREFULLY through the wooden doors and stepped into the cavernous silence of the church. It was a blessing that these churches were so dark inside. She paused in the shadows inside the door. Nicholas Warre was nowhere to be seen. A woman knelt at a shrine to the right, and two people prayed in a pew near the back. Banks of flickering candles glowed around the perimeter of the sanctuary.

"He must be somewhere at the front," she whispered to Millie.

Millie rubbed her arms. "It's cold. I'll wait here."

"I need you to come with me," India hissed.

"I'll be right here," Millie hissed back. "You know I don't like churches."

Ever since she'd met Nicholas Warre, India didn't care for them much, either. Already Millie had scooted into the near darkness behind a massive stone pillar.

India held her breath and veered left, tiptoeing toward the front, staying in the shadows. If she presented herself at the wrong moment, the marriage might take place here and now. Nicholas certainly cared more about the money he would receive than he cared about Auntie Phil's wrath.

There was no sign of him. She glanced back. Millie peeked from behind the pillar in the back, likely thinking that India had made a mistake and whomever she'd seen was not Nicholas Warre.

It was no mistake. She would recognize him anywhere.

She was nearly to the front now. A door at the side stood ajar, and the quiet murmur of men's voices drifted through the corridor behind it. She crept as close to the gaping door as she dared and paused, straining to listen.

"It is all very doubtful," a man with a heavy French accent was saying.

"I'm sure her mother could lay those doubts to rest."

It was Nicholas Warre's voice, clear as day! Her pulse raced.

"Perhaps so," the Frenchman said, "if she could be trusted—and if she still lived." If who still lived? "But alas, she does not. *C'est tragique.*"

"Oh, yes." Nicholas Warre's tone dripped with sarcasm. "I can see how tragic you find it."

"Is this why you came to see me? To inquire after the welfare of an urchin laundress?"

"That 'urchin laundress' is my *sister.*"

His *sister.* India's heart lodged in her throat as she realized suddenly, sharply, that whyever Nicholas Warre had come into this church, it had nothing at all to do with a marriage.

"Forgive me." The man with the accent again. "I fail to see what you want from me."

"I don't want a bloody, goddamned thing from you." Nicholas Warre's voice was ice cold. "What my mother could possibly have seen in you, only God knows."

His mother!

"Mon fils—"

"Do not *ever* call me your son. I may owe my birth to you, but I'll be damned if I'll allow you to acknowledge it."

"I am a priest," the other man said, laughing. "Everyone is my son. It was not meant to be personal—a slip of the tongue, *c'est tout.*"

India's pulse raced wildly. *I may owe my birth to you*...Nicholas Warre? Owed his birth to...the man in that room? A priest?

If he found her here, listening—

She backed away from the door, only to cry out and

whirl around when a hand touched her back. A young priest steadied her elbow.

"Mademoiselle, *puis-je vous aider?*"

She shook her head in a panic. "No. *Merci.* I am fine." Footsteps! Footsteps in the corridor! She pulled away and hurried down the side aisle in a deafening rustle of skirts. If Nicholas Warre found her here, if he suspected she had overheard—

"India."

She kept going, pretending not to hear him.

"India." He was right behind her now.

She stopped. Fear pounded in the base of her throat as she turned.

Nicholas…the French priest's son? She stared at his face, desperate to look away but unable to.

"What are you doing here?" he demanded in a low whisper.

She swallowed and lifted her chin. "You know very well what I'm doing here," she said as furiously as she could. "Just as I know very well what you are doing here—the same thing you've been trying to do all along. You can't imagine I will believe your lies now, Mr. Warre. But know this—I'll not allow you to bribe that priest into performing our wedding."

"Our *wedding.*"

"You can't fool me, Mr. Warre. Our marriage is worth too much money to you to let it go so easily." Behind him, an aging priest came through the door and walked toward them, looking on with interest. And there was no doubt, in that moment, that everything she'd overheard was true, and that the priest standing there was Nicholas Warre's father. "I did not believe that piddle about helping me with my *technique,* and I'll not believe whatever tripe you may offer me now about your reasons for being in this church. But I shan't go through with any wedding to you—not ever."

He pointed behind him, his expression thunderous. "Were you listening outside that door?"

"All this lack of concern, all this proffered *assistance*," she went on, ignoring the question. "You are a consummate actor, Mr. Warre. I am quite certain there is a special place in hell for men who force women into marriage. And for the priests who consent to it. I only hope he's taken you for twice as much as the priest in Marseille did. But rest assured I shall be doubly on my guard now." His chin was as far as she could make herself go toward looking him in the eye.

"Against a forced marriage," he said.

"Precisely."

She held her breath, willing him to believe her. His stare penetrated to the tips of her toes. Every pounding heartbeat chanted, *Bastard, bastard.*

Finally he smiled—an indulgent curve of his lips that signaled a lie was coming. "Your capacity for misunderstanding is limitless, Lady India."

"As is your capacity for deception, Mr. Warre." When had those shadows appeared beneath his eyes? He looked exhausted. Weary.

"I have any number of business acquaintances in Paris that I plan to confer with before I leave," he explained dispassionately, "in an effort to salvage at least part of this journey from being a complete loss. Père Dechelle happens to be one of them."

The *business acquaintance* behind him smiled a little and turned away, moving toward the altar.

Do not ever *call me your son.*

She made herself scoff. "Very well, and as I have business of my own to attend to—I have a very important appointment tomorrow, if you'll recall, for which I must prepare myself—I shall leave you to your... *business*. Good day, Mr. Warre."

Outside, she practically ran back toward Auntie Phil's.

She'd thought she knew everything that mattered about him. That she understood him. But she'd been wrong.

Very, very wrong.

"What happened?" Millie asked, following close on India's heels. "Why are you in such a hurry?"

I may owe my birth to you....

"Why was he so angry?"

Nicholas Warre was not an earl's son at all. Which meant... What? What did it mean?

Very little, if nobody ever discovered the truth. He'd been born within the bounds of matrimony. As far as the world was concerned, he *was* the Earl of Croston's youngest son.

But he wasn't. And he hadn't gone into that church looking for a priest to bribe.

"India, slow down!"

India slowed a tiny bit.

"For God's sake," Millie said. "You're acting as if he tried to drag you to the altar!"

"He would have," India lied, hardly knowing what she was saying. He had to realize that she'd heard more than she admitted to. The way he'd looked at her, as though he could read her very mind...

As if he was caught in a torment of shame that nothing could ever remove.

And then, after less than a heartbeat, his expression had changed to anger.

"If I had stayed a moment longer," she repeated, "he *would* have forced me to the altar." Except that he probably wouldn't have. Not just then.

"Bollocks. He expressly told you he was meeting with a business acquaintance."

And that had been an utter lie. He'd been meeting with his father. His *father!*

That 'urchin laundress' is my sister.

And he had a sister, right here in Paris. A *laundress.*

Had he known all this time? Did his family know? If they did know, they kept the secret very well. She'd never heard so much as a suggestion of scandal connected with Croston.

But if there *were* a scandal…

She ground to a halt right there, two houses away from Auntie Phil's.

"Are you all right?" Millie gasped, out of breath.

If there *were* a scandal, Father would not want to be connected with it. Father hated anything shameful, and this was incredibly, irrevocably shameful.

More shameful than a daughter who couldn't read.

If Father knew, he would undo his agreement with Nicholas and turn his back on him completely.

NICK'S HEART THUNDERED as he watched her all but run out the church door.

Bloody *hell.*

This was what his foolishness had gained him—the shame he should have left well enough alone, discovered.

There was no doubt she'd heard every bloody word

he'd said to Père Dechelle. Perhaps she had followed him into the church thinking he sought to arrange their wedding, but by the time he'd caught her, she'd been thinking something else entirely.

Nicholas Warre is a bastard.

All that babbling about catching him in the act… She hadn't looked him in the eye even once during that entire speech.

The India he knew *always* looked him in the eye.

He exhaled. Rubbed the back of his neck.

Devil *take* it. She knew everything. There was almost no doubt.

"Une amie?" came Dechelle's amused voice behind him.

"Go to hell," Nick bit out, and headed for the door. No, India could hardly be called a friend. She was…an acquaintance. One who now knew that not only was he a debtor, he was a bastard debtor who didn't deserve his own family name.

Even she, with all her hoydenish adventuring, did not carry *that* shame.

And there might have been desire in those eyes before, but it bloody well hadn't been there just now. Instead, there'd been shock. Horror. Fear.

Fear, no doubt, of the consequences of being married to a French priest's by-blow. He could only imagine what she must be thinking.

And since when have you cared what Lady India thinks?

He exited onto the street, looked to his right and left. There was no sign of her. Would she run straight back to her aunt with the news? Perhaps by the time he returned to his lodgings, there would already be a note waiting for him: *I must insist that you have no further contact with my niece.*

But no note awaited him after his slow walk back to the hotel. And none arrived that evening or the next morning. Which meant…nothing had changed. Yet.

Except Lady India's opinion of him. As if that could have sunk any lower in the first place.

CHAPTER NINETEEN

THE ARTIST'S STUDIO was on the third floor of a building that apparently had stood since the earliest days of Paris. India started up the stairs, acutely aware of Nicholas a step behind her, and continued the chatter she'd begun in the carriage in the hope of making him believe she hadn't heard what he certainly thought she'd heard.

"I shall warn you," India told him breezily, not quite daring to glance over her shoulder, "this is bound to be tediously boring. '*Un peu au droit...au gauche...* Hold *still,* mademoiselle.' That sort of thing. I hardly know how I shall stand it myself."

"I feel certain you'll manage," he murmured, and nerves tangled in her belly.

A day ago, she'd thought he was someone else. Now...he almost seemed like a stranger.

A day ago, the surprise she had planned for him today felt triumphant. Now it felt foolish, which only made *her* feel foolish, because nothing had changed. He wasn't a stranger. He was Lord Taggart—he was, wasn't he?—and he was here. Escorting her to the portrait sitting, which he would have no reason to do unless he still planned to also escort her to the altar.

She should have told Auntie Phil what she'd learned in that church. Immediately, as soon as she and Millie had returned yesterday.

Instead, she'd pleaded a headache, shut herself away in her rooms and sat there like a ninny hugging a pillow and imagining she was holding *him,* kissing him, somehow easing from his face that awful expression that had etched itself into her mind.

It had only been the shock of the whole thing. She *would* tell Auntie Phil, and soon—perhaps just as soon as the portrait sitting was over.

They'd climbed halfway up the first flight when the door opened below and her surprise began to unfold.

"Mademoiselle India," a man called up. "It would seem we are just in time."

She turned to see the Comte d'Anterry and his friend, Monsieur Pisannes, two acquaintances of Auntie Phil's she'd met last night at yet another soirée—where Nicholas had made a point of ignoring her.

Nothing has changed, she reminded herself sternly, and smiled the way Auntie Phil might have done. "Messieurs. I am so pleased you could spare me a few moments of your afternoon."

"You are too modest, mademoiselle," the comte said, kissing her hand. "Nothing could have kept me away."

"Nor I," Monsieur Pisannes agreed.

The two of them bowed to Nicholas, who bowed in return with a perfunctory, "Messieurs."

And then they continued up the stairs, with the comte and Monsieur Pisannes continuing a small debate that had apparently been interrupted when they entered the building, while Nicholas helped ensure she did not trip over her skirts. The maid she'd brought from Auntie Phil's house trailed behind.

Already, butterflies threatened the satisfaction of seeing her invitation had not gone ignored.

"You've invited spectators," Nicholas murmured.

"Oh, yes— Did I not mention it?"

"Perhaps you did," he said mildly, "and I've merely forgotten."

If she *had* told him—which she had not—he most certainly would not have *forgotten*. The question now was, how much clothing would he let her remove before he confessed his intentions and put a stop to everything?

"I believe you're acquainted with most of them," she told him. "What a blessing you will have company and conversation during the tedious wait."

"Oh, I don't intend to stay," he said just as they reached the artist's apartment, where the door stood ajar.

She looked at him. He didn't?

"But I did promise your aunt I would see you safely to your destination," he added, and then they were inside the studio, where two of her other invitees relaxed at a table by the window and a third conversed with the painter, who was busy setting out his brushes and paints, and there was a round of greeting and hand kissing and general admiration, and then the painter was guiding her toward a red chaise longue nestled against a waterfall of gold draperies, asking her a half dozen questions about exactly how she would like to be painted.

"Avec des fleurs?" He added a vase of silk flowers to a small pedestal at the foot of the chaise, then whisked it away and stood back. *"Sans?"*

Nicholas was leaving?

"Avec." Flowers seemed appropriate. But…she turned, only to find Nicholas standing right behind her. Across the room, the other guests were opening a bottle

of wine, laughing at something the Marquis de Bravard was saying. It took all her willpower not to ask whether Nicholas really intended to leave. No doubt he *wanted* her to ask, which was why she couldn't.

"If you are in a hurry, Mr. Warre, by all means go," she said instead.

He checked his pocket watch. "I have a few minutes."

The painter gestured for him to make himself comfortable in a nearby armchair. Nicholas made no move to sit.

"You said you have a costume I can wear?" India said to the painter.

"*Mais, oui. Oui!* Behind that screen, mademoiselle."

"Oh, I do hope there is something exotic." She surveyed the collection of portraits around the room— women who had reclined in this very studio. Some watched her with brazen, *Do you dare do as I've done?* gazes. Others posed with eyes averted. "Or perhaps I should choose something more traditional," she added, noting a common theme of soft, draping robes. She laced her fingers together, more to hide a sudden trembling than anything else.

"Or perhaps you need not make a decision at all," Nicholas said, nodding to a large portrait on the far wall behind the painter's canvas. The woman in that one preserved her modesty with nothing more than gently bended knees and a hand resting in her lap.

"Mmm. An interesting possibility. But—" she looked up at him "—I worry you might regret allowing your wife to pose *entirely* nude in front of spectators."

"Forgive me," he said in a low voice, "has there been a wedding I'm unaware of?"

She beckoned the maid she'd brought and disappeared behind the screen, where she inhaled deeply. Twice.

Nicholas was acting as if yesterday had never even happened. Of course he was—what choice did he have? It wasn't as if he could hide himself away in shame and embarrassment. Not and pursue his intention of maneuvering her into wedlock. And it certainly wasn't as if he would allow her to glimpse such aching torment again.

The only reason she'd witnessed it at all was because she'd caught him by complete surprise. The depth of that pain was proving impossible to forget.

"Mademoiselle?" the maid prompted.

"Oui." India breathed deeply. She wasn't here to think of *his* difficulties, but hers.

Likely he was amusing himself at this very moment by imagining that now would make her excuses and explain that she'd decided to be painted fully clothed.

Have you learned nothing at all about me in these past weeks, Mr. Warre?

She fingered the variety of fabrics and costumes draped over the top of the screen and ignored the little voice reminding her what she had learned about him. If anything, the revelation should make her *more* determined to be rid of him.

She chose a soft blue wrap that looked like something from classical Greece.

The maid helped her undress and put on the wrap, draping it around her hips and over her shoulders. With nothing underneath, the wrap clung to India's curves and slid sensuously across her skin. She unpinned her hair and shook it out, letting it fall over her shoulders and breasts. A few more tucks for security and a dozen strokes through her hair with the brush, and she was ready.

She felt nearly naked, and with the feeling came a fresh resolve. When Nicholas saw her like this, he would put a stop to their game. With his true intentions out in the open, she could set about recruiting Auntie Phil's help to thwart them.

She took a deep breath and stepped out from behind the screen.

Nicholas was sitting in the armchair. And she knew, now, that he'd lied when he said he was leaving.

"Ah, mademoiselle," the painter said, kissing his fingertips at the sight of her. *"Venez..."* He guided her toward the chaise. A low, appreciative noise came from the direction of the card table where the men were seated.

Nicholas's gaze followed her impassively. He assessed her choice of outfit with a tiny furrow between his brows, the exact way she'd seen him assess a questionably aged roll at one of the inns where they had stayed on the road from Marseille.

She walked to the couch, conscious of her bare feet on the wooden floor, aware of every place the soft fabric whispered against her skin. Any moment he would stand up. Announce that the portrait would not be painted.

The *comte* and Monsieur Pisannes wandered closer, while her other three guests watched from the table by the window.

"Magnifique, n'est-ce pas?" the *comte* said to Nicholas.

"Ravissante," Nicholas agreed.

India sat down. Uncurled her body across the chaise

longue and draped one arm over the top like the women in the other portraits.

"Là," the painter said. "Just there."

"Surely you will be late if you stay any longer, Mr. Warre," she said.

The painter assessed her critically, ordering her to bend one knee, straighten the other, lean this way, then that way. Beneath the fabric, the tips of her breasts puckered. They jutted out visibly, and her cheeks warmed, but there was nothing to be done about it now. She looked to see if Nicholas Warre had noticed.

He was checking his pocket watch. "Not just yet." He flipped it shut and raised his eyes, leveling them at her.

Butterflies collided.

The painter stepped back. *"Voilà.* Perfect."

"What do you think, Mr. Warre? Perfect?"

"I shall defer to the artist's expertise on that score." He pulled a sheaf of papers from inside his waistcoat and unfolded them, leaned back in his chair and began to read.

"I shan't," the marquis said, sipping a glass of wine and observing her appreciatively from another chair nearby. *"Parfait."*

Nicholas wasn't even going to *watch?* She fumed silently while the painter took his place behind the canvas. Her irritation went unnoticed as Nicholas studied his papers.

At the table by the window, the *comte* and Monsieur Pisannes exchanged cards with two of her other guests. They'd probably seen dozens of scantily clad women. Perhaps hundreds. Maybe Nicholas had, too. The marquis continued to sip his wine and observe her. She didn't want to look at him—not now—but she needed to.

Devil take it, she needed to act as if reposing in a state of undress in front of these men was giving her no end of delight and was exactly the kind of thing Nicholas could expect from her for years to come. As if there was nothing she wanted more than to crook her little finger and have half a dozen gentlemen falling at her feet.

Of which Nicholas would not be one, because he would never fall at anyone's feet, and—

Oh. The room around her faded.

Because he wasn't looking away anymore.

And she wasn't breathing anymore.

And his eyes moved lazily across her torso, and her breasts came alive beneath his gaze, tingling, and suddenly she was more aware of herself than she could have thought possible. Other places stirred deeply—intimate places, ones that would never be painted. And now it was as if he was touching her again the way he'd done in that hayloft, except that he wasn't touching her, he was only looking.

Admit that you want me, Nicholas. The words winged through her mind out of nowhere—or perhaps not from nowhere. Because desire burned hot in those green eyes, desire and memories of what they'd done together.

And it was very, very clear that he *did* want her.

CHAPTER TWENTY

HE'D BEEN SO bloody sure she wouldn't do it.

That evening Nick lounged carelessly in an armchair while Madame Someone-or-Other kept up a lively debate about whether the work of a certain young Genovese poet merited the regard of a rational thinker.

After staring at India's barely contained breasts for the better part of the afternoon, Nick didn't imagine he would ever think rationally again.

Across the room, the Comte d'Anterry was likely having the same reaction. The man had spent nearly the entire evening staring at India, who was seated in a chair next to Lady Pennington, who shared a small settee with a young man who seemed slightly less enthusiastic about poetry than he was about Lady Pennington's figure.

He would have laid *money* India wouldn't do it.

But she'd done it.

And now there were three other men in this room alone who knew exactly, precisely how that swathe of thin blue fabric had molded to the perfect roundness of India's curves—and clung to their peaked crests. And it was his own bloody fault. He could have stopped the entire thing.

But he'd been so sure *she* would stop it.

And when she hadn't, a morbid fascination had

gripped him because she was so completely unlike any young woman he'd ever met. So utterly dogged in her purpose. So...*herself*.

And because even after what she'd surely overhead yesterday, he still recognized the smoldering desire in her eyes—for *him*.

He'd be a fool to read more into that than it merited. But one thing seemed clear: she hadn't told her aunt what she'd heard in the church. If she were going to tell, certainly she would have done it by now. Wouldn't she? Rather than go through all that scheming at the painter's studio, trying to convince him that marriage to her would be an endless festival of cuckoldry?

It was an effort that continued even now, as she paid not one whit of attention to the discussion, but a bloody lot of attention to a Monsieur LeGrand, who crossed his legs carelessly and toyed with his signet ring while he contributed the occasional offhand remark to the conversation. LeGrand was one of those self-styled intellectuals whose arrogance would get him killed outside the safety of a salon.

India cast occasional glances in Nick's direction, apparently to be sure he wasn't missing any of her flirtations.

Meanwhile, she had contributed nothing to the conversation. Not a consumer of poetry, apparently. It was a good guess neither was Lady Pennington, and Nick would lay a large sum on the prospect that Lady Pennington had skimmed just enough of the poet-of-the-evening as she prepared her toilette to be able to contribute the kinds of vague yet acceptably relevant comments she did now.

Monsieur LeGrand expressed an uncharacteristically

long opinion about a particular opening stanza, and Nick studied India's carefully averted gaze and oddly rigid posture. The moment LeGrand finished speaking and the debate flared up on the other side of the room, she relaxed.

Interesting. Why had she not done as her aunt clearly had and read a little of the poet's work so as to chime in?

He watched LeGrand bestow a moment of attention on her, and he followed the direction of the man's gaze directly to the swell of India's breasts above her stays.

Nick's jaw tightened. He could end this game they were playing tomorrow if he chose. Everything was all arranged with Père Valentine, who stood at the ready to perform the ceremony at a moment's notice. Winston and Vernier had agreed to be available as witnesses under the same terms.

There was no reason to wait.

Except that the possibility of his seducing her into compliance seemed more promising than ever. And the idea of her coming to him willingly—even if only driven by desires of the flesh—appealed in a way that caught him down deep, and that he'd do well not to examine too closely.

He leveled his eyes at her, met her gaze the next time she looked his way. *I'll gladly show you where all these flirtations can lead, India.*

Her cheeks pinkened, and her eyes darted away, and now he wanted nothing more than to take her away from here, find the nearest secluded spot—perhaps an enclosed carriage—and—

"Mademoiselle India, surely you agree that this poem on the whole has a romantic, and not a rational, theme," their hostess said.

India's attention snapped to the group, and for a moment she stared like a rabbit flushed into the open. Nick sat up a little in his chair.

"I would agree with that," India said. "Yes."

A gentleman across the room laughed. "Preposterous! Tell us a single verse that is not brimming with rationalism."

India hesitated, and then, "I believe that what is romantic is also rational."

That was the wrong, wrong thing to say.

"Pass her the book," the gentleman suggested. "Read the third and fourth stanzas aloud, mademoiselle, and let us see whether that might be true."

India paled, and now Nick sat fully upright in his chair. "Certainly there is something of the rational in the romantic," he said casually, "else mankind as a species would die out."

Their hostess arched a brow at him. "Would it, indeed?"

He couldn't imagine why India did not want to read, except that perhaps she worried she would be subjected to further questions along the same vein. But if India didn't want to read aloud to the present company—and he could hardly blame her for that—then by God, these self-important intellectuals were not going to force her.

"Without romance, the required act would be rather…perfunctory, would it not?" he asked. "Which might be satisfactory for the male of the species, but would hardly be acceptable to the female—but forgive me, perhaps you would disagree on that point."

Laughter went up, and now the attention was fully off India. The hostess gave a witty retort, and the gentleman fired a new line of questioning at Nick, and while he answered, he glanced at India.

And the expression on her face caught him straight in the gut.

Thank you.

She couldn't have said it more clearly if she'd stood atop Notre-Dame Cathedral and screamed. Inside him something shifted. Surged. And if he never saw anything else in his life, he wanted to see her look at him like that again.

He wanted to be her protector.

The one she ran to when she was afraid.

And God help him, because he wasn't anyone's savior. He was barely managing to save himself, and only thanks to this distasteful agreement with her father.

She bloody well wasn't going to thank him for that.

"YOU DIDN'T TELL me you'd invited guests to your portrait sitting," Auntie Phil said later, standing in the doorway of India's bedchamber. A small edge in her voice warned of displeasure.

India sat in bed, dressed for the night but not tired at all, and wished there were even one soul in all the world she could talk to about what Nicholas had done tonight. About how she felt. But nobody except Father knew she couldn't read—not even the many servants she'd cajoled into reading notes and letters aloud to her over the years after she'd pleaded a headache or eye strain.

"Spectators are all the mode, are they not?" she said, arranging the covers over her lap.

"Not for young virgins. And now I hear you've arranged to meet the Marquis de Bravard tomorrow at the Tuileries."

She certainly couldn't tell Auntie Phil how she'd felt. It was becoming more and more apparent that Auntie Phil might actually approve of a match between India and Nicholas. Inviting him to that soirée—there *hadn't* been a need for that, no matter what Auntie Phil said— allowing Nicholas to escort India alone to the painter's studio…and tonight, more than once, calling India's attention to Nicholas in not-so-subtle ways, trying to get them to strike up a conversation.

It was time to tell Auntie Phil the truth about Nicholas.

"Never fear," India said a little testily, "I made sure Lord Taggart overheard every word of my plans, and I'm certain we can count on him to make a very coincidental appearance."

"No doubt we can. But what I'd like to know is what you imagine will come of this little game you've been playing with him. A man will only stand to be toyed with for so long, India. There comes a point where he will either leave or make his move. And under the circumstances, I daresay Lord Taggart will not simply leave—which means he will make a move, and it may be one you won't like."

India yanked the covers a little higher. "He can't possibly imagine I will roll over like a dog at the threat of his intentions."

"Good heavens." Auntie Phil laughed, toying with a ribbon at the neckline of her dressing gown. "That would never do. But given the inevitability of the situation—"

"It *isn't* inevitable."

"—what you *can* do is turn things around and gain

the illusion of control, so that when the inevitable happens—"

"It *can't*."

"—it happens precisely the way *you* want it to happen, and not the way *he* wants it to happen."

It being their marriage. Hers and Nicholas's. She saw him in her mind—felt the way he'd looked at her, the way she'd fought herself to keep from looking at him in return.

Felt that overwhelming relief and gratitude when he'd intervened and kept her from having to confess to the entire party—including him—that she couldn't read aloud, not even if they mocked her and laughed at her. Not even if they withheld her suppers and banished her to her rooms.

She could not tell his secret to Auntie Phil now. She owed him a measure of protection after what he'd done tonight. Didn't she?

"I shall accompany you to the gardens tomorrow," Auntie Phil said now. "Clearly I should have been accompanying you all along, although it appears Lord Taggart has done an admirable job of protecting his interests. No doubt any number of admirers will have decided to join the marquis tomorrow, and we cannot expect him to fend them all off on his own."

"But—"

"And thus tomorrow we shall begin turning this ship around, so to speak."

She needed to tell, force the words out quickly while the time was ripe. Auntie Phil would certainly write the news to Father, and then this sham of an engagement would quickly be over, and then there would be no ship in need of turning, and she would never need to associate with Nicholas again.

A small ache opened up behind her ribs.

"Now sleep well, dearest, and pleasant dreams." Auntie Phil came forward and pressed a kiss to India's forehead.

With Auntie Phil gone, India sat alone, hugging her knees in the light from a single candle flickering on the nightstand. Why hadn't she *told?*

She was such a ninny. It wasn't as if Nicholas cared even one whit for *her* feelings. There was no reason she should care about his. He was merely following her around Paris to protect his investment while he arranged a wedding that would succeed where his other attempts had not.

Perhaps arranging a clandestine wedding was more difficult than she imagined, even in Paris. Perhaps it really was taking this long, and he wasn't toying with her because he wanted to but because he had to.

While she...

She couldn't seem to stop wanting him, no matter how much she didn't *want* to want him. The feeling was so much stronger now than it had been a week ago when the carriage had whisked them through the countryside and she'd spent too many hours watching him, indulging in the memory of his touch even when she knew she shouldn't.

But now...

Now he was more than an indulgence. It was as if everything had changed in those moments in that church when she'd glimpsed the shame and horror she knew he hadn't meant for her to see, and suddenly he'd seemed so much more...human.

Fallible.

Susceptible to shame. Weakness. Burdens.

Oh, she knew all about shame and weakness and burdens. And she knew *all* about a father's rejection and scorn.

And she was so, *so* tired of defiance.

She dropped her head to her knees and dragged in a breath through her mouth. Her chest ached so badly it hurt to inflate her lungs.

There was a horrible part of her that didn't even care how Nicholas really felt about her. That just wanted to give in and accept the marriage so that he might hold her and she might feel that sensation again of being wanted, being protected, even if he only gave his attention because of the money and his lust.

And it made her feel so, so ashamed.

She should want to run away like she'd done before. Like she'd always planned. It was possible—*anything* was possible, if she was willing to endure the hardships that would be required if they ever hoped to locate William and the *Possession*.

The Mediterranean seemed so far away now. Everything that mattered seemed far away. Unreachable.

If only she could go back in time to that gazebo in the woods at Auntie Phil's country house and curl up on that bench seat in the dappled sunshine and never leave.

But strong, brave people didn't want to hide in wooded gazebos. They wanted to sail the seas and shoot cannons and swill grog in taverns and take Egyptian lovers.

The only lover she wanted to take—and oh, God, she longed for his embrace so fiercely—was Nicholas.

MILLIE TRIED TO concentrate on a book she'd found in Philomena's library about a French physician and his experiments, but it was impossible to think of anything but how she might confront Lord Taggart about their agreement.

She glanced at the shrinking candle. Before long, nighttime reading would once again become a luxury.

From the floor above came the rumble of male laughter from Philomena's dressing room, and Millie closed her book. Philomena toyed with men because she could—she did not need them for anything.

If this plan did not work, Millie would be in a very different position.

Her stomach turned, and she squeezed her legs together inside her voluminous nightgown. There was nothing—*nothing*—she wouldn't do to prevent that. But time certainly was running short—certainly Lord Taggart did not intend to wait much longer before carrying his plans through.

She had to speak with him before that. Once he and India were married, he would have no reason to pay her what he'd agreed. Every day that passed, it seemed less likely that he planned to keep his end of the bargain. He might be waiting for the marriage to actually take place—which was not their agreement—and she couldn't let him do that.

She imagined confronting him. *You've been of little use to me,* he might say. *I owe you nothing.*

What would she do then? She had nothing to hold over him. No way to force the money from him. All she had to rely on—all there'd been from the beginning— was his honor.

A man's honor meant very little.

Just then, there was a knock at the door. Millie glanced at the mantel clock: ten minutes past one. What was India doing awake so late?

She went to answer, and admitted an India who looked decidedly strained.

"What's happened?" Millie asked, hoping—please, God—the answer wasn't a wedding. Not yet.

"We have to *do* something," India said. "This can't go on. I can't let him take my dignity—I won't." No, definitely not a wedding.

Millie shut the door. "What are you talking about? What has he done?"

But India was in one of her not-listening tizzies. "I can't let him make me feel like this," she raged. "I'm not vulnerable—not anymore. We may not have succeeded, be we captained that ship all the way to Malta, Millie. And perhaps we had some trouble, but we did it, and we could do it again. *He's* the one who's vulnerable. Only think what will become of him without Father's money. He should be *begging* me to marry him."

"Is that what you want? Him to beg you?" Because if that was all it would take—

"Of course not."

"You're not going to convince him to change his mind. Surely you've realized that much."

"I'm not completely dim-witted."

"Then the sooner you accept there's nothing you can do about it—"

"But there *is* something I can do about it."

"India, posing half-nude for a room full of men was never going to work, and neither will whatever you've thought of now."

"It isn't something I've thought of." Millie knew

India well enough to know when India had latched on to a silly scheme and when she was considering something very serious. The look on India's face said this was no silly scheme.

Millie stilled. "Then what is it?"

"You must promise you won't breathe a word to anyone. Ever."

God in heaven. If it wasn't something India had thought of, it had to be something she'd done. "Of course."

"Promise."

"I *promise.*"

"I never imagined..." India started, then stopped. "I just never would have thought."

Dear God. Millie imagined India in a room somewhere with a stranger—

Millie couldn't help it. She threw her arms around India. "Just put it from your mind. It will be all right.... Nobody needs to find out. Some women do not bleed the first time, so Lord Taggart need never know, even if there are no stains on the marriage bed—"

"What are you talking about?" India pulled away.

"Did you not part with your virtue?"

"No! For heaven's—*no.* And with him following me everywhere, I would hardly be able to even if I wished it. Which I don't, not anymore, because— Never mind why. Millie...Nicholas Warre is not what he seems."

Millie waited.

"That day we followed him into the church, I overheard something that could change everything if I told Auntie Phil. It could stop all of this. Father would never approve—not ever. I know he wouldn't. But if I tell... it would ruin Nicholas Warre forever."

And India proceeded to divulge information that would ensure Millie would not have to rely on Lord Taggart's honor to get what she'd been promised.

Millie sat down. "I see." The news was...unbelievable. Suddenly it was impossible to look India in the eye.

"Father would never want our family connected with Nicholas Warre if he knew," India said now. She sat down, too, and hugged herself, rubbing her arms a little. "I could go to Auntie Phil right now. Well, not right this minute, but tomorrow morning. Then we would see who had the upper hand." But India's tone had lost its fervor, and it was obvious that India wasn't sure she could ruin Lord Taggart, not even if it meant she would end up married to him.

Millie said, a bit hesitantly, "No wonder he is so desperate to save his estate. If what you say is true, without it he would be little more than a misbegotten good-for-naught." She glanced at a scratch on her finger. Looked up, smiled a little. "You would certainly have your revenge by exposing him. Only think how it would destroy him."

Already India was shaking her head. "I can't, Millie. I've got to find another way to stop the marriage, because I simply couldn't do that to him. To *anyone*."

And Millie felt about as honorable as a maggot, because if Lord Taggart refused to pay her, she would not have the same qualms.

CHAPTER TWENTY-ONE

By THE NEXT day, despite being somewhat comforted by Millie before finally returning to bed, India was in no mood for a stroll in the gardens with Auntie Phil and a bevy of admirers.

Auntie Phil made flirting look like such fun. But it wasn't, not anymore. India was so tired of this. She didn't want the marquis' attentions, didn't want these other Parisian gallants flocking around her the way they gathered around Auntie Phil—the way they were doing now, while Auntie Phil laughed with them as if she hadn't a care in the world.

All of India's flirtations weren't even having an effect on Nicholas. Perhaps because everything she told him was a lie. She didn't plan to have an affair. She only wanted him to *think* she planned to.

But if her strategy at the painter's studio hadn't affected Nicholas…what possibly would? How outrageously would she have to behave in order to crack his mask of indifference?

The sun filtered through high, hazy clouds as they stood in an opening where several paths converged. Auntie Phil entertained the men with lighthearted nothings, fluttering her fan and touching it occasionally to her décolletage. India didn't have the heart to follow suit.

Perhaps she could feign a terrible illness and be finished with all this nonsense. Nicholas could hardly force a marriage if she were confined to her bed, sick with a possibly contagious disease. It could last for days. Weeks, even. And by the time she was well enough to accept visitors, Nicholas would—

"Lord Taggart," Auntie Phil said, and now India heard the crunch of footsteps behind her. "What a relief to see you. I daresay my niece has been pining over that pond these past fifteen minutes—" she pointed across the clearing with her fan "—and you are just the man to escort her. Do take India to see the ducks, will you?"

No—

"A pleasure."

Nicholas offered India his arm, and there didn't seem a way to refuse—*because you don't really want to refuse*—and moments later they were walking together toward a pool where a group of ducks paddled peacefully, poking in the water for food.

She reached deep for the will to continue the game. "The number of times we've been thrown together by chance since arriving in Paris is positively uncanny, Mr. Warre," she told him.

"I was just thinking the same thing." He smiled a little. "Uncanny."

"Imagine, you deciding to take some air in the gardens at the exact same moment my aunt and I planned to meet the marquis. If one did not know better, one might almost think you wanted to interfere in our fledgling *amour*."

"Spoiling your plans for an intimate rendezvous was the furthest thing from my mind, I assure you," Nicholas said. He glanced over his shoulder. "Although it would seem your plans were already spoiled."

Being this close to him was madness. It took all her concentration not to simply stare up at him. Every sense seemed focused on the point where her fingers touched his arm, on the solid flex of muscle beneath her hand.

"The more the merrier, I always think."

"Indeed," he murmured, "you've demonstrated that opinion quite successfully." His tone left no doubt that he was thinking of her portrait sitting. Remembering.

Her body's secret places stirred.

"I only wonder that you did not seem as enthusiastic last night as you did earlier in the day," he added. "Perhaps studying modern philosophers is not a favorite pastime?"

Just that quickly, her secret places were forgotten. Too late she realized she'd tensed her fingers around his arm. Deliberately she relaxed them. "Mr. Warre, based on your knowledge of me—" she laughed "—would you expect me to be interested in philosophy?"

"I might have expected you to prepare for the evening, as your aunt did."

And now Nicholas was looking at her more intently than he had before, as if perhaps he knew there were things India wasn't telling him—personal things she would *never* tell him.

She waved his notion away and looked at the ducks. "After my grueling afternoon yesterday, I was hardly in any condition to study." She looked up at him brazenly. He couldn't possibly have figured out her failure from that single incident. Could he? "Sitting for a portrait is more tiring than one might expect."

"Mmm." His eyes were so green, so full of temptation. "I can certainly confirm that *watching* someone sit for a portrait is tiring."

She raised her chin. "You needn't have stayed."

His gaze touched her cheeks, her lips. "I daresay we both know I did need to."

A keen yearning curled inside her, tight and warm and wanting. If they were married, if she simply let this happen, the fight would be over. And there would be nothing to stop her from reaching out to him. Touching his face. Tracing the line of his jaw or the curve of his lip. Nothing to stop her from simply staring at him for as long as she wished.

As she watched, the calculation in his eyes softened.

"India," he started—in a new tone, a quiet and serious tone she'd never heard him use— "I want you to know that, as your husband, I shall never do anything to hurt you."

She stared at him. The look in his eyes—the tone, those words, they wrapped around her. Tempting. Making her heart beat faster.

"Don't…don't be ridiculous." Certainly his idea of *hurt* was different than hers. Obviously it was. "Only look at all you've done already, and without the benefit of that title. Need I remind you about the ribbons? And in any case, we both know you've changed your mind about…that agreement."

Would he finally confess—here, now—that he hadn't changed his mind?

If they married, and there would be no more India. There would only be Lord and Lady Taggart.

Which was why she needed to turn around, have him walk her back toward Auntie Phil and the men, and resume showing him exactly what kind of Lady Taggart she might become.

Nicholas's lips tightened. "India—"

"Taggart," a familiar voice called, and his gaze shot behind her, to the speaker, whose voice she recognized easily. She glanced over her shoulder at the Duke of Winston, ambling toward them. Relief tangled with frustration—what had Nicholas been about to say?

"Good afternoon," the duke said, joining them at the pond's edge.

"What a pleasure to see you, Your Grace," India said, and the two men began a conversation about the merits of the day's light cloud cover.

Whatever Nicholas had been going to say, she did not want to hear. And the duke— Yes, she realized now that the duke presented the perfect opportunity to turn the conversation in a new direction.

She waited until a few more pleasantries had been exchanged, and then she asked, "Have you been enjoying your evenings at Madame Gravelle's?" Her heart raced a little faster.

The duke's brows edged upward. He looked at Nicholas, then back at India, and amusement touched the corners of his mouth. "Evenings in the plural may be taking things a bit far," he said. "I doubt even I could survive such entertainments on a nightly basis."

Good. Excellent. Madam Gravelle's, she'd learned, was a house of ill repute. That made it the perfect subject to show Nicholas she wasn't interested in his declarations.

That you're afraid of them.

Oh, fie. "What a fascinating thing to imagine. I've

been thinking of attending myself, despite my aunt's opinion, and now I am all the more intrigued."

She felt Nicholas looking at her but refused to turn her eyes in his direction.

What if he's sincere?

It wouldn't matter. It wouldn't change anything. It couldn't.

"Far be it from me to dissuade you, Lady India," the duke said, humor dancing in his dark eyes. "But I fear you might not find it to your liking. It appeals to women with an entirely different sort of…shall we say…education."

Finally she looked at Nicholas, making herself smile up at him—but she could hardly breathe, and now her entire mind seemed filled with what he'd actually said to her a few minutes ago and how he'd said it. "I'm quite certain Lord Taggart would wish me to be well educated," she said as saucily as she could manage.

"Absolutely," Nicholas said. His lips curved. "I've always viewed education as most valuable."

And now they were back to pretending, and she would never know what he'd been about to say.

She was supposed to feel relieved. "Then you won't have any objection to my visiting Madame Gravelle's with His Grace."

"Not at all," Nicholas said evenly.

The duke made a noise and rubbed his hand over his jaw, and a quick cut of dimple gave away that he was only hiding his laughter. "As a compromise," he said to her, sobering, "perhaps Taggart will join me there in your stead—say, tonight?—and he can pass along the essentials."

"I feel certain that solution would never suffice for Lady India," Nicholas said.

"Certainly not," she agreed. "I suggest we make it a threesome."

"Good God," the duke said, looking at Nicholas, who only smiled pleasantly.

"We can hardly refuse a lady's wishes."

The duke shook his head, laughing, and bowed quickly. "Until tonight, then. This has been most entertaining."

"What an excellent plan," India said the moment he was gone, hoping to cut off any more talk of marriage. Pretending, which was so much better than...

I want you to know that, as your husband—

"I simply cannot wait," she added. "What fun we shall all have."

"I'm sure the visit will be most enlightening for you." India stared at him. He was going to allow this?

"And diverting," she agreed. "Perhaps the very kind of diversions a married lady might take advantage of."

There was a moment of something in Nicholas's eyes—a weariness that said he'd grown tired of their game. And yet, "The company at Madame Gravelle's will certainly put your 'the more the merrier' maxim to the test," he told her.

A nerve pulsed at the base of her throat. She raised her chin. "Excellent. I hope there are dozens of people there. *Hundreds.*"

"No doubt there will be plenty—" he stepped closer, so they stood face-to-face with barely a hairbreadth between them "—all expecting to see a good deal more than the outline of your breasts through a swathe of blue fabric."

"I shall look forward to it." Her breath turned shallow. If he hadn't been concerned enough to stop the portrait painting, what else might he stand by and allow?

"You'll need an excuse to escape the Comte d'Anterry's ball, of course," he pointed out reasonably.

"I shall sneak away and hire a chair. Balls last for hours—I can return before I'm missed."

"No need for that." Now his eyes roamed over her, dark with a hunger she recognized too well. "We can escape the ball together, and I will take you to Madame Gravelle's myself."

"Indeed? Or will you escort me back to my aunt's?" *Tell me again,* she thought. *Tell me again how we might be married and you'll never hurt me.*

Instead, he turned finally and offered her his arm once more. "Lady India," he said, starting back toward Auntie Phil and her admirers, "you have my word I will do no such thing."

THE MOMENT HE got India into the carriage tonight, Nick would instruct the driver to take a long and winding route through the city, and he would seduce her.

Right there, in the carriage. Never mind that despite everything she was a lady, and a virgin, and she would be his wife, and that plundering beneath her skirts in a moving carriage was not the way a woman fitting any of those descriptions should be treated.

She'd been so bloody close to acquiescence. He'd seen the way she'd been looking at him—the desire in her eyes, the softening of her face.

She was nearer to being a willing bride than she'd ever been. If Winston hadn't come along when he had…

There was no certainty Nick would have convinced

India of anything. He hadn't even planned exactly what to say. The words about not hurting her—they had risen up from somewhere deep inside him.

And the next thing he'd known, she'd been proposing a debauch with Winston.

He escorted her back to her aunt, made his excuses and left the gardens, imagining India at Madame Gravelle's amid all that raw sensualism, and—

God.

As he walked back to his hotel, his mind took him to that dangerous place where India was beneath him, wide-eyed and gasping as he stoked her desire, readying her, introducing her to all the things she claimed she wanted to know, sinking into her and hearing her cry out as he took that damnable virtue she spoke so carelessly of tossing away.

God.

He inhaled deeply and turned the last corner before he reached his hotel.

It was time. She wasn't going to Madame Bloody Gravelle's, and they weren't playing this game anymore. It was clear enough that given the opportunity, he could stoke India's desire until she was begging him to take her, just as she'd begged that night in the hayloft.

Letting her glimpse his feelings just now had been a mistake. He already knew that touching her would not be. She would respond—there was no doubt about that—and soon she would be standing in front of Père Valentine, saying the necessary vows without any coercion except the promise of more pleasure to come.

He opened the door to the hotel, nodded to the hotelier, started up the stairs.

India wanted him to admit he hadn't changed his plan to marry her? Very well.

He would show her tonight—very, very thoroughly—exactly what he intended their relationship to be.

FROM THE SHADOW of an alley, Millie watched Nicholas Warre disappear through a pair of doors with peeling blue paint and almost—*almost*—felt sorry for him. Hôtel Bernard looked like a medieval seedbed for the plague.

But his own desperation didn't change the facts. He'd made her an offer, and she'd fulfilled her end of the bargain. She picked up her skirts and hurried across the street, feeling comfortingly nondescript in the old brown cloak she'd bought from a woman selling secondhand clothes at the market.

The door stuck a little, but she let herself into a worn reception that smelled of tallow and whale oil smoke. The hotelier eyed her from behind the desk.

"The man who just came in," she said, producing a key she'd taken from Philomena's maid. "I saw him drop this in the street."

The hotelier grunted his disbelief and jerked his head toward the stairwell. *"Numéro 34, au troisième."*

He assumed she was a prostitute. It made her feel sick as she climbed the stairs, but it was a small price to pay. She could not let Nicholas Warre off the hook now.

She had to knock twice, but suddenly the door flew open. He stood there half-dressed, shirttails hanging out of his breeches and his waistcoat draped across a wooden chair behind him. The room was barely big enough for the bed and his trunk.

"What are you doing here?" he demanded.

She made herself look him in the eye. "We need

to discuss our arrangement. I've done everything you asked."

"Have you?"

She narrowed her eyes at him. "Yes."

"Aside from a few halfhearted attempts, I'm not sure you've been of much use to me at all."

"You owe me a hundred pounds, Lord Taggart—"

"Do *not* speak of such sums here." He pulled her into the tiny room and shut the door. "It seems to me, Miss Germain, that my success has been largely my own doing. Yet I'm to understand that you still expect full payment?"

She *needed* full payment. "Yes. And the letter."

"Ah, the letter."

Yes. The letter. God help her—he could not renege on that now. She would not allow it. "The money *and* the letter, Mr. Warre. And I'll not leave here until I receive it."

"Lady India and I are not yet married."

"Through no fault of mine—and waiting until the wedding was not our arrangement!"

"Perhaps it should be."

"You and Lady India won't ever be married if your true paternity comes to light—which it will if you do not fulfill your end of our agreement this instant."

His eyes turned cold, and his face turned to stone, and Millie wished the threat back but it was too late. And now he was turning to his valise, digging, coming up with a small piece of paper.

"Payment," he said flatly. "For services rendered."

One hundred. She stared at the bank note in her hands, giddy and sick all at the same time. She wanted to ask about the letter—she needed that letter—but after what she'd just threatened, she couldn't imagine him still vouching for her character.

Better to leave, quickly, before he changed his mind about what he'd already given. "Good day, Lord Taggart."

She took the bank note and fled. Down the stairs, past the hotelier—

"*Attendez!*"

She stopped. He came out and blocked her way to the door, holding out his hand and wiggling his fingers. "*Donnez-moi. Donnez.*"

He wanted her to give him money? Because he thought—

"*Non*—that isn't what I—"

"*Donnez!*" He reached for her arm, and she had fled so quickly she had barely stuffed the bank note in the pocket of her cloak and he reached inside, pulling it out.

"*Non!*"

The hotelier laughed.

"*Donnez-le-moi!*" Millie cried, lunging toward him, but the hotelier pushed her away. And now he was looking at her as though he might take something else, as well—something she would rather die than give him.

"*Putain.*" The hotelier laughed. *Whore.* "You will get more where this came from, eh?" he said, pocketing her bank note.

Millie didn't wait. She ran.

CHAPTER TWENTY-TWO

HE WAS DOWN to half the money he'd had when the day began.

Which made it even more nonsensical that now, three hours after he'd parted with what some might consider a fortune—despite the fact that she'd threatened him with a secret she could only have learned from India, which proved that India had heard exactly what he'd imagined—he stood near the river, half-hidden behind a hay cart, and watched the women and girls washing clothes aboard the laundry boats moored haphazardly along the banks.

This was folly. Utter, complete folly.

He'd planned to leave Paris without doing this.

And now the sun was sinking below the horizon, and nearly two hours of searching and asking had turned up nothing. How he thought he would ever find one girl among so many boats and laundresses, he had no idea. He didn't even know what she looked like.

It was past time to give up. It would be dark soon.

But he couldn't walk away.

Two boys ran by, laughing and shouting, chasing each other with sticks. Nick surveyed the women, looking for glimpses of dark hair beneath the rags and kerchiefs tied around their heads.

This was going to drive him mad. He was exhausted.

He should leave now, go find something to eat. His stomach had been rumbling for two hours.

Just one more. The words that had driven him for hours drove him toward the water's edge once again. He spotted a woman in a boat—stout and industrious, with strands of dark hair falling from beneath a dirty white mobcap. She was almost within speaking distance, so he moved a little closer. Children carried armloads of clothing hither and yon, followed by shouts from their mothers.

He was just about to call out to the woman when a sharp reprimand from somewhere to his left froze him in his tracks.

"Emilie!"

His attention snapped to the side, searching.

"Emilie, *non!*"

He found the speaker, a gaunt woman with thin, angry lips teetering purposefully toward a girl in a boat—a small girl of perhaps ten or eleven, who had paused her washing to reach out toward a mallard paddling closer to investigate the activity. The girl ducked her head and instantly resumed her washing, but it wasn't enough. The woman yanked her by the arm, smacked her across the face. The girl barely flinched.

"Lazy, useless girl," the woman spat. "You think the ducks are going to do the washing for you? Eh?"

"Non, Tante Marie—"

"Ne dit rien!" The woman gave the girl a shake. "Always excuses from you. *Toujours les excuses. J'en ai assez!"*

Nick hardly realized he'd moved until he was standing there, shoes sinking into mud at the river's edge.

"Pardonnez moi," he called sharply. "Is there a problem?"

The woman's gray eyes snapped in his direction, narrowing. "Not that concerns you."

But already he was looking at the girl in the woman's grip, who was staring at him through wide brown eyes that were...too familiar. His gut clenched.

"Emilie?" he asked.

The girl's nod was barely a movement.

"What do you want with Emilie?" the woman demanded, releasing her now to face him.

He looked at her sharply. "Is there another Emilie here?"

"Why do you ask?"

"Do you know another Emilie?" He barked it this time.

His tone had its effect, and he could see the woman calculating. *"Non."* And then, with a contemptuous glance at the girl, *"Merci, Dieu."*

Tante Marie, the girl had said. This woman was the girl's aunt. "Where is her mother?" Nick demanded.

The woman grunted. "Dead. Of course. And leaving me with Emilie, as if I don't have enough children of my own." Her eyes shot daggers at the girl.

At Emilie.

Nick looked at her, too. She stood in the boat, dirty skirts drenched, hands red and chafed. Thin, much too thin. Ruddy cheeks. Hollow brown eyes a little sunken in her face. Everything about her screamed laborer. Commoner. Urchin.

And everything about her screamed Yves Dechelle. He didn't need to meet the man twice to see the resemblance to their father. To Nick himself. The set of her brows, the shape of her chin, the tilt of her nose.

His chest filled, squeezed, so full it made his throat tight.

"How old are you, Emilie?"

"Eleven," she said in a small voice.

Eleven. He turned to the aunt. "Who is the girl's father?"

"What business is that of yours?" the woman snapped. "Who are *you?*" Already now she was looking him up and down, assessing the value of his clothes. And then, at Emilie, "Stop staring and return to your washing, you lazy little—"

"No." Nick waded into the water and grabbed the edge of their boat, reaching out and curling a hand around Emilie's arm, as gently as he could, to stop her turning away. "I am your brother," he told her in a voice he had to work hard to keep calm. Nonthreatening, when he wanted to yank her aunt out of the boat and show her what it felt like to be slapped. "*Je m'appelle Nicholas.* I won't hurt you." It was the second time today he'd said those words.

A little cry escaped Emilie's lips, and her aunt's face twisted contemptuously. "*Son frère.*" She laughed, clearly believing that, more likely, he was trolling the river for a virginal plaything. The very idea enraged him.

"And I am taking her with me," he said flatly.

"You'll not take Emilie anywhere without paying." She held out her hand. "*Deux écus.*"

"*Tante Marie, non!*" A terrified Emilie cowered in his grasp. Two *écus*...for less than a pound, the woman would simply let him—let *anyone*—take Emilie away?

"Don't be afraid," he told Emilie again. "I will make sure nobody ever strikes you again."

A spark of hope in Emilie's eyes faded as quickly as it appeared.

Nick turned to her aunt. "I *am* her brother, and I owe you nothing."

She grabbed Emilie's other arm. "*Deux écus,* or I shall make such a scene you'll not have her at all."

Already they had attracted attention, or he had, and more than a few of the washerwomen were looking their way. Listening. Thinking, most likely, exactly what Emilie's aunt thought. He could feel Emilie trembling in his grip.

He told himself to let her go. Walk away. Nobody would ever think he was more than a man with a taste for young girls but not enough money to pay the price.

Instead, he reached into his pocket. Withdrew a coin. Let them think what they would. "One and no more."

The woman's eyes turned hungry as she snatched the silver coin from his fingers. "Good riddance," she said, and turned back to her washing.

Nick lifted Emilie out of the boat. *"Tante Marie!"*

NOT A SOUL interfered.

Nick spoke reassuring words until he'd said *I won't hurt you* every way he could think of, but still Emilie's hand trembled in his as they hurried toward the street, and tears streamed down her cheeks. He reminded himself—again—to slow his pace so she could keep up.

She was small—too small for a girl of eleven? He didn't know.

A girl of *eleven.*

Panic welled up inside him. He bundled her into a

chair, barked the address at the driver. Ushered her past
the hotelier, silently daring the man to object.

His rented room seemed half the size with Emilie in
it. She stood in the only free space—at the foot of the
narrow, sunken bed—in her soggy clothes, with her
arms hanging at her sides, watching him through terrified brown eyes that could eat a man's soul.

The gravity of the situation closed around him like a
hand around his throat. Good God. What had he done?

"Tu as faim?" he asked. She only stared at him, but
then he heard her stomach rumble and knew the answer.

He took her to a bakery on the corner, the charcuterie
across the street, purchased a bit of cheese to go with
the bread and meat. Back in the room, he fashioned a
simple meal. Emilie sat in the single, crooked chair and
ate tentatively at first, then ravenously. He considered
offering her more, but worried it might make her ill.

The slow rage that had already lit inside him burned
hotter. Had she gone her entire life without enough to
eat?

The window was completely black. Night had fallen,
and what the devil was he supposed to do now? He
surveyed the tiny room, hating that he had to think
twice about moving them somewhere better. He simply couldn't afford to lodge them both properly in Paris
for…

How long? Days? Another week?

Already time was closing in on him, while Holliswell rubbed his hands together in England, salivat-
ing over Taggart. At this very moment, India would be
at d'Anterry's ball, waiting for Nick to show up so they
could continue their ridiculous pretense about Madame
Gravelle's.

He wouldn't be seducing her in any carriage now, not with Emilie to think of.

And he couldn't stay with Emilie in Paris, not like this. She would need her own room. Clothes—an entire bloody wardrobe, and not the washwoman's rags she wore now. She was his *sister,* for God's sake. She deserved...

Everything.

Tutors. Dancing masters. Drawing instructors. Libraries full of books. Dolls, toys...all the things she so obviously had never been given.

Emilie needed Taggart, perhaps more than he did.

And there was only one way to give that to her.

"It's time," Nick said, finding Vernier at home and still readying for the evening.

Outside, Nick's trunk sat atop a rented carriage in which Emilie waited, bundled inside one of Nick's jackets, with the rest of the bread, meat and cheese wrapped inside a cloth in case for later. Once they got to Taggart, he would hire a cook and give instructions that Emilie was to be fed whatever she wanted, whenever she wanted, even if it was three o'clock in the bloody morning.

"Tonight?" Vernier asked, while his valet fastidiously brushed his coat. "Are you certain?"

"It's imperative," Nick said. "I can't wait any longer."

"Mais, oui. Bien sûr." He dismissed his valet, then turned to Nick. "Tell me what I am to do."

"Lady India is at d'Anterry's ball as we speak," Nick said, and told Vernier about the conversation with Winston earlier.

"Madame Gravelle's—*Dieu*. I hardly know what to say to that," Vernier exclaimed with a laugh.

"I had no plans to see it through," Nick said.

"*Mais, non*. But her expectation will work in our favor."

Precisely. In the next minutes, they worked out their plan: Nick would go to the ball as planned, while Emilie waited safely outside. Vernier himself would make an appearance at the ball, too—just long enough to surreptitiously notify Winston, if he was there—and would leave quickly to alert Père Valentine.

Nick would secret India away from the ball as planned—and drive her to the church, where weeks of game-playing and obstruction would finally end.

WINSTON WAS NOT at the ball…and neither was India.

Nick stood in the shadows at the edge of the ballroom, having checked every corner of d'Anterry's lower floors and torchlit grounds, and looked at his pocket watch.

He'd been more than two hours late to the ball. Vernier had left twenty minutes ago to finalize arrangements for the wedding. Nick sank farther into the shadows to avoid being noticed by Lady Pennington, and told himself the thing he suspected could not possibly be true.

India wasn't stupid.

She would not go to Madame Gravelle's alone.

But she *was* determined to show him she could not be controlled, and his gut told him that was exactly where she'd gone.

He pushed his way through the crowd, heading for the door.

"Lord Taggart!"

God. God. He stopped abruptly. "Lady Pennington."

"Have you seen my niece?" A tiny furrow creased gracefully between her brows. "I can't seem to find her anywhere."

"I was just looking for her myself," he said. He had to go. Now. "I shall let you—"

"Do let me know when you find her—"

"Of course."

"She was dancing with the marquis again earlier, but surely he knows the wrath he would face if I discovered he had spirited her away." She smiled knowingly. "As I'm sure he would face yours, as well."

"Most certainly." He bowed. "If you'll please excuse me…"

"Are you quite all right? You seem out of sorts."

He tried to smile. "Not at all." Except that in the time it was taking to exchange these bloody pleasantries, anything could be happening to India at Madame Gravelle's. "If you'll excuse me—"

This time he didn't wait. He raced out to the carriage, thanked God the driver was already familiar with the famed house of pleasure's location, and hoped that Winston—whom Nick could be certain had not actually *taken* India there—was at least not too preoccupied to notice that she had arrived on her own.

CHAPTER TWENTY-THREE

INDIA LURKED IN the shadows at Madame Gravelle's with her pulse thrumming and her fingers folding pleats in her sleeve.

There were so many people here. In an adjoining room, an orchestra played a lively and lilting tune. There were bodies everywhere—people drinking, laughing, fondling.

From behind the shelter of a faux column, she watched a woman push her breasts into the waiting hands of two men.

Perhaps coming here had been a mistake. She'd been so certain Nicholas would be here—so aggravated, awaiting him at the ball, *knowing* that he was playing some new kind of game wherein he imagined he could stop her from coming here simply by not showing up at the ball. But she didn't see him anywhere.

She edged a little farther behind the column. Even the Duke of Winston was nowhere to be seen, but with so many bodies, there was no knowing for sure.

She should leave. That had been her plan—come to Madame Gravelle's as she'd told Nicholas she would, knowing at least the duke would be here, and if it was a disaster, she would leave quickly and nobody would ever be the wiser.

But now the entrance was three rooms away, with

dozens of shocking activities taking place between her and the door, and—

"Bonsoir, mademoiselle." A man had approached from her other side, partly blocking her escape from behind the column.

She tried to smile. "Bonsoir, monsieur."

His cheek dimpled. "You are enjoying the party?" He was blond and handsome, laughing and open with a wicked light in his blue eyes.

No, I was just about to leave.... She glanced at the crowd again. After everything that was said at the gardens, surely Nicholas would be here.

"Mais, oui." She swallowed, buying herself a moment, keeping her eye on the crowd, but not *too* closely, because— Good God. Did that woman just— "I always enjoy this kind of party." She shifted her attention fully to the man.

He laughed. "I have been watching you, mademoiselle, and I am convinced you have never attended this kind of party before." He reached out and fingered a lock of her hair. "Tell me…what drove you here tonight? Curiosity, perhaps?"

Stupidity. Even if Nicholas had been here, what had she really thought to accomplish? *Don't be a ninny,* she scolded herself. *He could yet arrive.*

Proving to him that she would be a terrible wife, that's what.

"Yes…yes, curiosity."

The man edged closer, even though there was barely a foot of space between them to begin with. Now there was barely an inch. He caught her hand and kissed her fingertips. "Then perhaps I may satisfy it for you."

"No, I don't think that will be necessary, monsieur—"

"Pardon me," a man interrupted, joining them in a very cozy threesome. India looked up into—oh, thank heaven—the near-black devil-eyes of the Duke of Winston. "I'm afraid you've chosen the wrong entertainment for the evening, Giroux."

"Bah!" the blond Frenchman said good-naturedly. "I should have known you would have a claim to such a one as this."

"The daughter of a friend," the duke told him, "who has somehow found her way here and must now find her way back."

"Ah, I see."

India's relief edged into irritation.

"I couldn't possibly leave when I have just met such a charming acquaintance," India told the duke, tucking her hand into Monsieur Giroux's arm now that the duke was here with Nicholas surely nearby.

The duke ignored her and ordered Monsieur Giroux to leave with a quick jerk of his head. When the man had gone, the duke looked down at her. "Where is your fiancé, Lady India?"

"I have no fiancé, and in fact I was only just beginning to enjoy myself with Monsieur Giroux when you interfered—"

"Do not play games with me," the duke said in a low voice, curling his hand around her arm. "This is no place for an innocent. Where is Taggart?"

"You do not know? I assumed you were together."

Those devil-dark eyes narrowed. "No."

Beyond him a woman in a sheer toga began to dance. He glanced over his shoulder and moved to block India's view. And then, "Oh, heaven be praised," he said, and she saw Nicholas shouldering through the crowd.

The sight of him nearly made her light-headed.

"I've never been so glad to see anyone in my life," the duke said as Nicholas joined them.

Nicholas turned his head and murmured something to the duke—something India could not quite make out. The duke nodded once, said "Certainly," and disappeared into the crowd.

"I did not see you at the ball," India said now, raising her chin at Nicholas. "I feared you had decided to entertain yourself without me."

"You should not have come here alone," he said flatly. He was angry—she saw it in his eyes.

That only irritated her more. "I thought I had an escort for the evening," she said. "But no matter...as it turned out, I wasn't completely alone. Before you arrived, I was having a very pleasant tête-à-tête with a Monsieur Giroux."

"Indeed."

They were both wedged behind the column now, and there was no place to put her hands except on his arm and chest, and the heady feeling of being this close to him combined with the security of his presence emboldened her.

Every heartbeat seemed crazed with his nearness. "A very fitting introduction to married life, I should say, although *married* may not be precisely the correct—"

Nicholas took her by the arm and pulled her out from behind the column.

"Wait—stop."

"We're leaving."

"We are *not* leaving." She dug in her heels next to a love seat where two men and two women were— Oh.

She looked away and lowered her voice, hissing in

Nicholas's ear. "I'll not allow you to drag me hither and yon as you see fit. You have no right. What about the *education* you seemed so eager for me to pursue?"

"You've had all the education you require." Now he had his hand on the small of her back and was pulling her away from the love seat, away from the crowds and toward the edge of the room, still veering toward the doorway that would lead into the adjoining room and the exit.

"Indeed—at the hands of Monsieur Giroux, whom I shall never forget as long as I live—*never,* Mr. Warre—" her pulse raced as they skirted the edge of the room past couples in various states of dishabille, engaged in every variety of intimacy "—not even when you and I—"

She cut off when he stopped suddenly and turned.

"You want an education?" he said, inches from her face, and oh—she recognized that look. The wild light in those eyes. "Do you, India?"

"Yes," she managed thickly.

He moved a few feet, pulled her into a darkened corridor. Murmurs, laughter and a throaty cry drifted from deeper in its recesses. He pressed against her to allow someone by, pushing her against the wall.

"Then perhaps you could help me understand exactly how Giroux compromised you," he said against her ear. He was pressed flush against her, chest to knee, with her skirts crushed between them. His face was so close, and his lips—oh, she wanted to kiss them so desperately. "Like this?" he asked, and bent down to brush his lips across the curve of her left breast.

Her knees threatened to buckle beneath her. She couldn't speak.

"And perhaps like this." He moved his lips to the swell of her right breast.

"Yes." She could barely breathe the word. Her pulse was chaos. Her breasts longed for his touch. He straightened, and she looked up into his eyes. "Yes—precisely like that."

Nicholas moved closer—so close that his lips brushed hers when he spoke. "Then I suppose he did this." He grazed her breasts with his fingers and slipped his fingertips inside her stays, pushing her nipples up and into view—right *here*. In the corridor. "And this." He bent down and suckled, and she gasped.

His breath came hot against her skin as he nipped, pulled, flicked with his tongue. Pure, sinful pleasure shot straight to that bud of pleasure between her thighs. People passed by the corridor's entrance but she closed her eyes and clung to him, straining into pure sensation and the sweet pull of his lips on her flesh.

She heard herself moan.

Heard him mutter, "Bloody hell."

And then his mouth came down on hers and he was kissing her, with her exposed breasts pressing against his jacket and her fingers digging into his sleeves. He kissed her hard, uncontrollably, and suddenly her eyes flew open and she realized he was pushing her farther down the corridor. They bumped into a couple coming the other direction, and Nicholas gripped her to keep their balance. Out in the main room, she glimpsed a woman shaking loose a voluptuous mass of auburn hair that rippled over creamy décolletage.

Nicholas pulled her impatiently though a doorway and stumbled with her into a draperied alcove with a small, upholstered stool and a gold-framed looking glass. There was just enough light to see her pale pink-tipped breasts reflected in the glass, and his hands cover them as he dipped his head to her neck.

She thought of the auburn-haired woman, and recklessly she reached for her pins while Nicholas pressed hot kisses to her throat and piqued her to pure need with his circling thumbs.

He looked up, met her eyes in the glass the moment her hair came tumbling free.

"Good God," he said roughly, and moved behind her so that now they both faced the glass and there was no choice but to watch him hold her breasts and pull her nipples with his thumbs and forefingers while pleasure seared between her thighs.

Shrieks and wild laughter drifted from the main room. There were voices in the corridor.

And Nicholas, yanking up India's skirts that seemed to take up the entire alcove. Hooking a hand under one of her legs, lifting, setting her foot on the little stool. And then—oh, *yes*—he was touching her there again like he had in the hayloft, only this time—oh, *God*—he was watching himself touch her—they *both* were—because he was holding up her skirts so the V of her thighs was fully exposed, and even in the near darkness the triangle of her woman's hair contrasted starkly with the pale skin around it.

She felt more than saw his fingers splay her folds. Lost herself in the utter wantonness of his touch, of the sight of him touching her. And it felt delicious.

Naughty.

Shamelessly, wonderfully wicked. Words she never would have spoken anywhere else rolled off her tongue. "You want me, Mr. Warre. Only try to deny it now."

"You're damned bloody straight I want you," he said against her ear, while below his fingers delivered pleasure that left her scarcely able to think. "I want you screaming my name when I fill you." Those fingers plunged inside her deeply.

"Nicholas."

His hand stilled, and he stared at her in the glass.

She stared back.

"Are you expecting me to hesitate, Mr. Warre?" Her voice felt thick. Seductive.

He made a feral sound, and his fingers left her. He reached for his placket. Seconds later he turned her from the glass and curled her hand around hot, solid flesh.

His cock. The feel of it in her hand startled her—hard yet soft, strong yet delicate, unlike anything she'd ever touched. And warm—almost hot, pulsing against her skin.

She closed her fingers around it, and he groaned.

She stroked, emboldened by the bawdy sounds around them, as if the primal knowledge she needed was carried on those murmurs and cries.

He pulled from her grasp and sat abruptly on the upholstered stool. Pushed her skirts up and gripped her thighs, urging her over him, suckling her breasts and—

Oh.

There was her reflection behind him, shrouded by shadows but clearly visible, with her hands on his shoulders and her lips parted and her hair falling around them while he feasted on her. She caught a glimpse of pale thigh, of dark hand gripping fair skin, and it didn't seem possible to want something as much as she wanted to give him her virtue right here, right now.

And then he was reaching for her, bringing her

mouth down to his, and nothing existed but him. Heaven was his tongue invading her and his hands urging her wider, wider, pulling her over him until she felt something pushing against her opening.

Breaching.

Piercing—*oh*. It *hurt*.

Spearing up inside her—*"Nicholas!"*—thick and full into her yielding body while his hands moved to cup her breasts and he rolled their peaks between his fingers and pain turned slickly, exquisitely into pleasure.

Her hips moved against the buried pressure of him. His hands left her breasts and dug into her hips, guiding her up, and then down—hard—onto his shaft, and up again. And down.

Again.

Again.

Their mouths tangled in desperate madness. She gripped his shoulders while he plunged, thrust, drove into her blossoming channel. Her bud of pleasure pressed and rubbed against the juncture of his legs, and the sensations from the hayloft began to build again, only sharper this time.

Fuller.

Rising, spiraling, surging.

Her legs splayed wide across him, and she took him deep. Deeper. Stretched open around him as he stroked her to womanhood.

Felt herself slipping.

Heard him whispering. "Ah, devil—yes."

Teetered on the edge of release.

And then it came, and she fell with it, gasping, clenching him with her whole body while her thighs gripped his and he pounded up into her and for a moment the world went blank except for the crippling pleasure between her legs. He gave a ragged cry against her skin. Bit his teeth into her shoulder. Strained hard inside her now, and she felt him pulsing, pulsing, pulsing.

Holding her so tight she couldn't breathe.

And then he slackened, just a little, just enough so her lungs could work again. For a long, tilting moment the entire universe seemed centered where their bodies were joined.

She opened her eyes. Saw herself in the glass, tangled and bedazed.

Virgin no more.

He let his forehead fall against her shoulder. His breath came hard, labored. His hands still gripped her hips beneath her mass of skirts.

More drunken voices came from the corridor. A woman's squeal, a man's bark of laughter. A great cheer went up from somewhere farther away.

Nicholas cursed and raised his head.

She looked in his eyes, and a protest keened inside her. It was too soon to let go.

You could tell him you'll marry him, and then he would be yours.

No—*No.* If they married, *she* would be *his.*

And yet...

"Let us go to your lodgings," she whispered. "We could send word to Auntie Phil that I'm safe—" oh, his arms *did* feel safe "—and we can...continue." Did people continue?

Nicholas gave a strangled laugh. Lifted her off him, his cock softer now but still thick and full as it left her.

He tugged her skirts down. Stood up, pushing himself inside his breeches, while the aftermath of their love-making seeped warm and damp between her thighs and she tried to rearrange herself inside her stays.

He tried to help, and she might have laughed but he seemed agitated suddenly. "Christ," he swore softly. "Is there anything to be done with your hair?"

And she realized, now, that he hadn't meant for this to happen any more than she had, and that he was in a hurry to leave.

"It's too dark to find the pins."

He gathered her hair in his hands anyway and twisted as if trying to tame it, but gave up and let it fall. "Here—" He yanked off his jacket, draped it over her shoulders, covering her hair and buttoning it over her breasts that didn't want to go back into their stays as easily as they'd popped out. "Keep this around you, and do not let go of me until we've left this place."

They pushed through the crowd, and she nearly tripped over her skirts keeping up with him down the stairs. Below, they exited Madame Gravelle's onto the dark, quiet street. He paused, and then—

"Over here."

He practically ran with her toward a carriage. The coachman saw them coming and jumped to open the door. Nicholas handed her up—practically shoved her in his haste—and she stumbled onto the seat while he crowded in behind her. The door slammed shut, and the carriage jerked forward.

"Where are we— Oh." She saw, now, that they were not alone. A small figure shared the bench with her, huddled on the other end, looking at them wide-eyed.

It was a girl. A young girl—perhaps nine? Ten?—huddled in a blanket and wearing a ratty mobcap.

The carriage rattled and shook as it raced through the city.

"Who is this?" India asked.

"This is Emilie. Emilie, this is Lady India."

And India knew that this was his sister. The laundress.

A girl of this age?

"Bonsoir, Emilie," India said.

"Bonsoir," came an almost inaudible reply.

"T'as mangé?" Nicholas asked her, in the same voice one might use to coax a stray kitten.

Emilie nodded, and now India saw a crumpled cloth on the seat between them. It was folded neatly around a lump of something, no doubt the remains of whatever Nicholas had given her to eat.

India looked at him across the carriage. A dozen questions that could not be asked in front of Emilie crowded her tongue and sat there, mixed with the lingering taste of him. How had she come into his care? Where was her mother? What did he intend to do with her?

What did this mean for the secret he carried?

And all the while their own secret ached sweetly beneath her skirts—the tender pain of fresh womanhood that gave rise to hopes she scarcely dared to consider.

Perhaps he did not want a marriage of necessity. Perhaps he felt as passionately toward her as it seemed—felt everything she was feeling. Desire. Tenderness. A yearning to be close.

Perhaps this would change things between them.

The carriage slowed. Stopped.

A coachman opened the door.

Nicholas leaned across the seat. *"Attends,"* he told Emilie, and then, almost as if an afterthought, touched her cheek. "We shan't be long."

The coachman helped India out of the carriage with Nicholas right behind her, and India now saw that they had not arrived at Auntie Phil's, where she had assumed he was taking her.

Instead, they had stopped in front of a simple door at the back of a stone building. India glanced up, saw the unmistakable heights and arched windows of an old church.

"No." She tried to stop, but Nicholas's hands on her arm and waist kept her moving toward the door. She struggled against him. "No, you can't be doing this now."

"Stop—not where Emilie can see." But a moment later they were through the door and into a darkened corridor, out of Emilie's view.

"But I thought…" Clearly she'd been wrong.

The lingering soreness between her legs screamed betrayal.

"You can't do this," she said a little frantically, planting her feet to fight him. "There must be some other way for you to repay your debts."

A murmur of voices drifted down the corridor as they approached a lit doorway. "India—" she struggled harder *"—stop."*

They reached the door, and Nicholas turned her suddenly to face him. "I can't wait any longer, India. Holliswell will take ownership of Taggart in four weeks.

He's likely already measured the rooms for new furniture." She didn't want to hear this. She wanted him to tell her he'd changed his mind. That he wouldn't marry her for the money, that she meant more to him than that. "We still have a journey to London ahead of us, and now I've got Emilie to care for, and I don't know what the devil I'm supposed to do with an eleven-year-old girl, but there it is. And I don't have to tell you what Emilie is to me, do I, because that day you followed me into that church you heard every bloody word."

Her heart pounded. What was she supposed to say to that? "It doesn't give you the right to force me into captivity."

"Bit of an exaggeration, don't you think?"

"No. I don't. I shall be trapped, and I shall despise you, and you shall come to hate me. I can't possibly imagine that's what you want."

"What I *want*—" he cut short and glanced through the door they were about to enter "—is irrelevant. I've played your game, India, but I can't play it anymore. I've got too much at stake." He eased his grip a little. "You have my deepest apologies. *This* is the last thing on earth I would choose—" the truth of it was etched into the hard planes of his face "—but that's just the trouble. I have no choice."

And he pulled her through the door.

Inside were the Duke of Winston and a man she didn't recognize.

"For God's sake, Taggart," the duke said, "what could possibly have taken so long?" He glanced at India, and comprehension lit his eyes. "Ah— Never mind."

Next to him, the other man observed her with a

combination of reservation and interest, as if he knew exactly, precisely what she and Nicholas had done at Madame Gravelle's.

A wizened priest stood near the wall next to an ancient wooden table with crosses carved into the legs. A large book bound in wood and metal sat on the tabletop. "We are ready?" he asked.

No. No, she wasn't ready. She fixed her eyes on the duke. He merely shrugged. "I owe Cantwell a favor." Next to him, the other man blocked the door.

And India knew there was nothing more she could do. This was going to happen. Here, tonight, despite everything she and Nicholas had done not half an hour ago. Or perhaps as part of it? God help her—perhaps *this* was why he'd pulled her down that corridor.

An awful ache settled into her chest. "Does my aunt know about this?" she asked Nicholas.

"Winston will tell her."

"And Millie—"

"Is perfectly astute enough to make her own way," he said with a tone of finality, and turned to the priest. "We are ready."

He'd known. He'd looked into her eyes, urged her to offer herself, and all the while he'd known what he was about to do.

She was such a fool.

Already the priest was intoning the vows, as if even paying attention was optional. He asked for promises. Nicholas gave his. The priest turned to India, repeated the questions.

And now she could continue to fight a fight she could not win, or she could hold her head up as the man on whom she'd just bestowed her virtue laid his final claim to her.

The world inside her went numb.

She raised her chin, barely recognizing her own voice as she spoke the words. "I do."

CHAPTER TWENTY-FOUR

THEY RACED OUT of Paris, headed north to the Channel, and Nick tried not to think about what he'd just done.

He'd done what he had to do. And now, finally, he would be able to resolve things with Holliswell. There would be enough left over to invest in the new mill projects, and then he could turn his attention to Emilie.

Everything that would entail was more than he could contemplate now.

Which left him contemplating India. His wife—who had said the vows after all. The memory of her voice sent a chill across his skin even now. *I do.* Toneless. Flat. Quiet, but not a whisper.

And now it was done.

As was the consummation, which was the bloody *last* thing he'd intended when he'd gone into that hellish place.

Perhaps he'd succumbed to the environment. Been momentarily debased by the erotic activity assaulting them from all sides.

But whatever the reasons, one thing could never be changed: he'd taken her virginity.

The moment burst to life in his mind at the same time the carriage hit a particularly nasty pothole. The jarring only seated the memory more firmly at the front of his thoughts.

A woman's virginity was supposed to be taken, at the very least, in a bed. Beneath concealing covers to help her preserve her modesty. In the traditional position, where a man could more easily control his rhythm and use the strength of his arms and the leverage of his knees to avoid penetrating too deeply or powerfully.

At least, that was how he would have envisioned the proper way to do it. Claiming a lady's virtue wasn't something he'd ever actually done.

Until now.

And he definitely had not done it that way.

But devil take him, when he'd pushed up against her in that darkened corridor, with the sights and sounds of sex all around them and her own lips weaving preposterous fictions about a Mr. Giroux, something inside him snapped.

And given the opportunity, he would do it all again.

But there wasn't going to be another opportunity, because after what he'd done tonight she bloody well wasn't going to give him one.

India sat across from him now, silently staring out the window while Emilie slumbered innocently, her head lolling to one side and bobbing a little with the motion of the carriage.

The very sight of her made him want to hurt someone. And perhaps he didn't know the first thing about raising a child, but he would never—*never*—sell one to a stranger for one bloody pound.

But you'd marry a woman against her will for fifty thousand.

He reminded himself India faced no less than what hundreds of other young ladies faced every year as they were married off to men of their parents' choosing—men much uglier and crueler than he.

He wondered why she wasn't screaming. Threatening to load her pistol and shoot him in his sleep, toss his body to the fishes in the Channel.

But he knew. He knew why, and the truth made him feel more weary than he had during his entire effort to find her.

He'd defeated her, and nothing would ever be the same between them from this point forward.

MARRIAGE CHANGED EVERYTHING.

India stared out at the gray sodden city and felt a chill creep across her skin that had nothing to do with the weather.

He'd done it. He'd forced her to become Lady Taggart. And now all hope of ever determining her own destiny was gone. And the small hope she'd begun to reach for that perhaps being Nicholas's wife would not be so terrible… That was gone, too. In the days it had taken them to journey here, there'd been no banter with Nicholas. No innuendo, no semi-accidental touches.

And she felt so, so betrayed. And so very stupid, because it wasn't as if she'd believed he had abandoned his idea of their marriage. Hadn't that been precisely the game they'd played in Paris? More the fool, her, for imagining he might be wishing for something more than a marriage of necessity with her.

Next to her, Emilie put a finger to the glass and traced the path of a dirty raindrop sliding down the outside of the pane. Nicholas's sister looked so small, so lost. During the journey here, India had come to know Emilie as a shy, quiet girl who was much too serious for her age.

I don't have to tell you what Emilie is to me, do I, because that day you followed me into that church you heard every bloody word.

India stroked Emilie's hair and put an arm around her shoulders, hugging her close. *"Ça va?"*

Emilie nodded, staring down at the street below, where carriages clattered and splashed along just as they might on a rainy day in Valletta or Venice or Constantinople. Yes, everything may have been all right, but India could only imagine what Emilie might be thinking. There were no clothes to wash, no work to be done, no hordes of people crowding along a dirty river. The town house where they stayed—Nicholas's brother's house—was a temple of splendor even by London's standards, but compared to what Emilie was used to...

India had checked the wardrobe in the room where Katherine and Captain Warre's daughter Anne stayed, but Anne was several years younger and much smaller than Emilie. None of the gowns were appropriate for a girl Emilie's age anyhow.

"Un chien," Emilie said, pointing to a dog nosing through refuse.

"Oui," India said brightly, though it took all her effort. She pointed out a man with water running off the brim of his hat, and Emilie smiled—but still no laughter. Emilie never laughed.

"What will we do here?" Emilie asked, looking up at her.

Worry was so plain in Emilie's eyes, and it mirrored too closely India's own fears. Very shortly, what India would do was accompany Nicholas to visit her

father. Already she felt sick. Imprisoned, this time by
a new gaoler.

India shrugged lightly, hoping Emilie would not
sense her fear. *"Rien."* She walked to the door as she
spoke and opened it. It was unlocked, so she could do
that much—for now, at least. She left it open wide and
returned to the window, taking Emilie's hand. "We are
guests here, and guests may do anything they please.
Even nothing at all. Come here," she said, and climbed
onto the bed. "I'll show you." She scooted up against
the pillows, or as much as she could with her skirts tan-
gling around her legs and her panniers tugging awk-
wardly this way and that, and patted the spot beside her.

Emilie climbed onto the bed next to her.

"See?" India said. *"This* is what we do." She settled
against the pillows, looked at the room and prayed this
was not what she would be doing for the next fifty years
of her life. She'd done plenty of it already, during the
first fifteen.

She looked at Emilie, who was looking up at her.

"Fun, *non?"* India said, and couldn't help laughing,
because this wasn't fun at all. And for the first time in
all these days, Emilie laughed a little, too.

At that exact moment, Nicholas appeared in the doorway.

Next to her, Emilie started forward. "Nicholas—"

"Vous vous amusez bien?" he asked them, but mostly
he asked Emilie, who nodded—still a bit shy of her
brother, but already full of adoration.

"We most certainly are having fun," India told him
in French, hating that she still felt something when she
saw him. More than something. She felt *everything*—
the same excitement she could hear in Emilie's voice,

coupled with so much more. "I've been showing Emilie how to do nothing."

"Mmm. A very important skill. And I expect you to master it," he told Emilie with a wink and a quick smile that wasn't meant for India, but that she felt in her toes, anyway. The smile dimmed when he shifted his attention to her. "Are you ready?"

The moment of joy she'd experienced at Emilie's first laughter faded as she rose and made her way to the door. "Yes." It was the answer she'd been giving him ever since Paris.

Yes, she slept well at the inn he'd chosen in Calais.

Yes, the cabin she and Emilie shared during the Channel crossing was comfortable enough.

Yes, she was warm enough in the carriage.

It was the only answer she could afford to give now. Perhaps, if she were compliant enough, he would allow her a measure of freedom as his wife.

She felt him behind her on the staircase, too aware of him, while the possibility that he might touch her tangled with the nerves already cramping her belly at the idea of facing her father. A thought flew in from nowhere: *please don't let Father change his mind and declare the marriage invalid.* She foolishly wished he would reach for her. Touch her. Reassure her.

She stepped into the entrance hall, and panic flared up. But there was no time to think of it, because a guest was just being admitted, a beautiful, dark-haired woman in a gorgeous floral gown—

"La, Nicholas! What a relief to see you in London again!" She swept toward him, and he kissed her cheeks. "I've been so terribly worried about you, traipsing halfway around the world. And this must be Lady India," she said.

"My sister," Nicholas told India, "Honoria, Lady Ramsey."

India curtseyed and murmured all the right formalities.

"Why did you not send me a note immediately?" Lady Ramsey complained to Nicholas. "I had to hear the news of your arrival from a servant."

"I'd planned to write you this evening," he told her. "At the moment, I have a pressing need to pay a call on Lord Cantwell."

"Lord Cantwell. But—" She looked back and forth between them. "Well, of course, you wouldn't have heard. He sailed for the colonies a fortnight ago."

"The colonies," Nicholas said sharply.

"I understand he's been sent as an ambassador or some such—political unrest or something of that nature. I can scarcely follow all the twists and turns of it. But the fact remains, Lord Cantwell is not in London."

Not in London.

But…Father wouldn't have left without making arrangements, would he? Already India could see that was exactly what Nicholas was thinking.

"I must speak with his man of business at once. Excuse me."

He strode out the door, leaving India standing there with Lady Ramsey, who stared after him for a moment, then turned her stunning green eyes on India.

"I'd hoped we might have a moment to speak privately," she said.

And now India realized that she herself was the hostess—no matter that it was Lady Ramsey's brother's house—so she led the way into the nearest sitting room and called for tea.

"Please, Lady Ramsey," she said, "do sit."

"Thank you. And I shall come straight to the point," Lady Ramsey said, seating herself on a nearby chair. "Lady Croston is a dear friend, and I am outraged on her behalf that you and your friend stole her ship. But more than that, my brothers mean the world to me, and Nicholas is especially dear to my heart. I begged him to reject your father's proposal, but Nicholas is nothing if not strong willed, and he refused to listen. But that doesn't mean he doesn't deserve happiness. It's what I want for him more than anything in the world."

What about my happiness? India wanted to ask. But it was too late for that now, and nobody cared about her happiness, anyway. "I'm sure Nicholas will be happy the moment he receives what my father has promised him," she said.

"La, that dreadful agreement! *Our* father would turn in his grave to know what Nicholas has resorted to— and through no fault of his own."

"Except for his debt," India couldn't help reminding her, even as she thought how Nicholas's father was not in any grave, but was in Paris probably reciting a mass.

"Is dear Nicholas to blame for tempests? Pirates? My brother's debt is the result of a string of unfortunate circumstances and nothing more. Nobody expects every single investment—every last one—to fail. Diversification is supposed to mitigate the risk." Lady Ramsey accepted a cup of tea and sipped. "But it didn't, and now Nicholas has been up to any number of things to try to right himself, such as this silly new investment consortium—mills or some such."

"Nicholas doesn't think it's silly," India objected, thinking of all the hours he'd spent studying those plans during their journey.

Lady Ramsey cocked her head and looked at India. "No, I suppose he doesn't."

"Nicholas is very hardworking."

"*Too* hardworking. Both my brother James and I think so. There's no reason for it, all this scrapping about."

"Perhaps he enjoys it."

There was a soft noise from the doorway, and India saw Lady Ramsey's attention shift curiously past her. India turned.

Emilie!

Quickly she set down her cup and saucer. "A moment, please," she said, and hurried to the door.

"Qu'est-ce que c'est?" she asked Emilie in a hushed tone, bending down and touching her cheek. "Are you all right?"

Emilie nodded, casting a worried glance into the salon. "I should not have left my room. I only wondered where you had gone."

"Shh. It's all right. Only return upstairs, and I'll be there shortly, and I shall teach you a new game to play. All right?"

Emilie nodded, her eyes full of fear and guilt even now.

India reached for her hand and squeezed it. *"Bien. Va-t'en."* Emilie hurried toward the stairs, lifting her skirts to practically run up them, and India turned back to the salon and Nicholas's other half sister, who sipped her tea and regarded her curiously.

"Who on earth was that?" Lady Ramsey asked.

What would Nicholas want her to say? She knew very well what he would *not* want her to say. She smoothed her skirts and returned to her seat, trying to act as if it hadn't been Nicholas's sister who had just run up the stairs to hide.

"A young girl Miss Germain and I took aboard the ship," she explained, reaching for her tea. "An orphan." She made herself smile at Lady Ramsey. "I told Nicholas I would raise hell if he did not agree to give Emilie a home."

"La, Lady India—it is my very great fear you will raise hell regardless."

CHAPTER TWENTY-FIVE

THIRTY MINUTES LATER, Cantwell's man of business stared at Nick blank-eyed from behind a pair of spectacles and a desk that looked as if it had sustained an assault by the entire French army.

"I have a contract with Lord Cantwell for payment of fifty thousand pounds," Nick told him.

Ludlow dipped his pen and added words to a half-finished letter. "He said nothing to me about it before he left."

"All of bloody England knows about this contract."

"What I mean is that he left no specific instructions about satisfying the contract should it be fulfilled." He dipped his pen once more. "I had the distinct impression that he did not believe it would be."

"But it has been," Nick said flatly.

Scribble, scratch, scribble. "Fifty thousand is a very large sum for me to be making decisions about without his lordship's express direction." *Dip, dip, scribble.*

A pit opened up in Nick's gut. This could not be happening.

Nick planted his hands on the mess of documents littering the desk and leaned close. "I have the contract right here. Surely you do not imagine Cantwell intended for you to leave his business *obligations* unfulfilled."

Scribble, scribble, scratch.

Plunk.

The man jammed the pen into its stand and leaned back in his chair. "How well do you suppose that contract would stand up in a court of law, Lord Taggart?"

It wouldn't. There had never been any question about that—it was just an agreement between himself and Cantwell. Which meant if Ludlow refused to honor it, Nick couldn't even petition a court to demand performance.

"Forgive me," Nick said now—quietly, feeling bile rise, "but it sounds as if you are questioning my arrangements with your employer. As that cannot possibly be the case, I must insist that you draft the bank note immediately."

"I'm afraid I can't do that."

"It isn't your place to interfere."

"On the contrary, Lord Cantwell relies on me to manage his affairs. This one, I daresay, has been badly mismanaged. You have my deepest apologies." Oh, yes. Ludlow looked nothing if not apologetic. "I'm afraid you'll simply have to wait until he returns and discuss it with him then." *Dip, dip, scribble.*

By the time Cantwell returned from the colonies, it would be too late. Every method Nick could think of that might change Ludlow's mind would also ensure that Nick would end up in gaol.

Nick stalked to the door, feeling as if he were suffocating. "You'll regret this decision. And when Lord Cantwell returns, you will likely find yourself without employment."

"I doubt that very much, Your Lordship," he heard Ludlow say as Nick slammed the door.

Out on the street, the full meaning of it sank in like

the steady rain soaking his greatcoat. There would be no money from Cantwell. He shouted directions to the driver and raced to see Holliswell, but met only false sympathy and a smug smile on Holliswell's fat lips. There would be no more extensions, no more so-called favors.

And now, Nick's only hope of having anything at all was to find a buyer for Taggart quickly—in a fortnight or less. He could sell the place, pay Holliswell and at least have a little left over. Otherwise, Holliswell would simply take Taggart as payment.

Now, either way, he would lose his only legitimate home.

Either way, he would be a man who could lay claim to nothing—not even his own name.

And either way, he would still have Emilie to think of—and India.

Good God. India.

The carriage rolled through the streets toward James's house, and Nick rubbed his hands over his face. Bloody hell. He'd married India thinking at least she would be mistress of Taggart. But being Lady Taggart would mean nothing now, and instead she would be mistress of...what?

He did not even know that much.

But one thing was sure: whatever situation he found would be painfully modest. At least anything he gave Emilie would be more than she'd ever had before. But to see India as Lady Taggart, up to her elbows in wash water...that was a shame he couldn't bear.

But there was a solution. He looked out the window, thinking of it. Hating it. But India had never wanted this marriage, anyway. Had been crushed by it—hadn't he seen enough evidence of that since they'd left Paris? The fight had left her, and he hadn't realized how much he would miss it until it was gone.

And it hurt like the devil to do what needed to be done—more than he would have expected it to—but it was the only way.

AFTER LADY RAMSEY left, India found Emilie and taught her to play pick-up-sticks. And then she ordered a fresh pot of tea, and they sat against the pillows on the bed and drank, and India told Emilie that ladies of leisure mostly talked of gowns and fashion. And even though India had not thought much about either for years, she made a game out of playacting dramatic statements in nasal French like *I daresay I shan't live unless I find a bolt of lace in the exact shade of peacock-green* and *That horrid brown silk won't do—it simply won't do!*

And they giggled and laughed, and India imagined that this might be what it was like to have a sister. She got the idea to begin teaching Emilie some words of English, so she started with the things around them: teacup, saucer, coverlet, pillow, shoes.

India looked at her feet next to Emilie's, two pairs of toes pointing in the air, and felt less alone than she had in a very long time.

The slam of a carriage door drifted up from the street, and moments later came the faint sounds of someone being admitted below.

"Mon frère," Emilie said hopefully. *"Il est revenu."*

"Yes—I believe so." It sounded as if Nicholas had indeed returned, and India wondered with what news. Had he secured the money? And if he hadn't…

A wild imagining planted itself in her mind: that

there would be no money. That he would finally see
how wrong he'd been. That the money was not the important thing, and he'd already received the real object
of value—her—and that their marriage meant nobody
could take that from him. *I have nothing to offer you
but myself,* he might tell her. And perhaps he wouldn't
care about shame anymore—only about her, and Emilie,
and the three of them would live together somewhere
cozy and happy and safe.

Moments later, the butler appeared in the open doorway. "Your ladyship is needed in the library," he said.

She left Emilie with the reassurance of a quick return, and went downstairs to find Nicholas sitting on
the corner of the desk with his hands clasped lightly
between his legs, staring at the carpet.

He looked up at her through hollow eyes. "Your father's man of business refuses to honor the agreement
in your father's absence," he told her. "I've spoken with
Holliswell—he's not willing to wait, even for correspondence from your father. My only option is to sell
Taggart immediately if I can. Otherwise…"

Otherwise Mr. Holliswell would take ownership of
Taggart.

No money. It was a fact—there would truly be no
money. Her heart raced, and all the things she'd thought
of mere minutes ago took wing on fresh hope.

Just then, the butler appeared again. "Bishop Went-
worth, Your Lordship."

A distinguished man of the church entered the room.

"I appreciate your coming on such short notice,"
Nicholas said to him. "This is Lady India…" He made
the introductions.

"I read your note explaining the situation and that you wish to proceed with an annulment," the bishop said.

"An annulment," India echoed. Nicholas wanted to annul the marriage? There was an initial moment of shock, and then...

"If ever a marriage deserved to be treated as null and void, it is ours," Nicholas told the bishop. "The agreement I made with her father—of which I'm sure you are aware—had no legal footing. Lady India has voiced her objections clearly and consistently."

And now—*now*—he was prepared to honor those objections? She stared at him, hearing the words while pain began to pool inside her, filling her, rising mercilessly as he continued to speak.

"The marriage ceremony itself was of questionable validity," Nicholas went on, "ashamed as it makes me to say it—"

Ashamed? *Now* he was ashamed?

"—and of course, the marriage remains unconsummated."

Unconsummated!

She couldn't stand it a moment longer. "What the devil are you about?" The words ripped out of her. It hurt—oh, God, it *hurt*—and she should be relieved—she should be *rejoicing*—but an awful outrage gripped her instead. "It wasn't enough to force me into marriage? Now you think to cast me aside?"

Nicholas looked at her sharply. The bishop's brows dived.

"I concede to your well-reasoned arguments that I had no business attempting to marry you in the first place, and that the marriage we have now is a sham," he said.

Of course. Of course he did. There was no money now—no *reason* to keep her. He didn't want her anymore. Not without the money.

"Now that you won't be receiving your reward from my father, the marriage is a sham. You were perfectly happy to pretend this marriage was legitimate when it served your purposes, but now that it does not—"

"Don't be ridiculous."

"—you'll do what? Send me into the street with my trunk and a pat on the head? After everything you've done?"

"Oh, for Christ's sake—"

"After I gave you my *virtue?*"

"Lord Taggart," the bishop interrupted, frowning, "with all due respect, this is not what I expected to hear."

"I'm sure Lady India is only having a momentary lapse of reason," Nicholas said through clenched teeth. "We have discussed the possibility of a separation endlessly."

"I am not a jacket, to be worn when it pleases you and then tossed aside when you decide it no longer suits."

"I was under the impression that my *jacket* wished to be liberated to choose its own wearer," he ground out.

The bishop cleared his throat. "With all due respect, Lord Taggart, I'm afraid this…ah…*fashion dispute* is hardly a proper situation for annulment. I'm needed back at the church, so may I suggest, if the jacket fits—" he looked at India "—wear it."

CHAPTER TWENTY-SIX

"WHAT IN GOD's name did you think you were doing?" Nicholas demanded irately the moment the bishop was gone.

"I might ask the same," India shot back, somehow able to speak past the terrible ache in her chest. "You will certainly never get your money from my father if this marriage is annulled."

"You do realize," he said darkly, "that we will never put this marriage asunder now."

Yes. That was precisely what she realized. "If that is what it takes to prevent you from using me at your convenience and then tossing me aside without a penny, then that is the price I shall pay."

"Without a *penny?* Are you saying you objected because you thought you would receive no *money?*"

That wasn't it at all, but it was better than letting him know the truth and risk exposing feelings she didn't fully understand. Let him believe it was money she wanted—for once, let him believe *he* was not enough.

She nodded.

He stared at her. "You can't be serious."

"Believe it."

"I would have given you something if you had but asked!"

"When would I have asked? In the mere two hours

you've spent busily arranging the annulment of the marriage that a week ago you wanted so desperately that you enlisted your friends to *trick* me? With this marriage set aside, you would not feel beholden to offer me anything at all for the trouble you've caused me."

But she didn't want him *beholden*. Ninny that she was, she wanted him to have taken her virtue because he wanted her for his own. To have married her because he wanted her for his wife.

The shame that had attacked her in Paris squeezed her now. She still wanted him, even though he did not want her.

"I can hardly feel beholden now, can I?" he said angrily. "You had your chance for freedom, and now you have chained us both for life."

"How fascinating that you now abhor the very plan you conceived," she told him. She thought of Emilie waiting upstairs, trusting them both, fearful for her own future. "I only hope you don't plan to cast Emilie aside, too, if she fails to live up to your expectations."

Nicholas stalked to the desk and opened a lockbox. He reached for a pen, and after a few angry scratches he thrust a paper in her direction. "Five hundred pounds. You may pack your things and return to your aunt in Paris."

India stared at the note in her hands. Five hundred— "You cannot afford this."

"What I cannot afford, Lady India, is *you*."

His words dug into her heart like cruel fingers. "You will have to do much better than this to be rid of me," she made herself scoff. Only a few weeks ago she would have taken this money and fled gleefully back to the Mediterranean. Now all she could think of was what it meant that he was willing to pay such a huge sum to be rid of her, and that he would have nothing left for Emilie if she took it. She tossed the bank draft onto the desk. "You stole my living out from under me when you took me from Malta—"

"A living you yourself had stolen!"

"—and we shan't be even until you provide me a living to replace it."

"Even."

"What good is Paris to me? When you found me, I had a ship and a crew, with the Mediterranean waves beneath my feet, billowing sails to take me where I pleased, and a hundred possibilities waiting in my future." And she'd never known a man's touch, never known how it might feel to be wanted. Protected. Well, he wasn't trying to protect her now. "I had the means to make my own living without having to be mistress to *anyone.* How do you propose to replace *that,* Mr. Warre?"

"If I could afford it, I would buy you a ship of your own and happily watch you sail away to the West Indies or wherever the hell you bloody please." The lips that had once kissed her senseless were thin and tight now.

She should want to sail to the West Indies. But she didn't. She wanted to close the distance between them and feel his arms come around her. But that distance seemed as far as the West Indies themselves.

"Then you won't mind putting that in writing." She forced a smile. "For the day when you *do* have the funds."

"Ah, yes. A promise for that happy day when I regain my fortune and all is well again. Whyever not?" He slapped a scrap of paper onto the desk and snatched the pen from its stand. He dipped it and scratched words across the paper. Handed it back to her with a crooked, self-shaming smile. "There you are. My promise, in writing, to buy you a sailing ship the moment I'm able."

She slipped it from his hand, folded it carefully. "In the meantime, I shall have no choice but to stay with you and share in whatever living you *can* afford."

He stared at her, and for a moment she thought he might say that he wanted her to stay. She held her breath, watching a muscle work in his jaw, trying to interpret what she saw in his eye, almost hoping—

"On the contrary," Nicholas said. "By the end of the week, I expect you to have packed your things and arranged passage back to your aunt in Paris."

INDIA TOLD HERSELF she didn't much care what Nicholas expected. She wasn't going anywhere—not now. For once, let *him* suffer the consequences of what he'd done.

She tried to ignore the feeling that she was doing most of the suffering.

Eventually Father would return, and Nicholas would likely get his money—even if he no longer had Taggart. He would also no longer owe a debt, so he would keep the entire sum. He would be able to afford to give her a nice living of her own.

By then, she would certainly be finished with all this silly pining after him. All these absurd fantasies about the three of them. By then, she'd likely be as anxious to see the last of him as he was to see the last of her.

And when he did give her a living, she would be prepared to make the most of it. Which was why, now, she was nervously creasing a scrap of paper as her chair stopped in front of a small town house…number fifty-three.

This was useless. If Mr. Wiggins were a magician, he would have worked a spell years ago.

She almost pulled the bell to leave, but then the carriage door swung open. The footman stood waiting. And she was so tired of being stupid that she reached for his hand and climbed the short steps.

An older woman answered the door almost immediately. India cursed the shakiness in her own voice. "Is Mr. Wiggins at home?"

The woman frowned. "Who is calling, please?"

"I have no card. Please tell him it is Lady India, Lord Cantwell's daughter."

Immediately the woman curtsied and opened the door wider. "Do come in, my lady. Through here—you may wait in the parlor. I'm afraid Mr. Wiggins is just preparing for an appointment, but I shall let him know you are here, and I'm certain he will see you if only for a few minutes."

The woman left, and suddenly India felt as if a huge burden had lifted off her. In a moment she would see Mr. Wiggins, and he would help her.

Everything would be different now. She was older, more determined. And there may not be much time—any day, Nicholas might force her to leave—but she could make use of the time she did have. Kind, gentle Mr. Wiggins, with his whiskered jowls and his spectacles and his patience, would know exactly what to do.

"Lady India?"

She'd been studying her fingers, and now her head

snapped up at the male voice. The *young* male voice. "Yes?"

"My housekeeper said you wished to see me."

Good heavens, no. India stood up. "Do forgive me. I asked to see Mr. Wiggins." This man was everything dear Mr. Wiggins was not—athletic figure, waistcoat in the latest mode, dancing eyes. "He was my tutor when I was a girl."

The young man smiled a little. "My father. I'm afraid he passed away winter before last."

"No." India's heart sank. "How dreadful. Please forgive my ignorance."

"Not at all, Lady India. Might I inquire the reason for your visit?"

Still shocked by the news, she reached for an answer. "Merely to visit an old acquaintance who meant a great deal to me." She could not tell this man the truth. "He was the most patient tutor I ever had."

"And you had many?" The young Mr. Wiggins smiled. "Forgive me. That was terribly rude. Your compliment means a great deal. I only hope my own pupils will say the same of me one day."

"You're a tutor?" Of course he was. He had followed in his father's footsteps.

"Yes." He cocked his head a little. "Do you have children in need of one?"

Yes. She had Emilie. But she couldn't hire a tutor for Emilie without talking with Nicholas, and now young Mr. Wiggins was frowning inquisitively at her delayed response, and…

"No, I…" *I'm the one who can't read.* She tugged

nervously at her sleeve. "Actually, I confess that I…I'd hoped to hire your father myself."

She didn't leave.

Nick gave her a day. Then another. Her trunks arrived from Paris, along with a nasty letter from Lady Pennington blasting him for his treachery, marrying India in the manner that he had.

He'd been so certain India would leap at the annulment. When she hadn't…

For a moment he'd thought it was because of him.

But of course, it had been exactly as he'd thought. *Worse* than he'd thought. Certainly, India wanted exactly what she'd always wanted: a ship. The freedom of the high seas. A life of waterfront taverns and men's clothes and swilling grog atop the waves.

And she thought she would wring that life from him.

She had to know he would never be able to make good on that promise. That it hadn't been serious—how could it? Men who scraped by in cottages could not afford to buy ships.

The thought of losing Taggart ripped through him like a dull knife hacking at his insides. He'd already begun making inquiries, trying to find a buyer for Taggart. He would have to sell the house along with everything in it. All he would take were his clothes, a few personal items, and some of the lesser quality furnishings for a home he and Emilie would share. A cottage, most likely. Modest, small, inexpensive to maintain.

He and Emilie. Alone. *Not* he, Emilie and India.

He would not be the man who had to house an earl's daughter in a smoky, mouse-infested cottage because he hadn't been man enough to hold on to his fortune. Bad enough that if all had gone as planned, he would have housed her with her own father's money.

No. Better to be the man whose wife lived her own life because she hadn't wanted the marriage in the first place. Somehow he would find the means to send her on her way.

But thank God India hadn't accepted that bank draft he'd offered in the heat of anger. He didn't know how he would have covered it—more debt would have been the only way. He hardly had anything left of the money Cantwell had fronted him for his journey to find India. This morning, he'd used part of it to outfit Emilie.

He passed the drawing room now, after returning from an early afternoon meeting that proved productive, and stopped short. Spun on his heel. Went to the doorway.

"*What* are you doing?"

India pushed a needle through a piece of fabric and drew the thread through, glancing up with a smile that went straight to his gut. "Emilie is sleeping—you'd think she never slept a wink in all her life, with how easily she drifts off for a nap—and I discovered a *fascinating* pattern for a pillow cushion in that drawer over there." She nodded toward a chest at the side of the room. "And would you believe it, the fabric and thread, as well. I only hope I am doing it justice." She held out her work for him to see, as if he had any interest whatsoever in a bloody pillow cushion. But— Good God. He'd never seen such poor stitching in his life. She wasn't doing it justice at all.

"I meant," he said tightly, "what are you still doing *here?* I told you to be gone by the end of the week."

Her brow furrowed the smallest bit, as though she had no idea what he meant, and he suppressed an urge to yank her off the sofa and march her to her rooms, where he had no doubt he would find no trunks packed—but where he *would* find a bed, on which he would be mightily tempted to lay her back, strip away her clothes and remind her exactly what had happened between them in Paris.

She hadn't been thinking of any ship or living then. And now he wanted her again so badly it physically hurt.

"You could not really have expected me to leave by today," she said evenly. "Plans must be made."

"And I expected you to be making them."

"And I shall. I most certainly shall. Just as soon as you provide my living."

He leaned close. "Hear me well, India.... There will be no living. You need to leave *tomorrow.* There can be no further delays." Because having her here was killing him.

Watching the way she indulged Emilie, seeing India's bright smile once again—so different now from the frightening numbness in the days after the wedding—as she chattered away to draw Emilie out...

Lying awake at night, on fire with the knowledge that India lay just across the hall, alone in her bed, and all he had to do was go there and the flames would ignite between them again, and for better or worse she'd be unlikely to turn him away...

And that she was truly *his,* and there wasn't a bloody thing anyone could do to put that asunder.

"Oh, but there *is* a living, Nicholas," she said now,

poking the needle through the fabric, then checking beneath it. "With you."

He couldn't stand it. All this was doing was prolonging the agony. He jerked the fabric from her hands, and now—finally—had her full attention. "Do you have *any idea* of the gravity of my situation?" he demanded harshly. "What kind of life Emilie and I shall have after Taggart is gone? Heaven knows the kind of cottage I shall be able to afford—and that's if I can find someone to buy Taggart. If not—" He couldn't stand to think of what would happen then. "Either way, there will be no soirées, no balls...there likely won't be any damned *meat* on the table. God knows there won't even be any ladies' maids." He gestured at her angrily. "You would have to coif your own bloody hair."

She gave an exaggerated shudder. "Stop, Mr. Warre. You're terrifying me."

"You find this *amusing?*"

"Not at all. I've endured worse, as you well know. Sharing your embarrassed circumstances while we await my father's return is a small price to pay."

He wished suddenly, painfully, that all of this resistance was because of him and not because of the living she believed he owed her. "The longer you stay," he said now, "the harder it's going to be for Emilie when you leave."

The truth of that hit its mark. He saw it in her eyes— a flash of concern, a dampening of her spirits. And now he almost wished he'd let her continue this ridiculous drama until twenty years had gone by and the living she demanded from him became the life they shared together, whatever and wherever that might be.

But that was only a fool's fantasy. India wanted her

freedom, and the shackles of genteel poverty would only crush her spirit.

"I doubt I'll ever be leaving," she retorted with noticeably less vigor, "since you'll never be able to afford to send me away." She set her godawful needlework aside and stood up, moving past him to leave. "How will you like that, Lord Taggart? Only imagine being stuck with me as your wife for the rest of your life."

INDIA SHUT THE door to her room and, this time, bolted the latch herself.

He was right. And it hurt so much she could hardly see through the swim of tears filling her eyes. She leaned against the door, staring up at the ceiling, blinking furiously.

Of course she had to leave. She could tell herself whatever she liked, but staying with him would be impossible if he truly didn't want her here.

And she was such a ninny, because he'd made it perfectly clear from the beginning that he needed the money. Only imagine what he would say now if she told him the truth: *Surely you didn't think—for God's sake, India, you've known all along my reasons for this marriage.*

A tear leaked from the corner of her eye, and she brushed it away furiously. She couldn't even blame him for what they'd done at Madame Gravelle's. Hadn't she been telling him for weeks that she wanted to be rid of her virtue? Hadn't she tried to seduce him herself?

And heaven help her, she wanted to feel that way with him again.

But he didn't. He wanted her to leave. And he was right about that—she needed to return to Auntie Phil's, for Emilie's sake. Insisting on staying, continuing this game about wanting a living from him…it wouldn't even salvage her pride. All it would do was hurt—a little more, each time she heard him say how much he wanted her to go—until she ended up entirely crushed.

Thinking of leaving Nicholas, leaving Emilie, she felt crushed already.

CHAPTER TWENTY-SEVEN

THE AFTERNOON'S MEETING, it turned out, had been even
more productive than Nick expected. The man was interested in Taggart. Nick spent the evening with him,
discussing possible terms and arrangements, and returned late—spent, exhausted and with an ache in his
chest that made it difficult to breathe. Tomorrow, he
would need to leave for Taggart to take care of things
before the sale. He would take Emilie with him. But
he'd made arrangements for India to stay with Honoria.

James's town house was silent as he climbed the
grand staircase, on his way up to tell India the news.
That his brother was not in town was more of a blessing
than Nick could have hoped for. It made their stay feel
slightly less like charity, and it saved him from James
offering to help the situation.

James didn't understand why Nick so stubbornly refused assistance. But James had no idea they were only
half brothers, not full. That only James Warre could
trace his heritage to Croston.

Nick paused on the familiar landing and remembered
those weeks he'd spent so much time in this house,
when all of Britain thought James had perished after
the Royal Navy ship he'd been captaining had wrecked
off the coast of Spain. Nick had been next in line to ac-
cede to the Croston title.

Those were the worst weeks of his life.

And with James rightfully the Earl of Croston once more, Nick would never accept Croston assets. Not ever, and it didn't matter if James thought he was clubbing himself in the ankle out of pride.

Upstairs, he started toward the rooms where he was staying, but thought better of it at the last minute. He should look in on Emilie. But as he approached her rooms, he noticed the door standing open and candlelight flickering from within. He paused outside and heard India's voice speaking softly.

"Oh, *yes*," she was saying. "He is *very* courageous."

"Really? Tell me."

"We sailed together on a ship once," India said.

She must be telling Emilie about James. Devil take it—he didn't want Emilie to know about James. Not yet, not until she was old enough to understand. Too late now, thanks to India and her blasted loose tongue.

"A ship like the one we sailed on from France?" Emilie asked.

"Oh, much grander than that. It had three masts and great, white, billowing sails that stood out like clean linens against the blue sky. She cut through the sparkling sea like a warm knife through butter."

India had a way of making the sea sound so much more magnificent than it actually was. But then, India loved the sea. It was where she wanted to be, and if he'd never attempted this fool's errand she would be there still.

But she wasn't, and the clarity of hindsight couldn't change that now.

"Dit-moi," Emilie pressed. "What did he do?"

Good God. Listing James's seafaring accomplishments could take all night.

"He did something very brave, after I'd done something very foolish and I was in grave danger. He stood up to an angry mob of sailors who were very upset with me."

Nick's heart stopped. She wasn't talking about James.

"Did he fight for you?"

"He would have, if it had come to that. But your brother is a very intelligent man. He knew exactly the right things to say. He defended me ferociously."

"And he saved you?"

"He did."

"Just like he saved me."

"Yes, *exactly* like that. Now. No more stories. It's time for you to go to sleep."

Nick backed away from the door, his pulse thudding so hard now he could feel it in his throat. She'd been talking about *him*. Telling Emilie he was all those things. That he had been her savior.

He turned toward his rooms. Didn't quite make it before he heard Emilie's door click shut behind him and a soft, "Oh. Nicholas."

Hearing her say his name did something to him on the inside. He was such a damned fool.

He turned, mere feet shy of his own door. She held a candle that flickered over a billowing white nightgown. Her hair fell over one shoulder in a gleaming, golden braid.

"I was just…saying good-night to Emilie," she told him, taking a few steps forward—her door was across from his—and he could see the question in her eyes.

The fear that he might have been listening. "I kept her up much too late playing pick-up-sticks."

"I've just returned from…some business," he told her.

"Yes. Of course." She was looking at him with eyes that held none of her usual taunting combativeness. None of the careful calculation that had marked their games in Paris.

She looked so vulnerable without it. So real.

"I've found someone interested in Taggart," he said. "I met with him tonight to discuss the arrangements." Saying the words out loud was harder than he'd anticipated, and his throat suddenly felt tight.

"Oh," she said, looking almost…sad. "That didn't take long."

Perhaps she'd been holding out hope that there would still be some other solution—one that would produce more money.

"I need to go to Taggart tomorrow." *Emilie and I, while you stay with Honoria.* "For a few days. To make preparations."

"Of course."

Was this more of the numb compliance he'd seen on the journey from Paris? Where was her belligerence? The jabs about demanding a living? Perhaps she was embarrassed that he'd so obviously overheard her wild exaggerations.

Honoria's coach will be here for you at noon, he needed to tell her. *She will help you make arrangements for Paris.*

India picked at a fingernail. Her nightgown nearly swallowed her figure, but hints of curves taunted him. He didn't want to send her to Paris—he wanted to take her to his bed, remove that nightgown and lose himself inside her.

"I'll expect you and Emilie to be ready by seven." The words came out, surprising him, and—from the way she looked up suddenly—surprising her, as well.

"But I thought—"

"I've nowhere for you to stay while I'm gone—" *liar* "—and we've outstayed our welcome here." Totally untrue. Good God. What was he doing? He needed her *away* from him.

But he just wasn't ready to let her go.

I've decided to *return to Paris.* That's what she'd meant to say. But then she'd realized he'd overheard her talking to Emilie, and suddenly there she was in her nightgown and there he was staring at her, and her mouth had gone dry. And the last thing she'd wanted in the entire world was to return to Paris, and so she'd let him speak first, and now...

Now their carriage was arriving at Taggart. And one look was enough to know that coming here was a terrible mistake. The carriage emerged from the woods into a clearing, and her heart squeezed. Taggart was everything a dilapidated old country house should be— rough, brown stones with tendrils of ivy creeping all the way past the uppermost floors. Great chimneys that spoke of warm fires on cool days. Rows of windows that would brighten the rooms inside.

A long drive led directly to the front in a big loop, inside of which a flower garden bloomed. Someone had been caring for the place. In the distance, beyond the house, she could see the edge of a pond—not the formal, geometric kind, but a natural one surrounded partly by a wood and edged with grassy slopes where wildflowers grew.

Sunlight cast a warm glow over the meadows, the house, the flowers, the soft grass at the pond's edge. And India wanted to stay here more than she could ever remember wanting anything in her life—even her adventurous life aboard the *Possession*.

She hardly dared to breathe. They *couldn't* stay here—not even if she told Nicholas she didn't want Paris, didn't want a ship, didn't want a silly living that he could not afford to give her.

She dared a glance at him, but his gaze was fixed out the window at the road behind them.

The carriage stopped in front of the house, where a great wooden door looked as if it hadn't opened in half a century.

India kept Emilie's hand tightly in hers as they walked into the entry. Nicholas had already explained to Emilie that this was a house he would be selling and that they wouldn't be staying here. But Emilie's brown eyes went just as wide here as they had at his brother's house in London.

It was clear the house had been closed up. There were sheets draped over furniture. Nicholas grimly directed the footmen upstairs with their trunks, as if he would have preferred to stay elsewhere.

"The rooms won't be ready," he said now, as if he'd only just thought of it.

"We can find the linens," India said. "Emilie will help me."

"No," he said sharply. "Miss Ursula will find them."

He stood staring—at what, she couldn't be sure. His eyes drifted over everything: the beautifully carved banister, burnished with age. The modest but stately plaster work on the ceiling.

Emilie let go of India's hand and walked timidly toward an open pair of doors that led into a bright salon. "Pretty," she said to India—one of the words India had taught her.

Nicholas looked at India. "Please take Emilie outside." His distress was palpable. His voice sounded too thick. His face was strained. "There's a gazebo by the pond—perhaps she would like to see it."

A gazebo. India's heart squeezed a little. Of course there would be one.

"Certainly." Entertaining Emilie was something she could do.

"You'll likely run into Miss Ursula—if you do, ask her to come to the house."

"Certainly." And she wished there was something she could do, some comfort to offer, but she didn't have the first idea what to say, and he hadn't even wanted her here in the first place.

She took Emilie's hand and turned to go, but at the last minute turned back and reached out to touch his arm.

His eyes shot to hers.

She drew her hand back quickly and took Emilie outside.

NICK WATCHED INDIA and Emilie walk hand in hand out the door, and it took all his effort to drag a breath into his lungs. His throat was so tight it hurt. His skin burned where she'd touched him, even through layers of clothes.

And he never, ever should have brought India here. He should have left them *both* in London with Honoria.

Made up some story about Emilie—something Honoria would believe.

And now he would never erase the image of the two of them standing here witnessing his shame.

He'd needed them to leave—if only to take a turn outside—because he'd wanted to reach for India so much he wasn't sure he'd be able to keep from actually doing it. What he wouldn't give for even a small taste of her devil-may-care spirit. The we'll-make-do stubbornness that had her hiding in a hayloft covered with straw or making plans to sneak aboard a vessel in Marseille.

But even India would find little to hope for in this situation. It had never been more clear that he had absolutely nothing to offer her. All he'd ever really had to offer anyhow was her own father's money.

As soon as this was over, he would make sure she returned to Lady Pennington in Paris. And he would keep his distance in the meantime. Because if he held her now, he wasn't sure he could let her go.

THEY FOUND THEIR way toward the pond. India tried to be cheerful for Emilie's sake, but every word was an effort. Her heart was breaking for Nicholas, imagining him wandering alone through Taggart. As they walked, she kept her eyes open for any sign of Miss Ursula, but the only person she saw was an old man down at the far end of the flower garden fussing with the plants.

"My brother is sad to leave his house," Emilie said quietly as they walked down the sloping meadow toward the pond.

"Yes, he is." And he did not want her adding to his shame. It would have been one thing if he'd received the money from Father as expected. He could have kept

Taggart, and then she would have been the only shame he would have had to hide.

But to add having her for a wife on top of losing Taggart—not to mention the terrible shame she knew he felt because of his parentage—it was too much.

She was too much.

And he didn't even know everything.

A short path through a wooded grove led to the pond—she could see the water sparkling through the trees, rippled by a light wind and dappled with sunshine. They emerged at its edge, and—

Oh. "Look," she said to Emilie. "The gazebo."

It sat on its own little knoll jutting into the water, so that when they stepped into it the pond surrounded them on three sides. The house was not visible at all from here, but it would be from the other side of the pond, where a grassy meadow stretched to another wooded grove.

They walked toward it, and India thought of the little gazebo nestled by the stream at Auntie Phil's country house.... This one, quiet and peaceful, had its very own pond.

They went inside, straight to the back railing to look at the water.

"Des canards," Emilie said, pointing.

"Yes. Ducks," India gave her the English word. She wondered if maybe they could have tea sent to the gazebo, but it didn't seem there was anyone at the house to bring it, and Nicholas would certainly object. Below them, a rowboat sat on the shore with a pair of oars nearby. Perhaps—

No.

They weren't here to enjoy themselves.

They were here so Nicholas could finish his business and say goodbye. And already she was realizing—too keenly, and much too late—how awful that must be.

"Ducks," Emilie repeated carefully, trying to mimic the sound exactly. And then, "*J'adore les*...ducks."

India couldn't help laughing. "I...love...ducks," she translated slowly.

Emilie repeated it back. And then, a bit haltingly, "I love...my brother." She looked at India, waiting for confirmation that she'd said it right.

But suddenly India couldn't speak.

"*Nicholas,*" Emilie said, pronouncing it the French way. *Nee-koh-la.* "I love...*Nicholas.*"

"*Oui, je sais,*" India said, pulling her into a hug. *I know.* "And he loves you, too."

"And you," Emilie said, looking up at her.

India looked away quickly. No, no he did not. She squeezed Emilie's shoulders and pointed at the ducks. "Look, I think they're having an argument."

Emilie smiled at the ducks' antics, and India breathed a little easier.

Love.

She chatted with Emilie about the ducks and what they might be saying to each other, and about the scenery and the grounds and everything they'd seen on their journey, even as Emilie's innocent words took hold inside her.

Nicholas didn't love her. He couldn't, not after he'd seen her dressed in her tricorne and breeches in Malta, watched her climb the yards aboard William's ship, found her hiding in a hayloft covered in straw just to escape him.

But she...heaven help her, because she...

She loved *him.*

"Ye're out of yer bloody mind. Do I look like I know the first thing about bein' a lady's maid?"

India stopped short halfway through Taggart's front door a while later, startled by the gravelly female voice booming through the entrance.

"I'm not asking you to be anyone's maid," came Nicholas's remarkably calm voice. "Only to make up the rooms."

"And then ye're going to bring out Mrs. Potts to cook," the woman accused. "I can cook." And then, "Who's that?"

It was much brighter outside than in, but India saw the two of them standing at the foot of the stairs, and now she realized they were looking at her and Emilie.

"This is...Lady India," Nicholas said. Lady India, not Lady Taggart. "And Emilie." He made the introduction. "Miss Ursula, Taggart's caretaker."

This was Miss Ursula? She took Emilie's hand and walked forward, seeing now that the person standing with Nicholas was almost certainly the same gardener she'd seen earlier—and was definitely not a man. Curly gray hair puffed out from beneath a woven cap. A dirty old jacket was buttoned over a dark waistcoat and a pair of smudged brown breeches with dark stockings. On her feet she wore a bulky pair of scuffed brown shoes.

And perhaps Nicholas did not want to be married to her, and perhaps she wouldn't be allowed to stay—not at Taggart and not in Nicholas's life—but she *was* his wife.

And she loved him. And looking at him knowing that, hurt much more than she'd guessed it would.

"Lady *Taggart*," India corrected. She ignored Nicholas's quick frown and offered her hand the way she might have done aboard the ship. Let Miss Ursula think what she would. "I'm very happy to meet you."

Bright blue eyes peered skeptically at India from a ruddy face softened with peach fuzz. "Ye didn't say anything about getting married," Miss Ursula accused, scowling now at Nicholas.

"That's because I feared a jealous rage," he said drily.

"Stuff!" She brushed her hands vigorously on her jacket. "Couldn't you have stayed away longer? Now you're tracking mud through the hall, and it's me that's going to have to sweep it."

India glanced down, but there wasn't a speck of mud to be seen.

"Very well, I'll make up the beds." Miss Ursula pointed at him. "But don't expect me to be doin' hair and the like—roses I'll coif, but not a lady's hair." With that, she harrumphed up the stairs.

India looked at Nicholas. And right there, at the base of the stairs, she made a decision.

She would not let him send her away.

He could scowl all he liked, but she wasn't going.

"Should I be worried about a jealous rage?" she asked now, feeling a little giddy over her decision.

He looked up the stairs in the direction Miss Ursula had gone. "Miss Ursula has been in my employ for twelve years. I haven't yet told her about the sale... I would appreciate it if you wouldn't say anything."

The giddiness faded a little. Poor Miss Ursula would be at the mercy of the new owner for her employ. And Nicholas would be without any help at the cottage.

She reached for Emilie's hand. "Come, Emilie—let us go upstairs and find our rooms." *And help Miss Ursula with the linens,* but she kept that part to herself.

Upstairs, India found Miss Ursula grumbling to herself with an armload of bedsheets. "I could put out me back this way—egad, don't ye take those!" But it was already too late, and India plucked half the stack from Miss Ursula's arms, ignoring her.

"Emilie and I will make up the bed in here." She swept into the nearest room. Immediately she spotted Nicholas's trunk on the floor. Her gaze flew to the bed.

His bed. The one he'd always slept in here at Taggart.

The one where, if they were truly husband and wife, he might—

"Ye'll not be making up 'is lordship's bed," came Miss Ursula's gravelly voice as she stalked into the room, waving her hands at India. "Shoo! Go on with ye."

India plopped the linens onto a chair and didn't leave. "I've made beds before—" well, her own bed aboard the ship, and only rarely "—I know what to do." Sort of.

"Don't make no difference if ye know what to do. Ladies don't make beds." Miss Ursula pushed past India and yanked the covers away from the mattress.

India debated whether to press the issue or—

"Well?" Miss Ursula fisted her hands on her hips. "Do ye plan on standing there holding it all day or are ye going to help put it on?"

—or help.

India unfolded the sheet, and together the three of them smoothed it across the mattress, while Miss Ursula muttered about ladies making beds and working as if they were common folk.

"I did a lot more than this when I lived aboard a ship," India told her. "Although it's a sight easier in breeches."

"The devil ye wore britches."

"Only ask Lord Taggart."

Miss Ursula snorted in disbelief.

But India only made up her mind even more firmly that she would not be made to leave. Nicholas would not be able to afford to keep servants. He did not need a wife on a pedestal. He would need a helpmeet. She had too much experience in the world to be put off by making up beds and washing linens and cooking, even though she'd never cooked a day in her life—

"Miss Ursula," she said as they moved to the next room to make up Emilie's bed. "Would you teach me to cook?"

"Cook! Egad no, I won't teach ye to cook. Ladies don't cook."

But she wasn't going to *be* a lady. She was going to be a *wife*. Just an ordinary wife. Nicholas's wife.

How could he be ashamed of her then? It would be exactly as he'd once said—there would be no soirées, no balls, no dinner parties. No public life in which her history would bring him shame.

And if she could be enough help at the cottage, perhaps he would overlook her inability to read.

He would have to overlook it, because she wasn't going to give him a choice. He could use the nastiest tone, give her the coldest looks, but she was going with him and Emilie to the cottage. If she could pull lines and rig sails and swab decks, she could feed chickens and make boiled potatoes and scrub floors.

He needed her. He did. Only let her prove it, and he would see it, too.

CHAPTER TWENTY-EIGHT

"I TOLD YOU I did not want you to help Miss Ursula make up the beds," Nicholas told her later when she found him in the library, going through paperwork at his desk.

"I wasn't going to stand by and watch her do it alone, when Emilie and I are perfectly capable—"

"I don't want Emilie making up beds," he said sharply.

"So what do you expect us to do? Sit and drink tea while Miss Ursula does everything alone? Except we can't even do that, as all the furniture is covered—or do we have your permission to remove *those* linens so that we may sit?"

He raised his eyes—only his eyes—and his hand stilled. She narrowed her gaze, refusing to look away. "There must be something I can do to help."

She watched him and felt the weight of what needed to be done here. *I wish you didn't have to endure this,* she wanted to say. *I wish my father had been here so that you could keep this place.*

And even after everything he'd done, everything she'd endured herself because of him...she meant it.

"All right, then," he finally said. "If you want to help..." He reached for several sheets of paper, glanced through them and held them out to her. "Take this list.

Make sure everything is accounted for. If you find anything that isn't already listed, write it at the bottom."

India stared at the papers in his hand.

"Or perhaps you didn't contemplate doing *that* much
work," he commented.

She took the papers. "Of course I did." She leafed
through them the way he had, as if she was skimming
through the words. But her heart was pounding, and
all she could think of was whether he could tell she
wasn't really skimming. Her nerves stretched tighter
and tighter, and reading was impossible now—even
the words she did know, of which certainly there must
be some.

"Mark everything off as you find it," he told her. "If
the numbers are different—forty forks instead of thirty-
five, for example, make the correction."

India nodded, still staring at the paper, terrified now
that something in her demeanor would give her away.
There was nobody here but Nicholas and Emilie—
nobody she could secretly go to for help. Except, possibly, Miss Ursula, and it was too easy to imagine her
booming voice announcing India's failings to the entire county.

*Ye want me to read this to ye? Can't ye read it yer-
self?*

She inhaled, looked up and tried to smile. And Nicholas was so handsome that her heart ached just looking
at him, wishing he wanted to keep her half as much as
he wanted to keep Taggart.

THERE WERE A few words on the list India did know. *Fork*
was there, and *spoon*. Perhaps a dozen others—short,
single words. The kind that were easy to remember.

But there were so many other longer ones she wasn't sure of. She could guess, but what if she was wrong? If only there'd been more time for visits to the young Mr. Wiggins in London.

It would have been so much easier to help with the linens, or perhaps packing away whatever Nicholas planned to take with him, or even helping Miss Ursula outside.

A letter had arrived from Paris. India had recognized Millie's handwriting. She was able to hide the letter away before Nicholas asked her about it—thank goodness Miss Ursula had been the one to receive it. But there hadn't been time to do more than study it and apply a few of the techniques the young Mr. Wiggins had begun teaching her. Her priority was the inventory list.

Over the next day, India started with the things she could read. Emilie followed her from room to room, helping her count. And the more time she spent inside this house—old as it was, and in so much need of care—the more she wished they could stay here.

She sat now in a storage room on the very top floor, counting sheets. Small windows overlooked the grounds. From here, she could see the treetops, the pond, the flower garden at the front. It was perfectly quiet.

Safe. Peaceful.

And then...footsteps. Heavy ones that she recognized instantly as belonging to Nicholas. She stepped away from the window and resumed her work, but lost count immediately, focused entirely on the *thump-thump-thump* of his approaching footsteps.

And then he was there, in the doorway. He had to

duck through the door, and his head nearly touched the low, slanted ceiling.

"How is the inventory coming?" A hint of roughness touched his voice.

"Well." He seemed to fill the room, watching her with troubled eyes, green like the sea on a stormy day. "Very well," she added. He wasn't close enough to touch her, but she felt him on her skin as if his hands pressed into her flesh.

"I need to check something on the list," he said.

"Oh." She looked down at the pages in her hand. Held them out to him.

He stepped forward and took them, and now he was even closer.

He studied the list, leafing to the second page. She watched his hands—those strong, sure fingers that had touched her so intimately in France. And it was impossible not to imagine, now, what might happen if he touched her again. Perhaps even here. Now.

Her breathing turned shallow.

"The candelabras are in the dining room," he said suddenly, looking up. "I saw them only this morning."

Candelabras? Her attention shot to the list in his hand. "Yes…I saw them, as well." Candelabras.

"You inventoried the dining room yesterday," he said. "You didn't count everything?"

"I must have forgotten to mark them." She kept her eyes fixed on the pages he held. "I'll check them again as soon as I'm finished here."

Her insides felt suspended while he glanced over the list. "I saw the silver braziers, as well. And—for God's sake, India. No wonder this is taking so long. You didn't finish the pantry, either, or the downstairs linens."

Oh, God. She backed up a step.

"Now look here," he said with irritation.

Numb. She felt herself going numb.

"I expect this finished by the end of tomorrow. If you're not going to do this efficiently—"

Then you'll stay here without any supper until you do.

"—then return the list to me and I'll do it myself."

She stared at him.

He frowned and held out the papers. "Are you feeling unwell?"

Was she— "No. No, not at all. Of course I'll finish by tomorrow," she said, taking the list and setting it aside. "I told you I would do it." Now she raised her chin, even as a knot twisted on the inside. "But of course if you would prefer to do it yourself, you have only to say the word, and I'm quite certain Miss Ursula can find a way to keep me busy in the gardens. Or the kitchen."

"You're not going to work in the goddamned kitchen."

She couldn't even do the one task he'd given her. Only think how much more he would regret her staying when he found out how little help she really was.

Then suddenly he looked past her, toward the small window. "A rider."

INDIA EXHALED WHEN he left, shaking with relief. She counted the rest of what she knew to count in the storage room, then returned to the dining room and counted the candelabras and silver braziers, writing the numbers very small on the bottom corner of the list since she didn't know exactly where to put them.

The rider had left, but India had heard nothing of what he wanted.

Just as India was leaving the dining room, Emilie came from downstairs. "Where is my brother?" she asked.

India didn't know, so they looked in the library and walked out to the stables, but he wasn't there, so they decided on a visit to the pond.

They spotted him through the trees, standing where the path broke into the open, with his arms hanging at his sides. Motionless. Saying his goodbyes, she supposed, to this beautiful place he must love more than anywhere on earth.

She slowed, held Emilie back, suddenly feeling as if they were intruding. But he must have heard them, because he turned.

Emilie waved at him.

He smiled a little at her—at Emilie, not at India—and they started forward again, joining him in the sunshine. India hardly dared look at him. Her mind raced for something appropriate to say, something that would not make it all worse.

Emilie took his hand. India glanced down, watched his large fingers curl around Emilie's small ones. Her own fingers tingled with wanting to take his other hand. She made a fist instead.

"Could we go in the boat?" Emilie asked, pointing to the rowboat.

"Bit windy today," Nicholas told her.

"Only think if we had a small sailboat," India said, "what fun that would be."

Nicholas looked at her. Too late she realized her thoughtlessness. "Of course, a toy one would be much better," she said quickly. "One would never get wet, and it could be the most magnificent ship ever, with three masts and fifty little guns, and you could take it wherever you go—even to a cottage."

He was staring at the water again. A muscle in his jaw flexed.

"Must you sell this place?" Emilie asked him in French.

"Yes." He looked down, touched Emilie's cheek. "I must. But we shall have a cottage of our very own, snug and safe. You needn't worry."

"Only think how much fun a cottage will be, Emilie," India said. "Perhaps there will be a giant tree, and Nicholas will fashion you a swing, and you can glide for hours upon hours watching the birds play in the branches. And we can plant beautiful flowers all around the house, and you will have a room all your very own where the sun will shine in. And on gloomy days, the smell of bread baking in the kitchen will fill every room."

"Really?" Emilie said, looking up at Nicholas.

Can India come with us? India imagined her asking. But Emilie didn't know India would not be joining them—Nicholas hadn't told her yet.

And now he was looking at India with an expression she couldn't quite identify. Perhaps she'd made another mistake, describing cottage life that way.

But he put his arm around Emilie and rubbed her shoulder. "Yes, really. The cottage will be great fun. You'll see."

LATE IN THE night, Nick stood in his bedroom in his shirt, breeches and stockings, rereading the note the rider had delivered, wondering what the devil his solicitor could want so urgently.

There wasn't time for a trip to London, but he would have to make one tomorrow. He would go on horseback in the morning—early—and be back by evening.

Another wasted day, on top of so many others.

The business here needed to be finished quickly. Two days hence at the latest. Then they would return to London, and he would begin looking for a cottage, and India—

God. India.

She made cottage life sound so fantastical he almost believed it himself. Any other young lady would have been horrified by the state Taggart was in. Mortified by the task at hand and what it meant. Any other young lady would have wanted to stay at James's house in London—would probably be begging for them to live there, just to keep up appearances.

But India had helped Miss Ursula change the sodding *linens* on the sodding *beds*.

India wanted to *help*.

And Nick wanted her so badly he'd considered shutting the door to that damned attic room and taking her right then, right there. And he wanted it even though he knew bloody well she didn't want to be here. Even though he could see her fading before his eyes, just as he'd known she would.

Wandering about the house, taking a haphazard inventory hither and yon?

He thought about her blank stare when he'd questioned her about her methods. And perhaps she didn't *want* to help at all. Perhaps she was only trying to find some way to occupy herself, absent the busy labor aboard a ship.

A sailing boat on the pond. Good God. Only imagine

if he did have one, and if they were going to stay here. Only imagine her trapped forever on his little pond in a tiny sailboat.

But they weren't staying. She wasn't staying. She would return to Paris, and if nothing else, she could have excitement there. He might have the legal right to stop her, but he had only to think of her trapped in some gloomy cottage to know he could never, ever do that to her.

She was sunlight and freedom.

And he was a man with no home, no place, no name.

Yet somehow, now, he found himself tossing the letter onto his dresser and lifting a candle. Opening his door, padding barefoot across the corridor, knocking on hers…looking for some of that sunlight, even if only for right now.

Her door opened, just a little—just enough for him to see a long section of billowing white nightgown—and she looked up at him. Her eyes were so huge, so blue. And her lips—his tongue remembered her taste.

"Is something the matter?"

"No." He barely recognized his own voice, thick with desire and need. "I'd like to come in." Even though he knew better, even though he'd promised himself he wouldn't touch her again because he shouldn't—not after he'd ordered her to leave.

But he had to. He *had* to.

In the candlelight glow, comprehension darkened her eyes. Those lips parted, and—acquiescence. She stepped back, opened the door wider.

He stepped through it. Set his candle on a side table and faced her. She looked more like a virgin now, in her billowing nightgown and braid, than she'd looked that night she *had* been a virgin and he'd so mindlessly plundered her.

And it was wrong—so bloody wrong—but he wanted to make love to her with nothing between them.

He wanted to feel her bare skin against his.

He wanted her to part her legs for him, even knowing everything about him—his heritage, his financial embarrassment, his hopeless future.

And so he reached for her.

Kissed her.

And Christ—now she was kissing him back, not like she'd done at Madame Gravelle's but more sweetly, more thoroughly, more...

Everything.

He framed her face in his hands, drinking deeply of that sweetness. Her arms came around him, and she was so damned soft and pliant, pressing herself against him with an intoxicating little sigh, and he may have ordered her to leave but right now he was so bloody glad she hadn't.

Stay, he wanted to say. *Stay with us. With me.*

Instead he hooked her under the knees and lifted her into his arms. Kicked the door shut behind them and carried her to the bed. Laid her across it and stretched over her, kissing her harder now, deeper, filling his hands with flesh covered by soft cotton.

He rolled with her so she lay on top of him and he could pull her braid apart, shaking her golden hair loose to fall over her shoulders and onto his chest. Touched her face, brushed his thumb across her lips, dug his hands into her hair and pulled her down, kissing her with a need so strong it scared him.

He pulled at her gown, needing to touch bare flesh.

Felt her pushing his shirt up—Christ, he wanted her touch. Craved it. He pulled at her gown, pulled at his own shirt, and then—

Yes.

God.

She was naked. Full, uninhibited breasts. Pale, curving hips. Smooth belly above the softest patch of dark golden curls that he already knew hid a channel that would accept him with a slick, hot resistance.

He pulled her to him. Felt her breasts against his bare chest, her hard nipples pressing against his skin. She was all softness and curves, and he touched her everywhere—breasts, belly, hips, thighs.

He slipped his fingers into her folds and found them already damp with anticipation.

And touching her wasn't enough. He trailed his lips down her neck, across her collarbone, while he filled his hands with her breasts and pushed them high, kneading, glorying in the beauty of those pink crests.

He took one in his mouth. Savored the tautness of it between his lips and pulled. Heard her cry out, felt his cock pulse in response. He took the other.

Turned her again so she lay beneath him. Pushed her breasts together and suckled each in turn, then began teasing her with his thumbs, knowing a deep satisfaction when her thighs parted and her hips strained upward.

He kissed his way down her belly. And God—*God*—her petals were so pink, so open. He pushed her thighs wider, dipped in for a taste, and her ragged response inflamed him. Made him want to devour her more than he'd ever wanted anything, and he did—his tongue circling over her pleasure, dipping into her channel, finding her tight bud once more. He gripped her hips, but she strained hard, panting, gasping, signaling that she was climbing closer to climax, closer, closer....

And she was there, fisting the covers in her hands, throbbing and pulsing around his tongue as she peaked, and it was too much.

He had to be inside her.

Now.

Immediately.

He stripped off his breeches. Rose up over her, let his erection find the sweet spot where his tongue had just been. And her hips surged upward, and he slipped to her opening, entering her, and he drove himself forward—

OH. OH! INDIA felt him thrust into her, tasted her own musk in his kiss, sighed as her channel stretched full and tight around him the way she'd longed for it to do ever since that night in Paris.

Nicholas.

Her husband.

Her love.

Her heart seemed to swell as he moved powerfully between her legs, pushing himself inside her again. Again. Again. She tangled her tongue with his, felt him dig his fingers into her hair, welcomed him with open thighs and tilting hips that she pushed up, up, up to meet him.

He was so beautiful—eyes dark, lips gasping against the intensity of the pleasure. She kissed them, and he responded instantly, and she tried to press herself closer, hold him tighter, bring him deeper.

I love you.

Each thrust drove the fact more deeply home.

I.

Love.

You.

And oh, heaven, he was rolling with her now so that she lay on top of him again. His hands guided her hips up…down… *Oh.* And she moved on him that way harder, faster, watching him strain upward to take one of her nipples into his mouth, and pleasure spiked below.

Spiraled higher.

And she felt him fully inside her—all of him—and now the intimate muscles between her thighs clenched him, seized, pushed her over the edge into sweet oblivion that left her panting and calling his name.

Nicholas.

He was there, holding her hips, taking over, straining up into her.

And she collapsed onto him, breathing hard against the crook of his neck, inhaling his scent while her thighs still straddled his body. For the longest time they lay there, before he finally turned with her to the side, and she felt him slip from her body. She looked into his face—his beautiful green eyes, his perfectly sculpted nose, his firm lips.

His arms came around her, holding her fiercely as if he would never let her go.

If only it were true.

NICK SLOWLY CAME awake and opened his eyes, feeling India next to him with her arm draped across his bare chest. It took a moment for the memories to come, but they did.

Lovemaking. Never in his life had he done anything

like what they'd done tonight. He hadn't known it was possible to be that...*close* to a woman.

He turned his head on the pillow, looked at her lips curving peacefully in satisfaction and slumber.

At least, for now.

A feeling stirred in his chest—a desire to pull her closer, hold her, wake her up and make love to her again only more slowly this time. The look in her eyes when he'd been buried inside her...

He'd be seeing those eyes in his memory for the rest of his life.

Already he was half-aroused. He pushed himself slowly, carefully to the edge of the bed. Thankfully she did not awaken.

This never should have happened again. Now that it had...

Damnation.

They would have to pretend that it hadn't. Nothing had changed—he still had no money, and she still wanted her freedom above all else, except perhaps some of the money he didn't have....

And wasn't that going to be entertaining.

He took his breeches off the floor and quietly pulled them on.

A candle flickered on the writing desk, burned so low that barely an inch of wax remained. He walked over to snuff it out and saw a letter lying there. It was to India, from Miss Germain, dated after he and India had left Paris.

He started to blow out the candle.

Skimmed over the first sentence, then the second. A few of the words had pencil marks on them. Odd.

A third sentence, and then he was reading the entire blasted thing.

…a terrible confession to make, and I fear you will never forgive me. From the moment we met with William and Lord Taggart I knew there was nothing to be done against them, but that is no excuse…. My only defense is my desperation. You know optimism is not my strong suit. I helped him, India. Lord Taggart came to me while we were aboard William's ship and offered me one hundred pounds in exchange for helping make sure you did not escape him in France. And God help me, I was so terrified that I agreed. I know our friendship can never be repaired after what I've done. Perhaps it will be of some comfort to know that what money he did eventually give me was stolen from my hands no sooner did I leave his presence. Right now I am dependent entirely upon Philomena's generosity, which I fear will end very soon. I hope to find a tolerable position in Paris very quickly….

There was sudden movement from the bed. His gaze snapped up.

"What are you doing?" India started to scramble from the bed, apparently realized she wore no clothes, then grabbed the covers and pulled them up to her chest. "That letter is private!"

It was, and he hadn't meant to read it.

But— Bloody hell. She knew that he'd bribed Miss Germain. She hadn't said a word about it earlier—but then, he'd hardly given her the chance.

"Forgive me," he said.

"I'll not forgive you for that."

He tried to determine whether she meant she wouldn't forgive him for reading her correspondence or for paying Millie to help him in France.

"India, about what Miss Germain wrote—"

"I know what she wrote."

"You should know that I took advantage of her desperation. If anyone is to blame, it is I."

"I never doubt that you are to blame for anything, Mr. Warre." She scooted to the edge of the bed and got out, dragging the covers with her, and snatched her nightgown from the floor.

Mr. Warre. A few short hours ago, it had been Nicholas. Not that he should have expected that to last, even under the best circumstances, which these decidedly were not.

If nothing else, he owed her an explanation. India held the covers with one hand and worked the nightgown over her head with the other. Her head poked through the neck hole, then an arm wiggled through a sleeve. "I knew when I asked her to help me that she would never turn down what I offered her," he said.

She stopped with her other arm halfway through the sleeve and stared at him.

She was furious, of course. She had a right to be.

"I knew she was my best hope of keeping you with me."

She finished pushing her arm through the sleeve. He waited for her attack as she let the nightgown fall and pushed the covers into a heap on the bed.

"I don't expect you to forgive me," he said. "And perhaps there's no reason to forgive her, either—" he wouldn't mention that Miss Germain had tried to black-mail him with information India had surely divulged in confidence "—but as she told you, I *was* the one to approach her with a proposition she was hardly in a position to resist."

"I see." She looked drawn. Almost…stunned. If he didn't know better, he would think she hadn't known until this moment. "And how much did you offer her?"

Nick stood there, half-naked at the foot of the bed that was rumpled from their lovemaking, from sleeping in each other's arms, and realized…

She *hadn't* known. The letter was there—she'd obviously been reading it—but she hadn't known.

And he thought of Paris, of that night at the salon when the gratitude on her face had been so out of proportion to what he'd done.

He'd saved her from having to read aloud. That's what he'd done.

And there was the list—the inventory of Taggart she'd so haphazardly begun, shifting from room to room without finishing what she'd started.

Not because she was inefficient or making light of the situation, but because—

She couldn't *read* it.

And what in bloody blazes was he supposed to say now? *Pity you can't read. Excellent job in bed, though.*

"One hundred pounds," he finally answered. And the sum had been *stolen.* He felt a little sick.

He wanted to reach out to India, hold her. Had she been so rebellious, even as a child, that she had refused her tutors? Had Cantwell denied her an education?

"I see," she said woodenly. Her eyes were full of

pain and betrayal, and it made him want to hold her all the more.

"It was supposed to secure her a future after you and I were married."

"How very kind of you."

"India—"

"I would like to be alone, please," she said, standing rigidly next to the bed.

And with no words to justify what he'd done, and no idea how to acknowledge what surely she realized he now knew...he chose to honor her request.

SHE CRIED WHEN he'd gone.

He'd seen the letter. Assumed she'd read it.

He'd seen the stupid, useless markings that Mr. Wiggins was teaching her to make and that might have helped, eventually, but she was only just learning to use them and there hadn't been time.

And now Nicholas knew. He hadn't said as much, but she'd seen it in his eyes.

Which meant that any hope she might have had that he would change his mind and want her to stay—which was a silly hope to begin with that only the silliest ninny in the world would have—was gone.

Millie had been helping Nicholas. Had accepted *money* from him.

India thought back, walked through their journey from Marseille. There'd been the dressmaker—India's plan to seduce Nicholas that had gone oh, so very awry.

Millie had not objected. India had just assumed it was because of her desperation.

And then there was the morning after the maid had

set her free. It was Millie who'd talked her back into the carriage with Nicholas.

And there's been the sudden headache and disappearance from the Pont Notre-Dame.

India sat down.

Millie had betrayed her. The truth of it sat heavy in her chest, but there was little point in being upset now. Millie's deception had led her into the arms of the man who'd just made love to her. The man who held her heart but didn't know it.

The man whose eyes had gone soft with pity at the realization that she could not even read a simple letter, that she couldn't be the helpmeet he would need.

India put her head back down on the damp pillow and wept until she fell sleep.

CHAPTER TWENTY-NINE

MILLIE STARED AT Philomena in the upstairs drawing room Millie had shared with India before Lord Taggart had whisked her away, hardly comprehending what she was being told. "Employment?"

"Yes. It's an excellent position, too—possibly better than you deserve."

Even though Millie knew better, a spark of hope lit inside her.

"The Duke of Winston—" Philomena began.

"Duke," Millie interrupted sharply. The spark snuffed out.

Philomena arched a brow at her. "Yes. He was injured a few days ago in a terrifying incident when a piece of facade fell off a building near the palais." Philomena shuddered. "So tragic. The man standing next to him was killed. I can only imagine the effect that knowledge has had on poor Winston's psyche." Millie suppressed a horrified shiver, but could not quite accept that *poor Winston* would be an accurate description. "In any event," Philomena went on, "the injuries have delayed his plans to travel to Greece, and he requires an attendant with medical knowledge to accompany him. I've told him I know the perfect candidate."

Millie was already shaking her head. She could

not—*would* not—be a personal servant to a duke. "I can't do that. You know I can't."

"I'm not entirely without sensitivity to your feelings," Philomena said. "I told him the candidate was a certain Mr. Miles Germain, who I know from London and who I encountered by chance here in Paris. If you're careful, he never need know you aren't what you claim."

"Unless he has a penchant for young men," Millie said sharply.

Philomena laughed. "Let me assure you in no uncertain terms that Winston is a consummate connoisseur of females."

Which was *worse.* "It couldn't possibly work." Already a panic was beginning to rise. "I haven't the disposition to jump at the bidding of a spoiled, self-indulgent—"

"The question, Millicent, is what choice do you have? You need employment," Philomena said, "and the duke will pay you handsomely."

"But what will he *want* of me?"

"Heaven knows! No doubt he'll want you to mix up concoctions and poultices, that sort of thing. Listen while he airs his complaints. But of course I don't know *precisely* what he will require—you'll have to learn that from him, which you will do tomorrow. I told him you would be there at half past eleven for an interview."

An interview. *Tomorrow.*

"And I would suggest you put on your best manners," Philomena warned, then smiled. "But only think…when your employment with Winston is finished, you'll be in Greece—practically next door to Malta and that surgical school." She reached over and patted Millie's hand. "I can't think of a more perfect situation, can you?"

HALF AN HOUR after arriving in London, Nick stared at his solicitor, dumbfounded. "I don't understand."

He tried to comprehend the words the man had just spoken, but couldn't.

The man frowned down at the papers in front of him, spread out amid a clutter of files and books. "This is your thirty-fifth birthday, is it not?"

Nick nodded, and thought he might be sick.

"Then the funds may be distributed."

The funds. "Are you…quite certain there hasn't been some mistake?"

He could see the solicitor quietly taking stock of his reaction, of the fact that Nick hadn't had the first idea. "Your mother was very clear. Hold the property in trust until you reach the age of thirty-five."

"James never mentioned receiving anything at thirty-five. But I suppose only Honoria and I—"

"The only trust your mother's solicitor spoke to me about was this one, for you alone. I've brought a list of the trust properties and other assets…." He shuffled through the papers. "You'll find the holdings are quite significant, sir."

Nick heard a rushing in his ears. "How significant?"

BY THE TIME Nick left the solicitor's office, he hardly knew what to think. His mind raced, trying to grasp what he'd just learned.

Significant did not begin to describe what Mother had left him. How could he never have known?

He stood outside the building, too dumbfounded even to call for a chair. He would need an extra day in London—at least. He would need to talk to Holliswell. And Cantwell's man of business.

Right there on the pavement, Nick started to laugh.

Holy God—he needn't concern himself with either of them after today. His debts would be gone, Taggart would be secure and India...

The laughter faded. India would still want her freedom. The very freedom he'd promised he would give her should he ever acquire the means.

A chill ran though him, and he finally got in a chair and headed for Holliswell's.

Freed from that burden, he stopped to tell Cantwell's man of business that no further dealings between himself and Cantwell would be necessary, and that Cantwell should be informed that Nick had no more use for their agreement.

Just before exiting Ludlow's office, Nick stopped. "What can you tell me about Lady India's education?"

The man frowned. "Very little."

"It has come to my attention that her education may not have been...complete."

"Oh?"

"Or perhaps she was a less than diligent student?"

"Does that trouble you?"

The man knew something, and Nick decided he wasn't leaving this office until he discovered what it was. "As a matter of fact, yes. It troubles me greatly to imagine that perhaps she was *denied* an education."

He could see Ludlow considering how to answer that. "Not all children absorb their tutors' teachings like a sponge, Lord Taggart. I ought to know—I've a boy of ten at home who would sooner fence with a pencil than write with it."

"Are you suggesting Lady India had trouble with her tutors?"

The man looked at him. "Lady India's education—"

"My daughter's education," came Cantwell's derisive voice from behind him. "An oxymoron if ever I knew of one."

Nick turned abruptly. Cantwell. Here? "I'd been told you left for the colonies."

"I did. Storms the moment we left the Channel… We put in at France, and I booked passage home. The colonies can wait." He walked into the room. "Why are you inquiring about India's education? She comes as-is, Taggart. You'll not be giving her back because of any shortcomings."

The man's tone had Nick clenching his jaw. "Why is Lady India's education an oxymoron?"

Cantwell reached for a newspaper on Ludlow's desk, gave it a once-over. "India never would learn a bloody thing. Not a tutor in London hasn't been in my employ at some time or other. Not one did any good. Lazy child. Never was one for learning." He tossed the newspaper aside.

"Am I to understand that despite having every tutor in London, India never received an education?"

"Oh, she received an education. Whether she accepted it is another matter. Such crying and fussing… you would have thought I was forcing her to submit to the rack. Even the much-touted Wiggins could do nothing with her. And of course I tried everything I could think of to impress upon her the importance of her studies—withheld anything that could possibly be used as a toy, even went so far as to withhold meals… Good God, only Henry VIII's wives spent more time locked away. But that's neither here nor there. She's your problem now, Taggart."

Something Miss Germain had once said to him came whispering back...

Will you promise never to lock her away?

"Yes," Nick bit out, needing to leave—quickly—before he blackened the eye of a man he would see session after session in the House of Lords. "She is." He left quickly and ordered the chair to return to James's house.

He could hardly stand to think what she must have suffered as a girl at Cantwell's merciless hands. And it was too easy to imagine what India had been thinking last night when he'd so unwittingly discovered that she couldn't read. Did she imagine he would treat her the same way Cantwell had?

He guessed now that it was exactly what she feared. And he could either return to Taggart now and tell her he would never, *ever* imprison her for that or any other reason and spend the rest of his life trying to prove it was true, even as she wilted in the confines of Taggart's boundaries...

Or, he could do what he'd promised.

He could give her the freedom she wanted.

NICK ARRIVED AT his brother's town house to find that James had returned to London the day before. He told James what he'd learned from the solicitor—there would be no hiding it. But he didn't tell his brother the reason he suspected Mother had left an inheritance of this magnitude just for Nicholas.

If James knew anything about Nick's parentage, it didn't show. No doubt James assumed Mother had wished to provide for her second son.

And so they sat in the library with glasses of cognac while Nick tried to imagine telling James the truth—but he couldn't bring himself to do it. All he could think of was that he was about to lose India, and he couldn't stand to lose James and Honoria, too.

"You've gone mad," James said now, looking at him with raised brows and doubting eyes. "Give India a ship? Of her own? She'll be dead within the year."

Irritation flared. "She's got more skill than that."

"Forgive me if I don't agree. A young lady of nineteen does not belong on the high seas in command of her own ship." James, of course, would know, being a celebrated naval captain himself.

But, "For God's sake, James, your own wife did exactly that."

James gave a sharp laugh. "Katherine and India are very different."

Nick remembered how easily India had gotten along aboard William's ship and wondered exactly how different. Given her own command now, by the time India was Katherine's age she could well have all the expertise that Katherine did.

His mind drifted forward. By that time, Emilie would be India's age, perhaps even married.

And Nick would be alone at Taggart.

He took a drink of cognac. "She says I've ruined her life," he said, shifting his glass in small circles on the table. "I'm inclined to think she's right."

"Giving her a proper home is ruining her life?"

"My keeping Taggart won't make a difference to her. You know her—you've sailed with her. She's too free-spirited, too…enamored by the wonders of the world. To India, life at Taggart is like…being locked away."

"Oh, for Christ's sake—"

"She never wanted this marriage, James." Nick

sat forward. "I forced it upon her. Literally. I literally dragged her into a bloody church with Winston and Charles Vernier as my henchmen and forced her to say the vows. Our marriage isn't even legal."

"Who's to challenge it?"

Nick gave a laugh and drank more. "How many times did I threaten India with those exact words?"

James sighed. "So you give her a ship. She sails away, and six months later you learn she perished in a wreck. How will you feel about your decision then?"

He would never forgive himself. But, "I've been watching her these past days—it's unbearable. The light has gone out of her. If I force her to stay at Taggart, I'll watch her perish as well, only much more slowly and painfully. And I'll know it's *my* fault—every last bit of it." She'd made a tremendous effort for Emilie's sake— they both had—but somehow that only made the whole situation more tragic. "She'll never be happy with me, James. My sins against her are too great."

WHILE EMILIE DUG the soil in a small garden plot of her own Miss Ursula had given her, India drifted farther down the garden to where Miss Ursula trimmed dead roses off the bushes. Millie's letter was tucked up her sleeve. India stood there watching Miss Ursula work.

Snip. Snip.

This was a bad idea. There was no telling what Miss Ursula might say. Perhaps she couldn't even read herself.

Snip. Snip-snip.

India slipped the letter out. It trembled in her fingers as she unfolded it, and the entire situation Nicholas had described about Millie replayed in her mind. She wanted to hear Millie's words.

Miss Ursula tossed a handful of dead flowers into a bucket. "Well? Are ye going to stand there waffling all day, or are ye going to tell me what's in that letter?"

India swallowed. "That's…just the trouble. I…I'm not sure what's in the letter. Precisely."

Snip-snip-snip. A trio of dead roses flew into the bucket.

India fidgeted. "I was wondering if perhaps…you could read it for me."

Snip.

Miss Ursula tossed a final rose into the bucket and reached for the letter. She squinted at first, then frowned, then frowned more deeply. "Ye want me to read it aloud?"

"Yes, please."

Miss Ursula looked at her—hard—and shuffled toward a nearby bench, grumbling, "Can't read all this standin' up."

India sat next to her and listened to Miss Ursula read the letter aloud, and India's heart broke for Millie. "Poor Millie." She sighed when it was finished.

It hurt—it did—but she knew Millie too well to hate her. Millie feared being alone and powerless in a world of cruel men. There was no way she could have resisted Nicholas's offer.

She told Miss Ursula about Millie, about taking the *Possession,* about the plans they'd had. "Suppose I can understand it," Miss Ursula said. "Suppose I can at that. But I never would have pegged 'is lordship for something like this," she added, still frowning.

"It hurts, but…I can't hate her for it."

"And 'is lordship?"

India looked at her hands. She couldn't hate him, either—not even after this. Offering Millie that money…it was all part of the same thing, his desperation to keep Taggart. "No, I don't hate him."

Miss Ursula snorted. "'Course ye don't *hate* 'im. Seems more to me like the opposite, what with ye both creeping 'round each other like foxes circling a hen-house."

"Taggart is going to be sold, Miss Ursula," India said now.

Miss Ursula made a noise and waved the fact away.

"And even if it weren't, Nicholas doesn't want me as his wife."

"Now ye listen to me," she said, pointing a weathered finger. "I've known 'is lordship these many years—twelve, to be exact—and I know when he's happy and when he's not."

"He doesn't want me. Once Taggart is gone, he and Emilie will move into a cottage, and he's already ashamed of me—"

"Ashamed of ye!"

"—and he doesn't want me to go with them. He never wanted me for anything but the money he thought he would get from marrying me. He's made that clear enough. And now he knows I can't read, and you should have seen the look on his face—I don't think I can ever face him again." She stood up. "I need to leave Taggart. I need to leave before he returns."

"Ye've gone mad! Leave Miss Emilie?"

No. No, she couldn't do that. But—

Across the garden, Emilie stood up and pointed toward the drive. "Nicholas!"

India turned. Saw him riding toward them. Her heart leaped and sank all at the same time.

India watched from the garden while Emilie rushed to meet him. Nicholas slid from the saddle and grabbed Emilie around the waist, lifting her into the air and turning in a circle as he hugged her.

She could see his smile from here. Could see him telling her something, and Emilie growing excited and throwing her arms around his neck.

He led his horse toward the stables, holding Emilie by the hand, and India watched them go, wanting more than anything in the world to join them.

But she waited until they came into the house and Emilie ran upstairs to change out of her dirty gardening apron, and she approached him in the entryway.

"How was London?" Seeing him now, everything they'd done the night before he left came rushing back—every last touch, every brush of his skin against hers, every intimate movement.

"It was…surprising." He tilted his head back, looking up at the ceiling, the windows at the front of the house. "I have good news."

"What news?" He didn't look like a man with good news. He looked…sad.

Almost as sad as he'd looked before he'd left.

"I shan't have to sell Taggart after all."

The news struck India breathless. "My father's man of business—"

"Hardly." His greatcoat swirled around his legs as he turned in a circle, as if seeing Taggart for the first time. "It would seem that my mother set aside something for me, and as yesterday was my thirty-fifth birthday—"

"Yesterday was your birthday?"

"Yes."

"Why did you not tell me?"

"It didn't signify."

It signified to her.

"In any case," he went on, "it seems I have come into a considerable fortune through a trust my mother set up for me."

"Oh, Nicholas, that's wonderful!"

"Yes." He stopped looking around the entry and looked at her. "Yes, it is. I have more than enough to pay my debt to Holliswell, keep Taggart and…about anything else I fancy, I suppose." He paused, looking at her. "Such as a ship."

A ship—

"I stopped to see a man who manages the London affairs for a friend of my brother who has shipyards in Turkey and London. As luck would have it, they've nearly finished construction of a small brig for an investor whose funds fell through at the last minute, and I was able to make an advantageous bargain. I'm told she will be seaworthy in a fortnight."

"Seaworthy…" He couldn't possibly mean…

His ridiculous promise, made—she'd thought—in the heat of anger. She'd nearly forgotten. But now…

Blazing pain spread out behind her ribs as her mind grasped what he was telling her.

"And to further compensate you for the upheaval I've brought to your life," he went on before she could think what to say, "I intend to give you five thousand pounds instead of the five hundred you found so insulting." He looked down at her, his expression carefully blank. "I only regret that I cannot give back the liberty I've stolen from you these past weeks. I cannot undo it—nor can I undo the marriage—" there was a pause, a memory of that awful meeting with the bishop in London "—but I can do as you've asked."

He was giving her a *ship*.

He had money now, money of his own, and Taggart was secure. And he was sending her away. Of course he was. He knew the truth—knew she could never be a fit mistress for Taggart.

Her plan to insist that she go with them to the cottage crumbled. That was so different from insisting she stthaay here as Lady Taggart. She might have made a fit mistress for the cottage, but now there wouldn't be any cottage.

Now there would be balls. Soirées. There would likely be a house in London, dinners with his compatriots in the Lords, entertainments to be hosted.

This is my wife—you remember, Cantwell's daughter, the young woman I agreed to marry in my desperation, she imagined him saying. *I had to drag her away from her stolen ship, you know. She was in a tavern when I found her, dressed like a man. Tried to gut-shoot me with her pistol. Oh, yes—and she won't be reading us any poetry tonight. She can't.*

Of course he'd bought her a ship. It was the one thing he thought she wanted more than anything. The one thing guaranteed to have her packing her things and setting out from London posthaste, never to return.

Except…

She didn't want to sail away on a ship, never to return.

"Are you feeling all right?"

No. She was breaking inside. But, "Yes. Yes, of course. I…" She couldn't tell him that she loved him.

That she wanted to stay at Taggart. "I'm just surprised. After all that's happened, I despaired of ever returning to the sea."

Despair of an entirely different kind keened inside her. But she couldn't refuse the ship, the living, without telling him her heart.

And if she did that, he would laugh, or perhaps pity her, or worse.

There was a sound from outside. The unmistakable clatter and clop of an approaching carriage. Nicholas went to the windows.

"Are you expecting visitors?" India asked.

"No." And then a muttered curse. "It's Cantwell."

CHAPTER THIRTY

FATHER.

But— "I thought he'd gone to the colonies," India said, hearing the edge of panic in her own voice.

"I saw him in London," Nicholas said grimly. "Go into the library— I shall deal with him."

India hesitated. Through the windows, she saw Father approaching the door.

"India, go."

So she did. She hurried past the staircase to the library and ducked inside the door, just as she heard Nicholas admit Father.

"You're not giving my daughter a goddamned ship."

"The gifts I choose to bestow on my wife are between her and me," Nicholas said flatly.

What if Nicholas decided to send her back with Father instead? Hiding in the library, she felt nine years old instead of nineteen.

Stop being a ninny and face him.

Her feet wouldn't move.

"When you propose to give my daughter the means to her own death, Taggart, it bloody well *is* my business. I asked you to marry her and return her to England— *safely.* Implicit in that arrangement was the idea that you would not then send her back out to perish on the seas."

"Forgive me," Nick said coolly, "but we no longer have any arrangement at all."

"Is it the money? Are you trying to blackmail me, Taggart? Because it's worked. I'll give you the bloody money."

"Perhaps you ought to offer it to India instead. She was making her way splendidly when I found her, and I expect she'll do so again."

That wasn't exactly true.

"My daughter belongs in a drawing room, not on the deck of a sixteen-gun brig!"

"Then you'll be happy to know the ship she'll be sailing has a mere ten."

"She's a girl—and not a very intelligent one at that. She can't command a ship."

"The fact that I had to pursue her all the way to Malta proves otherwise."

"You do realize that India can't even read—"

"Most likely thanks to you."

"Me," Father thundered. "I did every bloody thing I could think of to take her education seriously. Only imagine how easily such a foolish girl will be taken advantage of. Does she imagine anyone will deign to transact *business* with her? Good *God.* Tell me what it will take to change your mind."

"I'm not going to change my mind. India will have her ship, it will be hers to do with as she pleases, and that's the end of it."

It was too much. India rushed out of the library and into the entry. "What did you expect, when you decided to find me a husband this way?"

"India," Father said sharply.

"He only agreed to your horrible arrangement because of the money, and now that he doesn't need your money anymore, you're surprised that he doesn't want me? And you call *me* foolish."

"India!"

But she was already halfway up the stairs. Devil take Father and Nicholas both.

NICK WATCHED INDIA hurry up the stairs.

He doesn't want me. What the devil—

"India!" Cantwell shouted, starting past him, but Nick stepped in front of him.

"Your business here is finished."

"It won't be as easy as you imagine," Cantwell said. His eyes hardened—blue eyes the same color as India's. "Do not expect that ship to be ready anytime soon."

Suddenly Nick wasn't sure it mattered. *He doesn't want me?* Above, his eye caught Emilie's aghast face peeking over the rail, watching India hurry out of sight. He made a motion for her to return to her rooms as he ushered Cantwell to the door. "I shall see you to your carriage."

Cantwell spun on his heel. Nick followed him outside— just in time to see a second carriage coming down the drive.

"Looks like Croston," Cantwell said, just as Nick himself spotted the crest on the door.

Bloody hell. It was James.

Worse, he discovered moments later as Cantwell's carriage pulled away and James's pulled up, it was James and Honoria. Both.

"La, Nicholas," Honoria said as Nick helped her out of the carriage, "what is this I hear about Lady India sailing away on a ship?"

Their evening meal was a sorry affair prepared by Miss Ursula, the only servant he had.

Nick dipped his spoon into a quick soup Miss Ursula had thrown together—thin and brothy, but full of meat and vegetables, and tasting better than it looked. He thought of Emilie, alone in her rooms with her dinner tray. He'd managed to excuse himself for a few moments earlier to go up and explain what had happened, but he'd bungled the whole thing because how could he explain without telling Emilie the whole sordid mess? It was hardly appropriate subject matter for the thoughts of an eleven-year-old.

To his left, Honoria set her spoon on the edge of her plate. The sound was deafening.

To his right, James ate silently.

And at the other end of the table…

India seemed to shimmer in the candlelight. She lifted her spoon to her lips, a perfect lady in one of her aunt's reworked gowns from Paris.

He watched those full pink lips close around the edge of the spoon and had to look away.

There'd been no opportunity to speak with her privately since her father's visit.

"Where do you plan to go?" James asked India now.

"Athens," she said, carefully tilting her spoon to let a swirl of soup pool inside of it, keeping her eyes carefully lowered. "Perhaps Constantinople."

"Katherine said to remind you of a merchant in Constantinople named Ashkan."

India thought for a moment. "Oh—yes. Thank you."

Honoria put down her spoon. "Staying with Nicholas would be an excellent plan, as well," she said crossly.

"Ree…" James said.

"Well, it would be. Certainly Taggart is grander than any ship, even if it does need a bit of repairing. Nicholas will have an army of servants in short order, and it will be as comfortable as anywhere. La, India, I simply cannot understand you."

"Honoria," Nick said, "she doesn't *want* to live in England."

"But the two of you are married."

Now India put down her spoon. "That may be true, Lady Ramsey, but this was never a love match."

The hell it wasn't.

The thought shot through Nick's mind, and his hand stilled with his spoon halfway to his mouth.

Slowly, deliberately, he lifted it the rest of the way. Tasted his soup. Put the spoon down.

Love.

He stared at India, sitting across from him looking at once vulnerable and defiant, and suddenly he saw her again perched on the table aboard William's ship with her toes on his chair, taunting him about loving her to distraction.

And damnation if it wasn't the truth.

He loved her.

And he didn't notice Miss Ursula approaching until she came up behind him and whispered in his ear.

He tossed his napkin aside and stood abruptly.

"What is it?" India asked.

"Emilie's gone."

INDIA REFUSED TO stay behind and let Nicholas and Captain Warre conduct the search. Emilie was nowhere to be found in the garden or even at Miss Ursula's cottage.

The cold grip of fear was the specter of what they

might find as they made their way down the wooded path to the pond. They hurried so fast that caution was impossible—India felt her skirts snag on a bush and heard the fabric rip.

Nicholas held a lantern, calling Emilie's name. Ahead of them, a rippling slash of moonlight cut through the inky pond.

India heard a splash. "She's there!" India shouldered past Nicholas and Captain Warre, hiked her skirts and ran. "Emilie!"

They burst from the woods onto the pond's grassy banks. And there was Emilie, crouched by the water with a great mass of soggy fabric in her hands...

Scrubbing.

She looked over her shoulder, seeing them, but she only scrubbed all the more frantically. India rushed toward her with Nicholas on her heels.

"Emilie, we've been so worried," India said.

"Qu'est-ce que tu fais?" Nicholas asked sharply, but it was only too obvious what Emilie was doing.

And now Emilie shot to her feet, recoiling, trying to drag the soaking fabric—the embroidered cover from her bed, India now saw—from the pond. The light from Nicholas's lantern reflected on Emilie's wet cheeks and illuminated her horrified eyes.

"C'est rien—c'est rien!" Emilie babbled. *It's nothing.* "I spilled my soup, but I've washed it. It's clean now."

Nicholas pulled her into his arms, and India pried the wet bedcover from her hand. Captain Warre joined them, taking the lantern from Nicholas.

"You scared me to death," Nicholas was saying to Emilie, holding her tight even though she herself was

soaked. "You must never come to the pond at night—
c'est trop dangereux."

"Mais le couvre—"

"You're not here to wash bedding." He pulled back
and took her chin gently in his hand. *"Comprends?*
You're not a laundress anymore. You're—"

"You're here to stay," India interrupted quickly,
putting a hand on Emilie's shoulder. "Not to do washing." She turned to Captain Warre. "Aboard the ship,
of course, she had a job to do, but here—"

"India," Nicholas said tiredly. "That won't be necessary."

She looked at him, looked at the dark wet blotches
on the front of his jacket and waistcoat where he'd held
Emilie against him. Looked into his eyes, and realized
what he meant to do.

"Forgive me," Captain Warre said, "but am I missing something?"

NICK SENT EMILIE upstairs with India and asked Honoria and James to join him in the library. He poured
three glasses of port, trying to formulate the words he
would need.

He was so, so tired of living a lie.

"La, what an awful scare," Honoria was saying. "One
never likes to think of children outside alone at night,
especially not in the country, where any kind of noc-
turnal beast could be lurking."

James just sipped his port, studying Nick over the
top of his glass.

"What on earth could have possessed the child to
go to the pond now?" Honoria went on. "Although
heaven knows, with orphans, how they're raised. One

can hardly blame them for having no sense of civility, poor dears. I'm sure she'll grow into a fine servant for you, though, with a bit of proper training—"

"Emilie is not my servant."

Honoria's brows lifted. "She isn't." And then comprehension filled her eyes. "Oh. Oh, Nicholas…" Her gaze shifted to James, whose expression didn't budge.

And Nick knew exactly what they were thinking. "Emilie is not my child." He drew in a breath. "She is my sister."

Now one of James's brows shot up. "Your *sister*."

"La, Nicholas, that isn't possible, unless Father— James, could Father have—"

"It wasn't Father," Nicholas said on a sigh, rubbing his forehead. "It was Mother."

"But Mother's been—" James cut off as Nick saw him putting the pieces together.

"Emilie is the daughter of a Parisian laundress, or so I assume—her mother is dead. She was fathered by a priest who is not averse to enjoying the delights of his city." Nick looked at them. "And according to Mother, so was I." There it was. The truth, out in the open after fourteen years.

Honoria stared at him with confused, disbelieving eyes. James only sipped his port.

Nick narrowed his eyes at him. "You knew?"

"No."

"When did Mother tell you this, Nicholas?" Honoria asked softly.

"The afternoon she died."

"And you've carried it all this time?" She reached for him, but he was too on edge to accept her touch—too afraid of what would happen when they really considered what this meant.

"I don't expect things to be the same between us," he said, looking at James.

"Christ's sake, Nick. Don't be an ass." James drained his glass and went for the bottle.

"Things aren't the same. And they never will be—it's a simple fact. But I thought you both deserved to know the truth."

"And you think you already know the effect it will have," James said, looking over with the bottle in his hand.

"La, Nicholas…what a terrible, awful thing. I hardly know what to say."

"You don't know what to say?" India echoed, walking into the room, and bloody hell, Nick knew that tone and that expression.

"India—"

"Let me offer a suggestion," India said coldly. "Perhaps, 'How wonderful that you have a sister,' or, 'You're still my brother, Nicholas.' If you reject him now—reject both of them—it would be because of something that isn't even their fault."

"India—" Nick tried again.

"And it will be your loss," India went on, moving directly in front of him as if defending him from attack, "because Emilie is the sweetest, gentlest girl ever born, and Nicholas is the most deserving of men." He was? "Even had he never received that money, even if he had to sell Taggart and live in the dirtiest hovel, I would be proud to call him my husband."

She would?

"How much more should *you* be proud to call him your brother?"

There was dead silence except for the thunder of Nick's pulse in his ears.

He looked at India.

Then at James and Honoria, and said, "Excuse us a moment."

INDIA'S HEART RACED as Nicholas steered her from the room.

He was furious. She'd seen that expression before. That day at the dressmaker's when she'd worn no fichu. That night at Madame Gravelle's. A short while ago, at the edge of the pond when they'd first spotted Emilie.

He stopped outside the room and turned her to face him.

"Please forgive me. I spoke without thinking—"

"I'm not giving you that ship."

And he kissed her. And it was as if he was giving her his very soul, which she wanted so much more than any ship, and she had to tell him how she felt, could not let him send her away without at least letting him know—

"I love you," he said roughly against her lips, breaking away enough to look at her. "I love your fearlessness and your loyalty and the heart you have for Emilie and even for Miss Ursula, and I don't want you off sailing the Mediterranean—I want you *here*. With me. Every day for the rest of my life."

She stared at him—at those deadly serious green eyes that held so much in. They held nothing in now... everything he was feeling for her churned behind them as he waited.

Waited for her to say something.

A hundred thoughts and emotions cluttered her tongue, but what came out was, "I can't read."

His hands tightened around her face. "I don't care, India."

"I've tried—I've tried so hard. I was seeing a tutor in London, but I could only see him twice before we came to Taggart—"

"I'll bring him here."

"But I'll be no good—"

"*I'll* help you. And if you can never do it, I'll read for you myself. I'll hire ten servants to follow you everywhere and read every damned word in the world. But I won't buy you a ship so you can sail away from me. If you want to leave, you'll have to find another way."

"I *don't* want to leave."

He searched her face. "I forced you to marry me."

"I don't care about that. I love you."

"I took your virginity in a damned *brothel*."

"I *gave* it to you in a brothel," she countered, scarcely able to comprehend what was happening. "And I would give it to you again if I could, ten times over, and anywhere you liked—at Taggart, in a cottage…even in a bed of hay. Because I love you. I love you, Nicholas, and I don't ever want to leave you."

His mouth came down on hers again—hard, possessive, demanding everything she had.

"La, James," came Honoria's soft voice behind her, "I don't think she'll be going to the Mediterranean after all."

EPILOGUE

INDIA SAT NEXT to Nicholas in the rowboat, laughing as she worked one oar and he worked the other, while Emilie sat giggling in the bow.

"On fait des circles," Emilie said.

"Yes," Nicholas growled, raising a brow at India, "we *are* going in circles, because *someone* doesn't know how to row."

"Of course I know how to row," India said happily, dipping her oar into the water. "I have a seafaring nature." Quickly she dipped her hand into the pond and flung a splash of water at him.

"You'll pay for that."

"I hope this isn't another one of your empty threats, Mr. Warre." India stretched up to kiss him loudly on the cheek, and Emilie smothered a new peal of giggles behind her hand.

"We shall see, shan't we," he said under his breath, and she flushed.

In the bow, Emilie reached for the sack of stale bread pieces Miss Ursula had given her and tossed one toward the ducks, who immediately flocked closer, and for the moment there was no need to row. The ducks quacked and splashed, chasing after morsels of bread.

India looked up at Nicholas, and it was as if the entire world lived behind his eyes.

He leaned down and touched his lips briefly to hers. "There's something I've been meaning to ask you," he murmured.

"What?"

He pulled back, touched her cheek, looked deeply into her eyes while Emilie laughed and threw bread, making the boat rock a little. "Will you marry me?"

India's breath caught.

"Qu'est-ce qu'il a dit?" Emilie asked excitedly, her attention suddenly on them, demanding to know what Nicholas had said. *"Qu'est-ce qu'il a dit?"*

"He wanted to know if I will marry him," India said, smiling ridiculously up at him. "And I am saying yes."

* * * * *

New York Times bestselling author

LINDSAY McKENNA

brings you into the line of fire with
Operation Shadow Warriors...

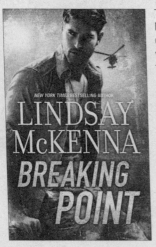

The Alpha Platoon. A unit of Navy SEALs stationed in the unforgiving heat of Afghanistan... who just learned that their newest team member is a woman. But Bay Thorn has a spine of steel—and the chops to prove it. Without a team to back her up, however, she's dead in the water. And her only ally is Gabe Griffin, a lone SEAL who is lethal, dangerous and unbearably attractive.

Between the open hostility from Bay's team and the harsh Al Qaeda territory, Gabe is a lifeline for her. But mutual respect quickly grows into mutual attraction. And with each day and every assignment, the longing only deepens. They mustn't speak of it. Mustn't act on it. Because in this line of work, falling in love can get you killed....

Available wherever books are sold!

Be sure to connect with us at:

Harlequin.com/Newsletters
Facebook.com/HarlequinBooks
Twitter.com/HarlequinBooks

www.Harlequin.com

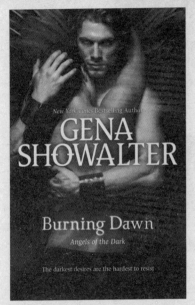

New York Times bestselling author

DIANA PALMER

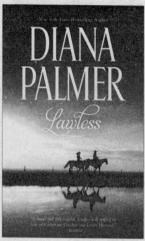

Five years ago, Judd Dunn, a hard-edged Texas Ranger, put Christabel Gaines's father behind bars—where he belonged. But Judd's involvement in Crissy's life was far from over. With their jointly owned ranch on the verge of bankruptcy, Judd wed her in name only, promising to save their land and vowing to ignore the sexual tension between them.

Now, just when Judd decides to release Crissy from their sham of a marriage, he is blindsided by a bloodthirsty foe who is setting the stage for unspeakable evil by preying upon Judd's greatest weakness— his wife. No longer a starry-eyed schoolgirl, Crissy's a smart, fearless woman with unfulfilled desires. And she will do anything in the name of love—including taking a bullet for her husband.

With their very lives at stake, Crissy and Judd must confront their darkest demons, their new rivals and their deepest desires—and face up to a mutual destiny they cannot outrun.

Available wherever books are sold!

Be sure to connect with us at:

Harlequin.com/Newsletters
Facebook.com/HarlequinBooks
Twitter.com/HarlequinBooks

www.Harlequin.com

PHDP842

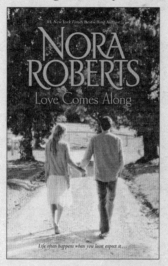

A no-nonsense female cop reluctantly teams up with the one man who makes her lose control in a deliciously sensual new novel from *New York Times* bestselling author

LORI FOSTER

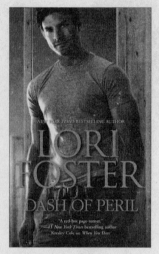

To bring down a sleazy abduction ring, Lieutenant Margaret "Margo" Peterson has set herself up as bait. But recruiting Dashiel Riske as her unofficial partner is a whole other kind of danger. Dash is 6'4" of laid-back masculine charm, a man who loves life—and women—to the limit. Until Margo is threatened, and he reveals a dark side that may just match her own....

Beneath Margo's tough facade is a slow-burning sexiness that drives Dash crazy. The only way to finish this case is to work together side by side…skin to skin. And as their mission takes a lethal turn, he'll have to prove he's all the man she needs—in all the ways that matter....